DOING THE HEART GOOD

DOING THE HEART GOOD

NEIL BISSOONDATH

A CORMORANT BOOK

The publisher gratefully acknowledges the support of the
Canada Council for the Arts and the Ontario Arts Council
for its publishing program. We acknowledge the financial support of
the Government of Canada through the Book Publishing Industry Development
Program (BPIDP) for our publishing activities.

Printed and bound in Canada

National Library of Canada Cataloguing in Publication Data

Bissoondath, Neil, 1955–
Doing the Heart Good

ISBN 1-896951-35-X

I. Title.

PS8553.I8775D65 2002   C813'.54   C2002-900036-X
PR9199.3.B457D65 2002

Jacket design: Tannice Goddard, based on an original front
cover design by Nadina Gray/Simon and Schuster UK
Text design: Tannice Goddard
Jacket image: Chaz Kibo/Photonica

Cormorant Books Inc.
895 Don Mills Road, 400-2 Park Centre
Toronto, Ontario, Canada M3C 1W3
www.cormorantbooks.com

For
VSN
who showed the way forward

A *breathless silence.* Night creeping in beyond the trees, sky a dapple of blue on the darkening leaves. Stars appeared. I went to bed. They burned my home.

So everything changes.

I did all I could to avoid ending up here. But I've ended up here anyway — in my daughter Agnes's home, I mean. Me, my medals, some knicks and knacks spared by the flames.

This evening marks the six-month anniversary of the night that brought me here, six months during which Agnes, her husband and her son have grown accustomed to addressing me in a low shout. This speaking to me as if I were at the far end of a large room no longer requires great effort of them, it now comes quite naturally. Even so, and despite the latest technological

1

contraption plugged into my ear, words reach me like a whisper through a straw. Mine is the only voice that resounds with any clarity in my head, the only voice I truly hear.

I used to tell my students, the undergraduates, I mean, that their essays should go from the general to the specific. In a curious way, the specific, *me*, is mostly what's left to me now, and I must go in search of the general.

Except for the night-clothes I was wearing when led from the duplex, I now spend my time encased in the unfamiliarity of new garments. For a man of my years — *advanced* is the way polite people would put it — this is no small thing. It's like assuming a new skin after decades of breaking in the old. Even my stick is new, a length of carved and polished teak Agnes picked up at an antique shop in Quebec City. There's no clearer way to explain what this is like than by saying that I've acquired a new leg which resists grafting itself fully onto me.

As for those night-clothes of faded cotton pyjamas, they now carry deep within their fibres the smell of smoke. They have withstood all attempts — multiple washings, perfumed fabric softeners — to extirpate it. Agnes would have me throw them out, but I've resisted, at times with the intemperateness of a child. I've even turned off the contraption on her, which is not unlike hanging up the phone in someone's ear, only ruder for the person is standing there in front of you. Agnes doesn't understand that it is just this scent — for her, a memory of destruction — that seduces me to sleep at night, that comforts me when I awake to the midnight darkness. She doesn't understand that when, in bed, I bury my face in the soft sleeve, I detect in its smokiness the very tinctures of the life — *my* life — now irrevocably gone.

Agnes has made inquiries on my behalf regarding my upstairs neighbour Tremblay. Apparently he suffered a few minor burns in the fire but was otherwise unharmed. He and his wife, who was at the time visiting their daughter in the country, lost every-

thing and have moved to a cottage they own far from the city. It
is, I am told, in a bucolic setting on the edge of Lake St. John,
surrounded by trees and attractive outcroppings of rock. They
no longer need much space, and are content to live out their lives
there. We have his phone number, and Agnes has transmitted
hers — ours — to him. But neither of us has yet made the effort
to get in touch. We always had such a difficult time with each
other face to face. Even with the help of the new telephone technology for the deaf, I fear I would catch only every second or
third word of his.

I am happier burying my nose in my sleeve, filling my mind
with the scent of the countless people who've entered my life,
stayed a while, then left.

The early weeks and months of the year of my birth saw the
wintry air leavened by regular and unexpected infusions of
warmth. Hope, then, of relief: My mother, grateful to the God in
whom she had only tenuous belief, loosened the button of her
too-tight collar.

In the year of my birth, the guns of the Great War, silent for
two years, were formally muzzled in Paris. Peace was ratified
without pomp — and without America, who could not bring
herself to cease hostilities with a defeated Germany and submit
to the world-weary optimism of the League of Nations. The year
of my birth, then, was a cradle of thwarted hope.

When, some weeks following my birth, my father complained
about my mother's tossing and turning in their bed — like an
unstable barge churning the waters, he said — she suggested that
he take himself to the bed in the guest-room. He thought it a
capital idea. I am, perhaps as a consequence, their final child.

In that year, Consuelo Spencer Churchill (née Vanderbilt),
Duchess of Marlborough, petitioned for restitution of her

3

conjugal rights. She had been separated from her husband, the Duke, for fourteen years, in an agreement concluded through the intervention of King Edward himself. Such a suit for restitution, filed by a woman, was understood by all to be the preliminary to divorce proceedings.

That year, the Roys' house, just a few doors down from ours, was reduced to its foundations by fire. Oil left heating on the stove burst into flame when, it was claimed, the young Mrs. Roy — unmindful, some said; indecent, said others, for it was the middle of the day — joined her husband in bed for a tryst. Sympathy for the unhappy couple was apparently not universal, for they were of a people, Tremblay's people, Jack's people, referred to as frogs but thought of as rabbits.

That was the year several inmates of the prison in Albany, New York, were mysteriously turned into human magnets by botulism ingested from canned salmon. Their fingertips caused steel to spark, the filaments of light-bulbs to vibrate.

In that year, an iceman's horse attacked an automobile at the edge of the financial district. The automobile won. When the animal had been dispatched, the automobile owner had its shoes mounted on the doors of the car. He had been, during the war, a member of the Royal Flying Corps.

That was the year the financial optimisms spurred by the demands of the war began a steady decline. Sales of coal and iron, the raw materials of armies on the march, fell off, the stilled battlefields of Europe bringing hardship and conflict to far-away Cape Breton. The price of wheat, lumber, fish and steel dwindled by half. New spectres arose, new kinds of battlefields.

Not, though, at our home. My father had done well in the boom times. Spared military service by the thumb he had been born without, he had "traded". When trade faded, he was comfortably cushioned.

Doing the Heart Good

꿈

In the summer of that year, rumours of a python on the loose kept doors shut and windows sealed on our part of the island. Many elderly folk were rendered insensible by heat, and more than one exposed tree-root found itself whacked at night by sticks and umbrellas.

It was in that year that one Onésifort Pronovost, a former bohemian become a convenience-store owner, swore to the newspapers that he had seen a cloud of roses in full bloom swoop past his window one night. He had watched as they shaped themselves into a v-formation and set course for the full moon.

This was the year our neighbour the widow Roberts, as genteel a septuagenarian as one could imagine, greeted a mid-afternoon thunderstorm by divesting herself of every stich of clothing and dancing a ballet in the street. My mother ran to her rescue with a coat, but the widow Roberts would not be rescued. She ran off, and was found some hours later, still in her natural state, offering lengthy confession to an unsuspecting priest.

That was the year my father began playing the stockmarket with the recklessness that would lead him three decades later — after he had recovered nicely from the Crash — to the only slightly greater risk, but far more volatile thrills, of the downtown gambling dens.

In the year of my birth, in Ottawa and in Washington, one lacklustre leader was succeeded by another, prompting my sister to remark years later on my birthday that it was the Year of the Forgettable. But it was, too, the year that Sandberg won the Pulitzer and Hamsun the Nobel; that Perez Galdos, John Reed and Alexandr Blok died; that the Yankees sold Babe Ruth to the Red Sox for $125,000.

꿈

❧

My mother read the newspapers. She told me later of these things. On the day of my birth, she declared, there was no event of momentous occasion. I have always assumed that she did not include my appearance in her dismissal.

My mother was a woman who knew much about the world without having experienced much of it, while my father was a man who knew little about the world despite his extensive dealings with parts of it. I've often wondered how it was that they came to make a life together, to have children, to seed the future.

But here I am now, over seventy years later, sitting in the twilight of my daughter's living room, her son, my grandson, nestled into my left arm. The boy has been scrubbed clean. He smells of soap and fabric softener, and even his nails — those six-year-old nails that constantly appear to have been grubbing about in dirt — are closely trimmed.

In the corner beside the picture window before us, the Christmas tree glows and blinks, the glow steady and diffuse from deep within the branches, emerging past dangling ornaments and strands of tinsel; the blinking more immediate, from bulbs less camouflaged and somehow less cheerful in their calculated rhythms. Were it not for its scent — a lingering of pine forest, a suggestion of earth, of the outdoors slowly expiring in an environment alien with forced warmth and dessicated air — the tree might be a fistful of some distant nebula wrenched from suspension in deepest space.

Through the window, a light snow drifts down in the early winter darkness, flakes flaring in the street-light, contracting surreptitious against the silhouetted branches of the oak which, when in full summer bloom, lends the living room the greenish hue of a fish-tank.

Agnes is a good daughter. In her uncompromising way, she has my best interests at heart. She's far from irreproachable — she works in a bank, for God's sake! — but I recognise that I have little, perhaps nothing, to reproach her for. A comforting thought.

I was not long in the hospital after the fire. Despite my being clearly intact, the doctors insisted on a two-day stay for observation, at my age not an unwise precaution. The nurses and their aides — women for whom I have long had a particular affection — were thoughtful and kind, their efficiency leavened with humour.

When my time was up, Agnes collected me and drove me here, to her guest room become mine. She would not drive me past my home, or what was left of it. She suggested another time, later, when the shock had worn off.

Her refusal made my heart pound. Was there so little left? Was the damage so severe? I had, lying in the hospital bed, speculated on the time that would be required to effect repairs. Agnes's attitude as she directed the car along the exit ramp to the highway was suggestive of debris, my house turned to jetsam. It returned to me the glimpse I'd had of the horrific voracity of flame. I felt then the peculiar grief I imagine grips the bereaved when they're told that the condition of the departed would dictate a closed-coffin funeral.

The room — Your room, she said; *My* room? I thought — is small. It was intended as a study, but has proven inadequate to Jack's purposes. A research fellow at some university institute, he's appropriated half the basement for his desk and his computer and the white Swedish bookcases which buckle under the weight of his books and journals. His field is physics, a subject of which I am wholly ignorant. He and I are unfailingly pleasant to one another. We have been so from the moment we met ten or eleven years ago when Agnes, on the flimsiest of excuses, brought him by the house one evening. He was a slender man with a shock of brown hair and stylish tortoise-shell glasses. We shook hands, exchanged wary smiles, made weak attempts at jocularity. His English was impeccable. Then they were off to a restaurant. I remember turning to Mary and saying a heart-felt, "Oh God, his name's not *Jack*, is it . . ." Mary shook her head. "No, dear. It's Jacques." Then she added, significantly, "Jacques. Get used to it." But he's remained Jack to me.

His career has been steady if unspectacular. His name graces an impressive number of scholarly papers that sit stockpiled on his bookshelves, but the walls remain unburnished by a gathering of testimonials. He is obliged to spend an inordinate amount of time, Agnes says, pursuing research grants.

All of which has led him to the basement from this little room become mine.

The room is pretty in a jumble-sale way, decorated in the claustrophobic style with a bed slightly too large, a chest of drawers slightly too high, a night-table slightly too rotund and a reading lamp slightly too garish. There is no closet. On the wall above the chest of drawers hangs a Krieghoff reproduction: snow and wood and colourful peasants charming only to behold. I've placed my medal-box on top of the chest of drawers, displacing Anges's vase of dried flowers.

On the wall above the bed, where some people place crucifixes, hangs a framed photo of Mary and me, black and white, faintly ill-focussed. The ground is awash with leaves. In the background, a tree raises bared limbs against a cloudy sky. We are both wearing coats, mine unbuttoned. Our arms are linked, and we look happy. This photo: it is an unexpected, iconic gesture from Agnes; it is meant to reassure and comfort. Even so, I must distance the sensation that I am camping in a motel room on the edge of nowhere.

The boy stirs in my lap. He gazes up at me, his little mouth yawning wide. "Grand-papa, m'as-tu acheté un cadeau?"

"A cadeau? Have I bought you a gift? Well now, let's see. A gift for François. Oh dear me, how could I have forgotten?"

"Grand-papa!" His eyes flicker from my face towards the kitchen, and I know that Agnes has called a warning about his protest — or perhaps just about its stridency.

"Now, now, young fellow," I say, "you'll just have to wait and see, won't you." I fake a pout, feeling like an actor ill-rehearsed, the falseness of the thing manifesting itself with a light trepidation. Like so much else in this new life, this role of grandfather, once occasional now perpetual, still feels assumed. It is for the most part more agreeable than not — but I know that, were Mary yet with us, I would be her understudy. I am not a sentimental man. Sentimentality, after all, is the raw material of self-delusion. All this newness, though, encumbers me.

François's lips stitch themselves together into a grimace that would not be inappropriate on a toothless and disagreeable old man. He is restless with anticipation, for tonight Santa Claus — *le Père Nöel* — arrives. François believes fervently, or at least he wishes to. Jack insists this is a sign of intelligence. The boy, he says, suspects that if he stops believing, the gifts too will stop. It's like religious faith, he says: Without the magic, the whole bottom falls out.

Not wishing to be a disloyal grandfather, I choose not to voice my scepticism as to whether this is intelligence or greed.

Yesterday morning Agnes was good enough to drive me to the local mall so I could do my shopping. A last-minute excursion, yes, but why change the habits of a lifetime? As we joined the serpent's tail of cars waiting to enter the parking lot, I mumbled something banal about the soul-deadening appearance of the place: massive boxes of concrete and brick clumped together with no aesthetic beyond the chaotic, rendered even drearier by the illuminated signs designed to entice the comatose.

"With our weather, Father," Agnes said, "malls are a godsend." Agnes, it must be said, has inherited much of her mother's contrariness.

"God made trees and flowers, Agnes. I every much doubt He can be blamed for suburban blight."

"God works in mysterious ways, Father. He gave us winter and the wind-chill factor, too. Malls might just be His way of making up for that."

And with that she pulled up to the main entrance and let me off. She took her time pulling out, despite the almost immediate cacophony of protest from drivers behind. She was reassuring herself, I knew, that I was steady enough on my three legs to survive the expedition without major incident.

I made little headway in finding a gift for Agnes, the search made arduous not only by the inadequacy of my notion of appropriateness when it comes to such things but also by the atmosphere within the mall: the heedless bustle of coats and boots, eyes wrung with desperation, the rabidity of constant "music", the wreaths and ribbons and balloons, signs screaming bargains and, at the epicentre, a hefty old man with alcoholic eyes bewildered behind his façade of red-suited gaiety.

Having considered and rejected possibilities ranging from a locket to a miracle toilet-bowl cleanser, I screwed up my courage and began venturing into boutiques dense with clothes and staffed by very young women armed with impossibly lithe bodies and ready smiles. *For your wife? For my daughter. A nice dress perhaps? Or a blouse?* But women's clothes make me helpless and I soon gave that up, relearning the lesson of the only time I gave Mary a dress for her birthday: "Do you really see me in *that?*" Forever after, selecting even a scarf has been beyond me.

I grew tired and found an unoccupied bench to catch my breath. Behind my closed eyes, the plethora of merchandise I had seen — all those dresses and blouses, sweaters, bracelets, earrings and necklaces — performed a manic parade, as if to mock my inability to choose. I began nodding off. It felt good, a downy space opening up, seducing me away from the simple task that was proving intractable. It was like playing hooky when I was a child.

Then a hand lighted on my shoulder and a man's voice said, "M'sieur?"

My eyelids rose slowly. A man in a uniform. A security guard. I looked around. I didn't know where I was, or why, or how I'd got there.

"M'sieur? Ça va?"

"I'm fine, thank you," I said. But I wasn't. I needed to be left alone, to search my mind for the information that would fill the *tabula rasa* that had intruded on me.

The guard asked my name. I told him. He asked if he could call someone for me. I thanked him and insisted it wouldn't be necessary, I was just resting. He was not reassured, but the walkie-talkie strapped to his belt crackled and he hurried off. What I didn't tell him was that the name I had given as my own was Kevin.

Then it all came back. Agnes, the shopping mall, the gifts. My home destroyed.

The information did not offer relief. I experienced instead a moment of fear, that not unfamiliar shower of ice that coated my heart and lungs and ribs. How could I have lost, however briefly, so much so totally?

After a few minutes, I consulted a nearby map of the mall and found my way to a bookstore, the only kind of store in which the cardinal points do not elude me. I picked up for myself a handsome edition of *A Tale of Two Cities*, on sale for a pittance. The desire to read has slowly returned and I know precisely on which page I stopped that evening six months ago when so many narratives — and not only those on the page — were interrupted by flame. With Agnes in mind, I scanned the shelves, my eyes blurring before the garish and the lurid, and soon encountered another kind of helplessness: I had no inkling what kind of book might give my daughter pleasure.

I could, of course, offer her the Dickens, as a way of

reintroducing her to the classics she struggled with in her early years. Although it smacks of the specialist in 19th century British writing I used to be, my love of Dickens seems the one precious thing I can pass on to a daughter with whom I have little in common. Might she have acquired over time the serenity that evaded her in youth to ingest through words, sentences, scenes and images, worlds and lives that appear destined to go on forever? Does she understand that, one day, Dickens will be read on Mars? Has she developed the ability to be astonished? My doubts are legion, for despite her many years of labour in a late-twentieth-century Dickensian environment, Agnes shows no sign of having developed the potential. She follows television serials, which she tapes every afternoon on a VCR in her bedroom dedicated solely to that purpose. Her fascination is with drama that glitters in ways that her life does not. She has no interest in the stories of those who rise from the depths, but rather in those who sink into them.

And so I turned away from the books, wandering disconsolate through the greeting-card and stationery section, a lengthy aisle which might once have been dedicated to the less popular literary arts of poetry and plays, neither of which is available with any ease today, least of all in an indifferent bookstore in a suburban shopping mall. Then my nose began to twitch. The musky scent of fresh paper and ink: it gave me pause. Such lovely things, packages of note paper and letter paper, of attractive design and colour, teal and rose and creamy almond and the shade of green seen only in early spring. The paper was of a kind that makes one wish to handle it, to seek out its textures. It makes one long for a correspondent. On a shelf above them, an army of boxed fountain pens — reds and greens and blacks and blues, some wood-grained, some mottled in shadow, some with silver bands and clips, some with gold, their triangular nibs wide and generous. The papers, the pens: they were suggestive somehow of elegance and agelessness; they were implements which, by their very essence, retained the ability to slow down time and impose contemplation in the same way that a good sherry can, for instance — and in a way that ball-points and note-pads and canned colas, all inherently dedicated to haste, cannot.

I wouldn't say that, standing there in the narrow aisle harsh with fluorescent lighting, I was bewitched. But I was in a state fairly close to it. And I knew, without knowing why, that I had found Agnes's gift.

Doubts have, however, since arisen. I cannot rid myself of the nagging feeling that the gift I've chosen is inadequate. Yet I've felt this way all my life — about myself, I mean. Mary and Agnes's ability to make me happy has always surpassed mine to do the same for them. Or, at least, theirs has been constant while mine has been sporadic. It's a dismal way to spend a life.

Doubts, then. The boxed paper — a light, luminous grey discreetly edged in gold — and the boxed fountain pen — also grey, with gold nib and trimmings — are not terribly feminine. And, truth to tell, it is my hand that I see wielding the pen onto the virgin paper, my words that I see being traced in a fine, classic, even stylish hand. Doubts, indeed . . .

Someone — I once knew who, but my memory has grown increasingly recalcitrant in recent years — this someone once said that the past is a foreign country. A lovely phrase, but woven from despair, for it suggests that the life one has lived is unknowable except in the most superficial of ways, that one is somehow doomed to be a tourist in the landscape of one's own past — and the tourist's landscape is one that exists only in his imagination, its objectivity suspect, its reality fluid.

I am on the whole a man of little religious feeling; I can't even pretend properly by respecting the conventions the way most people do. Yet for a long time I resisted this implicit despair; there was something distasteful about it. Now, though, the idea that the past is a foreign country — and foreign countries all have their fascinations — strikes me as being perhaps a touch optimistic. As one enters it, the past so often seems less like a foreign country than like the narrative of someone else's life, which is far more disorienting with its disorder of events that are alien, inexplicable and frequently untrustworthy.

I am, as I've said, a man of little, or to be truthful, of no religious feeling. Faith is such a fragile thing. Like a plant it must be cultivated — fertilized, watered, occasionally weeded. My parents were not diligent gardeners of this sort.

Despite his weekly poker games with our local minister, my father (who once said, "The way the reverend plays poker, he needs God on his side.") kept religion deep in his pockets with his keys and loose change. Later in life I asked him if he believed in God. He looked up from his game of solitaire and said, "Well, why not?"

As for my mother, her faith was satisfied with Christmas and Easter services at the church. She had no ear for organ music and she tolerated the sermons stuffed with half-baked homilies. But she liked the atmosphere, the social gathering. Whether she had any real belief, or how deep it might have gone, I cannot say. She never did.

And so I grew up with the idea that religious belief was something that everyone simply had, like clothes or shoes or a certain colour of hair. I suppose I believed, but in the way I believed that the Montreal Canadiens were the best hockey team in the world for all time. It was just a given.

It was the war that put paid to that.

One afternoon, after a brief but vicious skirmish, we came across a dead German sprawled in the underbrush. A bullet had gone through his left breast pocket directly into his heart. It had travelled through a small edition of the New Testament he had placed there. Some members of my platoon marvelled at the clean hole the bullet had made. I was impressed by the presence of the book itself. This sounds naïve, but it struck me full force that this man, like so many of my comrades, had carried the word of God with him like a talisman. In this conflict where brutality met brutality, *God was on everybody's side.* He couldn't be trusted. And a God that couldn't be trusted couldn't exist. That was it for me. God, and any feeling he may have inspired, became a casualty of war.

Since then, I have viewed with a certain equanimity the prospect of falling into a void after my final breath. Nothingness, non existence, does not frighten me. What does disturb me is falling into a void *in this world.* Turning to nothing *in this world.* Fading within a generation or two to just a name and a few photographs. The thought of such obscurity causes my heart to thunder. It coats my insides in ice. For only in the memory of this world is there an afterlife.

It's because of this — fear of it, resistance to it — that I've recently taken to jotting down some of the episodes of my life. When I find myself alone in the house, I get out pen and paper, make myself as comfortable as possible in this very spot, and I scribble. As my writer friend might have said, I scribble, therefore I am, and perhaps, later, I still shall be.

This is not the first time I've written. My *curriculum vitae* lists pages of articles and several academic tomes. They reside in libraries, and are of interest only to graduate students and others in the literary field. But my c.v. does not include work of more lasting importance to me. I twice took on the old saw which holds that those who can do, those who can't teach. As a result, two manuscripts lay for years in a storage box at home, hidden beneath a thick stack of old course notes. They were novels over which I laboured for many long hours of writing and revision, one a war story of accidental heroism, the other a story of love and its near loss. They were frankly autobiographical in nature, and perhaps because of this I revealed their existence to no one, not even Mary. What if, on reading them, she were not impressed? How foolish I would've felt, the academic reaching beyond himself, trying to emulate his writer friend. They were good books, I like to think. They might even have found some small audience. But they're gone now, fodder for the fire. I have only myself to blame, my lack of courage. Today, it's as if they've never existed. There's no point in regretting their loss.

In my present scribblings I am not, let it be clear, interested in The Good Old Days. In the good old days, when our teachers entered the classroom, we got to our collective feet out of respect. Most of the time we thought: *Here comes the arsehole.* The school authorities were satisfied by the show of obedience, and we learnt the fine art of hypocrisy. Those are the good old days. The phrase itself is an exercise in sarcasm.

When memory flows from my mind to my pen, it's like assuming another skin, one so obsolete it's as if fresh. My muscles grow taut again, or weary from battle, or rigid with the uncertainties of a life yet to be made. I become once more a dazzled lover, a clumsy father, the teacher who blew hot and cold. My hair darkens, my sight sharpens, my voice sounds like distant versions of the one that is mine today. I see me as I was, reinhabiting those skins and marvelling at how unrecognisable I am, even though I know that the boy I was then is within the man I am now.

I recognise the conceit of the enterprise, but I do not regret it. With age, one sheds many of the vanities that animate the younger years. It's reassuring to have one left. So I scribble in longhand on sheets of vellum — recollections of people who have been part of my life or intrusions into it; recollections that have come to me over the last months with no discernible coherence, some with the vivid immediacy of yesterday, others with greater distance. There are ten or eleven of them, I haven't counted, the number is irrelevant.

More pertinent is what's to be done with them. As Mary's friend Martha would have said, I haven't the foggiest.

Possibilities are legion. I could simply give them to Agnes, or leave them to her in my will. I would like my grandson to have them one day, they may prove of some interest to him as he reaches that inevitable point in his life where a grasp of the larger family picture acquires a certain urgency, but I worry that they might end up a mere curiosity in his hands, some kind of exotic bauble, un-decipherable cyphers whose flavours and subtleties would prove forever inaccessible because of what is already, to him, the passive, second-hand language in which they are written.

I toy with the idea of secreting them some place safe but not too discreet, so that they will one day be found quite unexpectedly, a treasure unearthed, as it were. I imagine Agnes discovering them many years hence. I see the pages delicately grasped in her febrile fingers, while François, grown into a young man, gazes over her shoulder at the precious anthropological find. A look of wonder crosses Agnes's face — in this fantasy hardly changed, as if my mind cannot conjure the ways time might sculpt itself onto her features — when she realises what she's holding.

A look of wonder? Really, Mackenzie, really! Such exaggeration, such immodesty! Mary often said it was a wonder I never dislocated my shoulder trying to pat myself on the back. One morning, wishing to loosen up my stiff, under-exercised muscles, I performed a few toe-touches before the bedroom mirror. Mary came in, took one look at me, and accused me of bowing to myself in adoration. I'm not a bad fellow, she always said, simply one whose attention and sympathy are most easily stirred by his own achievements.

So this writing paper I've purchased has been chosen, I'm beginning to suspect, less with my daughter in mind than myself. It may be, in some curious way, a vicarious gift.

But there's nothing to be done about it now. The paper will

have to do, as will the remote-controlled fire-truck I got for François and the bottle of very fine wine — at least, what the man at the wine store swore was very fine wine — that is my offering to Jack. I do wish that my gifts were more personal, more intimate, less generic. But this is a pleasure denied me. For this to happen, I would have to have known them as Mary did, on a wholly different order, in a wholly different way.

The boy sits up on my lap. "Grand-papa," he says, "j'ai soif."

"Your mother's in the kitchen. She'll give you something to drink." I help him to his feet and he runs off. Outside, the snow thickens, its descent through the windless night sedate and elegant.

Last night, I dreamed of Kevin. It was summer, the air warm and dry. We were eleven years old. We were standing at the edge of a grassy field, ten feet or so from each other. He was as usual facing away from me and seemed unaware of my presence. His hair was flaxen, plastered flat to the pate except at the nape of his neck, where it curled in tight, discreet rebellion. His shoulders were narrow, suggestive of a frailty that would have persisted. His frame was slight and fine-boned; he would never have muscled up. He merely stood there, my brother, gazing away, perhaps at the gentle undulation where field met sky. I had no desire to call out to him, no desire to have him face me, no desire to discover what his face might look like. It was enough that he was there, not far from me.

That's all there is to it — the dream, I mean. As always, an experience without narrative or exchange, static even, but remarkable as unsummoned moments of great peacefulness.

It was mere days after his eighth birthday, on a day of heavy snow, the kind of snow that obliterates the world, that Kevin went outside to play and never returned. There was no wind to whip the snow into chaos, there was no sense of havoc. Children play outside all the time in conditions less benign. His body was found the following spring as the deep drifts thawed in the fields that began, back then, only two blocks from our house. No explanation for what happened to him was ever found. My parents were told his body was unblemished; there was no sign of attack or accident. It looked for all the world as if he had stretched out in the snow and fallen asleep, for good. I have no memory of him, or of his funeral. I was too young. Except for his name, all I know — and precious little it is — is hearsay.

I no longer tell Agnes about my dreams of Kevin. They make her uneasy, and being uneasy makes her irritable. She's a modern woman, Agnes, a successful professional, but even the modern imagination falters before immemorial illogic: charms, jinxes, omens of one kind or another. Agnes will never admit to it, but each morning she reads her horoscope in the newspaper.

Some years ago, after I'd recounted one of the dreams to her, she said with something approaching anguish, "But father, how come you dream of someone you never knew, someone you can't remember? You don't even know what he looked like."

Agnes knows there are no photographs of the man who would have been her uncle. His appearance is all conjecture. I struggled with her question then, and I continue to struggle with it now. No satisfactory answer has ever occured to me. I simply know that my brother's appearance is not wholly a mystery to me. I dare not share this with Agnes. The dreams are not in the least discomforting to me, but to her they are a kind of unsettling magic, a mystery she cannot accommodate. I accept the magic. Now.

I was not a believer in magic as a young man. I prided myself that no one could pull the wool over my eyes. When I was a boy, perhaps seven, my father took me to see a magician. A *prestidigitator*, he said, teaching me the longest word I'd yet learnt. We went to a small theatre downtown. It seemed very far away. The crowd was large and animated, and my father seemed to know half the people in the lobby. Inside, on a stage, there was a man in a top-hat and cape, aided by an assistant, a young woman who appeared to have hidden a brace of rabbits in the top of her spangled evening gown. Apparitions filled the stage, objects appeared and disappeared, fire was swallowed and spat out. Everyone was impressed, or at least pretended to be. I refused to believe in the trickery.

I remember my determination being hard on my father. This was our first excursion alone as father and son, without Ruth-Ann or my mother, and he'd clearly invested a great deal in it. I felt that the gregariousness with which he greeted his friends was meant in part to impress me with his ease in the world, to suggest that he had a whole other life, a more exciting life, away from our home. I would not let myself be impressed, by anything. He felt he had failed. My scepticism extinguished his animation, and we returned home in a silence that acquired a certain permanence. It was as if he could never quite bring himself to trust me again. Did he feel that I'd judged him harshly?

Now, after decades, I too have come to a belief in magic of a sort, a febrile magic but the only one left to me. To be succinct, living in the present is becoming something of a struggle. As for the future — I've never been *that* optimistic a fellow! So what's left to me is the treacherous territory of memory, its magic which permits events a life long after they've ended, animates feelings long dissipated, breathes quickness into bodies from which quickness has fled.

My single wish is that this house — which Agnes and Jack have, objectively speaking, infused with a chaotic warmth: throw-rugs, cushions, books haphazardly shelved, stacks of magazines and financial reports, yards of music albums and compact discs — that this house had a fireplace. Flames, ironically, open up the pathways of the mind in the way that fish do through their hypnotic meanderings between glass walls.

But this retrieval of the past, the belief that one's perceptions and recollections are trustworthy — this is all tricky business.

꙳

Two days ago, preparing myself a cup of tea in the kitchen, I called Agnes "Mary". I pursued an entire conversation with her thinking she was her mother. And when she pointed out, gently, her palm pressed in reassurance to my arm, that she was Agnes, I laughed it off, made light of it, pretended it was just a slip of the tongue when it fact it was a slip of the mind. I covered up. I had no choice, for the truth was alarming enough to make me light-headed. My conversation had been with *Mary*, and it had been a shock to see her features reshape themselves into Agnes. It was like losing Mary, my dear Mary, all over again. I brought my tea here, to the living room — I remember mumbling to myself: Walk, Mackenzie, stop shuffling! — and took refuge in this very armchair that has yet to accommodate itself to the con- tours of my body. I sat here for a very long time, the tea untouched and growing cold, searching in vain for myself in the unreflective windowpane.

It was the scent of the Christmas tree that rescued me. Jack had bought it the evening before and stood it in the corner where, overnight, the branches had settled, restoring the shape it had had before being cut and bundled. As the tree opened up, stretching its limbs as it were, it released a rich and vibrant scent — and it was this scent, so redolent of the here and now, as if the tree knew that its future days hence was one of dessication and abandonment, that burrowed its way into my senses. *Here I am, Mackenzie*, it seemed to insinuate, *fragrant with life even now.*

That evening, fortified by a generous helping from the bottle of sherry Jack has added to his liquor cabinet for my benefit, I lent a hand with the decorating of the tree, helping Jack untangle the strings of light and replacing the burnt bulbs. Not even handling the old decorations — handed over years ago to Agnes when, alone in the house now gone, I had no use for them — could diminish my buoyant mood. Being close to the tree, touch- ing it, beautifying it with an extravagance only Christmas could justify, a peace such as I haven't known for many years came to me: as if a multitude of nameless essentials had secreted themselves into my blood, sweetening it with heady perfumes. Mary's voice guided me as I worked, reminding me that the big bulbs went deep, close to the stem, while the smaller ones were hung from the tips of the branches. *You'll remember, won't you?* I went to bed contented.

But the feeling has not lasted. By this morning it was gone, leaving me hungry for it. This, I imagine, is progress. Before last night, the hunger had been unknown to me.

The boy returns from the kitchen. He walks as if on a tightrope. In one hand he holds a tumbler, in the other a glass of sherry. I reach for the tumbler.

"Mais non, grand-papa!" he says in mock irritation. "L'autre c'est pour toi."

Taking the sherry, I pretend disappointment. I pat my lap, but he shakes his head and sits instead on the floor. He sips at his juice and stares at the glowing tree with an intensity that suggests he's trying to peer into the very heart of it.

I lean forward as best I can and point to a glass icicle hanging just above his line of sight. "François, do you see that decoration?"

"Celle-ci?" He indicates a red ball beside it.

"No, the other one. The icicle."

"Oui?"

"Do you know — the first Christmas after your mother was born, your grandmother bought that icicle and she hung it on the tree and said, when Agnes has her own life and she buys her own trees, this'll be hers. That was a long time ago. Remarkable it's survived all these years."

François says, "Grand-maman?"

"Yes. Your grandmother. Mary."

Mary, my dear Mary. Forever to him just a name. How I wish I could speak to him of her, that I could transmit the essence of the woman he will never know. But the words François and I share are few, they allow for no subtlety, and the many that we do not share stand between us like a darkened valley from which emerges not the merest echo.

Hazelnuts are round and smooth. They have no natural faultline like walnuts or almonds. They are therefore the most difficult to crack. For the third time this evening, I centre one badly in the nutcracker and send it flying like a musket bullet past Mary's head. She doesn't flinch, follows it almost idly, a veteran now, ensuring it avoids the more brittle of our possessions: windowpanes, vases, the television screen. They will slumber for months in corners or under rugs, one day emerging underfoot as you're walking by in stockinged feet with a scalding cup of tea in your hand.

I reach for another hazelnut but Mary, quicker, dips into the bowl and offers me a peanut in the shell.

Snapping the shell open between thumb and forefinger, I say,

❧

"The fact is, Mary, I do *not* remember."

"I don't believe you," she says in that nonchalant and infuriating way she has of calling my bluff. "Everybody remembers the day JFK died." Her gaze sweeps around the shadowed living room as if seeing the hordes, this "everybody" she has summoned to her argument.

"You remember, too, I suppose," I reply as drily as possible, placing a peanut on my tongue.

"Of course I do. I was in the kitchen, just about to start making lunch. Pot-roast and scalloped potatoes. Martha was coming over."

"You're either fibbing or you're showing off. Mary, that was almost thirty years ago."

"You asked. Why would I make it up?"

"To drive me crazy."

"My dear, there are so many other ways to do that. Why are you sounding so grumpy?"

"Perhaps it's that tone of triumph in your voice? You seem to be enjoying yourself rather richly."

"I am. I don't believe this amnesia of yours for a moment. What I can't imagine is why you insist on it."

"I insist on it because it is the truth."

"My darling, this little game has been fun. Let's not complicate it by bringing truth into it, shall we?"

"Mary, when will you leave it alone? When will you stop bringing up —"

"Ahh, so you do remember *that*, don't you? You know me well enough after all these years together, Alistair. You know I don't believe in forgiving, or forgetting."

Before she can stop me I slip a hazelnut between the teeth of my nutcracker and press hard. The damned thing cracks open.

～

My convalescence had gone well, although I had grown accustomed to the feel of civilian clothing rather more quickly than to the idea that the shell had damaged my ear and ruined my leg for good. I had bad moments, of course. Carousing had become a fairly sedentary activity for me and, in a city where nights were defined by the word even at the height of the fighting in Europe, what young man can shrug that off? This was a city that would romp its way into the Apocalypse. But on the whole I counted myself lucky. I had seen first hand how much worse it could have been.

My age and the pronounced limp marked me as a veteran. Normandy? people would say. Afraid not, I would reply. Later, deep in France. A bullet? A shell. And then I would enjoy a round or two of free drinks from people buoyed by the certainty that the Nazi back had been broken and our armies would soon be claiming Berlin.

One cloudy afternoon, I left a discreet establishment on Guy Street with my spirits well fortified and the contents of my pocketbook undiminished. I had hardly walked — or hobbled — a block when I ran smack into what appeared to be a couple's domestic dispute spilled onto the sidewalk.

The woman was a bit younger than me, and pretty, the man an older fellow in a worn grey suit and spectacles with lenses so thick they caused his pupils to bulge. He was red-faced, hands gesturing spasmodically as he berated her. Too many buttons! I heard him shout. Too many buttons, Miss! You should be ashamed! Then he reached out, seized one of the buttons on her jacket and began tugging at it, trying to rip it off.

I tapped the fellow on the leg with my stick. "You're lucky I'm not a cop," I said.

Blue patches appeared on his cheeks. "But look at her!" he shouted, as a crowd gathered. "Look at the hussy!"

I looked, her large caramel-coloured eyes meeting mine with a frankness that made my heart skip a beat. I saw that she was not in the least cowed. She did not fit my definition of a hussy — modestly dressed in matching jacket and skirt, light blue, the jacket neatly buttoned up to her neck, a simple brooch pinned to her left breast. Apart from the palest lip-gloss — an appealing suggestion of moistness — her face was unpainted. "Do you know this gentleman?" I asked.

"I've never seen him before in my life."

"That's neither here nor there," the fellow retorted. "Given the situation—"

"I think you owe this lady an apology."

"We all have a duty," he sputtered. "To do our bit. Even if we're not on a battlefield. This is the home-front. We have a duty."

He saw my puzzlement.

"Look, man!" he said, chopping his hand towards her jacket. "Count the buttons!"

Although now convinced I was dealing with instability, I counted. Ten. "So?"

"We are in a war, man. There are regulations."

People in the crowd started mumbling. One voice raised the question that I was struggling with: "That's all fine, but what in the world is he talking about?"

The fellow's head swivelled from side to side, searching for his questioner. "The regulations are clear," he said to the puzzlement now written on every face. "Women—"

"Ladies," I corrected him.

"Ladies are not permitted more than nine buttons on their clothing. This *lady* has got ten. See for yourselves."

All eyes turned towards her, and for the first time she seemed to quail.

"Even so," I said hurriedly, "what's the harm?"

"I'm no military man," the fellow said, tapping his glasses. "But there must be a good reason. Who knows what lives might be endangered—"

"Don't be silly," I said. "I am a military man, or was until recently, and one button is as vital to the war effort as, well, you appear to be."

This brought laughter from the crowd, some of whom started drifting away.

"If we all flouted the regulations—"

"But we don't, do we? And besides, what would you have the lady do? Compromise her modesty? Or are you some kind of pervert who gets his jollies by seeing ladies half-dressed in the street? Is that it? Perversion hiding behind patriotism?"

The fellow turned purple, and when two of the more rugged men in the crowd nosed up to him, he hurried away.

"Probably some government number-cruncher," one of the men said, tipping his hat to the woman.

I took her arm. "Are you all right?"

"Yes, thank you. But I really didn't need your help."

"When he touched you—"

"We're all living with a great deal of tension these days. He was harmless."

"Would you like a drink? To settle your nerves?"

"My nerves don't need settling, thank you. Besides, I make a point of not drinking in the middle of the day."

I wondered whether she could smell the whisky on my breath, and it was suddenly very important to me that she not do so. I folded a stick of gum into my mouth. "Are you shopping, then?"

"I just came out for a breath of fresh air. I'm on my way back to work."

"What do you do?"

"I'm a government number-cruncher," she said, disarming me with a smile that shone with the light of a thousand suns.

Four weeks later, to mark the first month's anniversary of our meeting, Mary bought me the stick that supported me for decades, until the night it was left behind in the house now reduced to cinders.

Mary fishes a chunk of walnut from its shattered shell. "You were already overseas the day the bomber crashed into Griffintown, weren't you?"

"When was that?"

"1944. April, I think."

"You think! Can't you be more specific?"

"The twenty-fourth, sometime in the morning."

Sometime? But I restrain myself. "Of course I was overseas. Waiting to cross the Channel. End of April, you say? So it took me another two months to get to France. I remember feeling let down. I'd dreamed of being part of the big show. You know, storming ashore and capturing a pillbox single-handed."

"Such a waste. They all died, you know. The crew. Five young men in their Liberator."

"You knew them?"

"Oh no. They were RAF. Not from around here."

"And you remember where you were and what you were doing when you heard about it, I suppose."

"Well, I was there, you see. Downtown. At the corner of Peel and St. Catherine."

"You were there, on the spot . . ." My tone is dryer than she deserves. Mary and I have talked about many things throughout our years together — and of many of those things many times over — but we have spoken little of the war. Once it was all over, it was something to put behind us, our lives no longer on hold.

"I was on my break. I was standing at the south-west corner trying to decide between a soda and a coffee, and I'd just decided on a coffee when people around me began stopping and looking up towards the mountain. This strange growl filled the air, an airplane no doubt but much lower than it had any right to be. And there it was, having just come over the mountain, descending, descending, following Peel Street towards the river. For God's sake, it looked as if it was going to land on Peel Street. I saw its belly so clearly I could almost count the rivets. And my first reaction was anger. Some hotshot flyboy, I thought, buzzing the downtown, getting his kicks from startling the civilians. But there was this yearning in the growl of the engines, and then a kind of cough. And then, not long after . . . I didn't see it, of course. But I heard it. Horrible, horrible. Ten people were killed on the ground too, you know. When the victories began to come a few months later, I wasn't quite as thrilled as I might have been. I was too aware of the cost, for those up there, for those on the ground. It was like the *Athenia* back at the beginning of the war. D'you remember that? I knew people who'd taken that ship to England. I'd never been on it, I'd never even seen it, and I didn't know anybody who went down with her. But the day she was torpedoed I learnt not to underestimate the power of the vicarious. Just knowing that people I knew had spent weeks on board — it gave me the shivers. And the *Liberator* — well, it was the tiniest taste, but enough, of what Europe must have been like."

"Do you remember the date?"

"Of the *Athenia*? September fourth, 1939."

"Third, Mary. September third, 1939."

"Yes, you're right. I heard about it the next day."

A nut cracks open in my nutcracker. "Almond?" I say.

She shakes her head. "I think it's time for a bit of sherry, don't you?"

"It's the middle of the day, Mary."

"See what you've done to me?"

There was as yet no ring on her finger, but I was thinking about putting one there. The war in Europe was as good as won. The Japanese would be left but there, too, we had little doubt as to the outcome — the only question being how much blood would be spilled before Tokyo surrendered. I tell myself now, as I told myself then, that I was waiting for the official end to hostilities before presenting Mary with the ring I had already bought, at discount and on time, from a jeweller friend of my father's.

One evening, I accompanied Mary to a party, a birthday celebration, I believe, friends of hers. There, for the first and only time, I met a man who very nearly changed the course of my life forever. He went by the unlikely name of Norman Landing, and he was an acquaintance of Mary's. She introduced me to him shortly after our arrival, a tall, somewhat gaunt fellow with a striking resemblance to Leslie Howard. I offered him my hand, but his was not forthcoming. I saw too late that he had only one — hand, I mean — and it was occupied with a drink.

Mary said, "Norman was at Normandy."

Norman said, "Only briefly. 82nd Airborne. We went in just after midnight, from three hundred feet on a moonlit night. The drop didn't go my way, I'm afraid. Came down in trees. I broke through branches and hit the ground hard. Only, my arm didn't make it all the way. It stayed up in the tree."

I winced — and not only because of the nonchalance with which he had described the wrenching-off of his arm. I winced because I could feel myself diminsh before him. Here he was, after all. Movie-star looks. Urbane. An American paratrooper, a Pathfinder yet, the first wave of the first wave into Normandy. And here I was limping around, unable to summon the courage to give Mary the ring I carried around constantly in my jacket pocket.

The party did not improve for me after this. Norman took Mary off to get a drink and for the next hour or so I managed only to glimpse her through the crowd, laughing, chatting, always at Norman's side. She seemed — and she was not the only one — to hang on his every word, to bask in the reflected glamour of Norman from Normandy. I would have liked to ask him what had happened to the arm. Was it still hanging there, waving in the breezes? Or had it been retrieved, so to speak? I enjoyed the grimness of the pun, but I knew, too, that my questions would remain unspoken. I had been unnerved by Norman as thoroughly as he had been disarmed by the tree.

I wandered around the apartment doing as lost people do in such situations — examining the furnishings, fingering the fixtures, developing an interest in art and artifacts which would not normally interest me. Mary's friends were artists and their own ridiculous inventions — their *oeuvres*, as they referred to their crackpot canvases — littered the walls of the apartment. I found myself fleeing one silly conversation after another.

Who's this Harry Truman guy anyways?

Anybody know what the S is for?

Yeah, I do. Sergeyevich. Harry Sergeyevich Truman.

He's Uncle Joe's second cousin, Uncle Sam's brother.

One has to be under the influence of something strong to appreciate such pathetic humour. I was under the influence of nothing. This conversation occasioned much honking and braying. I'd had enough.

I went in search of Mary. The cavernous living room — the place was a converted warehouse — was now thick with people. I had last seen her on the other side, in the far corner. I pressed my way through, past backs and arms and hands clutching drinks, and was about half the way there when a path cleared before me, fate opening up a view, and I entered that moment — that awful, awful moment — which told me everything; that moment which remains in memory as it occurred at the time: the sense that something — but what? — was not quite right; that reality was turning fluid; that the moment required humour of me — but what was the joke?; that time was slipping inexorably away from me, like an ice-cube dissolving on a hot grill.

What I saw was this: Mary and Norman coming together, her back pressed to his front, his arm encircling her belly, her hand reaching up to clasp his.

Then fate closed the view, and I was left shattered, with only this view of public intimacy.

Oddly enough, I felt embarrassed, for Mary, for Norman, but mostly for myself. How badly I had miscalculated, how close I had come to making a fool of myself by offering a ring to a woman who would then have been forced to tell me how much she liked me as a friend . . .

As I let myself out, a headache coming on, I reflected that my father's friend would probably agree to cancel the deal and, with any luck, might even refund my down-payment. After all, the ring had never even come close to being used.

For days afterwards, I went around feeling as if someone — Mary, Norman — had excised the bones from my body and drained off my blood. Several times I fled the flat I was renting, fled the ringing of the telephone.

When, after a week or so, I summoned the courage to return Mary's many calls — I was sure the calls had been from her, and I was beginning to feel cruel — I told her I had not been well, a flu that had suddenly come on at the party.

From the silence that followed my weak explanation, I understood that she did not believe me. I hadn't expected that. The conventions to which I was accustomed dictated the acceptance of white lies; they were a way of saying, I offer this flimsy excuse so that we may get gracefully beyond this by subsuming our embarrassment and hurt. But Mary would not play along and in desperation I told another lie: I swore it was the truth. I had been to the doctor, I said, I was on medication. I had no idea what I would do or say next.

Mary's silence deepened, and I could feel the telephone line sizzling in the heat of my lie.

Then she said, "When you're ready to tell me the truth, you have my number."

"It is the truth," I insisted, even as a voice in my head warned that I had already gone too far. Then, without premeditation, I blurted out, "How's Norman doing?"

"Norman?"

"Yes. Norman from Normandy."

"He's gone back to Washington. He— Is that what this is all about? Are you jealous of Norman?"

I said nothing, but I thought: Yes, yes! I'm jealous of Norman. I'm jealous of his damned lost arm and his good looks and his charming conversation and his arm around you . . .

"Tell me, Alistair. Is that it?"

"Yes," I admitted, feeling myself deflate in the way I had when meeting him. "I saw him put his arm around you at the party. I saw you embrace."

"You stupid ass. You stupid, stupid ass. He was telling some silly Army story, that's all he ever talks about, and he used me to demonstrate— But this is all beside the point, isn't it, Alistair? Now, I mean. I've done nothing wrong, but you've gone and done something unforgiveable."

"What in the world are you talking about?"

"There is no flu, is there? Your voice, it's as clear as a bell."

"No."

"You lied to me, Alistair. Instead of simply coming to me and asking me what was going on, you ran off and hid and lied. This won't do, Alistair. This won't do at all."

Then she hung up.

She serves the sherry in the glasses we reserve for special occasions — of crystal cut in such a way that the play of light causes the amber liquid to appear alive.

"What's the occasion?" I ask.

"The time of day."

We touch our glasses, take a sip. I hold up my glass to the stray beam of late afternoon sunlight idling in through the open windows, watch the sherry leap and sparkle with the liveliness of the North Sea on a clear day.

"Do you know who I was just thinking about?" she says.

"I would if I could read your mind, wouldn't I."

"Norman Landing."

"Please Mary, don't—"

"I wonder if he's still alive?"

Who cares? I think but dare not say. Mary does this on occasion. She finds a way to bring up my lie, forces me to relive it. She has neither forgiven nor forgotten — and she wants to be sure I don't either. I find myself squirming when she does this — discomforted by the memory of what I did, disconcerted by the ability of old guilt to unnerve, dismayed at the hatred (not too strong a word) I still feel for Norman Landing. Even innocent, Norman has become inextricable from my shame.

"You know what I think?" she says. "If he's still alive, he's probably a bitter old man. He was so taken with his lost arm. Jumping from that plane and losing his arm were his only heroics in the war. Hardly heroic at all if you ask me. But he was obsessed by it. He traded heavily on it. But you can trade on a story like that only for so long. Peace must have been a great blow to him."

I am overjoyed to hear this, but my joy does not last.

"And to think," she continues, "that you thought I could possibly be interested in him, of all people. And then to go and invent your story of a flu—"

꒜

"Mary, it was all so long ago—"
"Glad to see you haven't forgotten that."
"How can I? I almost lost you."
"Yes, you almost did. You jackass."

꒜

For weeks, it was my turn to collect unreturned phonecalls, weeks in which I was haunted by the pain I imagined in her caramel-coloured eyes. I became a prisoner of the flat, never daring to stray too far from the phone in case it should ring. I slept badly, dozing off at irregular intervals through the night — yet making a point of always keeping myself presentable, showering at odd hours, 3:00 or 4:00 am, when she was unlikely to call, shaving several times a day, brushing my teeth so often my gums hurt.

And finally one day the phone rang. She said, "You've been calling? You have something to say?" I asked if we could meet. The phone, that sizzled line, would not do. She snorted in derision when I mentioned dinner, and at the mention of a drink she said, "I'm not thirsty." But she would meet me, she said, that evening at seven at the chalet on the mountain.

I got there early. Fall was just coming on, leaves turning dull on the trees, the air with a bite to it. I didn't hear her walk up and when I sensed her presence I saw that she had established a great distance between us. We stood for some minutes, separated by an unbridgeable arm's length, looking out at the lights glimmering downtown, at the river the colour of pewter, at night enshrouding the horizon beyond plains and distant hills.

When finally she spoke it was in whispers lofted away in the light breeze. She spoke of the pain my lie had caused her. She spoke of trust and of its banishment. She spoke of feeling hollowed out, emptied, disembowelled, as if she were indeed the fool I had taken her for.

Her words were simple, and not numerous, but they lashed at

me, peeling skin. I heard her out.

When I found my voice, I spoke of the pain my lie had caused me. I spoke of hurt and bewilderment, of fear and loss, and of an overwhelming sense of stupidity. I begged her forgiveness.

No, she said, her face afire. Never.

The word ate its way like a voracious worm into my brain. Never: such a little word, with such big implications. I could feel a door thundering shut on me.

Then, unexpectedly, she took my hand. *Promise me,* she said. *Swear. Never again.*

Hungering for absolution, barely able to withstand the rage in those caramel eyes, I pressed her hand to my heart. I promised, I swore, I pledged my word with my very soul. A shudder ran through me, and I became tremulous. The stick slipped from my grasp, clattered to the ground.

Mary curtsied, reaching a hand out for the stick, but I caught her by the elbows, raised her up.

Then, in the grip of a moment I can describe only as a form of stasis, a moment when the breeze stopped moving, the lights froze, the night hung itself on a breath, I took the ring from my pocket and slipped it on her finger.

⌒

"What are you thinking about?" she asks.

"How close I came to losing you."

Her eyebrows raise sceptically over the rim of the glass at me. Perhaps it's just me, perhaps just my sense of guilt, but I don't think Mary has ever quite lost the distrust I created over Norman Landing. Truth has remained a touchy subject with us. She does not quite believe that I know the meaning of the word — and to be truthful, neither do I at times. Is truth found in impulses formed in a moment of anger or hurt, or is it found in the quiet moments later, when the heat has cooled and perspective is no longer ragged? Or might they both be moments of truth, as a volcano is a form of physical truth both when dormant and during eruption? I have no answers to these questions, for the tranquil aftermath always makes the previous wrath seem a lie. But one thing I can say with a clear conscience: I have kept the promise I made to Mary that fall evening at the chalet on the mountain, when stasis ended in a swirl of arms and a breathless blending that caused the world to race. That moment that was like a natural convergence of streams.

I reach for her hand. There, in my palm, are the years made manifest — the wrinkles, the spots, the tracery of veins rising through skin turned papery. There, too, the ring that came so close to remaining unused, the ring she has never removed in all these years. I press my lips to it, revelling in the warmth that her body infuses into the metal, and in the hardness that speaks of indestructibility.

And in a quiet voice, I say, "November 22nd, 1963. I was in my office at the university. The departmental secretary came to tell me the news. She was sobbing. I thanked her, suggested she take the rest of the day off, saw her out. Then I sat at my desk and let my tears overwhelm me. It felt like a foolish thing to do — but it was the only reaction I was capable of on the day that hope died."

Mary sighs. "So you do remember."

"No. I just know that's what I did when I heard that Kennedy'd been killed. But remember? No. I've never wished to. Only a foolish man would treasure such a memory."

Her fingers close on mine. "And you are," she says. "A foolish, foolish man."

"*Father?*" Agnes calls from the kitchen, her voice reaching me as if through several padded walls.

"Yes, Agnes?"

"Everything all right? You're terribly quiet."

"Everything's just fine."

"Should we be looking in on Aunt Ruth?"

The boy looks expectantly up at me. He likes Ruth-Ann, his great-aunt. He's entertained by her unpredictability, her vagueness, her inability to respect convention. And Ruth-Ann likes him. If she's here now in this house, if she's been allowed to spend the night away from those trained to offer care, it's because of the effect François has on her. His presence soothes her, it creates a space within which the ellipses of her mind become less abrupt, less jarring.

"She's probably all right, Agnes. They gave her a little something before she left, it'll probably keep her out for a while yet. Don't worry. She'll let us know when she's awake."

Agnes peers around the kitchen door. Her eyes — large and dark and, as Mary often claimed, not unlike mine — squint with the anxiety Ruth-Ann inspires in her. "I just wouldn't want her to wake up frightened. You know, unfamiliar surroundings?"

"Unfamiliar surroundings, yes, I know all about those. But I think it'll be all right. Ruth-Ann's more likely to be intrigued than upset."

She considers this for a moment. She knows the essential sweetness that has come to characterise my sister. It is the practicality inherent in my remark that causes her eyes to lose their anxiety. "Guess you're right."

"Of course I am. I've known Ruth-Ann for a long time. Her independence is, you know, a kind of fearlessness. Thank God she hasn't lost that. Got it from our father, I think, although he'd have been mortified to think that."

Agnes mouths something at me that I do not hear — I only see her lips moving — and withdraws back into the kitchen. François, who has fetched himself paper and crayons, is absorbed in a drawing. The house is silent, or at least I assume the silence I hear to be that of the house. Jack is downstairs in his study working on an article he wishes to finish before the week of vacation he's allowing himself between now and the new year. And in my bedroom, her brain venting memory into a void, my sister lies deep in narcotic sleep.

How like our father she is, Ruth-Ann, not in any immediately obvious way — she, too, would have been mortified by the thought — but in her undying wish to search out the sparkle in life, and to create it when there's none from material sometimes bizarre, sometimes innocuous. Once, he was her unwitting accomplice.

My father, for as long as I knew him, never shaved in the water-closet, a small, windowless room so cramped it seemed designed to do damage to elbows and knees. He preferred to prop up a small mirror beside the kitchen window and shave in the soft, early-morning sunlight. On cloudy days, he would sit at the dining table in the hazier light of the Tiffany lamp, his chin jutting stiffly above a bowl of warm water my mother had placed on a folded towel to prevent damage to the table-top. Squinting into the mirror held upright by one of mother's porcelain figurines, he would lather up with his brush and draw his straight razor, freshly stropped to a silvery keenness, down his cheeks and up his neck. He took great pleasure in this operation. He was deliberate and unhurried, each motion studied, as if he were sculpting his face afresh each morning.

One day, when I was still very young, Ruth-Ann nodded towards him as he stood shaving at the kitchen window. "Alis," she whispered, "d'you realise — one slip of the razor and, whammo!, it's arrivederci nose!"

I didn't know what *arrivederci* meant. When she explained that it was *Eye-talian* for goodbye, I was instantly flooded with apprehension. I pictured my father's severed nose winging its way from his face, his startled eyes following its trajectory as it ricocheted off the windowpane, careened off a cupboard and landed smack in the pan of eggs mother was frying for our breakfast.

Ruth-Ann, taller than me by a head, gazed at me with saucer-eyed significance, and gave a single, grave nod.

For weeks afterwards, not wishing to miss the moment when inadvertance might result in swift, radical rhinoplasty, I paid close attention to my father's morning ritual. After having watched me observing him for some time, my mother, misinterpreting my interest, patted me on the head one morning and said, "Patience, Alistair, you'll be shaving, too, before too long." She was beaming.

She could hardly have said anything more horrifying to me at that moment. My flesh was as if brushed by the iced wings of a thousand startled birds. Immobilized by this threat of unavoidable peril, I could barely bring myself to observe my father's morning ritual after this.

I was well into my teenaged years before I could appreciate the sheer cleverness of Ruth-Ann's trick. In its engagement with elemental fears, it was a play of imagination that would never lack for style or effectiveness. It had no expiry date.

And so, one Sunday afternoon not long ago, I called François to me. Struggling with the language, sprinkling simple phrases and words at him — *papa, barbe, rasoir, nez* — while shaping the air with wild gesticulation, I did my best to impress him in the way Ruth-Ann had impressed me. I gave it my all. I mimed the movements, my index finger the razor, my palm the mirror, exaggerating the slip, the excision, the flight of the wayward nose.

François frowned at me in puzzlement.

I repeated the performance, this time with a theatricality I hadn't employed since my earliest days of teaching, when impressing undergraduates still seemed important.

I was not a success. Despite my best efforts, François would not get the point. The child was obtuse. Nothing I did could convey to him the image of his father's nose fleeing his face. To his frustration and mine, he thought my pantomime suggestive of sneezing and skedaddled off in search of Kleenex.

Agnes, who knew the story well and realized what I was about, had eavesdropped with an enigmatic smile as she worked her way through a stack of ironing. When the boy trotted off on his self-appointed mission, she put down the iron, came up to me and whispered into my contraption, "Father, Jacques uses an electric shaver."

I did not thank her for this insight. There's an undeniably cruel streak to my daughter. She'd let me writhe through the entire faltering artifice, to the frittering away of inspiration, before pointing out the fatal flaw. I might as well have been mimicking the motions of scything to someone who knows only mechanical harvesters.

How foolish of me. How foolish. Ruth-Ann would never have allowed this to happen. She would have updated the details, she would have found a way to make the trick work — even now, in the endlessly remade geography of her mind. But she has far greater facility, far wider experience than I in this realm. My sister has, after all, composed a life out of what might be justifiably viewed as one little trick after another.

In the brochure, the gravelled drive up to the front door looked longer, wider, more elegant. Even the grass looked greener. In the last five years, however, they have planted more trees, the saplings, anchored by wires, suggestive of a frail rejuvenation; and they have replaced the heavy wooden benches scattered around the grounds with lighter ones of iron whimsically wrought.

All of this, along with the flowerbeds and birdbaths and patches of rockery, goes a long way in attenuating the unease I feel whenever I come here. For the large modern building at the end of the drive, three storeys of red brick and aluminum-framed windows, is a home — the final home — for people too old to have homes of their own.

My daughter drives slowly, following the arrows to the parking lot at the back. There is space for many cars, but it is usually empty, even on a day such as today, Saturday. The weather is simply too fine for visiting relics.

When Agnes turns off the engine, the quiet is unsettling. I will be some minutes getting used to it. The silence I'm accustomed to is a cocoon, its membrane constantly pressed by disturbance near and far. It is a silence rife with companionship. Here in the country the silence is breathless. There is something suspicious about it.

Making our way around the building, I become aware of the shuffle in my footstep, of the gentle click of Agnes's heels on the concrete path. I become uneasy. Perhaps this is what I find unpleasant about this silence: there is nothing distracting in its echo.

As we mount the stairs to the main door — Agnes gripping my arm, not seeking support but subtly giving it — a nurse known to me from previous visits bustles past and in her friendly, harried manner points past the wheelchair ramp to a clump of trees some distance away. "She's over there having a smoke," she says, hurrying on.

I turn to Agnes. "I can take it from here. I'll see you at the car in an hour."

"Are you sure, father?"

"Go on, run along."

And she runs along to find a quiet spot under some tree, hand already reaching into her purse for the paperback or magazine with which she will pass the time. It is good of her to take the time from her family in order to drive me all the way out here — as it is good of her to leave me to my business.

I find Ruth-Ann where the nurse said she would be, sitting at attention on a bench among the trees, a nurse dozing beside her. I can tell from the fullness of her cheeks that she is wearing her dentures today. Age has wizened her body, but her face retains a certain youthfulness. She would, if she could, be proud of that.

At my approach, the nurse opens his eyes, smiles, and with a little wave goes off. He, too, knows I prefer being alone with her.

"Ruth-Ann?" I say gently. "It's Alis."

She squints up at me, fingers pinching the cigarette holder protruding from her lips. "Alice?" she says. "Strange name for a fellow."

"Alistair," I say. "Your brother."

Her eyes narrow to slits and I see in the moisture flooding them that she is struggling with the word, as if she has lost its meaning.

Every family has its share of oddballs, and mine is no different.

I think, for instance, of the paternal great-uncle whose fear of birds grew so rabid he spent a long-weekend bricking up his country cottage from the inside. A superb mason, he did a thorough job. I imagine he felt an immeasurable safety until the day his food supply ran out. Only then did it dawn on him that he had left unbricked neither windows nor doors. Then he discovered he had left his sledge-hammer outside. A loner, it was over a month before he was released, a thin man turned skeletal but thankful that he'd had water-pipes run to the kitchen the year before.

And then there was my mother's cousin Edwina, whose experience of a mild earthquake led her, in later years, to reinforce her bedroom with transparent tape — reams of it firmly and carefully applied on the four walls and ceiling. It was said after her death that the tape, over three inches deep in places, had hardened over time into a tough internal carapace. "Just," I remember my mother saying, "like Edwina herself."

These antecedents — treasured parts of the family legend — may explain why my sister Ruth-Ann, without herself being one, was always attracted to oddballs. Exoticism is taken wherever it is found.

Let me be frank. Were she not my sister, Ruth-Ann and I
would not have been friends. The only interests we had in common were those given to us by shared blood and childhood
experience — and since Ruth-Ann is my senior by nine years,
even these were not numerous. She was attracted to the bizarre,
while I have always found the bizarre to be, well, merely bizarre.

I was half the way through my fourteenth year when Ruth-Ann,
in my memory of the time an ordinary-looking girl saved by
jauntiness (but I am speaking here of my *sister*, after all), ran off
with a fellow named Dalrymple. He was a circus performer,
an acrobat of some kind. My parents were devastated in their
understated way. Mother moved about with a stridency that
suggested anger but lack of surprise; father, dazed, was softened
by his hurt and bewilderment. For a long time, the house was
gripped in the peculiar silence that arises from mumbling and
seething whispers.

Some months later, we received by mail photographs of their
wedding: there, in the centre of the main ring, was my sister
resplendent in a traditional bridal outfit, her husband beaming
beside her in a white tuxedo and glittery top-hat. (He had borrowed the outfit, I found out later, from the ring-master). Around
them in full costume — standing on hands, heads, bicycles
and each other's shoulders; hanging from trapeze bars, ropes, an
elephant's trunk — were jugglers, trapeze artists, gymnasts,
lion-trainers, strong-men, clowns and a gaggle of monkeys. My
parents were not comforted, although I do remember being
cheered by the thought of free tickets should the circus ever come
to town.

And one day, approximately two years later, it did.

It is an unsettled day. High above, continents of white cloud
slowly give way to oceans of uniform blue, while lower down,

dark islands race by ragged and torn, edges fraying in violent winds.

Ruth-Ann is wearing the pink sweater Mary knitted for her many years ago. It is a little beaten now, a little misshapen, the wool loose in places, and it hangs on her whereas, new, it had been snug, but there is still a certain dapperness to it. Ruth-Ann would not wear it otherwise, even now.

She sucks hard on the cigarette holder, her cheeks collapsing, and an acrid burning reaches my nostrils. The tobacco is gone, the filter beginning to smoulder. I reach for the holder and ease its tip from her lips. She does not resist, her mouth working in disgust the way François's does when Agnes feeds him boiled carrots.

"Well, old girl," I say, "how are they treating you?"

Gaze somewhere in the far distance, she says, "Supercalifragilisticexpialidocious." Her voice remains strong, even though it is an instrument now connected only to brief moments of lucidity.

"Are you eating well? I must say, you appear to be in fine shape." My heart cracks a little when I say this, for Ruth-Ann remains robust for her age. No serious physical ailment has come to the fore, no organ has announced itself as the future agent of her demise. When the doctor suggested we attempt to wean her off cigarettes, I could manage only an astonished, "To what purpose?"

Overhead, an airplane banks gracefully, aligning itself with a runway at the international airport miles hence.

Ruth-Ann looks up, follows its progress until it disppears. "Supercali," she whispers as if sighting a miracle.

᭜

My parents, perhaps in an atttempt at pre-emptive self-defence, decided that the rigours of family reconciliation and meeting the son-in-law were best handled in public.

The company my father worked for was holding a picnic for employees the following Sunday at Beaver Lake. They instructed ("invited" is not quite the appropriate word) Ruth-Ann and Dalrymple to meet us there. I was at an age when I usually passed on such things as company picnics and Christmas parties, but this held such promise I eagerly tagged along.

The picnic had already begun when we arrived, my parents as usual seeking to be unobtrusive. Groups and couples wandered among the tables set up to feed the hungry masses, red and white chequered tablecloths lending an air of gaiety in the sunshine. Children ran around chasing each other and helping themselves from platters laden with sandwiches, bowls of salad, nuts and fruits, pitchers brimming with iced water and juices.

We found a spot slightly apart from the crowd, on one of the grassy slopes leading down to the water, sufficiently distant to establish a certain formality but not so much as to appear anti-social. We sat on a throw-cover my mother had spread, my father passing the time tipping his hat and waving at colleagues, his eyes and my mother's — and mine, for that matter — anxiously scanning the crowd and beyond for signs of my sister. Truth to tell, I was also on the look-out for a man in tights — I could picture Dalrymple only in what I conceived to be his circus costume.

We waited a long time, my mother growing impatient, my father and I making occasional trips to the food tables. Mother refused to eat, contenting herself with a glass of watery apple juice.

She had already suggested twice that we give up and return home when, from the top of the hill behind us, Ruth-Ann startled us with a joyous shout: "Mom! Dad! Alis!"

Mother, looking ambushed, grimaced and shut her eyes tight. Father heaved a sigh and tugged the brim of his hat lower on his forehead. I had barely stood up before Ruth-Ann wrapped her arms around me, picked me up and swung me around. When she

~

finally let me go I was breathless.

As she went to mother and father — a peck on the cheek for one, a brief embrace for the other — a shy-looking man standing just off to the side gave me an uncertain smile.

Dalrymple did not look in the least as I had expected. There was nothing remotely dashing or raffish about him. A decade or so older than my sister, he was hardly taller than me. His hair was neatly combed, his moustache trimmed, his cheeks chubby and closely shaved. He was wearing, of all things, a three-piece suit, the vest of which hugged an unexpected paunch. His shoulders were wide, though, and his grip, when he offered me his hand to shake, was powerful.

Father shook his hand in silence. Mother, in even greater silence, refused to do so.

Ruth-Ann took my arm and, whispering that she wanted to chat with mom and dad, asked if I would take Dalrymple to get something to eat. He was starving, he said, he always was. When I hesitated — I was more interested in eavesdropping on her conversation with our parents — she said in a girlish manner, "Pleeease, Alis?" Ruth-Ann has always known how to get her way.

"Come on, then," I called unhappily to Dalrymple and, without waiting, strode off down the slope towards the tables.

I was half the way there, stewing in my disappointment at having been denied drama and even more so at Dalrymple's conventionality, when he suddenly zipped past me, a spinning blur. Like everyone else at the picnic, I froze in my tracks, my mouth quite literally hanging agape.

For my brother-in-law was cartwheeling past me down the slope.

I watched, breathless, as he cartwheeled his way through the crowd, past children squealing in fear, past men puzzled to sudden silence, past women staring in shock, past the food tables, helping himself as he went, juggling sandwiches, carrot sticks, a chicken leg, past the croquet game, the water barrel of bobbing apples, the tethered pony giving rides in a circle, juggling and eating as he went. By the time he cartwheeled into the lake, he had consumed every smidgeon of the food, the stripped chicken bone tossed easily into a garbage can. When he emerged dripping from the water with a bottle of root-beer at his lips, shock gave way to a crescendo of applause ripping through the air like sails whipped by a powerful breeze.

Back up on the slope, mother was flat on her back, father crouched beside her furiously fanning her face with his hat.

Ruth-Ann, a few feet off, was jumping up and down. Her eyes were on her distant husband, her arms raised in triumph.

The nurse, who has remained at a discreet distance, fixes a new cigarette to the holder and lights it for her. Ruth-Ann's smoking is permitted only under supervision; she is allowed to possess neither cigarettes nor lighter — the danger of accident would be too great — and so is taken for a lengthy fix three times a day. Even under these conditions, I am told, she manages to consume a carton each week.

As the nurse takes his leave, Ruth-Ann gestures him back. "Give him one," she says, jabbing a thumb at me.

I shake my head. "It's all right, dear. I don't smoke, remember?"

"Give him one," she insists, suddenly angry.

The nurse extracts a cigarette from the pack and holds it out to me. "Just take it," he says. "It makes her happy."

"But I don't smoke."

"You don't have to smoke it. Just take it."

So I take it, and Ruth-Ann settles down, puffing happily away.

My fist closes over the cigarette, and it seems to radiate a kind of warmth into my palm.

Two days later, I met Ruth-Ann at the neighbourhood ice-cream parlour, a place where, younger, she had spent many an hour plotting adventure with her school friends. What for her friends had been a fantasy game turned out to have been, for Ruth-Ann, concrete plans. "Scooportwo, Tuesday, 2 o'clock", she'd whispered as we helped father bundle our greenish mother into a taxi.

We each ordered a cone — two chocolate scoops for her, one vanilla for me. Ruth-Ann insisted on paying. "My treat, Alis. It's about time, eh?" We took them outside. There was no place to sit, at least no place where we would not be observed, frowned at, reported on, so we wandered together through the unpaved lanes that provided passage between the backyards of houses. Later, those yards would be hectic with families pausing before supper as the heat of the afternoon waned, fathers still in sleeves and ties but jacketless, mothers cool and fresh after afternoon baths, the children neat and listless. Now, though, in the middle of the afternoon, the yards were deserted, fathers still in offices, mothers perhaps relishing a few moments alone while the children napped.

Ruth-Ann did most of the talking, filling me in on the last two years of her life.

For the first year or so, the circus had toured Canada, going from one small town to the next, one fair to the next. She had seen parts of the country she hadn't even known existed — and of most of them she said, "Once was too much." She had enjoyed Halifax, though, and Vancouver, and Toronto. "Guess I'm a big-city girl at heart, Alis. Once you've seen one mountain, you've seen them all." She had, she said, no feel for landscape. She kept busy doing odd-jobs, whatever needed to be done, from feeding the monkeys to cleaning out the elephants' stalls, eventually settling in as bookkeeper and ticket-seller. The jobs, she said, complemented each other.

"When we ran out of Canada, we headed down into the States." More small towns, more fairs. Her duties now included bookings and scheduling — and it was this that led to her big coup. She arranged for the circus to go overseas.

They had just returned from a year touring Europe, England first, then the continent. Several of those months had been spent in Germany — "They love a good show, Alis, noise and spectacle." She had developed great enthusiasm for the Germans. "You should see them, Alis," she said to me. "Strong and healthy. Determined. Disciplined. A force to be reckoned with. Fine-looking folk. Really fine-looking."

At the time, I knew little about the Nazis and could only nod. I had seen some photographs in magazines, but few people had any sense of the threat these "fine-looking folk" would present in just a few short years. Only in retrospect did this admiration strike me as curious — coming as it did from someone to whom discipline was a concept not far removed from the Spanish Inquisition.

Before taking her leave of me, she gave me four tickets to the circus. "Maybe mom and dad'll like to come," she said. I nodded, even though we knew the prospect to be unlikely. "And you — bring a friend, perhaps?" She cocked an eyebrow inquisitively at me. "Maybe a girlfriend?"

I blushed — such talk embarrassed me deeply at the time. She wrapped her arms around me and, just as she had at the picnic, swung me around and around. Then she hugged me so tight I gasped for air. Planting a kiss on each of my cheeks, she ran off.

Three days later the circus left town and I threw out the unused tickets. Imagining her looking out for us every night, imagining her scanning the crowd for our faces, imagining her disappointment, I have felt guilty ever since.

The following year, I received a short letter from Ruth-Ann. It was postmarked Juno. Dalrymple had left her and the circus, running off with the lion-tamer's daughter. She would remain with the circus for a while, until she decided what course to take.

৵৫

I was not to worry about her, she wrote. "You know me. I just keep on rolling with the punches and anything else that comes my way." This was the only hint she ever gave that her life was less than she would have wished it.

She asked that I give our parents the news. When I did, mother said, "So, he's cartwheeled his way out of her life, has he? I always knew he would."

Father, not looking up from his *Gazette*, grunted.

Mother said, "Is she coming home, then?" I could see she was already girding herself with righteousness; already she expected submission from the wayward daughter.

"No."

And that little word wounded mother in a way I had not seen since Ruth-Ann's first flight. It was as if an icicle had hit her in the heart.

"Ruth-Ann?"

She squints sideways at me, smoke billowing from her mouth and nostrils. "How do you know my name?"

"You're my sister."

"Are you Dalrymple?"

"No, I—"

"Are you Lardner, then?"

"No, I'm Alistair, your brother."

"Do you know Dalrymple and Lardner? I don't know who they are." Her gaze sweeps around, as if seeking the elusive among the trees and flowers and, more intently, a congregation of residents in wheelchairs some distance away. "Who are they?"

"They live here, as you do."

Her eyes swivel sharply towards me. "Not *them*. I know who *they* are. I mean Dalrymple and Lardner."

"They were your husbands, dear."

"My husbands." She speaks the word with the authority of

full understanding. Her eyes, glistening, reach up to the celestial drama of rushing cloud.

Sitting here in silence, allowing Ruth-Ann the pleasure of exploring what I imagine to be images suddenly ordered, I become aware of the slight chill that underlies the warmth of the day. I regret having gruffly rejected Agnes' suggestion of a wind-breaker.

Soon, emerging from reflection, Ruth-Ann turns to me and says, "And you — do you have a husband?"

Six months later, mother got her wish. Ruth-Ann came home. She merely turned up one day, a suitcase in hand, looking exhausted. "Hi, Alis," she said when I opened the door. "Mom home?"

She wasn't. She was out visiting a friend, and father was, of course, at work.

"Mind if I come in?"

Why would I mind? I was happy to see her, and as far as I was concerned, it was still her home too. She plumped herself down on the sofa and yawned. This was all very disconcerting to me. I had never before seen my sister listless. She accepted a cup of tea. I prepared a pot and while we waited for it to steep — she liked her tea strong and hot — I attempted to make conversation. "So," I said, sprawling in my chair, "how have things been?"

"Rough."

This was all she said — all she apparently wished to say — and I thought it prudent not to probe further. To fill the silence, I busied myself pouring the tea through a strainer.

As I handed her a cup, she looked up quickly at me and said, "One thing, Alis — don't expect to be an uncle, ever."

Stunned, I replied, "The thought has never occurred to me."

At that moment the front door opened and mother came in. When she saw Ruth-Ann, she lost control of her face: unguarded delight, to consternation, to a smile that turned to a grimace and, finally, to a mask.

Ruth-Ann said, plaintively, "Hi, mom."

The sound of her voice seemed to unlock something in mother. She held out her arms to Ruth-Ann and together they went up the stairs.

"Peaceful, isn't it?" I say.

She blinks rapidly, and arches her eyebrows twice, but whether this is in response to my words or mere reaction to smoke in her eyes, I cannot say.

Is it the place, I wonder, with the peculiarity of its silence? Or is it us, Ruth-Ann and me, with the peculiarity of our silences? During my visits, whether it be in sunshine, in rain, or beneath the indifference of clouds, our conversation tends to minimalism. With Ruth-Ann, conversation must be made. It is an art in which I am neither gifted nor versed.

I am not, at the best of times, a loquacious man. I dislike "running into" people, being obliged to make the space between us busy with questions and exclamations. Like most fellows, I find myself at a loss for words when visiting a sick friend at the hospital or paying respects at a funeral home. The brain seems empty, incapable of going beyond the social requirements. Small talk seems inappropriate, even though one knows that this is precisely what is required: chat about anything beyond the immediate that will relieve the innate tension of the moment.

Even now, as I try to puzzle through the reticence that comes to me, my thinking grows muddled: my words seem false and unwieldy even as they seek to understand why they become so.

Suddenly Ruth-Ann giggles. "You have funny eyebrows," she says.

I have grown to accept the fact that incongruity has become the major feature of her behaviour. Still, the smile that comes to me — that I let come — is thin. "Peaceful here, isn't it," I repeat, sighing.

I never did learn what Ruth-Ann did, how she lived, in those six months between her letter and her return home. Whatever her life had been like, the experience had taken a toll — but only temporarily. Within weeks, her vigour had returned. She found herself a job, called up her old friends, made herself new ones. Unlike me, she was rarely at home, which prompted an occasional grumble from my father but which my mother accepted with a new equanimity. "She'll come back," I once heard her say to my father. "She always does sooner or later." She sounded grateful.

Throughout this period, Ruth-Ann and I lived parallel lives in the same house, siblings bordering on strangers.

When, a year and a half or so after her return, the fine-looking folks she had met in Germany rode tanks and armoured vehicles through several countries to the English Channel, Ruth-Ann was too preoccupied with her social life to pay much attention. I do not mean by this that she was insensitive — she did once express concern for the many Karls and Günters and Hermans she had met in the embryonic Reich — but it was as if her lengthy proximity to Dalrymple's constant cartwheeling had turned her into a rolling stone determined to gather no moss. So busy was she rolling through the fields bumping into other stones — tongues wagged, rumours of Ruth-Ann's good times reached me weekly — that she simply could not conceive of anything, even the war in Europe, as laying greater claim to her attention.

I realize this makes my sister sound vain and shallow. She was at this time in her late twenties, that period of her life when she was perhaps at her most attractive: mature, fresh, with a glow no longer tarnished by the disappointment of Dalrymple, every faculty vibrating with the precision of a tuning fork, youthfulness still informing the laughter that would break out — genuine, frequent — in uncluttered delight. Certainly she was vain, but no more so than many her age. As for being shallow, Ruth-Ann was, in her way, one of the smartest people I've ever known in that she was always clear-eyed about herself; it was the world that gave her trouble.

I had decided to put off university until the war was over — or at least my service in it, which I secretly thought of as killing my share of Ruth-Ann's Karls, Günters and Hermans. I could have joined up immediately, but I wasn't in that much of a hurry. Everyone felt that conscription was inevitable. My turn would come. I would wait for it, enjoying in the meantime a raffish neighbourhood notoriety as a young man with war in his near future. I filled my time by reading through armfuls of books I borrowed from the library, mostly fat novels whose wor(l)ds evaporated at the final period, with the occasional "Superman" comic book thrown in for good measure.

One evening I was dozing over some fat tome in the living room when Ruth-Ann bustled in. She was all dolled-up, as we used to say, for an evening on the town with one of her stones.

Suddenly she reached down and snapped my book shut. "Okay, Alis, that's enough. It's time you went out and had some real fun!"

I gazed sleepily up at her. "Such as?"

"Such as?" she repeated. "Such as! Alis, you're spending far too much time with your nose buried in books. There's a whole world out there, you have no idea—"

I sat up, stung. "I have no idea? Ruth-Ann, answer me a question."

"Shoot."

"What's the Maginot Line?"

She shrugged. "A French conga?" she said uncertainly.

I was flabbergasted even in my triumph, but before I could respond, a cool smile crossed her lips.

"I'm not a fool, Alis. I read the *Gazette* too, you know." Then, bracing herself on the arms of the chair, she brought her face close to mine. "Listen up, little brother. Sure, the war's important. All of those books of yours — they're important too. But do yourself a favour. Call up a girl — if you don't know any, I've got friends. Go to any of the clubs downtown and just let loose for a few hours. Have a drink, have a dance, have some fun. And if you get lucky, have some whoopee. Because today's not coming around again, little brother."

I could smell toothpaste, powder, perfume — and, none too subtly, desperation. I resented it all. "Send it to Hollywood," I said. "Garbo. Dietrich. No, better yet — Jimmy Cagney."

In her eyes I saw her struggle to smother anger. Seconds later — that cool smile again. "Alis," she said. "Alis in wonderland."

Then her date was knocking at the door and Ruth-Ann, all aflurry, was rushing out.

It was our last fight and, I've often thought, a very good one to have. Nothing broke, nobody won, and out of stalemate arose a new kind of respect. My only regret was that I had not taken the opportunity — I never would — to tell her how deeply I disliked being called Alis.

She says, "Isn't it lovely?"

"Isn't it." My agreement is noncommittal: I am not sure what she is talking about.

Suddenly her words surge. "Ididn'tusedtolikehimyouknow. Toosugary. Eveninggownsandballrooms. Curtsying. Shit. Nevercouldcurtseyproperly. AlwaysfeltIwasgoingtotoppleover."

Good God, what is she talking about?

Suddenly, with the cigarette holder danging from her mouth, she leaps to her feet and begins waltzing around the bench, eyes closed, arms spread like wings, fingers stroking the air like a pianist's stroking keys.

Disconcerted, I call out, "Ruth-Ann, what are you doing?"

꒜

But she does not hear me for the music in her head — a music that hums faintly from her throat as she whirls around and around, the tune unrecognizable at first but then shaping itself into Strauss.

The nurse, leaning against a tree some distance away, smiles in delight — and his smile teaches me something. I feel my grimace melt away, feel myself grow happy for her happiness. And beyond all expectation, I hear myself humming.

Lardner entered Ruth-Ann's life when I was in Europe. He was an older man, a geologist by profession. Her rolling stone ran smack into his boulder and came firmly to rest.

Theirs, by mother's account, was a leisurely courtship. Lardner lived in Ottawa and travelled a great deal. He worked as a consultant to the war-time government, and not even Ruth-Ann was allowed to know the nature of his work. This, clearly, was part of his allure.

She never knew when he would be in town. He never called ahead, hinting that security required he not broadcast his movements — which must have given Ruth-Ann a shiver of excitement. He would merely turn up at the door bearing gifts — flowers, books, chocolates, bottles of fine French brandy that tasted even finer because of the mystery attached to their provenance. While Ruth-Ann hurried to shower and dress, he would relax in the living room with mother and father, charming them with stories of his pre-war travels to distant lands. Often, too, he spoke of the sensuousness of minerals and soil, their names rolling exotic off his tongue.

My parents were, by their own admission, enthralled.

One evening Lardner did something thoroughly old-fashioned. While Ruth-Ann was upstairs, he remarked to my parents that with the fall of Paris to the allied armies, the outcome of the war was no longer in doubt. This being the case, he said, would they object terribly to his asking Ruth-Ann for her hand in marriage?

Father, suddenly aware of the impediment of Ruth-Ann's marriage to Dalrymple and ignorant of what Lardner knew, mumbled something incoherent. At which point mother jumped in. "Mr. Lardner," she said, "do you do cartwheels?"

Lardner looked surprised. "Cartwheels? I've never done one in my life."

Mother — to hear father tell it — flushed with pleasure, for she knew that divorce was not an issue. Ruth-Ann and Dalrymple had had what Ruth-Ann called "a circus wedding". The ring-master had performed the ceremony despite his lack of legal authority to do so. There were no papers, nothing had been signed.

When Ruth-Ann came downstairs, she found Lardner alone in the living room, down on one knee and smiling up at her.

The dance ends abruptly, with no flourish, my humming, suddenly unpartnered, conspicuous in the silence.

Ruth-Ann remains five or six steps away from me, feet knitted primly together. I recognize the stance; it was how Dalrymple held himself that day at the lake. Her gaze is directed at the grass, her eyes only half-open peering as if into another world, perhaps at the world she has just been in waltzing away. She seems somehow depleted, her body hanging within her clothes.

Watching her, an ache rises in my chest. For the first time this visit, there is a suggestion of confusion — and although it appears a confusion that prompts not fear but wonderment, her awareness of it cuts me to the quick. At these moments — when she is like a child mesmerized by the world before her — Ruth-Ann knows that something is drastically wrong with her.

I limp over to her, take her by the wrist that is all bone and lead her, unresisting, back to the bench.

True to her word, Ruth-Ann never made me an uncle.

After their wedding she moved to Ottawa with Lardner, who continued visiting my parents whenever he was in town. It was on one of these visits, when I was still convalescing, that I first met him. It was not a particularly memorable encounter. I was in some pain that evening, my leg stiffened and throbbing as it would for years. Shortly after we shook hands I was obliged to retire to my bed. Even so, I took with me an impression of kindliness utterly devoid of pity.

After the war, they moved to Vancouver, where Lardner had been made senior geologist at a large international concern. His duties took them to the far reaches of the earth. The list of countries in which they lived for six months, a year, two, is simply too long to enumerate. Suffice it to say that, in the twenty-five years until his retirement, they were abroad more often than at home. For mother's funeral, Ruth-Ann flew in from Borneo; for father's, from Patagonia. Lardner, one might say, took her cartwheeling around the world.

His retirement did not slow them down. They continued to travel. Ruth-Ann had entered middle age with great vigour — and Lardner, naturally graced with the musculature of an athlete, remained physically preposterous as he aged. While normal men showed signs of decline, he retained his firmness and muscle tone, his posture military, his teeth so fine I once, wrongly, accused them of being dentures. True, his hair greyed — but to the colour of lustrous metal, rich and full and seemingly resistant to the ravages of wind. The grey, then, did not age him. It merely confirmed the general opinion of him as a jovial, cultivated, dependable fellow, spontaneous within reason, not the type — as father once said approvingly — to go off on a wing and a prayer.

Part of Lardner's attractiveness was his enthusiasm for the

future. He was an optimist who believed in a technological saviour. New gadgets dazzled him. He bought the first Walkman I ever saw and demonstrated it for me with a cassette tape of Dvorak's *From the New World* Symphony. My ears rang for an hour afterwards. However, when he tried to turn it off, he couldn't manage it. I located the stop button as he frowned in bewilderment at the "darn thing".

He bought a VCR, and eventually professed that he had to leave its operation to Ruth-Ann. "I've grown hitchhiker's hands, Alistair," he said with a wry smile. "All thumbs."

He bought a personal computer — "I feel like George Jetson!" I remember him exclaiming — but found its use beyond his comprehension. He believed that the personal computer was the harbinger of a new civilization, that it offered individuals an autonomy unparalleled in history — and so that failure, more than any other, shook him.

He was in his mid-seventies then. He remained clever, his memory sharp — he could describe in detail various manhood rites he had witnessed thirty years before in Central Africa — but decline was unmistakable, and the problem did not lie in his hands. I remember the awe textured with sadness with which he said, "The future is leaving me behind, Alistair." Then, blinking rapidly, he added, "As it should. As it should."

But still there was travel, always travel. And it was travel that led to his unexpected end.

Her wrist remains in my hand, a wrist so miniscule I fancy I could wrap my fingers twice around it. From deep within, from somewhere behind the bone, her pulse hammers into my palm.

If I could hear it, it would be thunderous.

We hadn't seen each other in some time and so, for the first leg of their trip, they spent a few days with Mary and me.

We settled into the living room with glasses of the wine they
had brought, something special chosen from the shelves of the
rare-wine store. The opening of the bottle had been ceremoni-
ous, with Lardner easing the cork out while peering through the
bottle backlit by a candle flame.

While Lardner and Ruth-Ann took gulps of the wine, Mary
and I were more judicious, fearful that we would have to render
judgement. After two sips, I decided that although it wasn't
"plonk" — a word favoured by my writer friend — I'd had
Burgundys more thrilling.

I sought Mary's assent — quickly given — in declaring the
wine delicious, then asked, "So, where is it this time? The
Himalayas? The Andes? The Bermuda Triangle?"

"Florida," Ruth-Ann said.

I was incredulous. "In the United States?"

"I've never heard of another, have you?" Ruth-Ann's gaze
held mine for a second longer than usual — a warning to temper
my reaction.

Lardner said, "We've never been there, believe it or not. I
know it appears conventional but for us, after all the places we've
been, well, one realizes exoticism is merely the unknown."

"Exactly," Ruth-Ann said excitedly. "At this point in our lives,
the pedestrian has become exotic." They would visit Florida for
two weeks of swimming and tennis. Having never had a conventional vacation, they wanted to see what it would be like.

"Good for you," Mary said, but I sensed there was more
involved than a sudden world-weariness. Just the year before they
had spent a month gathering honey with the semi-nomadic Raji
people in southern Nepal. This claim about the pedestrian
becoming exotic — it was, in its disingenuousness, unconvincing.

And indeed, before they left, Ruth-Ann took me aside and
explained that she had grown increasingly uneasy about taking
Lardner too far afield. In Nepal the year before, he had ignored

— or forgotten — instructions on not removing his face net and had endured dozens of bee-stings before being rescued. Luckily, he had suffered no ill effects apart from a face swollen almost beyond recognition. "We have to learn," she said, "to discover pleasures closer to home." With a twinkle in her eye, she added, "How do I go about making Niagara Falls fascinating, Alis?"

They took a taxi to the airport, Lardner in high spirits, Ruth-Ann more subdued.

That evening the telephone rang and a composed Ruth-Ann told first Mary, then me, of Lardner's death. Ruth-Ann blamed herself.

They had boarded the plane without incident, only to discover that their seats were several rows away from an emergency exit. "I've always been a nervous flyer, Alis, and thousands of hours in the air haven't helped one jot. So I prevailed on the flight-attendant to change our seats."

Lardner sat beside the emergency exit, Ruth-Ann beside the aisle. They had the luxury of an empty seat between them. Before take–off, the attendant explained to Lardner the procedure he was to follow in case of an emergency evacuation: how to unlatch the door and remove it, how to dispose of it. He had heard the explanation so often he merely smiled and nodded.

Later, I asked Ruth-Ann about the wisdom of allowing Lardner such responsibility. She resented my enquiry and replied with unaccustomed sharpness. "I'm not dense, Alis. If he'd shown any sign of confusion, I'd have insisted on changing seats with him. The other passengers' safety came before his pride, I was quite aware of that, thank you."

The flight was uneventful except for a difficult moment when Lardner returned to his seat from a trip to the wash-room. His sudden inability to buckle his seat-belt drove him to tears. "But on the whole," Ruth-Ann said, "the right spark-plugs were firing."

Eventually they landed and it was as the aircraft was taxiing to its gate that it happened.

Ruth-Ann had just tugged her large flight bag onto her lap in order to put away their books and magazines and travel-Scrabble when Lardner unlatched his seat-belt, yanked down the emergency handle and — with his great strength — removed the door and tossed it out. Then he followed the door through the aperture, stepping onto the wing of the swiftly moving aircraft. Ruth-Ann swore he actually managed four or five steps before falling from sight.

There always seems so much to say before these visits to Ruth-Ann. I store up a grab-bag of topics. News of the family, news of the world. I have brought books I thought she might like, even though she has never been one for books.

But it has all proven fruitless.

She no longer remembers the family, is barely aware of the world. And reading to her is like giving a speech to a blank wall; one's words, finding no validation, echo back, thinned and foolish.

So we sit like this, sometimes touching, sometimes not. And if we are lucky, as we are today, I will feel her pulse slowing, will sense her calming down, will sense the gathering of the self that remains to her.

Will see her turn to me, as she does now, and hear her say in startled recognition, "Alis!"

Joy surges within me. Her lucidity lasts for no more than a few seconds, but they are seconds of great and unalloyed pleasure. They are a gift which, as it ebbs, leaves me with the curious feeling that my sister's recognition of me is, even more than Mary's, confirmation of my own existence.

Afterwards, the life insurance company claimed that Lardner had committed suicide, thereby rendering void the hefty policy for

which he had been paying for decades. Ruth-Ann, well provided
for by Lardner's many investments, had neither the heart nor the
inclination to contest the decision.

From the mechanics of Lardner's last moments, though, there
was consolation. An autopsy revealed a massive heart-attack.
The doctors believed he was dead before hitting the tarmac.
There would have been, they said to Ruth-Ann, no fear, no pain,
no awareness: it was that fast.

Except that I refuse to believe it — this idea of an unconscious
death, I mean. Lardner was the kind of man who lived every
moment with his eyes wide open, alert to the nuances of life. I
prefer to think he remained so to the very end: that he saw with
cinematic clarity the stretch of silvery wing before him, the world
tilting as he fell, the grey tarmac rushing towards him. The way
of death should mirror the way of life, shouldn't it?

It's only fair, after all.

The nurse returns, cigarette pack in hand.

It is time for me to go — Agnes is likely to have been in the
car for some minutes now, impatient to return to her family.
Ruth-Ann has some time yet, enough for a couple more cigarettes, the nurse says. I regret this — Ruth-Ann seeing me walk
away from her, I mean. There has been quite enough of that in
her life.

Taking my leave of Ruth-Ann always feels to me like a kind
of abandonment. I must remind myself, forcefully, that she has
always preferred living among strangers; that it was only when
she identified the misfiring of her own mind that she thought
it prudent to return to her home town in the hope that long familiarity would extend awareness.

She lived for years in a little flat just off St. Louis Square. The
dining room and the kitchen were one and she shared the bathroom
with the tenant of another flat, but the place was full of charm and

꙯

Ruth-Ann was precisely where she liked to be, at the centre of things. Mary and I saw her only occasionally. She was always busy — volunteering daily at a soup kitchen, attending plays, raising funds for medical research, learning French, of all things.

All the new activity proved beneficial. A new clarity came to her, as if — to use her own metaphor — her spark-plugs had been cleaned.

But the deterioration — as she kept on reminding us — could not be stopped over time, and eventually the day came when she acknowledged that she could no longer fully meet her own needs. "Routine is what does it, you know," she said to Mary. "It deadens the soul and the cells." Mary asked her to move in with us. I found her offer to my sister deeply touching, but will admit to a feeling of relief when Ruth-Ann summarily rejected it.

It was Ruth-Ann herself who brought us the brochures to this place. Eyeing the elegance in the photographs, she said without a hint of falseness or self-pity, "It looks quite pleasant, doesn't it, Alis?"

She has been here ever since.

Leaving, then, is a difficult thing to do. Still, I must be careful not to abuse Agnes's generosity.

I press my palm to the back of Ruth-Ann's hand and, promising to return, take up my stick and wander slowly off towards the carpark. I glance backwards only once, at her sitting there under the tree, gaze directed at the sky, puffing vigorously away. Ruth-Ann, in wonderland.

François's hand moves briskly above the paper, his inexpert fingers bunched around the tip of the wax crayon. His intensity is startling, and I glimpse the fervour of a subconscious fed by the world, an imagination awoken, an interpretation of the natural world — both fresh and as old as humankind — pouring out in colour and shapes clumsily rendered.

Was Agnes like this when she was a child? Did she have this single-mindedness, this absorption in the creatures of her mind? I don't remember ever noticing that, don't remember seeing it.

I was not a negligent father, just one of thousands consumed with claiming a place for himself in the academic ranks. Could this explain Agnes's resistance to Dickens? After all that has

happened, I find my greatest comfort in *A Tale of Two Cities*.
How pedestrian it seems now, this urge not to make my mark on
the world but merely to carve out a nest within it. My ambition,
fully blown at the time, strikes me now as being of narrow gauge.
Yes, there is nobility in teaching — this idea of shaping future
generations, preparing the young to run the world and all that —
but within two years of my taking up the work, undergraduates'
idealism struck me as naive, their enthusiasm as puerile. The
bright eyes I saw struck me as being backlit through the ears.
And of course there came the decade of the Holy Sixties, when
that idealism metastasized into an unstable element, prompting
conflagration not only in countless cities around the world but
closer to home too, as close as my own institution where allega-
tions of racism led to occupation and, eventually, the wanton
destruction of computer equipment. One grows suspicious of
idealists. Time teaches that they cause as much havoc in this
world as cynics. Is it malicious to hold that the urge to change
the world, while innate to human nature, exists only because
of its failure to recognise the nature of the human? Horrors
centuries old have not changed in their essentials, only in their
manifestation: a man disembowelled by sword or by sharpnel
remains a man disembowelled. His disembowelment is no more
beautiful or no less savage because it has been achieved by
advanced technology. As for the institution itself, I saw it from
early on as a kind of Sinecure Central, as soul-deadening as any
other bureaucracy bursting with people determined to achieve
the wretched safety of untouchable permanence. I pursued it too,
of course. It was an inextricable part of the life I'd chosen. Still,
the feeling remained with me through it all, through decades, its
intensity undiminished to the day of my retirement. I am like
Lardner, who once told me of the realisation that came to him
one night that he'd invested his all in the wrong profession, and
how he regretted beyond words the oil paints he hadn't touched

𝓏

since adolescence. But it was too late. The path had been chosen for the best of practical reasons and had been pursued with great success. He was not given to folly: he sought no exit ramps. But he, at least, managed to channel his passion for the one abandoned into the one espoused.

François tosses the crayon aside and fumbles in his plastic box for another. He examines several, rejecting each. He is, in that deliberate way of his, after a particular colour. Even though his tree will turn out to be red, his grass orange and his sky green, there is nothing arbitrary here. He sees things in his own way, and to his eyes this is how the world is hued. I resist the urge to show him the error of his colours, for the error is mine, not his, and my intervening will only awaken his resistance. There's no point in merely tossing words at him. I must trust that he will one day see things for what they are.

But will he be able to? It's a question I've asked about my own daughter, though not of her. She once told me that never having known any of her grandparents — they all managed to die off before she was born — has always felt like a great loss to her. She never clutched at them, was never spoiled by them, never inhaled the scents and tasted the flavours of their worlds — a fibrous mustiness that arose from the floorboards, a suspension of talcum powder that followed in their wake, dry cookies that left a fine dust on your fingertips. And now that my house is gone, razed to its foundations by passions impossible to decipher, its very dust incinerated, François will imbibe such memories only from Jack's parents. At least, I tell myself, there are likely to be parallels. Still, Agnes feels that her hold on the past is tenuous — and this, growing up in a time and place where the past, or at least useful versions of it, was growing fetishistic. Agnes feels she has no secure family narrative to call her own. Perhaps this explains her lack of sentimentality, which has served her well in the professional world but which, closer up, resembles — not a coldness, no — but a kind of crackling practicality that is like distance.

I have on occasion glimpsed Agnes sitting alone in a plastic garden-chair out back or sunk into the leather sofa in the living room. At these moments — a communion with the self? the soothing of disappointments? perhaps a problem at work, or a fight with Jack behind the closed door of their bedroom — she holds herself erect with all the stillness and presence of an art installation, attractive but intimidating, radiating silence but hinting at secrets to impart, secrets which lay in territory stalked by some unnamable peril.

Agnes, it is fair to say, feels cheated. She takes them personally, these useless deaths. Jack it was who once insisted that there was no such thing as a useful death. Yet, as a man who has been to war, I know such a thing exists. Not in any grand sense of saving the world, but in smaller, more personal ways. Men in battle really have been known to throw themselves on live grenades to protect their comrades, to expose themselves to mortal danger by drawing enemy fire so that the rest of the squad could escape. Reflection has little to do with such actions. They simply happen, the product of instinct.

Still, though, life reserves for us all a drawerful of pointless deaths. I think of Jack's cousin, a lumberjack of a man who was skilled in carpentry, plumbing, brick-laying, electrical wiring — anything to do with construction. When Jack and Agnes bought this house, it was in fairly rough shape, it required a great deal of work, and Jack's cousin was the one to do most of it, repairing cracks, refashioning the bathroom, finishing the basement. He tore down old walls and erected new ones, finishing off the heavy work with a finesse remarkable in a man with hands the size of dictionaries. One day, at another private job renovating a cottage, he lost control of the electric saw with which he was cutting planks and amputated his left hand just above the wrist. He was alone in an isolated country area. Jack, who is not generally given to hyperbole, said that when the owners found him the following morning he had bled dry.

This idea of dying alone, with no witness to one's final moments, is one that has long haunted me.

My mother's favourite time of day was late morning, when she found herself alone at home. The neighbourhood was largely deserted then, the men at work, the children at school, her world grown so silent she imagined she could hear the flutter of butterfly wings, that she could hear, as she once said, the earth breathe. One spring morning, she wrapped a light shawl about her shoulders and stepped outside with a cup of tea to admire the last glitter of dew on the flowers. She had finished the tea when her heart turned itself off. She crumpled senseless to the ground, somehow cushioning the empty tea cup against her breast so that it remained intact while she did not. A neighbour found her some hours later.

On the day of her death, India and Pakistan raised new flags to signal their independence from the British crown. There were, then, events of momentous occasion, but no event was of greater occasion than hers.

Following her funeral, the cup, resolutely unwashed, came into my father's possession. For years, it occupied a place — not a place of honour, just a place — on the dressing table in the bedroom once theirs, then hers, now his. This gesture was so unexpected, so sentimental, it alarmed me. The reality of separate bedrooms and lives singular in their singularity had led me to conclude that theirs had become a marriage defined more by familiarity than by feeling — and, truth to tell, there was to me something reassuring in that. Feeling could always erupt, after all. It was an unstable element, untrustworthy in its essentials. And then, unexpectedly, this iconization of the cup from which she had been drinking in the moments before her death.

A new and anguished idea of my father then came to me. In the weeks and months following her death, he grew to resemble a reed losing its tautness. Mary said it was as if his very skeleton had gone flaccid. Indifference, or rather a certain stoicism, would have been easier to handle; it would have been more authentic, more typically him — or what I saw as being so. I could hardly bring myself to look at the cup, so naked a symbol of his long-camouflaged and now apparently self-predatory passion for my mother did it seem.

One day a year or so later, I found myself in the shadowy bedroom rooting around among his things — bottles of scent, loose change, match boxes, cinema stubs, sticks of gum — in an attempt to remove some of the dust he had let accumulate. As I went distractedly about my business, I knocked the cup over. I remember watching as it tumbled over the edge of the dresser and smacked onto the hard-wood floor. I took him the pieces. Pretending a greater penitence than I felt, I offered to glue it back together. "That old thing?" he said, grimacing. He turned from the shards in my cupped hand back to his newspaper. "Why bother? We've got lots more." It was a sign, I suppose, that in his quiet way he'd recovered from her loss, but I'd have been hard pressed to explain why the realization should have tightened a knot in my throat.

I was years in coming to the understanding that my father lived his life trying to impress my mother, as he'd tried through the magic-show to impress me. There are worse ways to spend a life. My father could have had other audiences — he surely did, at the tavern, at the gambling dens — but no other mattered to him in the way that my mother had. Without her smiles and laughter and applause, without her occasional booing and hissing, the theatre of his self-invention grew absurd and pointless. Hers was the gaze that gave shape and sense and consistency to his reality, the actor nothing without the chosen public of one. And yet, while she was alive, one would hardly have guessed it.

When, seven years later, his turn came to leave this world, his journey was more protracted, and more painful, than my mother's. For six months, a voracious cancer slowly gouged his insides with a red-hot rake. On the day he died, reduced dramatically to line and shadow, Mary and I learned that we would be parents in approximately seven and a half months.

That evening, once the arrangements had been made for the funeral and the obituary placed in the paper, I sat with Mary on the sofa, my palm on her yet unswollen belly, and thought that no child should witness a parent's withering. I swore then to do my best to spare the child whose name would be, in the fullness of time, either Arthur or Agnes.

But they've burnt my home. So I find myself in Agnes's house admiring labour performed by a man who will be remembered, if at all, for the absurd manner of his death, all the while withering in the sight of my child.

François's insistent call pulls me away from these sad reflections. I turn my full attention to the colourful world he's holding up for me to admire. As my eye drinks in the richness of his red lathered on the sky, the purple on the grass, the blue on the tree, my writer friend's cynical voice echoes in my head: *Writing, Mac? It's my version of a solo rush down the ice and whipping the puck into the goal. It's power, it's grace, it's that eye-blink of beauty. In front of the typewriter, my friend, I'm the Rocket. Shove aside the ugliness, Mac. Get to the beauty. And if you ever tell anybody what I just said, I'll disown you.*

"*D*an!" *Mary exclaims.* "How *are* you?"

Anyone hearing Mary's greeting fill the living room would assume she is welcoming a friend long unseen, but her enthusiasm — compressed into the verb with all the explosiveness of a hand grenade — does not fool me. Dan Mullen's presence always brings a grumble to Mary's voice, her dislike of him — which I sense; she rarely expresses it and I have chosen not to ask about it — lending an underground unhappiness to everything she says.

Mullen, with an animation so uncommon to him I suspect he is not fooled either, replies, "Mary, how are *you*?"

Mary places her hands on his shoulders, her touch so light her fingers make no indentation on the well-padded herring-bone, and presses first one cheek then the other to his. He is the only person she greets in this way. Others get either a handshake or a kiss, depending on their degree of closeness. It disconcerts him, which may explain why she does it.

Mullen is not a tall fellow — he and Mary are the same height — and his discomfort at Mary's greeting makes him awkward. His rotund body tenses, as if braced for a particularly nasty dental injection. Were Mary to press herself for a second longer against his bulldog jowls, his endurance might be breached and he would push her away.

When Mary draws back and steps away, Mullen blinks in relief and passes the back of his hand across his sweaty brow. Then, his sad, disquieted eyes sweeping around the living room, he turns to me like a man emerging from helplessness and says, "You got any plonk?"

I always do.

When I return with the "plonk" — an expensive scotch I reserve for his rare visits — he is sitting in a chair with one leg crossed over the other, the pant cuff rising to reveal a sock stretched shapeless and several inches of pasty, hairless shin. He is doing his best to appear at ease, but his face calls to mind a death-mask.

Mary, reaching for her glass of sherry, says, "I asked him."

"Did you?" I reply, aghast.

"Well, I knew you never would," she says, running her fingertip around the rim of the glass.

I turn towards Mullen, imposing on myself an equanimity I do not feel. Giving him his glass, I say, "I know you don't usually do this sort of thing, Dan, but would you consider it, this one time? As a favour to me, I mean? The Dean's been rather insistent. He knows we're friends."

He makes no response, not even the merest flicker of an eyelid, and the stillness that comes to him causes me to regret my request. This pause is not a dramatic device; he is, on the whole and despite his reputation, not a dramatic man. No, this quiescence surges from deep within him, from his all-too-evident sense that after all these years, I have, with my simple question, betrayed him.

Unexpectedly, he growls a question about payment.

"Payment?"

"Yes, Mac, payment. This writing thing, it's my job, you know. I expect to be paid."

"My dear fellow, when I attend conferences or publish a paper, do you think I get paid? The prestige is what counts. But we'll take you to dinner. I'm told there's a good Mexican restaurant nearby. You like Mexican, don't you?"

"I prefer my wife's cooking."

Mary rolls her eyes and makes a sour face. She has no need to mouth the words she is thinking for me to hear them with all the clarity of a shout. How often in the past that face has accompanied the words: *Mullen is so full of shit sometimes.*

Still, I have crossed a line. I have done so through ego: to snag Dan Mullen would add appreciably to my social standing within the department. Why I should care about such things I do not know. I have on the whole kept my gentle contempt for the place to myself. Such subterfuge, along with the urge to polish my profile, testify to the power of the culture within which I have so long laboured. It is not pretty. It is not commendable. It carries a whiff of hypocrisy. But there it is: I have not had the courage to resist its enticements. And so I have broached the subject not with the honesty of forethought but through opportunity rashly seized. Such self-knowledge is, however, no balm.

I sit beside Mary, sip at my glass of scotch. Even through my contraption, the rattle of my ice cubes seems very loud. There is no graceful way to change the subject. Mary has chosen to put it out there. I would have waited for an opportune moment; or I might have simply never brought it up. But there it is, out there between us like a viper on the loose — and it must be dealt with.

Mullen takes a long swallow of his scotch. He is letting the silence stretch out, letting it stretch thin; letting it grow as taut as a violin string. I am torn between fury and embarrassment: Dan Mullen is, after all, one of my oldest friends.

Mullen and I met one afternoon in a bookstore twenty-five years (and, for him, a baker's dozen books) ago.

That morning Mary and I had had a spat. She was at the time on a campaign to wean me off my habitual breakfast, a small bowl of cereal followed by two scrambled eggs with bacon and white toast, all washed down with several cups of black coffee. My heart and intestines had by this point replaced other parts of my body in her preoccupations. I was unwilling to be weaned. A bowl of fruit and yoghurt sprinkled with wheat-germ, accompanied by a *single* cup of coffee, left me ravenous — and hunger made me resentful. That morning, in a fit of defiance, I cracked open two eggs and swallowed them raw, shell shards and all, before her eyes. Tongue coated in slime, stomach heaving, I snatched up my briefcase and fled the house.

I made it to the department (housed at the time in facilities far less modern, and far less clean, than today) where five minutes of abject communing with the washroom gods settled my stomach enough to allow me to give my lecture. When I emerged from the stall, my colleague Professor Thrush was leaning against the wall beside the paper-towel dispenser, a look of sly amusement creasing his face. "Well, Mackenzie," he said, "had a few too many last night, did we?" In no mood for his banter, I turned on a tap and sought invigoration by dousing my face with cold water. "I must say I'm surprised, Mackenzie," he continued. "And delighted. Maybe you're not as much of a tight-ass as I thought."

Palming water onto my neck, I said, "Go to hell, Thrush."

"Careful, Mackenzie. Hell is a four-letter word, you know."

With a laugh, he made for the door. "Take it from someone with experience. Hair o' the dog."

By the end of the day, word had gone around the department that Mackenzie had gone on a bender the night before. It was not my imagination that people became friendlier; at least two of my colleagues suggested we go out for drinks sometime, and one mentioned something about a poker evening. I could not bring myself to admit that my performance in the washroom had been due not to a hangover but to raw eggs. Thus I ended the day feeling even more foolish than I had when rushing out of the house that morning.

Reluctant to return home, I wandered aimlessly for a while before drifting into a bookstore. I dawdled at the wall of classics (nothing new there, as Mary would say), then skimmed the poetry section (the *paltry* section: again Mary) and spent some time with literary criticism (the morgue). Finally, through no fault of my own, I ended up at the very back of the store, at three shelves dismissively labelled CANADIANA. A quick glance revealed the usual suspects. MacLennan, Mitchell, Grove, Callaghan, Moodie. They weren't even alphabetized.

Crouched before the last shelf was a tired-looking man with a frayed herring-bone jacket draped like a cape on his shoulders. A cigarette dangled from his lips, his eyes narrowed to the smoke. He held a stack of books in precarious balance against his chest. At first I took him for a store employee, but then realized he was too much of a dandy for that. He scooped up a handful of books from that last, now unburdened shelf and held them up to me. "Here, hold these for me for a minute," he mumbled between tightened lips.

I did as asked.

He stood up, ash breaking off the end of his cigarette, and bustled past me. He was a short fellow with curly black hair and a muscular build. He moved rapidly with sharp, ungainly steps, like a stiff man trying to catch up with tomorrow. I followed the trail of his smoke, my pace more leisurely.

I caught up with him at the front of the store. His stack of books secured between chin and forearm, he was shoving aside the bestsellers occupying the top shelf of the main display. A couple fell to the ground and he kicked them away.

"What are you doing?" I asked, glancing around uneasily for the manager who might object to having his stock manhandled.

He began filling the empty space with the books from his stack. "Taking these out of that fucking oubliette back there and putting them where they belong," he said.

I glanced at the title of the books in my hand. *Hot Nights at the Belvedere*, a novel by Daniel Jonah Mullen. "Let me take a wild guess," I said. "You're Daniel Jonah Mullen."

"Dan," he said, tossing his cigarette butt to the floor and stepping back to admire his handiwork before adding my copies to the display. The dust jacket showed a colourful frieze in the naive style of a musical sextet in full swing: a pianist with the obligatory cigarette growing from his lips, surrounded by a drummer, a tuba player, a trombonist, a clarinetist and a trumpeter in a fedora.

"What's your book about, Dan?"

"Just what it says. You remember the Bellevue Casino, on Ontario Street?"

"Near Bleury," I replied confidently. "Of course I remember it." Continuing the theme of the day, I did not reveal that if I knew about the Bellevue — that from the end of the forties to the middle of the fifties it was the biggest, brashest night-club in town where every month saw a new and elaborate floor show — it was from hearsay and the entertainment pages. I was a married man by then, and neither Mary nor I was inclined to carousing.

"It's about a place like the Bellevue," he continued, "and the lives of the people who spent their nights there."

꒳

"The Bellevue, eh?"

He cast a sharp eye at me. "My turn to guess. The Bellevue doesn't strike you as a fit subject for *literature*. A night club's just too banal for *literature*. One more guess. You're some kind of teacher, right? A *literature* teacher?"

"Wrong, wrong, right," I replied, merrily lying twice.

He lit another cigarette, tossing the match over his shoulder. "Don't let it worry you, friend. I'm not interested in writing *literature*. Tolstoy be damned. All I want is to sell a few hundred thousand copies and retire to some Greek isle. So, with any luck, my first born here" — he blew a stream of smoke at his displayed books — "just might pass for porn in this wild country of ours. I've thrown in enough tits-and-ass to send the entire population of distant, God-fearing Hogtown rushing off to confession. I'm hoping some good burgher'll try to ban it. Which'll give your modest author here a sure-fire hit, you mark my word."

The thought, it was clear, fired his imagination with Mediterranean fantasies which he allowed himself to indulge for a few seconds before continuing in a voice further sharpened by cynicism.

"Or, more likely, the *Gazette*'ll ask some egghead like you to review it. You'll come up with a few inanities, saying that it ain't Shakespeare and it ain't Dickens and it sure as hell ain't Jacqueline Susann or even, for God's sake, Harold Robbins — whom you all read late at night to put some wood in your peckers. And once you realize it wasn't written by some *furriner*, you'll lament the fact that it was ever published. So you see, my only hope is that my immortal prose'll give some reviewer a hard-on, which he'll resent, declare the book to be filthy porn — and then I'm on my way to join the sun-drenched fleshpots of Lesbos."

I said, "My dear Mr. Mullen—"

"What? You don't review books?"

"I was just wondering, who in the world is Harold Robbins?"

He grinned, as if he had unexpectedly encountered an innocent in a world he had believed to be irretrievably corrupt. "Robbins," he said, "is like a force of nature. Nature abhors a vacuum, and Robbins can't stand a hole that isn't filled." His hand grappled in his jacket pocket for his cigarettes. He offered me one.

I shook my head. "Thanks."

Tipping out one for himself, he said, "Do you drink, at least?" The question was like a challenge. "I've been known to."

"Well, let's go then," he said, turning around in a blossoming of smoke. "All this work's made me thirsty."

I have no memory of returning home that night.

But I do recall awakening the following morning, a steel-walled tornado banging around the inside of my skull. It gouged my eyeballs from behind, braided my neck and shoulder muscles into brittle cables, all the while its tail whipping my stomach into a frenzy of sour, heaving bile.

I was writhing in bed, fighting back the hiccups that were the precursors of the imminent eruption of my stomach, when Mary, my dear Mary, marched into the room, flung the windows open to brilliant sunshine and, banging a pot with a metal spoon, shouted, "Rise and shine, Sugar!" She had never before called me "Sugar". I thought it a most inappropriate moment to introduce the endearment.

I managed, barely, to moan her name in a plea for surcease — a plea that went roundly ignored.

She ripped my blanket away with a kind of ecstacy — I was still, I saw, fully clothed, thus explaining my sensation of being enshrouded — and I gagged at the smell that arose from me, an amalgam of stale whisky and musty tobacco smoke. In most unMary-like fashion she bellowed, "Come on, Sunshine! Up and at it! There's work to be done!"

I rolled to the edge of the bed and, with her help, made it to my feet on legs bereft of bones. With her hands jabbing insistently at the middle of my back, my stomach awash in bitter, rolling tides, I found myself in the dining room, leaning on the table still set for the previous evening's supper.

"I waited, *darling*," Mary said gleefully, "but I eventually got too hungry and went ahead without you." She gripped the handle of the china tureen sitting in the middle of the table and lifted it off. "But look, I kept yours for you."

My gaze sank heavily through the odour that rose from the tureen: fetid onions mingled with the congealed fat of greasy stewed lamb. The dish had clearly sat out all night on the table, oleaginous and suppurating.

My stomach heaved, a volcano whirling into eruption. I rushed off to bow once more before the cold and unforgiving porcelain gods.

When I was done, I found Mary standing behind me, eyes glittery with amusement and lips aflutter with contempt. Had she had a whip she would have cracked it. She poked me in the buttocks with her foot. "Into the shower," she ordered. "You stink."

A shower! God, the very thought of steamy water massaging my throbbing skull, washing my body clean of the toxins that clogged its every pore, was enough to prompt paroxysms of pleasure down my ropy spine. My fingers fumbled at my collar.

"Uh-uh, Sugarpie." Mary wagged a warning finger at me. "Into the shower this very minute."

"But my clothes—"

"Clothes and all."

"Mary!"

"Now!" she shouted, and the sound of her voice echoed around the vault of my skull like a spiky neuron gone wild. I turned meek, watching helplessly as she turned on the shower and pointed me to it.

With the smidgeon of dignity my condition permitted me, I stepped under the water. The experience was not nearly as pleasurable as I'd anticipated. I felt myself grow soggy from jacket-lapels to socks, and thereby experienced the enormous amount of weight clothes gain when soaked.

My one consolation, if it could be so considered, was that, even if a little late, Dan Mullen had made an honest man of me.

Two days later, a copy of *Hot Nights at the Belvedere* arrived in the mail. The sight of it caused me to gag: the cover, which now struck me as lurid, resurrected the physical gouging I had been a full twenty-four hours in surmounting. Holding the book in my hand, I found myself surrounded by whisky fumes and, for several seconds, I actually felt nauseous.

Mary, sifting through the bills, said, "What's that? You look positively green."

I passed it to her. "Ah, yes," she said. "Your drinking buddy." She opened it. "There's a dedication. 'To Alistair Mackenzie, who talks like a gentleman and drinks like a fish. And to Mary who sounds like a — *what?*"

I watched her turn scarlet, starting at her ears and growing rapidly to her cheeks and neck. Seizing the book from her, I read to my horror the rest of the dedication: *And to Mary who sounds like a sweet piece of ass.*

My first thought was: How dare he!

Then, as blood roared into my head, the second thought arrived on wings of ice: What in the world had I said to him about Mary to prompt such a vile phrase?

But I could remember nothing of substance, no words of praise (if praise it was) or damnation (was this an exercise in sarcasm?) on which I could hang an explanation. Relieved that the guilt was not mine — to the best of my recollection, at least — I spluttered, "A gratuitous insult. Unforgivable. Please don't take it seriously, Mary."

But Mary's face had already resumed its normal tint. "Daniel Jonah Mullen," she said, "must be a very lonely man."

"He's got a wife!" I suddenly remembered he had spoken of his "better-half by far", a woman named Karen or Karine or Corinne. "He seemed dazzled by her." In fact, a shard of memory reminded me of my impression that the only time Dan Mullen was to be taken seriously was when he spoke of the woman in his life.

Mary said, "Are you going to call him?"

"Call him? I should say not."

"He wrote a telephone number, it must be his. Looks like he's expecting a phone call."

"Well, I hope he's not sitting by the phone waiting. He'll be there for a very long time."

"Suit yourself," she said.

But I could see that my decision had met with disapproval. "What do you think?" I asked.

"He doesn't seem like the other people you know, not by a long-shot, and unless he's dangerous—"

"I think he's a harmless fellow, if somewhat uncouth."

"Then there's no reason you shouldn't call him up to thank him."

I knew instantly that she was right, and I wondered what intuition had revealed to Mary the glimmerings of an unlikely friendship which, up to that moment, had remained concealed to me. I didn't want to like Dan Mullen, but I did.

I was up the better part of a night reading *Hot Nights at the Belvedere*. I hadn't expected to devote quite so much time or effort to it. I'd planned to run through a few chapters, enough to get the gist and to be able to make a few intelligent noises.

I would, in imitation of the reviews published in the book pages, brew compliments with mild reservations before saying, with a certain pithiness, how much I looked forward to his next book. I would express my appreciation for his thoughtfulness in sending the inscribed copy to me — or, in view of the dedication, should that be to *us*? I planned to end by saying how unfortunate it was that he had included Mary in so grotesque a manner and that, given his fondness for anatomical metaphors, he would understand if I appropriated his colloquialism in suggesting that he take his book with all its immortal prose and stick it up his own —

But the book disarmed me.

Only the long-dead had never heard of the Belvedere, and even that was no sure thing. Scuttlebutt had it that at least one devoted patron had had himself laid to rest on the mountain with a spoon from his favorite nightclub tucked away in a pocket. Now *that* was loyalty.

Lips painted into a perpetual red smile, wads of cotton wool stuffed into her ears, Madeline Mayhew wandered among the tables with her tray offering fresh smokes to the high-rollers, the sports stars, the city-councillors, the bums, the geeks and the losers. On any night of the week, she recognized a dozen faces from the newspapers. Everybody came here, from the company president to the guy who sold his widgets. She wouldn't have been surprised to see St. Peter himself plop down his fifty cents and settle in at a table. This was the Belv after all, Madeline thought. Next best thing to Heaven if eternity was all you had left.

There was a charm to it, and an appealing gritty edge. The prose was straightforward — Hemingway without the self-regard — if somewhat derivative: one picked up echoes of, say,

Raymond Chandler. But there was skill, and a grasp of human complexity, with an underlying moral outrage that arose from a sympathy that understood everything but forgave nothing.

Many of the characters — Madeline Mayhew, the cigarette girl who was the centre of the story; Mac McAlister, the manager with a "lush" for a wife and the "hots" for Madeline; Tommy Mix, the teetotaling bartender; Richie Raglan, the bandleader and cocaine addict; the journalist Willie Avery, a "scribbler" who liked fine scotch and American cigarettes and who secretly pined for his wife every minute they were apart — were driven by impulse. This struck a note with me in that simple impulse was what had driven my sister Ruth-Ann in her days as a good-time girl. Simple impulse was also what I had spent much of my life avoiding. Reading the novel, I felt like a voyeur fascinated by the creatures of his attention precisely because they were so different from himself — a horrified part of him wishing to be more like them.

The next morning I recommended the book to Mary. "It's all right," I said. "See what you think."

She read it that afternoon — she has always been a faster reader than me — and when she finished, she was sniffling. Reaching for her hanky, she wiped her eyes, blew her nose and said, "Mr. Mullen may be uncouth, but he certainly gets to the heart of things, doesn't he?"

Mullen suggested breakfast. He was writing, he said — which was, for him, an all-night activity. "Seven too early for you?"

"Seven-thirty," I countered, for the pride of the thing.

He named a restaurant I had never heard of on St. Catherine Street. "Nothing fancy," he said. "Just your basic bacon-and-eggs joint."

A joint. I should have known. I sighed into the telephone. The advantage was that my office was only a short walk away.

The Rise 'n Shine turned out to be an all-night diner, longer than it was narrow, the lighting dim so as not to assault bleary eyes. The air was thick with the smell of sizzling oil, fried onions, eggs, bacon. My mouth watered.

Mullen waved wearily at me from the darkness of a booth towards the rear, and although it was only the second time I had seen him, I felt as if I were meeting an old friend. I slid onto the bench across the table from him. His eyes were narrow and bloodshot, the skin beneath darkened, as if his pupils had leaked into the flesh. His lips were greasy.

"Mac," he said. "Right on time."

Mac? No one had called me "Mac" since the army — unless he had that evening, of course, when my faculties were too weakened to object. But the name gave me a curious pleasure; its insistent informality put me at ease.

"I must look a sight, eh?" he growled. "It's these fuckin' all-nighters. I'm no kid anymore, but daylight just doesn't agree with my writing." His plate was a mess of sautéed onions, fried potatoes oozing coronas of oil, a pool of tomato ketchup. There was also a half-eaten sandwich, the bread showing oily indentations where his fingers had grasped it. With a self-deprecating guffaw, he added, "I suffer for my art. You're my witness."

"I liked the book," I said.

"Well, thanks." And he turned shy, eyes fluttering away on long lashes, fingertip flicking at the rim of his plate.

"Even Mary liked it. Despite the dedication."

He grinned. "Presumptuous of me, wasn't it?"

"Actually, you came across as a bit of a—" I paused, aware that the elegance with which I had planned to upbraid him had fled.

"Well, go on," he said impatiently. "A bit of a what?"

"An asshole, I'm afraid."

He grimaced — his face, it dawned on me, was a veritable theatre of exaggeration — and he exclaimed, "Is that the *best* you can do, Mac? Asshole? You've had all talent for vituperation sanded out of you, haven't you? Look, although I believe in going light on the adjectives, *puckered* asshole might have a touch more bite, don't you think, if that's the hackneyed route you want to take?"

His response took my breath away: I couldn't imagine how one would go about insulting such a man. And when my breath returned, it was in an explosion of laughter. "But why *sanded?*" I finally blustered.

"Because you're so fuckin' smooth, Mac. So fuckin' urbane. Nobody's born that way."

I conceded the point, even though our views on the matter were contradictory: smoothness and urbanity were clearly less virtuous to Mullen than to me. Then I said, "Look here, Mullen, before we go any further, about Mary — not to put too fine a point on it, that dedication was offensive. You owe her an apology."

"Consider it done." He wiped at his lips with a paper napkin. "But I meant it as a compliment, Mac, honest. Guess there's just no telling how a gal's going to react."

I was not mollified. "What about your wife?" I asked, wishing I could remember her name. "Is she, too, *a fine piece of ass?*"

He grimaced. "Not 'fine', Mac. Sweet. There's a difference." Leaning back and taking a deep breath he said, "That she is, my friend. That she is. In spades." He slipped a cigarette from the pack that lay open beside his coffee cup. "She's no ball and chain, my Kathryn. Uh-uh. If anything she's my wings. Big, strong, downy wings." He rolled the cigarette around between his fingers. "A man could do worse, Mac. And most fellows do. From what you said about your Mary, doesn't sound like you're one of them."

Two days later, Mary would receive a dozen long-stemmed roses and another copy of *Hot Nights at the Belvedere*, this one dedicated to "the lady who makes Mac a lucky man." There was also a scribbled note apologizing for any distress his previous dedication might have caused, and asking that the copy be "consigned to the closest garbage-bin, where it properly belongs." Mary would read the note twice, shake her head and mutter, "This Mullen is so full of shit." But she would do as he asked.

Mullen stuck the cigarette behind his ear; he had not, I saw, intended to smoke it. His reaching for it, his playing with it, had all been expressions of the agitation produced in him by thoughts of his wife.

The waitress came over, coffee pot steaming in her hand.

Mullen leaned forward, picked up his fork and speared a chunk of potato. "So, Mac," he said, "you hungry or you just going to sit there and watch me go at it?"

I indicated the sandwich on his plate. "What are you having?"

"Bacon sandwich."

Once again, my mouth watered. I thought of yoghurt and wheat germ. Not without some guilt, I said to the waitress, "I'll have the same." And when she filled the coffee cup she had placed before me, all I said was, "Do you have any cream?"

While my breakfast was being prepared, Mullen remarked that, although he wasn't "any Mona Lisa", he probably looked more haggard than usual. He had spent two days in New York haggling with his American publisher over his already completed second novel. They were unhappy with him, he said, because he refused to change his Canadian setting to an American one. "My Mountie for their FBI agent, the St. Lawrence for the Mississippi. I told them to go to hell."

Then, on the flight back home, he'd made a big mistake. The plane had been overbooked. Some passengers were, as he put it, "generously disposed of, which is to say bought off," the others placed pell-mell around the cabin. He found himself seated beside an elderly woman whose husband had been given a seat two rows away. The woman looked anxious and unhappy. Not relishing the thought of such a seat companion, Mullen gallantly

---

offered to switch places with the husband. The woman's gratitude was immediate and effusive. The husband looked dismayed. As he buckled himself into Mullen's seat, he thanked Mullen for his thoughtfulness.

"You should've seen his eyes, though," Mullen said. "Christ! The poor old guy was probably thanking his lucky stars he wouldn't have to spend the flight with his nervous-nellie of a wife, then I come along and screw it up for him." He told the story with no hint of amusement.

"You did what you thought was right," I suggested after a moment, wincing at the triteness of the comfort I offered.

"I'm no goddam boy-scout, Mac. Doing what's right isn't my mission in life. I leave that to the do-gooders. After my rumble in New York, all I wanted was a little peace on the flight back home — and a tumbler of plonk, of course."

"What does your wife think about all of this?"

"Kathryn? She says that, deep down, I'm a goddam do-gooder — and that I can't stand it."

"Wives like to think we're better than we are."

He took a long swallow of coffee. "Yeah. And I wish they'd stop it."

"But if they did, Dan, where would that leave us?"

"In the hole," he said. "Our natural habitat."

Over the coming months, Mullen and I had breakfast together several times, prompting Mary to remark, "My, you two certainly have taken a shine to each other, haven't you?"

He never spoke of writing, his or anyone else's, except for the time I broached the topic by asking the (apparently inane) question of where he found his ideas. He rolled his eyes. "Writing's not something I talk about," he growled, his gaze shifting away. "It's something I do." Since then, I have restricted any mention of his work to a brief compliment every two years or so, after the publication of a new book.

Once, the entertainment pages of the paper covered a launch party that had been held for him in a bookstore. The guest-list was long: book-page editors, well-known reviewers, several writers of local renown. There was a photograph: Mullen with a glass in one hand, a cigarette in the other, his shoulders crushed in the long arm of some local celebrity. Mullen looked wrung out and drunk, although the truth is that, except for the rare moment of excess, he scarcely drinks at all. The glass occupies his hand like a fixture; it has created for him an aura of alcoholic edge; it makes people wary — and so protects him from them. For all of his bluster and sarcasm and cutting wit, Dan Mullen is a painfully shy man.

I will admit that, on seeing the photograph, I experienced a pinch of — what? jealousy? — at not having been invited. But then I remembered Mullen's having told me that he loathed what he called "writerly get-togethers." When he wasn't at work, he wanted to talk about hockey or jazz or other men's wives. "You can't crib from other writers," he said. "Real writers haven't got much of a life. We're too terrified of the world, which is why we spend so much time trying to make sense of it, trying to tame it. As for the others, the ones who hack away at a typewriter for a couple of hours a day then knock off to some bar or café, they're just farting around indulging their idea of a writerly life. I prefer to spend my time with real people. People like you, Mac."

I was a few moments realizing he meant this as a compliment.

Mary, spreading jam on her whole-wheat toast, said, "So, you've become friends, have you?"

Her question gave me pause. In truth, I hadn't thought about it. When I confessed this, she said, "But you've been getting together regularly for months. Are you friends, or aren't you?"

"Well, I suppose."

"You *suppose*? Are all men like you, Alistair, or is it just you? You don't think, you just do."

"I don't think that's quite fair, Mary."

"Don't you? I know where people fit into my life. Ruth-Ann's your sister, she's not my friend. Marie-Angèle Tremblay's my neighbour, she's not my friend either. As for Agnes — don't make me laugh: a daughter's a daughter. Now Martha, on the other hand — Martha's my friend. I'd have no reason for knowing her if she weren't."

I found her approach exacting. Was friendship truly so complex a thing? The question of whether Mullen was a friend or not struck me as really quite immaterial. We met, we talked, we enjoyed each other's company. There were some things I would tell him and some things I wouldn't. To *suppose* that he was a friend was, to my mind, quite sufficient. Yet I protested: "But Lardner's my friend."

"Lardner's your brother-in-law. He may be a friend, he might even have become a friend had he not married your sister — but there's just no telling, is there? It's all about circumstance, isn't it?"

I gave her a sidelong glance. "Do you spend a great deal of time thinking about such things, Mary?"

"Yes. And so should you."

Her phrasing was that of suggestion; but her tone was more imperative.

And so I thought about it.

And I came to the conclusion that Dan Mullen and I had indeed become friends, and that what had made us so was that I had been "sanded" and he had not: each of us, I believed (although Dan would have scoffed at such psychlogical mumbo-jumbo), envied that very quality in the other. In a way, it made us rivals, cognizant of our many similarities, appreciative of our significant differences. We could learn from one another.

And so, for a quarter of a century, Dan Mullen and I have met occasionally for a breakfast that does my heart no good — but which does wonders for my disposition. When the Rise 'n Shine closed down fifteen years ago or so, he found another place, less conveniently located but serving the same, grease-drenched food. (The words "low fat" cause Dan to shudder.) We never treat each other. He pays his bill and I pay mine. I leave the bigger tip.

In all these years, Dan and I have rarely seen one another in the evenings — perhaps half a dozen times at most — and then only for a quick drink before he headed off to his typewriter. Each time he was edgy and distracted. He was between books, a place in which he does not enjoy finding himself. He is a disciplined, perhaps obsessive, writer; he writes all the time.

He talks little about himself — not through modesty, but by design. For a man whose career has such public dimensions, he displays a kind of genius in keeping his private life private without seeming to do so. The newspapers and magazines rarely mention his wife. After growing up in the inner city, he has chosen to live — as he puts it — a hop, skip and jump away from it, although I cannot fathom what lakes and farmers' fields can mean to a man who hardly even notices them — beyond solitude, I mean. For Dan Mullen's imagination remains in the geography of his early years. His are books of sidewalks and bars and interiors that echo with the sounds of ambition and loneliness.

In all these years, Dan has never invited me to his home — an omission that would never have struck me as curious had Mary not remarked on it. In the early years, she issued several invitations, through me, to Dan and Kathryn to come to dinner at our house. Their inability to accept — Kathryn would be out of town; Dan would be out of town; Kathryn's brother was visiting with his brood; Dan had to work — was never a disappointment to me. A question of context, I suppose: My friendship with Dan

Mullen has always seemed best suited to the smells of oil and grease and percolating coffee, our natural habitat. It has been many years since Mary's last, unrequited invitation. In all these years, then, I have never met Kathryn Mullen. And yet she feels hardly unknown to me. I have never seen a photograph of her, but I know that she is a woman of some beauty, with full eyebrows, sea-green eyes, and cheek-bones that could have by themselves ensured a successful modelling career. Her lips are perhaps a touch too thin for the fullness of her face, but she compensates with lipstick a bright shade of red. She is taller than her husband, a statuesque red-head who enjoys wearing shoes with heels that could dig holes for fenceposts, although the shoes and the lipstick and the matching nail-polish are the most spectacular of her accoutrements. In clothes, she tends to the conservative, simple dresses and pant-suits in muted autumnal colours. Her jewellery is fashionable but classic: modest earrings, a gold chain, perhaps the occasional brooch. One Christmas Dan gave her a set of emerald earrings the colour of her eyes. Like so many women of this province, she works wonders with scarves. At Dan's request, she never wears perfume. "I love the smell of her," he once said as we breathed the odours of frying fat. "Think of a shower in the woods, think of the scent of spring sunshine, think of the freshness of the air at 3:00 am on a clear autumn night." With a snort he added, "Perfumes are beneath her."

Perfumes are beneath her: I chose not to point out the irony which was so evident Dan would have scoffed at it. For Kathryn Mullen is Canadian vice-president of an international cosmetics company. They make skin creams and eyeshadow, mascara and bath oils, and enough perfume to smother half the stench of the world.

When Dan speaks his wife's name, it is as if he is pronouncing the name of some rare and precious elixir.

I once asked him what she thought of his books. "She's my

❧

biggest fan," he growled, "mainly because she's never read them. Says it's her way of keeping some mystery in our marriage." I was astounded. "It's okay by me," he added. "Whatever it takes."

Truth to tell, I have become somewhat fearful of ever meeting Kathryn Mullen. I have grown fond of her — or at least of this conception of her I have been given. I fear that I would not like the real thing, and where would that leave us?

Am I being unfaithful to a close friend when I wonder at times how in the world he managed to end up with a wife who appears to be the very incarnation of beauty, intelligence and graciousness? Dan Mullen is, after all, a man who would waddle bleary-eyed into one's living room, light up a cigarette and growl, "How about some plonk?" He is a man to whom a comb is a museum piece. His idea of athleticism is a dash to the liquor store before closing time.

Part of the genius of Dan's portrait of Kathryn is that she has over the years aged with us. He has, with some subtlety, painted delicate greys among her red hair; stencilled fine lines at the corners of her eyes; given her glasses. But always there has been the beauty and the grace, and the great strength that defines his sense of her. She would not use contact lenses; she would not have her hair tinted. Once he said, "Her back's been giving her some trouble." Another time, with the merest glitter of alarm: "She's having some tests done. Female problems." And not long ago: "She's thinking of retiring. While the going's still good." This he growled, signalling displeasure — but the smile that caused the corners of his mouth to twitch betrayed the pleasure he would not willingly reveal. Dan, who sees and appreciates all the minutiae of his wife, has been waiting years for this. I know that the time is not far off when our breakfast meetings will become less frequent, for he reminded me at that moment of the young Agnes on Christmas Eve. Like Agnes listening for the jingle of sleigh bells, Dan is already anticipating the gift to end all gifts:

the constant company of his wife.

Although I have not met Kathryn, Dan has met Mary several times. She joins us for drinks when he agrees to come over. He has never ceased being ill-at-ease with her, in all likelihood because he is aware of the scepticism with which she greets much of what he says. Mary has the tendency to ask pointed questions, her impatience barely concealed when she finds the answers unsatisfying. *She* reads his books, though, and passes on her compliments through me. I have never shared with him her occasional *Mullen is so full of shit sometimes.*

But Mary has never eaten with Dan. She has never seen him in performance, has never heard the tenderness that enters his voice when he speaks of Kathryn. Perhaps this is why she has never taken him as seriously as I have. Perhaps this is why, truth be told, Mary does not believe that Kathryn exists — not in the flesh, I mean.

Dan Mullen and Mary put up with each other because of me.

And it is right that they should do so. For if Dan and I have been friends for all these years, it is because of Mary. And if, today, I am deeply in love with Mary, it is because of Dan. Neither of them knows this truth about the other.

It happened one morning some years ago. Mary was in the kitchen preparing what had come to pass for breakfast in our home. She spooned yoghurt into a bowl while I waited impatiently for the coffee brewer to end its gurgling.

As I reached into the cupboard for the coffee mugs, I happened to catch sight of Mary out of the corner of my eye. The light of the rising sun was pouring in through the window behind her. The soft, yellow rays suffused her hair, startling the strands of grey. There were so *many* of them . . .

Then, as if with eyes freshly opened, I saw in the light how her skin, once so fine, had coarsened. I saw, with a kind of numb pain, her every wrinkle etched in relief: corded on her forehead, bunched at her eyes, radiating from the corners of her mouth and fringing her lips. I saw her roughened hands plucking an orange from the fruit basket, her fingers neither so slender nor so straight as they had once been. And I saw the fatigue that now clothed her as intimately, as innately, as another skin.

I was startled. I was moved. My jaw began to tremble and I felt my body engorge with sadness, with awe, with — finally — an overwhelming gratitude for the life she had willingly shared with me. This woman, like me suddenly no longer young, whose very age still revealed to me glimpses of youthful passion, had *decided* of her own free will to marry me. She had *decided* of her own free will to have a child with me. She had *chosen* to grow old in my company. Such faith. Such trust. Such loyalty. I was dazzled by the enormity of it.

I had never stopped loving Mary. My devotion to her never once wavered. But the years had made quiescent the passions of the early years. The active ingredient of *being in love* had lost its effervescence. I could not imagine my life without her, nor however could I summon the intensity of feeling that had made her irresistible to me.

At that sunlit moment, though, standing there in the kitchen watching her quarter the orange, I saw Mary's beauty in the way that Dan had taught me to see his wife's. And standing there, listening to the sputter of the coffee brewer, watching her years revealed by the sun, I once more fell deeply, and irrevocably, in love with my wife.

When I pressed myself to her and nuzzled her neck, Mary was puzzled.

"What are you doing?" she said with a slight stammer.

"I'm smelling you," I replied as my head swirled with the pure essence of her.

The silence in the living room screams, then screeches — but only at me. Mullen would sit there all night, letting that violin string stretch so thin it would become invisible, and sharp enough that anyone walking into it would be decapitated.

"Now, Dan, I've never asked you before, as you well know—"

"Your restraint has been remarkable," he growls. His lips, plump and wet, do not move as he speaks, the sounds formed only by the flapping of his tongue. His eyes stare past me. He is discomforted by the sarcasm with which he sharpened the blade of the sentence before slashing it at me.

Mary snorts. She has had enough. "For God's sake, Dan," she says in exasperation, "all he's asking you to do is give a reading at the university. What's so tough about that?"

"Nothing," he says, his voice like tumbling gravel. "It's not the reading, Mary. It's that he asked. I would never have expected that from a friend." He does not look at me as he says this, for the pushy and irascible Dan Mullen is as wary of confrontation as is a cat of water. "Problem is, friendship stops where the buck begins."

A quarter of a century is a long time. Throughout, Dan and I have argued and disagreed. We have often chided one another. But we have never wounded one another.

He neatly empties the whisky into his mouth, purses his lips and swallows with a deliberation that suggests he is following the path of the liquid as it runs down his throat. Then, placing the glass carefully on the table beside him, he presses himself up from the chair. The cuff of his pant leg catches on the top of his sock and remains there. It makes him look entirely dishevelled. Without looking at me, he makes rapidly for the door and, letting himself out, he mumbles, "I'll call you."

But I know Dan Mullen. I know his pride, and his powerful sense of place. I know that despite the decades, despite the pounds of bacon and gallons of coffee we've consumed together, he will not keep his promise.

The buzz of the oven timer — which comes to me like the distant whirr of a giant mosquito — brings Jack clattering up the stairs from the basement where he's finishing his article. The turkey, ready for one of its innumerable bastings, is his domain.

This morning, I watched him wash and dry it and rub it with butter and herbs, then stuff it to bursting with fistfuls of a gooey mixture comprised of breadcrumbs, onions, garlic, raisins, *herbes de Provence* and God knows what else. Finally, after sewing the cavity shut with a needle the size of a stiletto — just watching made me wince — he lathered the bird in honey and heaved it into the oven. An impressive show, performed with great dexterity, and with a grace I had never before witnessed in him.

107

As a young man, Jack had entertained ideas of medical school. Observing him prepare the turkey, seeing the gentleness in his hands, it occurred to me that he would have been a good doctor — but it all comes down to temperament, doesn't it? Is temperament revealed in gesture? I don't know why Jack chose another way for himself, but he has never spoken of regret.

He emerges from the kitchen a few minutes later, patting his hands dry with a kitchen towel and smiling over at me. Jack is not a tall man — indeed, Agnes in her pumps frequently appears taller — and his build creates the impression that he's even smaller than he really is. He is slight, with a body kept compact by jogging and tennis during the warm months and skating and skiing during winter, private enthusiasms to which he clings tenaciously. He has jogged in sleet and skied through snowstorms.

"How's the bird?" I call.

"Coming along well."

"And the article?"

"I wish I could say the same."

From the kitchen Agnes makes a comment that is too muffled for me to decipher, or perhaps it's meant for Jack's ears and not mine. In any case, he turns away from me towards the kitchen and promises in a chastened voice not to be long.

"Don't hurry on my account," I call. "I'm quite happy as I am. You go on, Jack. Wrestle the beast to the ground!"

With a wave of his hand, he trots back down the stairs to his books and his notes and his search for something original to say. This writing of academic articles does not come easily to Jack. He once described the process to me as one of "fighting with an animal". Most others take the accepted path of having a graduate student under their supervision do the research and the writing. They change a word here or there, add a phrase or two, then type their names first on the title page. Jack refuses to do this. He considers it exploitative and dishonest — antiquated notions in today's academic world. No wonder his career, while solid, has been unspectacular. Right now, Jack would much rather be out there in the darkness and the snow exerting his muscles than labouring over sentences few will read.

He will get his wish come New Year's Eve, when we set out for their cottage in the Townships. They will not countenance my remaining here alone and so I shall have to endure the snow-drenched hills and fields and deathly silence of the country. Many years ago it was the place for people of my ilk — the embryonic intelligentsia of novelists, moralists, poets and teach-ers — to spend the summers swimming, boating, playing tennis and interfering with other people's spouses. For a while, Mary and I toyed with the idea of buying a cottage. While Mary was enthusiastic, my heart was not in it, for among the summer hordes were many people I ran into professionally. Following them to the country would have been like following my work. I felt no urge and certainly no need.

One stifling day in the city, Mary, frustrated by my reticence, lost her temper and I lost mine in return. "For God's sake, Mary," I said foolishly, "the people out there, they drink rye of all things!"

"What's the matter?" she said. "You afraid they won't think sherry manly enough?"

As time went along the idea of a cottage died a natural death.

Later on, we had the opportunity, as many did, to move to a fancier part of town, or even to another city, as many more did prompted by our politics. But again, I saw no compelling reason. I liked our neighbourhood, was happy there. I had faith that things would settle down. We even had a chance to buy the duplex apartment above ours, but we had no need of further space and I didn't fancy being a landlord. How was I to know that Tremblay of all people would buy out the old couple who lived there?

And so things changed. Tremblay came to live above me and that summer society died off, their cottages going to another, altogether more sedate generation, to people like Agnes and Jack.

There is on the whole a kind of modesty to Jack. He is not the type to exult over a sporting triumph. Not that he's lacking in pride — only that he lets it show in discreet ways. For instance, he dresses modestly, simple shirts, unremarkable trousers, brown loafers over which he zips up black rubbers for snow. In the cold months, however, he favours form-fitting turtlenecks. They hug his torso in such a way as to reveal the firmness of his chest, the trimness of his waist, the tightness of his belly. They are a form of showing off. They assert that his is a well-exercised body. Come to think of it, though, does this seem an assertion only to one whose body is beyond beautifying?

François, stretched out on his stomach, is leafing through a picture book. He bears a strong resemblance to his father, does François. They have the same hair, the shade of which changes constantly, sometimes appearing a soft brown, at other times — as now in the twinkling light of the Christmas tree — acquiring a silvery sheen. In truth, though, their hair is almost colourless. It's wispy and thin and suggestive of transparency. This range of hair shades is a trick of different lights, the rays working their way through to the pate and reflecting back past the strands at themselves. Agnes, too, has noticed this quality in the hair of her husband and son. She's amused by it, says they will have no need of the tints that have become a standard part of her weekly visits to the hairdresser.

For some years Jack sported a beard, a moustacheless fringe that ran from ear to ear by way of the cheeks and chin; and he wore eyeglasses. He'd acquired the beard as a young academic just starting out. They were years of flirtation with politics — a heightened awareness, a restrained involvement — as an organiser and riding-association man, the beard almost part of the uniform, a sign of genteel radicalism. Now he's clean-shaven and has switched to contact lenses, which causes his eyes to appear smaller and softer than before, with a gaze that's slightly startled, as if the world constantly takes him unawares. His political ideas, rooted in notions of pride but developed beyond such narrow beginnings to pragmatic coherence, have altered somewhat with the years, although the essentials, that hard nut of pride, remain intact. Family, work and sport now occupy his time. A caution has grown in him. He has things to lose: a family, a house, retirement savings plans. It is not age that makes us cautious in life. It is success.

Still, he has his passions. Bach, recorded or live, seems stirringly conventional. The historical uses of tree-bark, on which he has assembled a small but impressive library, much less so. But the therapeutics of words — now there's where Jack awoke my wonderment.

Late one night I arose to visit the bathroom and glimpsed him sitting in the living room, precisely where I'm presently seated. He was bathed in the warm glow of a reading lamp. He had wrapped himself in a flannel blanket and his feet were bare. He was reading, his lips moving silently, in the way of a man who has difficulty reading. I was disconcerted — his struggle with writing flashed through my mind — until I realised that what I was seeing was far more complicated than that. It dawned on me that his involvement with the page was complete, that I was seeing a man for whom it was insufficient to read the words only with his eyes. He had to feel them gliding on his tongue, seek out their shape with his lips. He had to taste the words, savour them.

Agnes told me the next day that, late at night when Jack cannot sleep, he gets out an exquisite, leather-bound edition of collected verse — kept high on a shelf far from the reach of

François, who has been known to express himself on endpapers — and soothes himself with poetry. A startling habit, but one that made clear so much that I had failed to see.

Many nights since moving here I've lain sleepless in bed with the blankets tugged up to my neck. Being in this house, not just Agnes's but Jack's too, has brought back to me with renewed discomfort a tense discussion Jack and I fell into a long time ago, a year or so before François was born. A discussion occasioned by a man who believed deeply that the mind must rule the passions and who, nonetheless, will be decades safely entering history because of the passions he unleashed in others.

He had been around forever, this man, dazzling us, outraging us, nudging and bullying us from his prime-ministerial pulpit into a shape he believed worthy of ourselves. Then one night, almost on a whim, he took a walk in a snow-storm, and decided that the time had come for him to retreat from the limelight. He would give it all up — the power, the prestige, the influence that went beyond his office.

When I heard the announcement on the radio, tears came to my eyes. Not for the man, or for the future suddenly unpredictable without him. No, it was the snowstorm. The manner in which he had made his decision. He had walked out into a driving force more ferocious than the one that had claimed Kevin and returned with a new life. The image of this touched a chord within me that would remain sensitive for weeks. And it was in this period that Jack and I fell into the conversation we had studiously avoided. Neither of us had wished to venture into what we knew to be our personal no-man's-land defined by a figure I considered strong and principled, but in whom Jack saw arrogance and rigidity. Had Mary and Agnes not been in the kitchen putting the finishing touches to dinner, one of them would have spotted the red flag. One of them would have found a way — Mary forthrightly; Agnes, more attuned to the sensitivities, with an edgy humour — to steer us onto another, less treacherous path.

But they were not within earshot, and so Jack and I turned to the terrain of an event from early in the man's career, an event mythologised to a useful truthlessness, propagandised to multiple and contradictory realities. An event that could not be seen clearly for being sheathed in a welter of facts and non-facts. We careened down towards a place neither of us wished to go to, Jack and I, and we were, after those heedless minutes, like damaged goods.

I *imagine that in the distance,* across the ice and through the darkness of the clear night, he saw the lights of the other shore.

The bridge, a tracery of fanciful filament in the thickening dusk, is unlikely to have distracted him. It is hard to conceive that a man intent on taking his own life would, in those final moments, see beauty and not be seduced away from the abyss.

He drove far to come to this, two hundred and fifty kilometers east, along a ribbon of highway through mostly uninspired landscape. The occasional fold in the land, the occasional frozen stream, farms shrouded in the crackling white of deep winter. Thrush, I remember, was not an aficionado of the cold.

But why so far? The question nags at me.

I can only conjecture that he was looking for a place of a

certain beauty, and distant. Beauty that would be sensed but remain unseen: he had done it at night. And distance sufficient to separate him from his shame but not so great as to permit doubt to deter him.

I can only conjecture.

I followed the same path the week after he was fished out. I wanted to see where he had gone, picture what he had done: I felt I owed that to him. And to myself. The drive had seemed long, the landscape infused with a chill deeper than that of the season. I remember icicles hanging as large as broadswords from the eaves of farm buildings; and the way the crisp morning sunlight suffused the frosted wires.

He had chosen the beginning of a cold snap that followed the biggest blizzard of the season, −35 at midnight, with a gusting wind and a full moon in the sky. He had worn two thick, porous coats. He had removed his boots and socks. He had given himself no chance.

A fellow from the university here showed me the way. But we could go only so far. The way to the river was down the side of a cliff. There was a road, but the accumulation of snow and ice made it impassable in winter. There was a path, leading to stairs, but the way resisted me, the path deep beneath snow and ice. Footing was treacherous for a man on two good legs. For a man with a stick, it was foolhardy. Thrush had been in better shape than I, and his legs were sturdy. Still, it could not have been easy.

We turned and retraced our steps, following a railway line back to where we had parked the car. By the time we got there, my breath had grown harsh and I was leaning on my stick rather more than was advisable. Come back when it's warmer, my guide advised.

So I have returned now, in summer, to this spot beside the mighty river. The tide is out, the beach wide and pebbly, outcroppings of rock reaching out into the water. Closer to the far shore, a ship heavy with metal containers cuts swiftly through the water beneath the bridge. All around me families sit at picnic tables enjoying their evening meal: tablecloths and plates and cutlery, glasses of wine.

In my imagination the trees grow leafless, the shore ices up, the land grows stark and white, my skin prickles at a searing wind.

In my imagination he hobbles along barefooted, sinking to the knees in snow, and begins his walk across the ice, towards the sluggish, frosted water which, in the darkness, would have taken him by surprise.

The sound of a splash returns me to greenery and warmth. Fingers point to ripples on the placid river.

Un poisson. A fish.

I stare at the surface, hoping it will leap again.

But it does not. By the time I knew it was there it was already gone.

His body was found three days later by a professional photographer who had ventured out onto the ice with his camera. Luck, this. Without the search for art, he might have remained in the water until spring, when the runoff would have washed him away, perhaps forever. In his pockets they found his identification, for which they must have been grateful — for there had been no one to report Thrush missing.

Curious what we will remember from days which, later, mark themselves as memorable.

That morning, perhaps because of the tension of what I knew would be a difficult day, I awoke with an erection — a phenomenon which, I will admit, has grown infrequent in recent years. Daily living saps my reserves of vitality, in addition to which Mary and I have attained that stage of life when sexual intimacy — the anxiety of its delights — has mostly given way to a tolerant friendliness.

Mary, sitting up in bed, espying the phenomenon in the startled way she might an unexplained stain on the sofa, said, "Oh my! Is it real or do you have to go to the bathroom?"

Encouraged by the lack of sarcasm in her tone, I said, "Real, I think."

She ran her hands through her hair. "Are you just being hopeful?"

"No, I don't think so."

She considered it for a moment, as if assessing its veracity. "Well, then, what shall we do about it?"

Not wishing to appear uncouth with eagerness, I suggested getting on with our day. It would go away, eventually. "Or," I said, "we could deal with it in the time-honoured fashion. Are you prepared?"

Mary lay back onto the bed, removing her nightie as she did so. "My dear," she said. "I have been prepared for so very long."

Ahh, my Mary.

Always so full of surprises.

Only sometime later, when I was seated in the metro train after having fairly floated to the station, was my mind able to unencumber itself sufficiently of the lightness and thrill of Mary to prepare for the ordeal that awaited me at the university.

As I sat in waning thrall, a vision, as it were, came to me of Thrush as he had materialised beside me, here, one morning some weeks before. He was a squat and scruffily-attired man, silvered hair as if combed by his fingers alone, a briefcase sprouting papers clutched under his arm. But as he crashed uninvited onto the seat beside me, I noticed that he had shaved closely, with great care. I noticed, too, that he had been rather liberal with the after-shave.

Thrush (I use his real name instead of the anonymous T. only because he is now gone and his memory can be no more stained than it already is) was an acquaintance from the department, which he had joined the term before I arrived. He was a year or two my senior and had been a gunner during the war, which explained, I have long felt, a certain antipathy that defined our dealings with one another: I was not immune to the natural diffidence that infantrymen feel for those who frequently lobbed shells at friendly coordinates.

I was startled, therefore, to see that he had chosen to sit beside me when so many other seats were available.

"Mackenzie," he wheezed, hugging his briefcase to his chest.

"Good morning, Thrush."

"You look rather chipper this morning."

Chipper: I have never thought of myself as chipper. Being chipper has never been one of my ambitions. With restraint, I said, "And how are you this morning, Thrush?"

He yawned, passing his hand — thick fingers, gnawed nails — over his face. "I was up till all hours last night. Your fault. I should have been working on my paper for the review —"

"I wasn't aware that you still publish. Admirable."

"Habit, actually. Or perhaps vanity. I enjoy seeing my name in print, even if I'm the only one to notice."

His honesty so delighted me, I laughed. For most of us, our list of publications is little more than an intellectual obituary. "So tell me," I said, "why do you blame me for your lack of sleep?"

"It's that student of yours, the blind one."

"Elliot."

"Yes. Bright fellow. I was up all night wrestling with an essay he submitted for my seminar on poetic lunacy. Some theory he has about moonlight and sunshine —"

"Ahh, yes, Elliot is rather taken with the subject of light."

"Well, he caused me to burn the midnight oil, so to speak. And now here I am, all ragged."

"At least give the boy his due, Thrush. When was the last time a student challenged you with such rigour?"

He went silent, acknowledging, I felt, the justice of what I had said.

We changed trains, sitting once more together. The wagon was full of students — these students who are constant reminders that, while they are forever young, we are left with only dregs in our cups — and Thrush's eyes, rheumy and blood-shot as they were, began a wandering assessment of the females among them. I felt then that he was a man living with a great deal of pain, and that he was feeding that pain in what amounted to an exercise in self-loathing. I felt that his life-long bachelorhood was a great burden to him.

Thrush said, "You know, Mackenzie, the one advantage to age is that it removes all that sexual tension you battle with throughout your life. Know what I mean? The urge to pursue it, to acquire it — and then the pressure to perform with a modicum of talent. I was never much of a Don Juan, you know."

An extraordinary admission from a gunner, I thought. They were always so taken with the calibre of their weapons.

"It was all so time-consuming, wasn't it, Mackenzie? And then, the returns — do you remember the pressure to maximise the claims? But age takes care of all that, doesn't it? The desire, the ability. No one expects anything of us in that area."

Us?

"It's a kind of freedom, isn't it? I now dedicate all my energies to my work. I find myself more productive now than I've ever been. You know what I mean, don't you, Mackenzie?"

His question struck me as presumptuous, and it did occur to me to ask whether his gun had lost its firing pin. But he had spoken without regret or rancour, and so I had presumed at the time that he was merely trying to make the best of a bad situation.

As the train entered our station, I thought, with pleasure, of Mary, and though I could not tell Thrush this, I felt myself to be extraordinarily lucky.

I was slow that morning. The first snow of the winter had come down the night before, and what had been, as ever, enchanting at the moment had by morning become treacherous for me: on battened snow, two good legs are surer than three uncertain ones. I told Thrush that he should feel free to go on ahead without me.

He would not.

And so we walked in a companionable silence, he hugging his briefcase, I leaning on my stick, from the metro station to the department, where he went to his office and I to mine.

Only weeks and events later, as the train hissed to a stop in the same metro station, did it occur to me that he may, that morning, have spoken in pre-emptive self-defence.

For Thrush had to have known about the storm beginning to seethe around him. He had to have known it was merely a matter of time.

The university had put at our disposal a classroom in a rented building on the periphery of the campus. All around, and most particularly in the neighbouring streets, the sidewalks were lively day and night with bars, restaurants, nightclubs and their patrons. They were sources of light, movement, energy. But the intersection where our assigned building stood was a curious one. The nondescript buildings that occupied three of the corners, and the parking lot that occupied the fourth, seemed to repel or consume the light, so that even on the brightest days the inter-section was like a nexus of grimness, a no-man's-land through which pedestrians hurried, their sights set on elsewhere. The intersection offered no reason to pause, save for the strip club across from the parking lot if one was so inclined. While the other university buildings stood some blocks away in splendid integration with the downtown city core, the grey multi-storeyed

box where we were to hold our deliberations occupied its corner
like a prime candidate for sand-blasting or demolition. Both
physically and psychically, it occurred to me, our inquiry was as
removed as possible from the centre of things. Above us was an
empty floor long unrented, below us a beauty school that taught
ways and notions of glamour. We found ourselves ensconced,
then, between layers of urban schizophrenia.

The room itself was large but far from airy, and could be
viewed, optimistically, as historical: its floor was white with
chalk-dust generations old. With its windows long unwashed and
the view they afforded of the rear of various commercial establishments — red brick, grey brick, snow swept up into corners
and piled high against walls — the lights, necessary even on
sunny days, were indispensable on a day such as this.

My fellow panel members had already arrived, neither looking
— to use Thrush's term — particularly chipper. They, I saw
immediately, looked forward to this task with an enthusiasm
equal to my own.

Professor de Vasconselos and I arranged the tables. Professor
Goldman brought the chairs. Standing back, she said, "Must it
look so judicial?"

"You would prefer something more collegial, perhaps?" I asked.

"Less severe might be better, don't you think? Less intimidating?" She was the newest member of the department,
academically-gifted, highly accomplished, but yet with the
attitudes of a graduate student.

"My dear lady, this is an official hearing. But if you prefer, we
could probably find a quiet corner in a pub somewhere, would
that do?"

From over by the windows, Professor de Vasconselos laughed
heartily. "Have you brought your gavel, Mackenzie?" he said.

I suggested we take our seats and prepare ourselves.

Professor de Vasconselos, taking the chair to my right with a demeanour weighted by the world, said, "Let he who is without sin . . ." He was a man ageing well, with a kind of European finesse, the grey at his temples as if brushed in, the lines on his face finely carved. He could give elegance to such a remark.

Professor Goldman, taking the seat to my left, said, "All sin, Joaquim, or just this particular kind?"

"Sin is sin, is it not? Whether of this kind or another?"

Sin is sin. Indeed. I snorted in rather equine fashion. Catholic absolutism brings out the animal in me. I reached for a knob of chalk and flung it across the classroom. It clattered off the far wall leaving no mark. "Look here, my good people, I have killed men in battle. I have done, because of circumstances, a great deal of which I am not proud. Yet I believe myself to be without sin. For I have not wantonly, gratuitously, committed evil — evil in pursuit of gratification, I mean. That, to me, is sin. So I will happily throw any stones that require throwing. But that, let me remind you, is not why we are here. May I therefore suggest that we leave notions of sin to those authorities best equipped to deal with them and get on with the business at hand?"

I shall call her Miss R.

Miss R. entered the room with a becoming self-possession. She was a tall woman, taller than Thrush I daresay, well-dressed, with a seriousness that spoke of ambition and wariness underlain by a sense of insecurity: Everything about Miss R. said she did not truly believe in whatever talents she might have been blessed with. Her transcripts, which we had requested, had been deemed irrelevant to our purpose, but all my experience told me that she was a far from indifferent student.

She did not wait for an invitation to sit at the table facing us. "Look," she said, leaning forward. "I'm not here to beat around the bush. I admit it. I plagiarised the essay. It was stupid but I was desperate and so I did it."

Professor Goldman, taken aback, said, "So you don't deny having stolen—"

"I told you. I plagiarised it. What more do you want?"

"And Professor Thrush discovered this."

"He said he wanted to see me in his office after class. That's when he told me."

"Go on."

"He said plagiarism was a very serious offence, it could get me tossed out of the course, even expelled from the university."

"Yes, well . . ."

"And then he said it didn't have to go beyond these four walls — of his office, he meant. That we could keep it between us, if we could come to some . . . arrangement. Or maybe he said agreement, I don't remember." She waved her hands dismissively — elegant hands, slender fingers, nails moderately long and modestly painted.

Professor de Vasconselos, taking a note, said, "And did he specify the nature of this arrangement, or agreement?"

"Well, he gave me this look—"

"We're not interested in his looks, young lady," I said. "What did he say?"

"That's all. We could come to an arrangement."

Professor Goldman said, "So he said arrangement."

"Yes, I remember now."

"Go on."

"Then he started saying, oh, you know, he was a very lonely guy, his wife was dead or something, he hadn't been with a woman in, like, years."

Professor Goldman, scandalised, said, "He said that? That he hadn't been—"

"Not in so many words, but he kind of intimated it, you know? Talking about his loneliness and all that, and how his work kept him so busy."

Professor Goldman nodded, but my patience was being tried. "Young lady, what *did* Professor Thrush say?"

"All right, look. Let's cut to the chase." She abruptly leaned forward, palms splayed on the table top. "He didn't say much. He said we could come to this arrangement, he said he was lonely, then he stood up behind his desk and unzipped his pants. Okay? Is that clear enough for you?" Her neck reddened, her necklace of brown beads swaying forward, then snapping silently back onto her chest, a monitor of her emotions.

After a moment of silence, I said, "Is there anything else?"

She shook her head. "I walked out."

Professor Goldman said, "Thank you."

Professor de Vasconselos said, "Feisty. But she should enroll in one of those creative writing courses. Improve the verisimilitude."

Professor Goldman said, "You don't believe her."

"You do?"

Professor Goldman turned to me. I screwed the cap back onto my fountain pen. "Let's hear from Thrush," I said, troubled.

Contrition does not come easily to men of my age — if, indeed, it comes at all.

Thrush would not sit. He gripped the back of the chair in fingers that appeared bloated and vulnerable. He had, however, dressed for the occasion. His frayed herring-bone jacket had been replaced by a three-piece suit of a certain vintage yet still serviceable, and a tie now bound together the shirt-collar habitually left open. He aimed, I saw, to project an idea of dignity, but he had not succeeded. He had, as it were, bottled himself up. In the clarified grimness of the classroom, he appeared isolated and lonely.

"As you wish," I said, and proceeded to acquaint him with the wording of the accusation levelled against him.

He turned purple as I read.

When I fell silent, he said, "Calumny," his voice composed. "Fabrication. I deny it all."

Professor Goldman said, "Would you care to give us your version—"

"Not my version. What happened. The truth of the matter." He took a difficult breath, as if he were being strangulated by the necktie. "I caught the girl plagiarising. I told her so, in the privacy of my office, not wishing to embarrass her before the class. I explained the seriousness of the matter and its possible consequences. That's when she—" He jiggled the knot of his tie, wrenching, as it were, at his discomfort.

"When she what?" Professor de Vasconselos prompted.

"When she made an offer of a sexual nature. I was outraged. I ordered her to leave my office immediately and told her in no uncertain terms that I would be taking the matter up with the department. And now, as you see, I am here."

Professor de Vasconselos said, "What was the nature of the offer, may I ask?"

"I believe it's called fellatio in polite company. But she chose not to be polite."

Professor de Vasconselos, smiling, said, "I'm afraid Mackenzie here will probably ask you to state precisely what Miss R. said."

His colour deepened. "I'd rather not, if you don't mind."

"That's quite all right, Thrush," I said, with a sharp glance to my right. I am not a humourless man, but Professor de Vasconselos's idea of humour was becoming somewhat wearisome.

Professor Goldman said, "And your reaction was — outrage?"

"Are you questioning my word?"

"No. I'm just trying to get a clear picture of what occurred. You're saying you weren't even a little bit tempted? Professor

Thrush, you're no doubt aware that there have been rumours for some time—"

"How dare you!"

"You wouldn't be the first, Thrush," I said. And with a glance to my left: "Although I must insist that we restrict our comments to the matter at hand."

"I see," Thrush said. "So your minds are made up, is that it?"

"Our minds," I said with some severity, "are not here to be made up. They are here to ascertain the facts."

"Professor Thrush," Professor Goldman pursued, "you say you intended to bring the situation to the attention of the department. From our information, you never did."

"Are you familiar with the word compassion, Goldman? When I cooled down, I decided to give the girl a chance, perhaps allow her to redo the essay with the understanding that her grade for the course would not surpass a C. Standard practice, as I'm sure you're aware. She acted before I could."

I turned to Professor Goldman, then to Professor de Vasconselos. "Are there any more questions?"

They both shook their heads.

Then Thrush said, "Mackenzie, you claim you are here to ascertain the facts. But how do you intend to do that? It's my word against the girl's. I fail to see how I could possibly prove my innocence."

"It's not for you to do so, Thrush," I said.

He fixed a rabid glare on me. "If you really believe that, you are a fool, Mackenzie."

And I knew, of course, that he was right.

Outside, it had begun to snow, the flakes drifting and eddying down through a glazed daylight.

"Well," I said. "There we have it."

꙳

"Do you think so?" Professor de Vasconselos, elbows planted on the table, chin resting on his interlaced fingers, glanced slyly at me.

"What do you mean?"

Professor Goldman, suspicious, said, "I think Joaquim has something up his sleeve."

"There was a note in my box this morning, Professor Mackenzie. Someone else wants to talk to us."

"A witness?"

"Not directly. You know Collins?"

"I am acquainted with him." Collins was a part-time instructor in the department, a young man who wandered the halls enshrouded in his own, highly rarefied atmosphere. It was said that he constantly composed poems in his head. It was also said that he did not believe in committing his poems to paper. "Do you know what Mr. Collins has to say to us?"

"I spoke to him briefly on the phone. He's been agonising, it seems."

"About?"

"He's had dealings with the complainant."

"What kinds of dealings?" Professor Goldman asked unhappily.

"It seems he's had a similar offer to Thrush's."

"Can he prove it? Has he reported it to anyone?"

"Apparently not."

Professor Goldman turned to me. "Professor Mackenzie, I protest."

But my decision was already made. "There's no need to, my dear. Mr. Collins would no doubt relish the role of *deus ex machina* or some such thing, but I have no intention of offering it to him." I turned to Professor de Vasconselos. "Save your protests, my dear fellow. This amounts to hearsay, don't you agree? Hearsay that is prejudicial to the complainant, who would no doubt deny the allegation. I fail to see what bearing it could possibly have on the matter before us."

"It would establish a pattern of behaviour, I should imagine."

"Tell me, Joaquim," Professor Goldman said, "what did Collins do? Did he accept?"

"That's why he was agonising, you see."

"Lady and gentleman," I said. "I have already ruled all this irrelevant."

"Look, Joaquim, Ms R.'s a straight-A student—"

"That too is irrelevant, as you well know," I interjected.

"She's no fool," Professor Goldman nonetheless continued. "In fact, I gave her a couple of her As. What doesn't make sense is, why would she lodge a complaint against Thrush knowing full well Collins might come forward?"

"On the other hand," Professor de Vasconselos said, "why would Collins lie?"

"Enough," I said, at the end of my patience. "Whatever may or may not have transpired between Collins and Miss R. is none of our concern. Let us concentrate on the matter at hand. Our task is to ascertain the facts as clearly as we can and submit a report to the administration. We are not called upon to pass judgment. Indeed, I fail to see how we possibly can."

"So Thrush is finished," Professor de Vasconselos said.

"As is Miss R., Joaquim," Professor Goldman said.

"Nasty business all around," I agreed, not without a certain sadness.

I gathered my things. Outside the snow had grown voluminous — it would be several inches deep on the sidewalk — a wind wrenching the flakes about. The trudge back would be excruciating, and although I did not relish the thought, I did not delay.

I headed out. Back to the metro. Back home. Back, desperately, to Mary.

It was a storm of Biblical force: a rage of wind and snow before which the city quickly grew helpless. Cars became mired in drifts, students clung to each other for support, my stick probed, at times with uneasy success, for purchase. Only underground was respite to be found, the metro continuing unhindered, conveying damp and shivering thousands to destinations from which home was yet an uncertainty.

I was pleased, at my stop, to see that the buses were still operating. Indeed, I fairly shivered with pleasure, for I doubted my ability to see myself home otherwise. The labour of attaining the metro station at the university had drained my strength, so that my body had sunk to join my spirits in the abyss into which the morning's investigations had plunged them.

On the crowded bus — I was offered, and accepted, a seat — I thought of Thrush, and of Professor Goldman's parting comment: that she felt the years had made him foolish. I came close, then, to confessing that I shared her view of what had happened. I believed Thrush to be guilty of impropriety. I thought him capable of it. He had been a gunner, after all. But I restrained myself, given pause by her comment on the effect of the years. Was it that the years had betrayed Thrush or the other way around?

For I have found that the years lived, and the concomitant diminishment of the years yet to be lived, concentrate the mind. It sharpens one's judgement of worthiness, so that the medals one may once have prized, for instance, become, as the journey lengthens, valued in the main not for their prettiness or their testimony but for the memories — at times sharp, at times attenuated — they will entice from the mind. This, to me, is the gift of the years: a sense of the rightness and importance of things and actions. It is what some — and modesty prevents me from numbering myself among them — might call a kind of wisdom.

Thrush, I felt, had taken that gift and made nonsense of it.

The foolishness, then, the betrayal, was his own.

Mary met me at the door with relief. She took my coat, shook the snow from my hat and led me to the blazing fireplace. On the sidetable beside my chair sat the glass of sherry — my preferred restorative — she had poured in anticipation of my return.

She returned a moment later with her tea and sat with me. I related the morning's events, sharing my discomfort, and she was, as always, an attentive listener.

When I was done, she put down her empty tea cup and said, "You know, my dear, everyone always blames Eve, when the truth of the matter is that Adam was undone by his own weakness."

There she goes again, I thought. My Mary. Always so full of surprises.

We had barely finished dinner when the doorbell rang. I opened it.

"Mackenzie."

"Thrush?"

"May I come in?"

I stepped aside. "By all means. This is a surprise." Outside, the storm was still raging.

"This won't take long," he said.

At my insistence he removed his hat and coat, reluctantly stepped into the living room where he perched on the edge of the sofa.

I offered a drink.

He waved the offer off. "This won't take long," he repeated.

I sat across from him. "Look here, Thrush, if this is about Miss R., you know I can't —"

He again waved my words away and took a folded sheaf of paper from his coat pocket. "I wanted to give you this. It's that essay I was telling you about."

"Elliot's."

"Yes. He's really quite a remarkable young man. I wanted to be sure he got this back. I've appended some rather extensive comments."

"Why don't you give it to him yourself?"

"He's away as you probably know."

"Yes, he's in London doing some research. But he'll be back in a month or so."

He held the papers out to me. "If it's not too much to ask, would you make sure he gets it?"

"Yes, of course." I took the papers. "But I still don't—"

He got laboriously to his feet. "I'll be saying good night, then."

Putting on his coat, he said, "You know, Mackenzie, that committee of yours, the entire department. A self-righteous lot. And you know who the self-righteous are, don't you? They're the ones who haven't been caught yet."

It was as close as he would come to an admission of guilt — or, at least, so I took the meaning of his words.

I showed him out, then went to join Mary who had remained in the kitchen. She had heard everything. "Now what do you imagine that was all about?" I said.

"Neatening up," she replied. "He won't be around for long."

I snorted. "He'll still be around when Elliot gets back. The bureaucracy doesn't work *that* fast."

"He's not going to wait for the bureaucracy," she said. "Didn't you hear it in his voice?"

When the dishes were done we got into bed, and as we lay side by side under the covers — Mary engrossed in her book, me in Elliot's essay — the miraculous occurred once more.

I was dumbfounded, could only take Mary's hand — "My dear, what in the world are you . . ." — and place it on the spot where her fingers could discover for themselves the evidence of what had transpired.

"Oh my!" she said, incredulous. "Again?" She sat up, her grasp never wavering. "Are you feeling quite all right?"

"Never better," I assured her.

"But this—" And she gave me a rather painful tweak. "What's happening?"

"My dear Mary, if I could explain it, I would. But may I suggest that this may not be the most appropriate moment to seek explanation?"

She said, with wonder, "It feels . . . I mean, it's quite splendid. But twice in a single day! At your age! Might it be dangerous?"

"Dammit, Mary!"

"Shall we get on with it then?"

"Yes, I think that would be advisable."

And so we got on with it, Mary — as that morning — taking charge with a wondrous dispatch, she and I rubbing the genie bottle of each other's bodies, watching astonished as together we emerged as if from a thousand years of sleep.

That night I dreamed of Thrush, but the details of the dream have not remained with me.

Mere days later, as the city grew brittle in the grip of Arctic air, Thrush announced that he was taking early retirement, effective immediately.

There was no reception. There were no gifts, no speeches of thanks and farewell.

He simply emptied his office one morning and left.

In my pigeonhole that afternoon I found an envelope with my name printed on it. Inside was a photograph. A polaroid. Of Thrush. With no clothes on.

I was, to say the least, taken aback. And then I saw why he had put it there. His body was normal in all respects save one. Where the male appendage should have been, there was none. On the back, written in a strong hand, were the words THE WAR.

I hurried to my office, checked his home number in the university directory and tried to call him. There was no answer.

Then I dialled Professor Goldman and Professor de Vasconselos. I got their voicemails. To each I left the same message: "There's something I think you should see."

I dialled Thrush's number once again, to no avail. I went home, continued trying throughout the evening.

Days later I would understand that he had already left on his journey along the ribbon of highway through an uninspired landscape: a rendezvous with pride, and −35 at midnight.

A breeze blows over the water. It is warm, humid. Little white-caps dot the surface, and the wake of the ship, already far downstream, sends wavelets onto the beach. They make a crisp, seething sound, as at the ocean's edge.

Mary, who had wandered off, returns from her walk, hands clasped behind her back. "He chose a lovely spot," she says. "Even in winter it'd be enchanting."

She is right — I have had the thought myself — and yet her observation irritates me. "What does it matter, Mary? What he did was so—" The right word takes its time coming to me, and when it does it seems to me the truth of the matter. "—ugly."

"Are you talking about that incident with the girl?"

"No. That — The fact is, I don't know what happened there. I mean, you saw the photo. What would've been the point? And why didn't he — You know, there at the hearing—"

"What? Open up his trousers?"

"At least he should have made us aware of the information."

"My God, Alistair, are you being serious?"

"It would've changed everything."

"Exactly. Everything. And that's what he couldn't face.

Everone would've known, wouldn't they?"

"The process is confidential—"

"Yes, well . . ." she intones sceptically. Her eyes sweep away from me to take in the river, the bridge, the greenery of the far shore.

Mary has said that I have a highly developed idea of compassion. She recognises that I value it — but she insists that I do not feel it. I value compassion, she says, in theory but rarely in practice. Yet — who is it that makes a special trip to the supermarket a week before every Christmas to fill three, even four, bags with groceries for society's unfortunates? Certainly not Mary. But then I think of Thrush, and the horror in the photograph . . .

I walk over to her, take her hand.

"It's all so obvious, Alistair," she says. "There's no mystery here. That essay he brought you. This spot. What he didn't do, and the way he planned what he did do. You knew him for, what? Thirty years or so?"

I nod, with regret.

"And yet you never understood that your Professsor Thrush was a man who saw beauty in everything but himself."

The air stirs, a gust off the water, and it is as if legions of the wind are battling among the leaves.

What *I found myself* telling Jack that evening in our living room was a tale he already knew: of bombs in mailboxes blasting words around quiet neighbourhoods, of leather and fabric rent like flesh, and flesh — a janitor, a sapper — rent like fabric. *"Does the name William O'Neill mean anything to you, Jack? To anyone?"* Of a morning when a gift not a gift was delivered to a front door. Guns. An embrace to the wife, a ride under a rug on the floor of a car, he would not see his home again for two months. *There is a wind of madness blowing across the province.* Of an evening when a football flew across a well-groomed lawn. The squeal of brakes, and a ride on the floor of a car; he would never see his home again.

I spoke of an air of insurrection stifling the city.

And my pulse quickened when I spoke of the man's reaction. Fierce. Uncompromising. There was steel in the playboy after all. Helicopters. Soldiers. Police unconstrained. How far would he go? *Just watch me!* Arrests in the night. Jails overflowed, yes, most often without cause. But healthy tissue must sustain damage to eradicate the cancer, no?

In certain neighbourhoods wine glasses were raised to the man's health. Many a matron felt like hugging the armed men in combat fatigues. In certain neighbourhoods, people wanted to dance with relief. Not for us Belfast, Czechoslovakia, Vietnam! Not for us, as in the skies above, ultimatum at the end of a gun!

I spoke to Jack of evening in a small bedroom, a slender golden chain twisting and tightening, impressing its links into yielding flesh, constricting the windpipe. Gurgling, and a gathering of darkness, everywhere.

Then, eventually, flight from murder: Welcome to the sunny Caribbean!

I said: A stunned calm. No more words massacred, no more flesh flayed. The jail doors opened. Still: a victory that felt like no victory.

All this I spoke of to Jack — not wishing to, *needing* to for some unfathomable reason, regretting the words as they came but unable to stop them, hoping that he would understand those wine glasses and those toasts and the violence that had been done to us all.

He turned white. In a precise and raucous voice, he said, "They were a handful of misguided souls fighting for their language. It was a matter of survival."

"Their lives weren't threatened."

"Their souls were."

I leaned forward in my chair. "But, Jack, only one side killed."

He stared at me for a full minute, as if trying to puzzle out my equation. Then his eyelids flickered. A sadness shadowed his pupils. I saw that, at some fundamental level, a level perhaps to which I had no access, I had failed to grasp something essential — maybe even had understood nothing in the entire drama, now so many years later merely an episode in history.

Jack blinked once. Then he stood up, mumbled a brittle excuse-me, and quick-stepped to the bathroom.

A breathless silence.

He had conceded nothing, and neither had I. But perhaps this was an exchange — pointless variations on anguish rife with simple ironies — that required no concession. Perhaps, then, our exchange was one that required only statement, acknowledgement, Jack's wise decision to withdraw. Still, there was this rage in him, this vehemence all the more eloquent because unstated, that dismayed me.

In the silence that left me searching for air, it occurred to me that somehow, despite the endless trading in accusation, the point had been missed. The violence had been snuffed out not by the man or the army he sent in. It had been snuffed out, truly, by the common, human decency of a people whose idea of what they were had been profoundly offended. They were a people who saw themselves as rugged and gentle and hospitable, people proud of what had been evoked over centuries from the soil. Those who killed in their name would find no solace among them. Jack and I, jealous of our irreconcilable versions of the same story, were like blind men who knew a great deal but who understood little. Like the historians, biographers, film-makers who have ploughed and reploughed the same field. Like the man himself. *Just watch me!*

The man, I say. The man. Since that evening in the living room, I have not wished to pronounce his name. He remains for me a great man, with all the flaws that implies, but his name and the demons it calls forth are not worth the damage done to my relationship with Jack, whom I hold in great esteem. We spent a troubled evening, Jack and I, slightly wary of each other, both of us regretful.

Later that night, after Jack and Agnes had left, after Mary had gone to bed, I sat in the living room alone with my sadness and my unease. I saw that people live constantly with contradiction, I saw that we are all the time intimate with the irreconcilable. And I saw too that Jack and I cannot either of us be trusted to excavate truth from the past. I resolved never again to talk with Jack about the things that divide us. I chose that night to get along with my son-in-law.

More than six years later, the sight of Jack reading moved me. As I went about my business in the bathroom, the infamous conversation returned to me, arousing that sadness, that unease. I pictured him sitting at that very moment in the living room, in a light that had something of the dawn to it, sipping from the book through moving lips. And I knew then, with a suddenness that caused my heart to race, the intensity of the words coursing through his mind. I knew that at that very moment the essence of his being was being given shape and sustenance.

A moment of enlightenment. Nothing Jack said or did could have given me a more *intuitive* grasp — the words came in its wake, imperilling the moment — of the unfathomable fervour his language inspires in him. Other languages — English, Spanish, enough German to get by — are tools of his profession. But his language, that of the book, that of first endearments and early scoldings, the language that speaks to him beyond meaning, in which he dreams, is the language of his very breath. Swaddled in that blanket, bathed in that light, he was a man transported to another realm altogether, to the accents of childhood, yes, but also to whispers heard in the womb, and further back to sounds never heard: to centuries of stilled voices telling of struggle and hardship, of toil beyond imagining.

Alone at night, seeking a kind of solace he could not find even in the arms of his wife, Jack had turned to his language in its purest, most distilled form. This language that was like a cradle chiselled from crystal containing swift shards of light and edges of dreams, subtleties as surreptitious as salamanders.

His language is to him as my language is to me. Denied it, he would feel bereft, unanchored, without a place where his soul could find unconditional security. Possibly because I myself was feeling these things — this sense, overwhelming at times, that much of my life has evaporated, that my very reality was at stake — all this I came to understand with the intensity of a flash that evening as Jack sat there shawled in the golden light, his lips moving like a man saying a prayer. He was as I imagine myself at times in that very living room: plunged so deeply into *A Tale of Two Cities* that I feel my cares retreat and my self being remade.

I completed my business in the bathroom and made my way back to the bedroom. Treading carefully so as not to disturb him, I wondered how it was that History — that big, crushing H — had blinded us to this simple truth. I found myself wishing, for the first time without resentment, that Jack could find it in himself to appreciate my attachment to *my* language, which is for me, as his is for him, a kind of lifeblood, living and vital and pulsing with possibility. But it has taken me over seventy years to understand this — and my language, hardly a thing of beauty to someone who has always seen it as a threat, is for him too loaded, too barbed. My language is to him the way German is to me: made ugly by History. He can speak it, but he cannot revel in it.

On the floor, François shuts his book, rolls over onto his back and slides his thumb into his mouth. His face changes colour like a chameleon — red, green, white — as quickly as the tree-bulbs blink. I know I should warn him to remove the thumb, but I haven't the heart. The thumb in the mouth — bad for the palate, bad for the teeth — reveals a contentment felt in the bone. And watching him flush with that contentment, I wonder whether he, my daughter's son, repository of that whole other stream of unreconcilable history, will escape the bonds and barbs that encumber his father and his grandfather. I wonder whether he will be free to revel in the beauty that lies beyond our truths.

That night, when I finished in the bathroom, I did not flush, out of respect. The next morning Agnes, grimacing, reminded me of my omission. I pretended that I had forgotten to pull the lever. François still remembers the incident. When he forgets, as he often does, he gives his mother a look of wide-eyed innocence and directs an accusing finger at his grandfather.

Outside, the evening is cold and snowy, and even the moist warmth of the restaurant fails to banish the chill in Mary's hands. I enfold them in mine, rub them gently. When, after a few minutes, the chill enters my palms, I take a hot roll from the bread-basket and wrap her fingers round it. She shuts her eyes and smiles gratefully.

Across the table from us, Martha samples the wine and, after brief consideration, nods her approval. She ignores the cork that the waiter has placed before her; examining it, she says, is mere affectation. Randolph disagrees — the cork, he says, offers reassurance — but he does not pick it up.

The waiter fills Mary's glass, then mine and, last of all, Randolph's. Martha, as usual, places her palm across the rim of her glass. Having performed the little ceremony, she will have no more. With characteristic grace, she pinches the spongy middle from a roll, butters it, feeds it to Randolph. His tongue curls around the bread, pulling it into the cavity of his mouth. Before she can fully withdraw her finger, his lips close firmly around it at the first knuckle. Martha, to all appearances not in the least perturbed, immediately withdraws it, but his suckling is such that his lips make a plopping sound when her red-lacquered fingernail emerges wet from between them.

As Randolph chews at the bread with his accustomed vigour, Martha turns to us and says, "We have news."

We have news: This is the way she has, in the past, introduced gossip, tales of business triumph, the winning of a Caribbean cruise, the acquisition of a coveted antique milk-pail. Newscasters should borrow the phrase: "Good evening. We have news . . ."

"We're going to be married again," Martha says.

Randolph swallows, his lemon-sized Adam's apple jerking like a church bell in his throat.

"To each other?" I sound more incredulous than I intend.

Mary's eyes brighten at the news. "You're renewing your vows," she says happily.

"Not exactly. We've decided to take the vows we never did. We're going all the way, or almost. Church, dress, cake. We're even getting new rings."

"And the dress," I say. "Will it be *white?*"

Martha does not answer my question but she acquires a sublime, Virgin-Mary look — which is, I imagine, an answer of a kind.

Randolph sighs, claps his palm to his ridged forehead and draws it back along the shining pate, a fold of skin rippling before his fingers like a wave along the skull.

Mary, having deposited the now cool roll on the bread plate, fidgets with the stem of her wine glass. Her elbow discreetly grazes my arm, and I recognize the warning to let the question rest.

Martha says that the ceremony will be held in her childhood church. "It's astonishing," she says. "Nothing's changed. Even the priest's the same guy. Older now, of course—"

"Aren't we all," Randolph adds.

"Oh," Mary says in mild surprise. "You're to be married by a priest."

"Hallooo," Martha says, snapping her fingers before Mary's eyes. "A church? A priest is sort of part of the package, you know?"

"I'm just a little surprised, that's all, considering . . ."

"You shouldn't be," Martha says. "I haven't been to the club in years, but I never resigned from it." Then, with a touch of impatience, she adds, "What ever gave you that idea?"

Mary shrugs — quite uncharacteristic of her — and I hurry into the breach. "Are we to be invited?" I ask.

"Of course," Randolph replies with a haste that matches mine. "In fact — perhaps I shouldn't be telling you this — but if we were going whole hog, maids-of-honour, best man and all the rest, you'd be my choice. As it is, though, we felt it'd be a little foolish, you know, to go quite that far."

The church, the priest, the white dress: They seem to me to have already claimed quite a bit of the hog, and I'm relieved they've chosen to abandon the rest of the carcass. "I'm honoured, of course," I mumble. "But why me?"

"Who else, Alistair?" Randolph says. He has had only one glass of wine, but he has downed it rather quickly. He is already a little drunk. "You're just about my best friend. In fact, I'd say you're just about my only friend."

Something quails inside me. His admission strikes me as particularly bleak. For the truth is, I feel that I hardly know the man. My feelings for him, and for Martha, are at best ambivalent. Were it not for Mary, I would be unlikely to be interested in them — or they in me.

I am relieved to leave the subject behind when the waiter, linen napkin draped over his forearm, steps up to our table and, with a poetry of succulence, recites the specials of the day.

We are some minutes in sorting through his offerings — as so often, the poetics camouflage the reality. The waiter memorizes our selections, repeating each order once, and then goes off. He leaves behind at our table a curiously uneasy silence. Mary and Martha each seem to have retreated into a little corner of her own, neither of which affords access. Randolph, with a sigh of satisfaction meant only to fill the space, refills his glass and tops up mine. In the silence, the wine splashes with all the vigour and noise of water from a tap.

Randolph says, "Lively little bottle, isn't it?"

"Positively demonic," I reply, neither of us amused by the other's weak attempt at humour, but condemned both to our stilted efforts by the silence of our wives. We spend some minutes reading the label, information which, in our ignorance, is essentially meaningless to us.

Emerging suddenly from her corner, Mary blurts out, "I don't get it. Why a church? Why a priest?"

Martha's eyes flicker, startled, onto her. Then they flutter up beyond her shoulder to the approaching waiter. "Soup's here," she says.

When I first met Martha, her height astonished me. She was not outlandishly tall, but at 6' 1" was unusually so for a woman. While she was slender enough to flirt with skinny, she favoured padded shoulders, an affectation which, wed to her natural extroversion, lent her a slightly intimidating edge.

Martha is Mary's friend. They have been friends for a very long time. They met at work, nodding acquaintances for a few weeks, their exchanges not extending beyond pleasantries and such conversation as required by their duties. Had they not become convinced, like almost everyone else on the planet, that extinction in a nuclear war was imminent, they might never have become friends.

It was October 1962, and the Americans had Cuba in a vise, their navy intercepting all ships bound for the island and searching them for Soviet missiles. The folks in Moscow — referred to collectively by that dark and ominous word "Politburo" — were livid. Armageddon fluttered about on everyone's lips. Experts were telling us that we were the air corridor for Soviet nuclear bombers flying over the north pole and down to the American heartland, which suggested the unedifying spectacle of battle joined directly above our heads. I was surely not the only one to imagine bits of aircraft and body parts raining from the skies — not to mention the prospect of nuclear devices hurtling by. Would we see the missiles themselves? Hear them? Did they whistle? Childish, primordial fantasies. But how else was it possible to enter imaginatively the end of the world?

Life did not, of course, come to a halt. Mary was at the time teaching at a private school not far from home and although some effort was required to overcome the lethargy that crept gradually over us — the distillation of fear and helplessness and a bubbling uncertainty — we both carried on, neither of us giving in to the hollow that carved itself in us when we said goodbye for the day. It seems melodramatic now, but during those two weeks of tension one could not be reasonably sure that there would be a lunch-time or an afternoon, or a house or people to return to in the evening. You could not be reasonably sure that you and your world would still exist in an hour. Time itself, the ticking by of the minutes, seemed an absurd thing. Those mornings, I would stand at the window watching Mary and Agnes — at ten, almost as tall as her mother — set off together, the one with an airline bag of gym clothes, the other with a leather satchel full of school books. And watching them walk away from home, a part of me would mourn.

Mary was the school's instructor in, of all things, physical education. This was the source of some humour to those who knew her. Mary was not the least athletic person I have ever known — indeed, her badminton game was once quite decent — but she had never been terribly sports-minded. She never could understand, for instance, why hockey could play havoc with the emotions. A dazzling display of stickwork on the ice left her cold, so to speak. But she had a reasonable enthusiasm for physical fitness and this made her good at her job — getting the girls to run in circles, climb ladders, toss around medicine balls. Hers was a light hand. No one, least of all Mary, took the idea of exercise very seriously — she was not out to make athletes of them — and the sounds coming from her classes were more those of the playground than of the gymnasium.

But Cuba, for a while at least, changed all that.

These were — and it may seem strange to say so, but it strikes me as a defining quality — days utterly without humour. Laughter had fled, the very thought of it obscene. Smiles were rare. The pace in the streets was rushed, impatient, as if people were all hurrying somewhere, hurrying away, but undone by the knowledge that there was no place to go. The world itself was without haven. The anxiety made us grouchy. On the buses, normally voluble people sat in silence, hands clutching at bags and briefcases as if by anchoring themselves in this way they would avoid being blown away in the white blast that could come at any moment. My classes were half empty, people deciding, one assumed, that they would die somewhere other than in a classroom. One afternoon an academic disagreement erupted into shouting and clenched fists, but of course the hysterics weren't really about things literary. I sent everybody home, and when one student, gathering up her books, asked whether the class scheduled for two days later was still on, all I could do was shrug. She had been looking for reassurance, and my unthinkingly honest response brought tears to her eyes.

It was this — the impossibility of levity, I mean — that sparked friendship between Mary and Martha.

Martha, to whom avoiding boredom was as essential as earning a living, was employed by a company that specialized in temporary office-help. The work, unpredictable in content, never threatening to endure for more than a few months, suited her temperament, which — if her words to Mary are to be trusted — was proudly adaptable but, once the tasks had been mastered, easily distracted. It was in this way that she had ended up at the school, filling in for an ill office-assistant.

One afternoon in the middle of the showdown, as we all waited and wondered who would be the first to draw, Mary went to the office to check her messages. As she walked past Martha's desk, a heavy airplane rumbled by low overhead. Martha caught Mary's eye, wiggled her eyebrows like Groucho Marx and, between lips pouted into what the French refer to as "a chicken's ass", twittered, "Shouldn't we be getting under a desk or something before the bomb hits?"

Mary admitted later that her first thought was unkind. She frowned — only to find herself overcome a split second later by spasms of rich and boisterous laughter. Huge bubbles of it welled up irrepressibly out of her throat, as if a pressurized reservoir had been uncapped deep within her.

Martha herself was leaning back in her chair, shrieking uncontrollably. Her body shook. Her face turned red.

Mary doubled over, arms clutching at her belly.

When at last their laughter subsided, both were gasping and weak.

Martha wiped her palm across her forehead and said, "God! Best sex I've had in ages!"

Which prompted further gales of laughter from them both.

For years afterwards, the sound of an airplane flying by was enough to set them grinning at each other.

Randolph submerges his spoon into the soup — forest-green and creamy, with a spray of watercress floating in the middle — lifts it out and blows daintily at it.

Martha, swirling her spoon around in her bowl, says, "I grew up in the Point, Mary."

The Point. Point St. Charles. A neighbourhood which those of us who did not live there considered deprived — not desperately so like Griffintown and Goose Village, but sufficiently so that it developed a reputation for toughness. There were factory jobs, at Dominion Glass or Continental Can, and Martha's father was lucky enough to have one, at the Sherwin-Williams paint factory. But it was an area best avoided by those who enjoyed more favoured circumstances. I never set foot there myself — there was never a reason to — although some people I knew enjoyed the occasional rough-and-tumble Saturday night at the Bucket of Blood Tavern. I, however, have never seen the pleasure in bashing or being bashed, and during the war I had my fill of seeing other people bash away at each other, thank you very much.

Mary, in a voice edging on anger, says, "I know all that. You've told me all about it. That's the past."

"The past! You say that as if it's gone. Poof! Disappeared into thin air. We're none of us so lucky, Mary."

"So is that it? The priest, the church. Because of the Point?"

"Yes," Martha says sharply. "The Point."

Randolph, as uneasy as I, refuses to meet my glance and so, abandoned, I remark in as conventional a tone as I can muster, "They say it was a place of great community spirit, Martha. Neighbours always ready with a helping hand, street parties and the like. Is it true that doors were never locked?"

Martha's cheeks redden. "Poverty's never a pretty thing, Alistair." She rests her knife and fork on the plate with great deliberation. "I have no nostalgia, you know. Nostalgia's a noose around your neck. I can't stand people who look back on that place with fondness."

"She's fond of vengeance, though," Randolph mumbles inexplicably, gulping wine.

"Life there was hard, it was unpromising, no matter what those starry-eyed forget-me-nots might say. They've grown up and moved out and now they want to look back on the whole thing as if it was noble. It wasn't all that bad, eh? Not as brutal as some people like to say. Besides, a little suffering is good for the soul, isn't it? It's holy, it's worthwhile. Well not to this gal, it ain't."

Randolph places his hand on hers: a soothing gesture, a calming gesture. A reminder that he is there, and the Point distant.

Mary, sitting rigid in her chair, crosses her hands on her lap. She has not touched her wine since Martha's announcement, has had no more than a spoonful or two of the soup.

"My parents never thought much of education," Martha says. "At least, they thought that anything beyond high school was self-indulgent. Cash in hand was what mattered."

And so she left school before graduation. She had acquired some basic office skills — shorthand, filing, typing — and regretted that she had been graced with many abilities but no special talent. She feared that her life would always be ordinary. It was not great opportunity that tempted her into the work world, but rather lack of it. The sooner she found some little sinecure, the less uncertain life would become.

She quickly found employment in a hair salon as caretaker and general help, graduating after a few weeks to shampooist. She confessed to enjoying the work. It was soothing, she said, and sensuous, this running of the fingers through clients' hair. She had a particular liking for long hair, feeling the mass of it grow voluminous and silky with conditioner, feeling it undulate warm and palpitant between her palms like something newly alive: like something she had infused with life by this laying on of hands. The salon owner, however, was not kind. To hurry Martha along as she laboured at a client's head, she would meander by and jab at her with a nail-file.

At the first opportunity she accepted a temporary posting as a telephone operator. Although the job did not last long, it was the beginning of her way out. One temporary job led to another. It became a habit. And this eventually allowed her to step out of the Point to Verdun. Then, in a move so unconventional that Martha lost several long-time friendships over it — snobbery, some said; unbecoming for a woman alone, said others — she moved again, not farther west to Beaconsfield or Baie d'Urfé, but downtown, to a ramshackle apartment in the heart of the city, and eventually to Randolph.

"It was a scary time," Martha says almost in a whisper.

Randolph once more puts his hand on hers. "But they were good days too, weren't they, my love?" He speaks without a smile. His tone, untinged by nostalgia or celebration, is neither bitter nor sweet. There is, though, a hint of great weariness. Randolph strikes me suddenly as a man weighed down by those years — and perhaps, too, by their distance. He signals me for the bread basket. He breaks a bun in two, wipes up the last of his soup and consumes them. Then, bowl cleaned, he takes a large swallow of wine and presses his napkin to his lips.

For the first five years of their friendship, Martha introduced Mary and me to a succession of her boyfriends. There would be dinners, parties, dinner-parties, visits to night clubs, gallery openings, poetry readings. I would agree to be included in the dinners, the parties, the dinner-parties; Mary would go without

꿷

me to the gallery openings and poetry readings, events which frequently left her discouraged. As for the night-clubs, they held
little attraction for either Mary or me — indeed, Agnes in her
adolescence was the one who seemed most enthralled — and,
truth to tell, the thought of Martha's bony hips being forced to
spasm struck me as sad as it was embarrassing.

Martha's men were so numerous, and were changed with such
frequency, that on saying goodbye after a party or a show, Mary
and I learnt never to say "See you again" — for we almost never
would. There was an intense and desperate edge to Martha during this period of her life. She was happy conducting her search
for the perfect man — and hers was a happiness that required a
touch of desperation.

One day, Martha was sent to a temporary office job as assistant to the president of a small company. The president was
Randolph. His company produced and marketed household
cleaning products, the most successful of which was the atro-
ciously named dish-detergent "Absorba the Grease". Randolph
never shrank from admitting responsibility (or, as he thought of
it, claiming credit) for the name, one of several inspired by the
movies. He ran television advertisements for it showing a dark-
eyed, olive-skinned woman happily doing dishes to the sounds of
bouzouki music. I have always been astonished at the measure of
success, comparatively modest though it may be, that came
Randolph's way. The first time I saw the ad I thought: There are
certain businesses which do not deserve to thrive. But thrive it
did, and Martha found herself working long hours with
Randolph. Take-out shared in the office became late-night dinners in restaurants. They grew close.

The day before the regular assistant returned from her mater-
nity leave, Randolph proposed to Martha. Their wedding night,
Martha told Mary, was a true wedding night. She had withheld
her favours despite their mutual ardour, and then unleashed her

talents in a Bahamanian bridal suite. "He never knew what hit him," Martha said, which may explain the dazed look that creeps over Randolph's face at unexpected moments.

Not long after the bus-boy scoops up the bowls — Martha taking the opportunity to order a glass of mineral water with lime — the waiter arrives with the main courses. Although it is not my favorite cut (restaurants that call themselves bistros do not serve steaks that are called t-bone) my filet mignon looks fine in its sparse nest of vegetables and baby potatoes.

"It's the church's fault, you know," Martha says quietly. "All those priests and nuns running around promising the poor special consideration in Heaven. Be content with the little loaf destiny's offered you, for afterwards yours will be the kingdom of Heaven. Know what? The kingdom of Heaven's never appealed to me much. Who wants to spend eternity floating about on some cloud, sprouting wings from your shoulders? And just imagine trying to do the twist to harp music. I'd be bored stiff."

She speaks with great sincerity — there is no hint of humour or mockery — and I realize that the child's understanding has remained with her, what she felt to be an ugly message having grown no less trenchant with the years.

She sprinkles lemon juice onto her salmon. "Going to confession, now there was a thrill. What do you do when your only sin's masturbation? At fourteen I couldn't even begin to see the sin in something that was so much fun."

My mouthful of steak turns glutionous. I focus on the potatoes, small and white and perfectly round, until the images she has prompted dissipate in the flow of her words.

A weekly accounting of failure and weakness was nonetheless expected of her. She felt obliged to confess something, anything — and since the church considered the human being sinful by nature, pleading innocence would not fit the bill. The visits to the confessional grew burdensome. She would rack her brains looking for evil she had committed. "Once I kneed Tommy Ferguson in the privates when he tried to touch my bosoms: Was that sinful? What about the morning I accidentally saw my dad sitting hungover and *naked* on the edge of the bed: Did that qualify? Those didn't, by the way, but once in a while I'd hit the jackpot, a few Hail-Marys' worth anyway. Dipping six inches of snooty Mary Hanley's braid into a pot of black ink, now that produced a good little crop, seeing that Mary Hanley was as blonde as Marilyn Monroe." But fate and circumstance were not always so kind. Often, she entered the confessional empty-minded. One day, squirming wordless in the dark, glancing occasionally at the shadowed, patient profile of the priest through the grille, she did what so many of her girlfriends regularly did: She lied about having lied to her parents. It was innocuous enough to be plausible.

The following week she repeated the lie, with greater alacrity, and the priest — a youngish man who, exhausted by his labours in the parish, was said to doze off during long recitations by the incorrigible — noticed nothing.

By the third week, though, she was growing impatient with the game. The week after that, she said without forethought, "Forgive me, Father, for I have sinned. I've lied to you. Three times." She saw him blink, as if waking up. "My last three times at confession, I told you I'd lied to my parents, only it wasn't true."

He blinked again. "What wasn't true, my child?"

"That I'd lied to my parents."

"So your confession was a lie?"

"Yes, Father. But I'm telling the truth now."

"And why did you lie in confession, my child?"

"Because I had to confess something, didn't I? So I made up a lie."

"Are you telling the truth now?"

And on impulse she said, "No, I'm not."

"You're lying now? About lying or about telling the truth?"

"Yes," she said, savouring his confusion, feeling it as a victory. He hadn't been able to tell her truth from her lie; he depended on her to betray herself; he was, she saw, powerless without her complicity. Suddenly furious with him for having revealed his weakness, and at the same time ecstatic at having been freed from the charade, she pushed open the door and fled the confessional, the church and the little world she now saw as created in its image.

Martha spears the final asparagus tip with her fork. "And so that was that," she says, her voice unexpectedly growing frail.

The story is not new to me. I have heard it before, in less impassioned form, from Mary. Martha's retelling has given it greater shape and immediacy. She has turned it into a morality tale. Even so, I find it, in its way, quite moving.

Mary it is who, dissecting her veal, grunts dismissively.

Martha came up with the idea for the other business when sales of Absorba the Grease began to slip. ADAMANT EVE: *The Store for the Woman who Knows What SHE wants!* catered to the upscale whims of independent-minded professional women. Martha did all the buying herself and was determined to be unpredictable. Independent-minded professional women could never be sure just what they would find in the store — this was a large part of its appeal — but they were assured that the clothing and the jewellery, the household decorations and the *objets des arts érotiques* — frequently ornate and finely tooled, some of uses beyond imagining — would always be unique, chic, tasteful and expensive. The store flourished.

As, to the surprise of some, did their marriage. Even Mary, in a rare, unguarded moment some days before the wedding (a civil marriage, at Martha's insistence), confessed to me she would not bet a quarter on their union lasting three years. Later, as we sipped good champagne at the reception, Mary asked me to disregard what she had said. She was ashamed of what she saw as disloyalty to her closest friend. "I'm sure I was wrong, Alistair," she said without conviction.

"Sure you were," I replied, wanting to reassure her. But then, made unmindful by the wine and the cheery if contrived atmosphere of the restaurant Randolph had rented, I added, "They'll live happily ever after." The scepticism Mary detected in my voice caused her to frown at me.

But if that scepticism was there — and I am not denying that it was, I merely insist that it was unintentional — it was because of all that Mary herself had shared with me about Martha and Randolph and the shape of their relationship.

Martha early on confided to Mary that Randolph, for all his charms, was "a bit of a job". She didn't mean that he was eccentric or grubby or prim, which are qualities I associate with the men I have known who live long without the steadying influence of a woman. It was just that, having lived all his adult life alone, he harboured in his forties the absent-minded ways of the bachelor content with his life and not unduly concerned about impressing others. When he washed his socks, he did not turn them inside out, so that they had grown all nubbly with balled wool. His shirts hung listless and awry in his closet because he never thought to secure them to the hangers by doing up the top button. It had been with a *frisson* of distaste — *frisson* being, Mary said, one of Martha's favorite words, for its very sound suggested a chill cutting down the spine that "shudder" did not — that she discovered his coffee of preference to be instant. The indictment — for, despite Mary's denials, this was what it sounded like to me — reached a curious apogee with Randolph's candle-holder. Like, apparently, every bachelor in the history of mankind, he had as centrepiece on his dining table an empty, straw-encased Chianti bottle down the sides of which had dripped the melted wax of several cheap candles. What made everything worse, though, was that Randolph had not improvised the candle-holder. He had *bought* it.

I don't know whether Martha ever made the connection, but this candle-holder, I believe, proved providential. It gave her an insight. "Just goes to prove," she said to Mary. "You can sell anything if you position it right."

"None of this is new, Martha," Mary says impatiently.

Martha runs a fingertip around the rim of her water glass. "No," she says in a voice surprising in its moderation. "But why does it have to be new to count?" Her gaze rises from the glass. "Mary, how come you never guessed I had a crush on the priest, big-time?"

Randolph sloshes a generous helping of wine into his glass and drains it.

The vague frown Mary has been wearing subtly unfolds itself. She spears a sliver of veal. "How come you never told me?"

"Yeah, right. Hey, Mary, guess what? When I was fourteen I spent half my time dreaming up ways to boink the curé. That's hardly the kind of thing you confess to *yourself*."

"Let's cut to the chase," Randolph says wearily. He rubs his eyes. "Two years later, the guy deflowered her."

A silence envelops our table. It is as if we find ourselves in a universe of our own, the other diners, the waiters, the tables glittering prettily distanced to an illusory discretion.

Mary, leaning forward, whispers, "My! You *do* have news."

"Quaint word, isn't it?" Randolph continues. "Deflowered. As if the beauty's plucked from a woman the moment she's—"

"Shut up, Randolph," Martha snaps.

Mary says, "Let me guess — this priest who's going to marry you, he's the same one, right?" Martha nods and Mary, holding her eye, says quietly, "You're crazy, you know that?"

With a shrug, Martha says, "So what else is new? He doesn't remember me, of course. I'd be a fool to think I was the only one. But that doesn't matter. I remember him. That's what makes it right, his marrying us."

"It's like a homecoming," I mumble, but even Mary's elbow ignores me.

"And the church?" Mary asks. "You say you never resigned from the club, but I thought you'd left all that behind."

For the first time, Martha blushes. "I've been to confession a few times recently. It was hard at first, but it's getting easier."

"Have you confessed *that* sin?"

"Of course."

"To him?"

"No. Someone else."

"And?"

"Any sin can be washed away, Mary."

"How convenient," I remark.

"Shut up, Alistair," Mary snaps.

Randolph says, "Confessing your sins becomes easier the older you get. A question of quantity. There's an endless supply." He says this matter-of-factly, as if Martha's having an endless supply of sin does not disturb him. "It clears the air," he adds, holding up the wine bottle to see how much is left.

"So there you have it, darling Mary," Martha says in a voice turned steely. "The point is the Point. Surely you see that."

Mary centres her knife and fork on her plate and raises her eyes to stare unblinking at Martha. Suddenly, she smiles. Her eyes soften. "How about a Spanish coffee?" she says.

Randolph emits a great sigh, and it occurs to me that the point of the Point seems to him, as it does to me, as it does not to Mary, reason for despair. I try to catch his eye, but it is not there to be caught. I understand none of this. Perhaps sensing that,

Randolph mumbles to no one in particular, "That's my Martha.
Dot the i's and cross the t's." What I sense, though, is that the t's
are being dotted and the i's are being crossed. But, in this company, I have learnt to keep my counsel.

Martha began her remake of Randolph with a flanking movement.
Ignoring the socks and the shirts, the coffee and the candles, she
bought him a winter coat. Camel hair, of elegant cut. Randolph,
whose taste in clothes ran to the utilitarian, was dazzled when he
viewed himself in the mirror. He gazed and gazed until he could
see himself no more for the tears brimming in his eyes.

Everything else followed as a matter of course.

His was an extraordinarily tended body. He "worked out",
spending an hour every other morning — while Martha was
still in bed — huffing and blowing through a "routine" in his
basement gymnasium. He enjoyed, he once said, "pumping up"
his muscles. He swallowed fistfuls of vitamin supplements and
"protein drinks". Just a few years my junior, Randolph was
capable of contortions which would have maimed me for life.
Once, at a barbecue in their backyard, he put on a display of
handstands and one-armed pushups that brought a gleam to
Martha's eyes and made her distracted for the rest of the evening.

His clothes were tasteful and well-cut, shaped, it was clear, to
his physical lines. And yet he rarely appeared comfortable in
them. It was as if the clothes inhabited him rather than the other
way around. His hair, which had always been unruly, was done
away with the day he judged the salt to be overwhelming the
pepper. His teeth were white and straight and even and — it was
one of his boasts — all natural. Even his fingernails were always
trimmed to identical length and sanded smooth and buffed to
such a shine part of me suspected them of having been lacquered.

Randolph was not one to overestimate his talents. His success
alone was proof of that. The man himself, despite the boasts and

the obvious physicality, was not an exhibitionist. Indeed, were Martha not around, I suspect he would be only modestly proud of his accomplishments. His car would be high-end Japanese rather than low-end German. His house would be less grand, perhaps in an off-island suburb rather than within hailing distance of the city's old-money mansions.

But Martha was around, and her presence changed everything. She gave him an idea of glamour that brought him both pleasure and anxiety. She made him a better man than he would have been left to his own devices. And, perhaps most important of all, she gave him the knowledge that he had made her, too, a better person than she might have been without him.

So Martha ended up marrying the man she thought she should marry. She had made him perfect for her in every way, but I always suspected that it was his perfection — her creation — that she loved most of all. I believe Randolph suspected this too. It explained, I felt, why he worked so hard at it — being Martha's Randolph, I mean.

Their life, I grant, is a wondrous construct.

For dessert, Randolph elects a fruit plate while I decide to indulge in the profiteroles. Mary and Martha are content with their Spanish coffees. When the desserts are served, Randolph gazes balefully at his fruit and, with Martha's consent, calls instead for a slice of chocolate cake.

He has been talking about the early days of his business, when all he had was imagination, brashness, a product he believed in — and, on more occasions than he cared to recall, friends foolhardy enough to provide emergency financing with credit cards and personal cheques. His tone is one of disbelief.

Digging into the cake, he says, "I'm glad I'm not starting off now. I'm not sure I could hack it."

"Of course, you could," Martha protests. She turns to me.

"Don't you think he could hack it in today's world, Alistair?"

"I don't see why not. More and more it's becoming a place for those with entrepreneurial skills."

Mary says, "Your kind of talent never goes out of style, Randolph. You'll always be prized."

"Perhaps." He spoons chocolate icing into his mouth. "The world's becoming such a feminine place, though. In my day, you had a problem, you dealt with it. Some widget wouldn't fit, you hit it. It'd either fit or break. Either way, problem solved. You could afford to be brash. Isn't so anymore, I don't think. Not on the whole. All this new technology, for instance. It's not brute force that makes a computer work or gets a jet plane to respond. It takes a light, feminine touch." As if to seal the matter, he raises his hand and shows off the perfectly manicured fingernails, yes, but the wide palms, too, and the thick, muscular fingers: the hands of a carpenter or a pipe-fitter who has done well.

"So you get it at last," Mary teases. "We've taken over. That was the secret plan all along." Which brings to mind a comment Mary made on another occasion, that technology is like men, its performance rarely matched by its claims.

Randolph did not get the joke then and he does not get the joke now. Sadness shadows his eyes. "Back then," he says, "I had what it took, I had the balls."

Martha places a hand on his cheek, looks into his eyes. "You still do, dear." A rich laugh resonates up from deep within her. "I check them carefully every night as you well know."

A look of gratitude — or is that submission? — comes to Randolph's face, softening the flinty hardness I have come to associate with the well-to-do businessman he is. His tongue moistens his lips. Then his hand covers Martha's and draws it to his mouth. For some seconds he appears to chew on her palm, his need embarrassing in its intensity.

Finally, gently, Martha takes her hand away. "Naughty boy,"

she says. "We're not alone. And there's the honeymoon to come."

I am grateful to her for remembering that Mary and I are sitting here at the table with them — not to mention the dozen or so other diners at neighbouring tables and the waiters scurrying around.

Martha turns to Mary. "I warned you," she says. "It hasn't even been twenty-four hours. He gets so frisky! But you know what it's like. I'm sure that Alistair here's not immune to regular bouts of naughtiness, are you, Alistair?"

"Oh, Martha," I say after a moment, deliberately not tuning my voice to discretion, "I'm sure Mary's told you. Frisky's my middle name."

Martha's eyes register surprise. She's accustomed to a certain diffidence in my response to her more outrageous remarks. For once, the raucousness of her laugh is tempered by uncertainty. A fellow at a neighbouring table shoots an eyebrow up at me, whether in disapproval or envy I cannot say. Randolph pouts at the half-eaten wedge of chocolate cake on the plate before him.

From the corner of my eye, I see Mary reach for her purse. It is late — and she knows I have had enough.

Outside the restaurant, the city is unusually quiet, even for a weekday evening. The snow that was just tapering off as we arrived has turned Greene Avenue white. Shovelled off the sidewalks, battened down on the roadway by countless tires, not yet ploughed or sanded or ground into brassy sludge, it lends the street — with its dimly-lit boutiques and discreet bistros like the one where we have just dined with Martha and Randolph — aspects of the main thoroughfare in some small and picturesque northern town. One thinks of Rockwell (Krieghoff is altogether too rustic) and Christmas cards that stress the traditional scrubbed of soot.

Mary tugs her scarf higher onto her neck against the night air grown appreciably colder. Her gloved fingers nervously fluff it against her ear-lobes and under her chin. The packed snow squeaks beneath our boots, and fear of falling makes me judicious in the placement of my stick.

When I ask Mary to explain what Martha's marriage plans mean, my breath steams.

She says, "She sees a circle that needs to be completed. A way of putting a period to the Point. Unusual, I agree, but still, it haunts her, you know. Martha's needs are never obvious." After a moment she adds, "I didn't know this about Martha at first, but I learnt it fast enough. For her, if things aren't complicated, they aren't worth it. Friendship. Marriage. Complications create depth and texture. They give quality to the thing, and strength."

"Sounds burdensome to me," I can't help remarking.

"It isn't really," Mary says reflectively. "It keeps you on your toes, you see."

"Does she run her marriage that way?"

"Martha likes creating the unexpected. I suspect Randolph wouldn't have many complaints."

"But you haven't asked him, have you?"

"No, of course not."

"I'll tell you, my dear Mary — I'm not sure how many men enjoy being taken by surprise all the time. Surely Randolph must feel a little bit ambushed once in a while. This marriage thing — whose idea was it anyway? And then, does she expect him to be continually original and inventive and full of surprises? I'm sure he feels a pressure to. Surely he's said to himself: Christ! I wish she'd give it a break!"

"Maybe you should ask him, Alistair."

"I don't think so. I couldn't. It'd be like prying."

"That's the difference between you and Martha, you see. She wouldn't worry about prying. She'd just go for it. Martha's an open book—"

"A little too open if you ask me."

"—and she likes it when others are too. You know how she can be outrageous sometimes with the things she says. That's just her way of spreading open someone else's pages."

"Actually, Mary, sometimes it feels as if she's cracking your spine." The remark is not meant to be humourous, but Mary laughs anyway. "As for all that fawning and doting," I say over the measured crunch of our footsteps, "she hasn't changed a jot over the years, has she?"

"No, she hasn't."

"Still a prisoner after all this time."

Mary turns sharply towards me, breath turbulent in the glacial air. "What do you mean?" Her hands grip the edge of the scarf, tightening it around her neck as if in an attempt at self-strangulation.

"Don't be naive, Mary. She's always been a prisoner of Randolph's money. How else can you explain the way she's constantly throwing herself at him?"

"They're married, for God's sake. Throwing herself at him? Is that how you see it?"

"She hardly keeps her hands off him, even in public."

"*She* hardly keeps her hands off *him?*"

"However you look at it, she makes quite a spectacle of herself. What else could possibly account for it?"

She doesn't hesitate. "Love, perhaps?" she says, her breath billowing around her lips as she draws out the word, molding it in sarcasm.

"Love? Do you really think so? They've been married for years. Surely it's about time they—"

The steam clears from before Mary's eyes. They are hard with fury. "Martha's nobody's prisoner," she says with great deliberation. "And anybody who thinks so is a phenomenally bad judge of character."

I hold my breath. Dan Mullen's voice drawls counsel in my head: *Zip it up, Mac.* I know that withdrawal, hasty and utterly bereft of dignity, is now my most prudent course. I do not, however, wish to be prudent. Stung by Mary's accusation, I am too irritated to be prudent. "So what do you think of what Randolph did to Martha's hand? He was gnawing on her like a starved man going at a stripped ham-bone. I expect there was slobber all over her palm."

Mary's eyes fall to the sidewalk. After a moment she says, "Yes, I expect there was." Then: silence. She concentrates on her boots squeaking on the snow.

I suddenly feel monstrous. "Love, eh?" I say too quickly into the taut and frigid silence. "Yes, I see what you mean." But it is already too late. The wound has been made. I cannot heal it.

As I walk in step with Mary, or rather she with me, the sight of Randloph gnawing at his wife's hand returns to me: the working of his jaws, the spray of spittle. Why, I wonder, does passion's eloquence so often appear bereft of dignity? Is it an eloquence so particular to itself that I cannot read it? I choose not to put the question to Mary. "Yes," I repeat helplessly. "Yes. I see what you mean."

Her only response is a puff of breath that floats over her shoulder, like some ghost that can find no home. I reach for her hand, but do not find it.

$\mathcal{A}$*gnes, beaming, smoothes her dress* with her palms and sits on the sofa, a holdover from Jack's student days. Dark brown leather as intricately seamed as an ancient, dried up estuary. She's ready for the evening, her cream dress of such defiantly simple construction that her string of fresh-water pearls — a gift from Jack after François's birth — appears incongruous. Facing the window, she says to my profile, "If you blindfolded me and put me in a room with twenty freshly-baked turkeys, I'd bet you anything that my nose'd find Jacques's in two minutes flat."

Silence. Mine.

What in the world is she talking about? What's this about twenty baked turkeys in a room? Is there a point to her observation? These turkeys have fallen from the sky like some kind of celestial poultry. It's like a conversation with Ruth-Ann, where one sentence rarely connects to another with any kind of coherence. I continue to offer her my profile, for to face her would require a reaction of some kind. And I am quite at a loss as to how to react.

But I realize that she's making conversation. This is small talk. With me, small talk tends to grow smaller. It is one of my faults. I believe saying nothing when one has nothing to say is wise. Still, the professional life required a measure of it, and I grew into a certain proficiency. But after so many years away from the world, I'm rusty. I can't react gracefully, can't think of anything inconsequential to mumble about her husband's culinary prowess. Instead, I find myself saying, "Quite a conversation opener, Agnes. You should use it at those training courses you go off on, to break the ice."

She scowls at me. "Really, father, you've growing quite irascible in your old age. You're so prickly."

"Prickly. *You* think I'm prickly?"

"Sometimes."

"I roll with the punches, Agnes. I always have."

"There you go again, father. As self-aware as road kill. Must be all those years of living on your own. It's not good for anybody. You've become quite sharp with people. When I think of how you spoke to poor M'sieur Tremblay, especially."

Tremblay? Why should she bring him up? Some neighbours exercise a polite discretion. Other want to be chummy, with neighbourhood barbecues dancing in their heads. And then there are those like Tremblay, who lived with his wife in the duplex above ours. The fellow was the cause of constant aggravation to me. Always insisting on calling me miss-your. Needling me about my medals. Why shouldn't I have been sharp with him? One day, Tremblay, his sinewy arms easily bearing the weight of four heavily-laden shopping bags, ambushed me on the sidewalk

ๆ

outside the supermarket. It was a lovely day, sunny and dry. The outdoor cafés farther up the street were packed. He seemed delighted to see me and, to my alarm, declared we would walk back home together.

A slow walk with Tremblay was not an enticing prospect. My mind raced in search of an excuse. It was no good claiming to be pressed for time. We were of approximately the same age, but his two legs could out-walk my three any day. Besides, it was a ludicrous idea: He knew that mine was a life without urgency. I pretended, therefore, that I needed stamps at the post office a block away, and those bags of his appeared heavy. No problem, he said, they were lighter than they looked. Thus I was obliged to walk an extra block, and to buy stamps I did not need. There was no way to put him off.

He chattered all the way back, hardly pausing for breath — which was a bit of a relief, since my role was reduced to humming and hawing and the occasional grunt. He spoke with fondness of his daughter who was living a hard-scrabble life in the country; of the hunting trips he'd relished as a younger man, spending days in a forest blind waiting to bag a moose; of the several businesses he'd owned — bee-keeping, a convenience store, a small-appliance repair shop among others — each sold at a handsome profit when boredom set in and his natural restlessness sought some new challenge. And he spoke, most disturbingly, of his wife's ubiquitous breast.

"Ey, M'sieur Mackenzie—"

I let it pass.

"—you know, everywhere I go in t'e house, I find my wife's breast. Go to the bathroom, t'ere it is on the toilet tank. Go to the kitchen, t'ere it is on top of the *frigidaire*. One day, I find it in t'e fruit bowl, right on top of t'e bananas. You can imagine what t'at is like, you? Finding your wife's breast every where you go?"

I had, to put it mildly, no answer to the question. I didn't know what to do with this crazed version of Gogol's "The Nose". The best I could do after a few laboured steps was mumble, "No, I couldn't possibly."

"She can never find it," he exclaimed with a hint of exasperation. "One evening, ten minute before friends arrive for dinner, we running she and me all around the place, looking for the goddam breast. Finally, we find it, you know where?"

We were mercifully at our respective doors. I got my keys out. He did the same.

"In the goddam- How you call it? T'at place where you keep food in t'e kitchen? What in French we call *la dépense?*"

"The pantry?"

"Yes, t'e pantry. In the goddam pantry, wit' all the *boîtes de conserves*. Wit' peas and corn and tomato sauce!"

I hurried inside like a man pursued. Mary called from the kitchen that she'd prepared us a snack on the back porch. Taking the bag of groceries to her, I said that I didn't have much of an appetite. Allaying her concern — "Are you feeling all right?" — I told her Tremblay's tale of his wife's wayward breast. "The man must be off his rocker," I said.

The last reaction I expected from her was mirth. She leaned on the kitchen counter and howled in laughter. I was mildly offended — and, even more so, puzzled. "Get a grip on yourself, Mary."

She wiped her eyes. "Marie-Angèle had a mastectomy years ago," she said. "Gaston was talking about her prosthesis. She uses it to fill out her bra."

So convinced had I been that I was being treated to the ravings of a madman determined to discombobulate me, so intent was I on fleeing his clutches, that I had only half-listened to him. I had merely dismissed the absurdity of it all. I hadn't for a moment sought to make sense of his words.

For a long time after this, whenever I launched a search for my watch or my favourite pen, Mary would suggest I look in the pantry. It amused her to keep alive my sense of foolishness. Still, the grudge I held for months was not against her but against Tremblay. He could have done, I felt, a better job of contextualizing his story, but more than this, he was, truth to tell, simply the convenient recipient for my outrage. Why lay blame at home when he was available?

Agnes says, "Guess everything has a silver lining, eh? It'll do you good to spend your days around people after all those years of living alone." Suddenly she smiles. "Of course, it's been six months, and you haven't mellowed much. Old dogs, new tricks?"

Suddenly I too find myself smiling. Since my arrival here, Agnes has been fairly ginger with me; she's tempered her habitual sharpness. It's good to have a taste of it again. But, of course, I must acknowledge this only to myself — this pleasure her contrariant nature gives me, I mean. The strength of character it suggests. The glimpses of Mary it affords.

"Have you ever seen the Superman movie, Agnes?"

"Superman? The comic-book character? Hardly."

A wrinkle in her eyebrow reveals worry: She fears I may be having another unanchored episode. Although my question to her is no more incongruous than her comment to me, I am the one whose mental consistency is worrisome.

"You dragged mom to see it, I remember."

"Hardly dragged. I could never make your mother do anything she didn't want to. She wasn't an unwilling participant. As I recall she even got a bit of a kick out of it."

"I'll say! She told me all about Lois Lane's execution."

My neck and face grow warm. After the movie, Mary, analytical of films in a way I've never been (to me, cinema, while enjoyable, rarely rises above the level of literature for the lazy), remarked that she was puzzled by something.

We'd gone at my insistence, Mary somewhat incredulous — and highly amused — that I'd be drawn to such a film. As a

young man awaiting war, I'd been a fan of Superman, taken with
the notion of outrunning bullets, leaping tall buildings — and
saving Kevin. For a long time, swooping down out of the sky
and saving Kevin from the embrace of snow and ice — the only
time, perhaps due to the imminence of battle, that I was so
obsessed. I'd read most of the comic books and, later on, had
discreetly indulged in the television series, my mind painting
colours onto the black-and-white. There was, I was certain, no
question I could not answer about the Man of Steel. "Shoot," I
said confidently.

It didn't make sense to her, Mary said, that when Superman
and Lois Lane made love, he would have an orgasm.

Trust Mary to dredge up a question that no comic book had
ever covered. I was stymied. But only for a moment. Why on
Earth not, I said? I was certain that, as with everything else, he
would have a super one.

"That's just it," Mary replied with more thoughtfulness than
a comic strip character merited. "It probably would be a super
one — but then, all things considered, doesn't that mean that he
would blow Lois's head off?"

The image was, to say the least, startling.

"No," I declared with sudden inspiration. "He's a responsible
fellow. I'm sure he packs a super condom wherever he flies."

For once I'd got the better of Mary's contrariness. It was, sad
to say, the only time.

Agnes says, "Look at you. You're embarrassed, aren't you,
Father." She speaks with the same amusement that comes to her
voice when François does an entertaining turn.

I regret having brought up the subject. I don't even know why
I did. This is the sort of thing that happens to me when I try to
make small talk. I'm tempted to switch off the contraption, but
that would be an ugly thing to do. My face feels like it must rival
the large bulb that glows red at the foot of the angel crowning the

tree. I clear my throat. "You know, that silly remark of hers. Granted, it was funny at the time, but still. That silly remark about . . ."

"About Lois Lane losing her head?"

"Yes. It was the kind of thing Martha would have said." The thought had occurred only later, after the comedy had faded, leaving behind an image that was puzzling and vaguely disturbing. "Your mother picked up a kind of risqué edge from that woman. You remember Martha, Agnes?"

"Of course I remember Martha. She was one of a kind. Propulsive. Jet fuel. The kind of person who shoves you out of your little world. Try something different. Take a leap into the dark."

A variation of what Mary would've said. Except perhaps for the dark. Why the dark? Why not the light? So much more enticing, that. A blind leap into the light. Isn't it?

I took pity on Elliot the moment he entered my office.

I mean — the poor fellow. He bumped his shoulder on the door-frame, rather painfully, I fear. Then he dropped his stick and all his papers and stood there, aghast. I half-expected him to whimper.

Elliot, you see, is blind — blind as a bat, as the cliché goes. One could wag one's tongue at him in mid-conversation and he wouldn't raise an eyelid. But I suspect there is little satisaction to be gained in raising a middle finger at someone like Elliot, so he enjoys certain compensations: There is a host of ways in which he cannot be insulted.

I hastened to help him, apologising as I did so for my door-frame. I even found myself questioning why it should have been put there, and it was Elliot who replied that a doorway was probably a good place for it.

Now, blindness is not a sin. Indeed, these days it is hardly a handicap. But like many people I am discomfited when faced with the sightless. I do not know where to look.

I am not a squeamish man. In France, in the fall of 1944, I gazed frankly into the lifeless pupils of my best friend, fully aware that but for the luck of inches he would have been the one gazing into mine. And many a time after that, I gazed at the shut eyelids of my infant daughter asleep in her crib, and of my wife in bed beside me. As for sunglasses — on bright days they are, after all, ubiquitous.

But in an inappropriate context, these simple things all acquire a quiet horror. Elliot, in the penumbra of my office, has caused me to glance away from his lifeless pupils, his shut eyelids, his stylish sunglasses.

That day, he had a request. He wished me to act as supervisor for his Master's thesis. Two of my colleagues had already pleaded full plates. He named them, and I knew that their plates were indeed full — but only because they had taken rather small dishes.

I mumbled something mean-spirited about being his third choice.

Third choice, he said. And last hope.

I disagreed. There were other professors in the department who could do an adequate job of supervision.

Adequate, he said, would not do.

Which I thought rather impudent of him. In his condition, surely he should be grateful for whatever help he got. Happily, I did not voice that thought, for I was immediately ashamed of it. I also realised that, had he been a normal student, I would have refused on the spot: My plate — a large one, if I may say so — truly was full. Furthermore, I understood that, by seeking out a graceful reason for refusing, I was thinking myself into a corner. His proposed thesis was to be on the effect of sunshine in nineteenth-century American poetry.

Sunshine . . . But had he ever seen the sun?

"I wasn't born blind, Professor," he replied, and he explained that he had lost his sight as the result of a severe, nerve-damaging infection at the age of four. "I have memories," he said. "Or suggestions of memories. I *feel* what the sun looks like. Besides—" He had clearly thought about this. "Besides, you are an expert on the nineteenth century — but have you ever seen the nineteenth century?"

Hardly the same thing, of course, but I was not prepared at the time to challenge his cleverness. His eyes were in the way. I asked what he intended to do with his Master's degree should he be granted it, and he expressed a desire to purse a Doctorate and a teaching career.

And if he failed in this endeavour? What then?

"Then," he said savagely, "I suppose I could always sit at some street corner selling pens and pencils from a can."

As one might expect, that took the wind out of me — and shoved me firmly into the corner I had designed for myself.

Mary was not happy when I told her about Elliot. From everything I said, he struck her as a young man who was not looking for pity — and pity, she insisted, was precisely what I had offered him.

Well, yes. She was right, of course. I acknowledge that. But it seems to me that pity is as honourable a reason as altruism for undertaking good works — good social works, I mean. I do not for a moment believe that those of us on whom fortune has smiled — whether by birth, luck or hard labour — owes anything to anyone else in society. Social solidarity is merely a pleasing term for fascism, after all. An imposition. But pity — now that's something else altogether. Pity proceeds from the human heart.

And so, yes — why not? — it was pity that led me to agree to supervise Elliot. Pity got him what he wanted. What could possibly be wrong with that?

It was probably at our third or fourth meeting that I asked Elliot to speak to me of his blindness

Mary was quite put off by my curiosity. She felt that if Elliot wished to speak of it, he would, with no prompting from me. She thought my curiosity intrusive and, at a certain level, morbid. Mary's delicacy, it must be said, has always stuck me as admirable but useless. She had not been through the war. She had not sat outside a medical tent pitched in a French pasture, in the warm sunshine of early fall, the heavy guns too distant to be distinct, with Hurricanes and Spitfires racing high above to push back the aerial front. She had not sat there, surrounded by contradiction, smoking and passing the time with a friend aged overnight awaiting transport back to the coast, then to England and home. She had not made small talk in those marvellous and breathless moments, myself awaiting transport to where the guns were louder and where innocent hedgerows spat death in a parsimony of flying steel. And she had not had a friend grow silent in the fading whine of aircraft engines, his gaze rising unwillingly from the bruised grass to yours, to say, Why? Why do you pretend? Why do you not ease this new reticence between us by asking what it feels like? By asking about the pain and the shock — and the horror of trying to cross the leg which I feel to be there but which I see to be not? Then my truck arrived, and we waved a distant goodbye. He was soon lost to me in the dust — me with my unasked questions, he with the infection yet unsuspected and a constitution so weakened that within a week he would be laid to rest in England.

I felt that Elliot's disability, his handicap, had to be acknowledged in terms frank and unadorned. Only discussed and rendered ordinary could it be made unnoticeable, and so long as it remained noticeable it would be a hindrance to our work. Not to bring it up would have been false and dishonest on my part.

So I asked Elliot to speak to me of his blindness. And he slowly withdrew from his hunch — that hunch that comes so naturally to the tall and lanky — until his back was straight, his fingers loosely interlaced on his lap. He smiled. "I live," he said, "in a darkness alive with sound. And I dream of seeing that darkness erupt. I dream, Professor, of an understanding of light that goes beyond mere words."

I never found it necessary to mention his blindness again.

Elliot was a hard worker, and his progess was swift. I learned through the course of our meetings that we lived in the same neighbourhood. He enjoyed a fair measure of autonomy and knew the area well. He did not socialise a great deal, although he favoured the neighbourhood Ethiopian restaurant in summer. He spent much time studying in the apartment his parents had put at his disposal in the basement of their house. And every week he volunteered at the Institute for the Blind, a pleasant walk in fine weather, a short bus ride away in inclemency.

He once mentioned a girlfriend in passing, which, I will admit, aroused my curiosity — but I chose not to inquire, for the first question that occurred to me was unaskable: Was she, too, blind?

One morning I arrived at the metro and saw Elliot waiting for the train a third of the way down the platform. He stood with his bag and cane at the first emergency post, precisely the point where I usually stood: Two trains and several stations later he would find himself at the foot the stairs that led to the closest exit to the university. I knew immediately that I would not make my presence known, but that I would keep him within sight. I would observe him out in the world.

When the train arrived, he moved with deliberate precision: He knew where the open door would be, knew how many steps it would take him to get there. I was almost disappointed that there was nothing tentative about him.

When we changed trains amidst greater crowds, he moved with an assurance even I have never felt. People swirled and eddied around him, avoiding him and creating a corridor through which he strode to the train waiting on the far side. An old woman, a woman my age, offered him her seat — and he declined in a manner that disconcerted her: politely, with a smile, but never turning his face in her direction, so that he appeared to be smiling at the electronic advertisements flashing across the screen mounted on the wall of the train.

At the exit, I let him go ahead. He would be at my office within minutes. I stopped in at the magazine store and thumbed through a few obscure but earnest literary journals, and then made my way slowly to the office. He was waiting at the locked door.

As I approached, he said, "Why didn't you say anything?"

"I beg your pardon?"

"You were there, in the metro. You didn't say hello."

I fumbled with my keys, searching for an excuse: I was preoccupied, I hadn't noticed him, I was reflecting on a vexing problem, I wasn't feeling particularly well . . .

Elliot followed me into the office. He smiled. "Your shuffle, Professor, is distinctive. I would know it anywhere. What happened to your leg?"

And so, reluctantly, but comforted by the knowledge that I was making amends, I told him of the war.

"Even today, it remains in my mind as a mansion of a foxhole. Large and deep. Capacious. The earth almost finely excavated by the explosion of the shell. It was several weeks old, and dry, its sides powdery on the surface but battened down just beneath.

Compared to some of the towns we had passed through, towns from which the Germans had had to be driven with indiscriminate savagery, it was positively cosy, and certainly, as a structure, far more intact.

"No rain had fallen for weeks. I remember the sky and the sunshine as being particularly unsuited to war, remember thinking that on days such as these no one should have to kill, or to die — and, Elliot, yes, there were days which seemed more appropriate to death. Days when all was grey and the only colours were red, orange and blue, spurting from the barrels of guns or flaming across the sky, Hurricanes and Messerschmitts burning up with the incandescence of shooting stars. Sometimes there would be the miraculous blossoming of white silk, but more often, not.

"Red, orange and blue: They were ugly, ugly colours. Uglier still than the grey which lent them such effervescence. Grey was what it was, you see. True to its nature. But the others. It was their very gayness that made them intolerable.

"But this was not such a day. On the contrary. The Germans had withdrawn during the night — word had it that they were withdrawing all across the front, beating a hasty retreat across French soil — and Battalion headquarters had declared a bit of a rest, a few hours to eat and relax and wash up as best we could.

"It was the corporal, a fellow from Nova Scotia, Dartmouth or Sydney, who found the shell hole. McNally. Corporal McNally. Twice a sergeant, but that extra stripe had twice proved too heavy a burden. An unconventional fellow, a trait that proved useful in earning the stripes but inconvenient in keeping them. He led us down, into the shell hole. It was an exposed position to the skies — a passing Messerschmitt could have scored quite a kill with little effort but they, too, were in retreat.

"Once we had settled ourselves in, removing our packs, exposing our bruised feet to the air for the first time in days, he produced several bottles of wine he had liberated from a cellar in one of those ruined towns. This explained his curious choice of location. The lieutenant, a teetotaling Torontonian, would have seized them.

"We all followed McNally's lead, then, digging into our packs for whatever non-issue food we had managed to accumulate. Bricks of cheese, bread, sausages of uncertain provenance, even, I recall, a couple of hard-boiled eggs and a slab of cured ham. A feast! One bottle made the rounds, then another.

"And then . . .

"Where it came from I do not know. Indeed, which side it came from remains a mystery, one the authorities were not eager to solve afterwards. But suddenly, you see, we were staring at a freshly fallen shell half-buried in the soil no more than three feet away from where I sat. Not a large object — merely a slender canister two feet long. It had come without warning or report out of the sky and, miraculously, had failed to explode. But it could have at any moment. Time, as they say, froze.

"Now, I must ask you, Elliot, to keep in mind that none of what comes next makes sense to me either. It is simply a recounting of events that occurred within the space of seconds and which remain with me not in memory but as reconstruction. I do not recall these events from my own point of view, I mean. Rather, I see myself participating as I would have been observed by someone else.

"I see myself rising barefooted, my shirt unbuttoned, lunging, staggering, towards the shell. See myself taking hold of it, with both hands, withdrawing it from the earth and, in an unbroken motion, swinging it between my legs and flinging it up and away, back into the sky, up to the edge of the crater.

"Understand: All I wanted to do was to get it as far away from me as possible. Where it landed was no concern of mine.

"And where it landed was on the very lip. I saw it teeter there for the longest while, as if in indecision. And during that long while, I saw my mates gather, huddling as it were, below it, staring up at it as one might at a fearful idol. Why they should have chosen to huddle together in that particular spot is yet another mystery. But so they did. And I saw — as did they — the shell begin to tumble back down the slope of the crater towards them.

"I see myself turning in horror, see myself scrambling desperately up the slope, away from the shell, away from my mates.

"I didn't see the explosion, but I heard it, was deafened by it, and felt its concussive force. I was knocked flat, face first, my mouth and nostrils filling with earth. And then I lost consciousness.

"When I came to some days later, my leg and head were swathed in bandages — nothing life-threatening, but neither the leg nor my left ear would ever be the same again. My mates, I found out, were less fortunate. It seems the shell had exploded just feet from them. Four of them were killed, including McNally.

"I was patched up and shipped out, back to a convalescence hospital in the English countryside, where I spent some months. Before being sent home, I was given a medal and pronounced a hero. My surviving mates had told how I had, in disregard of my own life, attempted to throw the shell out of the crater.

"Hero, indeed . . .

"I said nothing. That would have been pointless, for such I suspect is the nature of much heroism: thoughtless action motivated by fear. Mere instinct, in other words. So I accepted the medal and my berth on the ship that would convey me back to Canada.

"I have since, as you see, acquired a walking stick, and my wife has begun dropping broad hints about a hearing aid. As for the medal, it is at home in a box, secured away with the other baubles that came my way.

"And that, Elliot, is the story of the leg that betrayed my presence to you."

After a moment, Elliot said, "You're good for me, Professor. You make me feel lucky."

I knew instantly what he meant, and was grateful to him for not making it explicit. And yet I couldn't help remarking, "If that's so, my good fellow, why do you sound so bitter when you say it?"

A smile came slowly to him. "Now we see," he said, "why you're a professor and I'm just a lowly student."

He could not, he said on the telephone, stop by my office as arranged. He said something about tests. Beth, however, had offered to pick up the package of reading material I had promised.

Beth: He chose not to place her, and I therefore chose not to inquire. I assumed her to be the girlfriend.

She was neither on time nor apologetic. She was rushed. Blonde, slighty-built, attractive in an unadorned way, she quickly identified herself and seized the envelope I indicated on my desk. She paused only on her way out, and then briefly, to say, "Professor Mackenzie, I just wanted to say thanks, you know, for Elliot, for all you're doing for him."

"I'm just doing my job, young lady," I replied.

Only in the wake of her departure did discomfort come to me, causing me some concern for Elliot. It was not so much in her words as in her tone: She had thanked me for my charity.

One day, he said, "My mom and dad just don't get it, Professor. They're not bad people, just the opposite in fact. But it's strange how wanting the best for someone — especially for your kid, I suppose — can seem so . . ."

"Confining?" I suggested. "For the child?"

He nodded, but hesitantly, the word no more than adequate. "I'm not with Beth for her sight, but for her insight. She's the smartest person I've ever met — beside you, of course. But for my parents, she's kind of the equivalent of a guide dog. They're just so happy she's not blind."

He had put it brutally, and yet I sympathised with his parents. "What does Beth do?" I asked.

"She's in the marketing program. But her real vocation is poetry. She writes, you know."

I thought: Oh dear. But I said, "Is she any good?"

"Oh, she's very good, Professor."

"Has she published?"

"She's not interested. For the moment."

"Yes, well, I suppose if she ever does, marketing skills will come in very handy. Not too many volumes of poetry make it to the best-seller lists these days. None, in fact, within recent memory."

"Professor! You surprise me. Best-seller lists. I didn't think you would pay attention."

I cleared my throat. "For your own good, Elliot, should you ever attain the pinnacle of academia you dream of, remember that we are not limited by our degrees or our specialisations. You will no doubt discover this for yourself as you grow older and lose some of that . . . youthful arrogance."

He laughed, and I understood that I had failed to see that I was being teased.

Not long afterwards, Elliot did precisely what I had hoped he would not do. He brought me a poem by his girlfriend.

It was handwritten in a beautiful script on an unlined 5 by 7 filing card. I set it aside on my desk, hoping he would not insist on my reading it immediately. "Well, then," I said, reaching for the paper he had submitted. "Shall we get on with—"

"Aren't you going to read it, Professor?"

Oh dear. "Yes, of course. Well now, let's see . . ."

lingering light
lightens lace
like lichen
lying lynched
upon
licentious lakeshores

I read it twice. To my shame. And the second time, to my greater
shame, I made a show of nodding my head — not that Elliot
could see the theatre, but still . . . — and pondering the words
and their rhythms.

Elliot said, "It's called 'Upon'. I told you she was good."

"Yes, you did," I acknowledged, careful not to commit myself.

"I mean, I know she's got work to do and all that. Her influ-
ences are still too obvious, she needs to develop a more personal
style, but still, the talent — it's really something, isn't it?"

I would have been curious to know which poets, in his estima-
tion, had influenced his girlfriend's style, but I was too forcefully
struck by Elliot's loyalty to her to spoil the moment for him.
Elliot's sensitivity to language was too fine, his knowledge of
literature too broad and penetrating — loyalty alone justified his
enthusiasm, and true loyalty is today a trait sufficiently rare to be
worthy of a certain reverence.

"May I keep this?" I said, knowing it would please him.

"Of course."

When he left my office after our session, I thoughtlessly spun
the card into the recycling bin.

A minute later, regretful, I retrieved it and pinned it to the
notice-board on the wall beside my desk.

Loyalty, you see.

Elliot arrived at my office one morning in a state of composure
which I knew to be, in him, a statement of disarray. It was as if,

when his world went into turmoil, his darkness demanded the imposition of a preternatural silence. Everything went silent about him — his walk, his movements, the fall of his cane on the ground. He became as soundless as shadow.

"Elliot," I said. "What is it? What's happened?"

He sat across my desk from me, arranged his things. Had my eyes been shut, I would have believed myself alone, so complete was his soundlessness, so complete his absence of presence. He said nothing, absolutely nothing, for at least three minutes. He might not even have been breathing.

I saw no reason not to play his game, so began thumbing noisily through a text on my desk, pretending to examine it in search of a particular passage.

Finally, Elliot said, "Professor . . ."

"Oh good," I replied without looking up. "It talks."

"Professor, Beth has left me."

"Dear boy, I am sorry."

"She said, I don't mind your not being able to see, Elliot, you know that — and I do know that, Professor — but I can't stand your blindness in other ways. There are so many ways you don't see, Elliot. I'm afraid one day you'll run me over — because you don't see me."

I waited for him to go on.

"And she's right, Professor. I don't see her. I can't see her."

He needed some comforting. I have never been very good at comforting. "But Elliot," I said, "how could she expect you to?"

"That's not the question, Professor. The question is, how could she not expect me to? And also, how could I not?"

He requested a postponement of our session and left my office, trailing his soundlessness behind him like Marley's ghostly chains.

A month, perhaps two, later, among the usual departmental

clutter and late essays in my pigeonhole, I came across a neatly typed note from Elliot. He apologised for having to cancel our next few sessions but something had come up. He would be in touch with me at the first opportunity.

It was Wendy — the young departmental receptionist who pronounced her name Windy, appropriate in that her hair always resembled a palm tree in a hurricane — who told me of the reason for Elliot's absence. It had something to do, she said, with his eyes and an operation.

The news rather startled me. I was of course aware of his occasional frustration, but nothing he had said or done would have led me to expect he would undertake such a step. Indeed, the very opposite was true. I had understood the nature of his problem to be irreversible — and he had never struck me as a believer in miracles. Even more disturbing was my realisation that the operation would make Elliot's blindness an issue in a way that it had not been since the early days of our collaboration. Now I feared it would come inevitably to define him.

Two weeks later, the telephone rang in my office. "Professor," Elliot said. "My apologies. I'll make up the work, I promise."

I assured him he would have nothing to make up. His hard work had already put him well ahead of schedule.

"Professor," he said, "I've had an operation."

"So I've heard. Was it successful?"

"We'll know tomorrow. The bandages come off in the morning." Even over the telephone, and despite the sounds of his speech, I could hear the greater silence of disarray.

"Elliot,' I said, "are you afraid?"

"I don't know what I am, Professor. I'm curious about one thing, though. If I'd told you about the operation — the odds aren't exactly in my favour, you know — would you have advised for or against?"

"I wouldn't have advised," I replied truthfully. "This was a decision that belonged only to you."

"But what would you have thought?"

"I would have thought it . . . unadvisable."

He took a deep breath. "I knew that. Just like my parents. That's why I didn't tell you."

"Have you given any thought to consequences, Elliot? Either way, I mean."

"Lots."

Then that silence interposed itself.

I was about to wish him good luck when he said, "Professor, I'd like you to be there. For the unveiling."

"Elliot, I don't know . . ."

"Think of it as a vernissage, Professor. One way or the other, it should prove entertaining."

Elliot was not prone to flippancy. I would have to cancel a seminar, but I promised to be there, and noted down the time and place. I was vaguely disappointed to detect no sign of joy or gratitude in him.

"Professor," he said, "what's the weather forecast for tomorrow?"

"I'm not quite sure. Sunny, I think, but on the cool side."

He pondered this for a moment. Then with a light chuckle, he said, "See you tomorrow."

Hanging up, I thought: Gallows humour.

But how hard I wished it to be so.

We were only four in the room. Elliot's specialist, a nurse, Elliot and myself. I did not think it appropriate, at that moment, to ask why his parents were not present.

Elliot, sitting in a chair, eyes bandaged, said, "Thank you for coming, Professor. I need to have some wisdom standing by."

"Elliot," I replied with some discomfort. "You overestimate me."

"I don't think so. You put up with 'Upon', after all." He laughed. "Remarkable forebearance."

"I've seen worse—"

"Professor, you're a liar."

This time it was my turn to laugh.

But levity could not feed on itself, could not grow. The energy, in that room, in that circumstance, was of a different and wholly unsuitable kind.

I kept my distance when the doctor, perched on a stool, began the careful removal of Elliot's bandages, peeling layers back one by one and depositing them in a stainless-steel tray held by the nurse. And I was reminded of waiting while Mary gave birth to Agnes, of the anticipation and the dread — I was not in the delivery room, of course, such things were not done at the time — and of the wish to flee from a spot to which I felt myself irrevocably rooted.

Finally the bandages were all off and Elliot sat there on his chair, eyes closed, the skin where the bandages had adhered looking red and raw, bruised.

The doctor said, "Open your eyes slowly, Elliot. They'll need a few minutes to adjust."

Elliot's effort was visible and wrenching, his eyelids more than unwilling to lift — fearful of doing so.

Then they twitched and rose.

And I saw that his eyes were frightfully bloodshot, his pupils lifeless, bereft of the brilliance of miracle.

He blinked.

I looked at the doctor, then the nurse, but they were looking at Elliot, with patience. Neither of them, I saw, knew more than I did.

The doctor held a silver pen up to Elliot's eyes. Light glinted off it. "Do you see anything, Elliot?" he said in a tone so clinical, so professional, I thought him a man of either great humanity or of no humanity at all.

Elliot made no reply.

The tension got the better of me. "What do you see, dear fellow? What do you see?"

Still Elliot said nothing.

And neither, for many minutes, did any of us. It seemed a holy silence, moments stilled by concerns greater than those of the world. It demanded respect.

The doctor slid his pen back into his coat pocket and reached for a flashlight.

Just at that moment, Elliot shut his eyes — and he kept them shut for several seconds before opening them again.

And none of us knew what to think — or what it meant — when he turned his face towards the open window, towards the sun raging in the morning sky, and from the outside corner of each eye rolled a slow and voluptuous teardrop.

Some stories have happy endings, some do not. Elliot's story, like so much in life, is more ambiguous.

For, eventually, he answered my question. He told me what he could see.

Elliot came face to face with his greatest wish: He could see the sun.

And then he came face to face with his greatest fear: He could see little else.

In the voice of a child, he said, "Professor?"

With throat tightened, I searched my storehouse of wisdom and found it meagre. History and decades, I understood, have not disarmed my helplessness.

I continued working with Elliot until my retirement — and even then agreed to meet with him from time to time, for discussion, advice. How could I refuse?

He completed his Master's thesis and decided to undertake the labour of a Doctorate. He no longer lives here. His subject took him to Columbia, in New York City. But whenever he was in town he would stop by for a chat and a glass or two of sherry.

The last time he was by, he asked me with amused directness whether I still pitied him.

The question robbed me of air. I could not bring myself to reply. My embarrassment was, I fear, palpable.

And once more, as so often before, Elliot came to my rescue. "I know, Professor," he said. "I've always known." And with a grin: "I took advantage of it."

I then told him the truth: that I no longer felt pity for him. A new fascination had arisen — a fascination that had not diminished with the years.

I told him that I enjoyed seeing the effect seeing the sun had on him. It made him at times arrogant, at times wistful. When the light filled his eyes, I saw him radiate anger and joy in equal measure — and I saw more than once the tumble of those voluptuous tears.

In Elliot's presence, I felt the warmth of the sun. I felt myself illumined by its rays. But I did not tell him this.

$\mathcal{A}$gnes says, "She was an inspiration to me, you know."

"Her? In what way?"

"She could hardly sit still, that Martha. A real live-wire. Not to take anything away from Mom, but I guess she showed me . . . Just watching her go-go-go. She achieved so much. Just look at what she did with the business. I remember thinking, that's how I want to live my life."

"So that's where you get it from. You do too much as it is, Agnes."

She gives me a tired, satisfied smile. "Hell, no, father. I love my job. I love puttering around the kitchen, working in the garden."

"That's not what I mean. I mean all the other things you do. That centre where you volunteer, for instance. It eats up an evening a week, and some Saturday afternoons to boot." I learned about this volunteering of hers only after moving here. She'd never mentioned it, and when she did one afternoon before setting off, I thought of the projects that Mary had enjoyed taking up, fund-raising for one cause or another. How much more of Mary's personality had she inherited? "Shouldn't you think about giving that up? Spending a little more time with François, perhaps?"

Her face drains of emotion. "So that's what this sudden concern is about. The centre."

She is wrong. My "sudden concern" — and her words are painful — is not meant as a way of bringing up the centre. I am less awkward than that. Still, here we are. "Well, I have rather wondered why there of all places. There's a slew of respectable charities looking for—"

"Why not there, father?"

"That's not an answer, Agnes."

"You want an answer? All right, here's one. I watch you sitting there reading *A Tale of Two Cities* as if you haven't got a care in the world. Do you remember how you used to try to get me to read Dickens? You only gave up a few years ago, and in all those years I only managed *Oliver Twist*. Ever wonder why?"

"Constantly."

"You know, there at the centre every week I come across Oliver Twists of one kind or another. Hundreds over the years. Runaways, pregnant teens, abuse cases you don't ever want to know about. And there aren't too many happy endings."

"You don't get along with Dickens because he liked happy endings? Are you a pessimist, then, Agnes? You've never struck me as—"

"Not a pessimist, father. Otherwise I'd have given up the centre years ago."

"What then? Help me to understand. Optimists believe in

happy endings come what may."

She shakes her head, looks away from me. Then — that determination, that challenge: Mary again — looks back. "This has nothing to do with spending more time with François, does it, father? So what's eating you? I've been doing this for years. Mom knew all about it—"

"Your mother knew?"

"She thought it'd be best if you didn't."

"You concealed it from me? A little mother-daughter conspiracy?"

"Not concealed. Not really. We just never mentioned it too loudly when you were around."

"I see. She was a smart woman, your mother. She knew I would have trouble with—" How to put it? Among the centre's services, Jack explained to me one recent wintry Saturday afternoon over coffee in the kitchen, is arranging for pregnant girls to dispose of the inconvenient consequence of their actions. This is not how Jack put it. This is how I absorbed it. At last, I complete my sentence: "— some of the things you do."

Agnes crosses her hands on her lap. The gesture, suggestive to those unfamiliar with her of contemplative retreat, like someone sitting in a church, is an unfailing sign of her anxiety. She does not merely cross her hands. She grips one with the other the way nervous people on airplanes grasp the arms of their seat. I see her steeling herself, and I know we're about to have a conversation she's rehearsed many times in her mind.

"Father," she says in a voice so composed the word sounds like a title, "I always thought you fought in the war so people would have the freedom to make choices for themselves."

"Well, yes, I did."

Or did I? Choice. Freedom. Democracy. All those big personal sacrifices those who were not there like to evoke. I suppose they're all true, in a way. They have a place and meaning in the larger picture. But for me? The young Alistair Mackenzie? Did I fight for freedom, democracy, this idea of choice Agnes talks about? The words never entered my mind back then. Not once did I hear them brighten the profanities that punctuated the running, the marching, the lancing of blisters, the oiling of weapons. Not once did I hear them uttered in the boredom and vomiting of the transport ship heaving on the Atlantic, or shouted in the pubs and dancehalls of southern England. They never entered the whispered prayers as the coast of France — where the only certainty was that death awaited countless numbers of us — emerged from the fog like a grim smudge materialising on photographic paper.

We were out to kick Hitler's ass, we wanted to splatter Fritz's brains. We wanted to survive. Freedom? Democracy? Perhaps some held fast to such ideas. But not my friends. Not I. It was a job that went beyond drudgery, although there was a great deal of that. It was a game that went beyond rules, although there were a great deal of those. But grand ideals? I don't know how many people were invigorated by Churchill's elegant bluster. We all far preferred listening to "Don't Fence Me In" or "That Old Black Magic". Most in my circle tolerated him at best, a lot of the English girls barely. I wasn't surprised when Attlee beat him in forty-five. People had had enough of being preached to. We don't remember these days that the fellow was half inspiration, half irritation.

If pressed to search for some higher purpose to my going to war, I would suggest that I did so to stop people from killing each other. But even that would be overstating the case. Even that, set against the all-too-simple truth, would be too grand. But how to tell this to my daughter? She has this lovely idea of why I did what I did during the war. She, like so many others, has invested me — not so much in my person as in the mythology of the time — with the status of crusader. It would take a far prouder man than I to disillusion her.

And so I decide to parrot the lie, in my own way. "I fought, we fought, for freedom, Agnes, not for licence. This volunteerism of yours, yes, it helps many, but it also sends all those babies off to be—"

"Father, when you joined the army—"

"But that was war, Agnes. This, what you help those young girls do. Don't you see? It resembles what we wanted to stop." We? I sound false to myself. We shall fight on the beaches, we shall fight on the . . . My opposition is formless, its basis essentially visceral, but it is not fabricated. The way I've cast it, however, is. There were few things Mary and I chose not to discuss; this was one of them.

"Don't you see they're two completely different—" Agnes's voice breaks in exasperation. Then, more bitterly: "And you wonder why Mom— She knew that's how you saw things. You wouldn't see it as saving lives, giving these young women another chance. Your war killed people, father. Terminating a pregnancy isn't like having a tooth extracted, you know, it's the most—"

She gets abruptly to her feet. "I'm not about to quit the centre, father. And it's clear you're not about to change your mind. For you almost everything begins and ends with the war. Things aren't as simple these days. So why don't we just give it a rest, all right?"

I nod even though her comment is unfair, and she turns away from me, her face marked by a quiet anguish, an anguish that shows me my daughter as the child she was so long ago, serious at times, carefree at others. And I feel a pain now, the same I felt when faced by her distress after a tumble from the tricycle or a shove in the playground: this tightening in the chest and throat, this eruption of helplessness from within my marrow. I've never known how to deal with my child's unhappiness. Indeed, I've had a hard time recognising unhappiness in others.

*W*hat a difference a preposition makes.

Those who did not like him — and they were not numerous — said of him: He spends his life looking up to everyone else. His friends, or those who owed more to him than they would comfortably acknowledge, were careful to replace that judgemental *to* with a more descriptive *at*.

In such small ways are fierceness and compassion sometimes measured.

This game of prepositions arose from one singular, inescapable fact. Antonio Gaudi Slovar, a man who laid credible claim to being the best accountant in the city, was short. Very short. Indeed, Antonio Gaudi Slovar, who has protected the tax-bracket of many a well-to-do professional, was a dwarf.

199

We met several years ago when some investments I had made proved lucrative enough to attract the attention of the tax people. The letter I received from them, a masterpiece of bureaucratese, came slathering at the mouth and with palms open. My return was clearly seen as a prime source of funding for social programs.

I am no right-wing zealot. My sense of compassion ensures that I support society's efforts to aid the unfortunate. The letter from the tax people, however, suggested subliminally that they wished to turn me from a contributor into a recipient.

Assistance was required.

I first heard the name Antonio Gaudi Slovar from Mary. Martha had suggested him as an accountant capable of maintaining my solvency. I was sceptical, partly because of pride — I had always handled my tax affairs on my own — and partly because his name was simply beyond the pale. He came highly recommended — Martha and Randolph attributed their ownership of two Florida condominium buildings and various other properties to his talents — and yet the name gave me trouble. Antonio Gaudi. Spanish, clearly, perhaps some kind of homage to the architect fellow. However, that would have been the intention not of the man himself but of his parents. Then Slovar: Clearly not Spanish, perhaps eastern European, it brought to mind the word "slobber". The name, then, hardly inspired the sort of confidence one would wish to have in the man to whom one planned to hand one's financial fate.

Mary told me I was being stupid. "It's a rather exotic name," she said, "but that's no disqualification."

Right again, as usual.

I called him up to make an appointment. He answered the telephone himself. After a brief introduction, I explained that he'd been recommended — "Who by?" he said suspiciously — and that I required his expertise to solve a problem with the tax department. He asked the nature of the problem and listened without interruption, asking only at the end for clarification of certain details. Then he said, "Fine, bring the stuff by."

Stuff? What stuff?

"Whatever you've got. All your documents. Your last return, receipts. You know, all that stuff."

I asked when would be a good time.

"Drop by any time."

I asked where his firm was located.

"Firm? Ain't no firm. Just me." And he gave me the address.

His office was in a begrimed office building downtown, not far from the university. My heart sank when I saw where it was, for the building seemed the home of establishments — small "trading" companies; a travel agency with a fly-by-night appearance; "immigration consultants" — which screamed *Buyer Beware!*

He was on the fourth floor and despite his gruffly-offered advice — "There's a lift but the stairs'll be faster." — my leg dictated a ride in the ancient, steel-walled elevator. The contraption shook and shuddered and groaned every inch of the way up, progress marked only by a sense of laboured movement since the numbers above the door remained unlit. It finally stopped, exhaling as if in exhaustion — and then paused for a startlingly long moment, gathering the strength to open the door.

The corridor was long and narrow, dustily lit. The walls, olive-coloured, were as scuffed as the rubber tiles peeling their edges from the floor. Every ten feet or so a closed door — some stencilled with an enigmatic name, some with numbers, some with not even that — suggested the surreptitious. This was a building, inside and out, that was difficult to imagine as fresh and clean and spanking new. Only the man's reputation prevented me from turning back.

His door was numbered, and a hand-lettered sign read:

A.G. SLOVAR, C.A.
"Trust Tony to Trim Your Taxes"

Oh God . . .

But I had already come this far, and I reminded myself that only the shallow prized style over ability. I knocked. A distracted voice called for me to enter.

The door squeaked open to an office plunged in twilight. Behind a long desk, just visible above stacks of folders, in the light of a single lamp, was the crown of a head. "Mr. Slovar?"

The head rose higher above the folders. Two dark eyes blinked at me. "About time. Where's my pizza?"

"Your pizza?"

"Aren't you the pizza guy?"

"Most assuredly not."

"So who the hell are you, then?"

"The name's Mackenzie. We spoke on the phone yesterday."

"We did?"

"I've got a problem with the tax people," I reminded him.

"So who doesn't?"

Wheels whirred on plastic as his chair moved with surprising speed to the far, unencumbered end of the desk. And it was then that I saw he was a dwarf.

"Sit," he said, pointing to a chair across from him, a miniature affair — a seat the size of a dinner plate, a back in the shape of a kidney bean, the two joined by a black brace that resembled a human spine — designed to discourage lingering.

"So tell me," he said, and I repeated all that I had told him the day before. He noted down the facts and figures. When I was done, he took the documentation I had brought, spread it all out on the desk before him and plunged into study.

His office spoke of an unsettling disorganization. A range of grey filing cabinets flanked the wall behind him, access to the upper drawers and the boxes stacked on top afforded by a step ladder. More papers sat in piles along the wall on the floor behind me and beneath the window. Outside, a penumbra reigned on what had only moments before been a bright morning. I was a minute in realizing that what I had concluded was a deep tint in the windowpane was actually the soot of decades layered and encrusted: Through it, a sunny day would appear grey, a grey day greyer.

Finally, he gathered up the papers and patted them neat. "Leave it with me," he said. "I'll be in touch."

"Is that it?"

"Was there something else?"

"No, I was just—"

"Fine, then," he said impatiently. "I'll be in touch." He swivelled his chair away and, pulling himself along by the edge of the table, disappeared once more behind the folders.

"By the way," he called as I opened the door, "if you spot the pizza guy, tell him to step on it. His tip's evaporating."

Two weeks or so later, Antonio Gaudi Slovar called and invited himself to dinner. Alarmed, I offered to stop by his office the following day. "I wouldn't want to inconvenience you," I said, but he was adamant. My house was on his way home. "Is everything all right?" I said. "With my problem, I mean."

"Of course. You should be getting the cheque in a month, two tops."

"What cheque?"

"Turns out they owe you. Not a king's ransom or anything but, hey, these days every penny counts, right?"

Mary, cheered by the turn of events, took the news of our unexpected dinner guest with good grace. "I hope he likes chicken," she said. Then she had me hurry to the wine store before it closed.

When the doorbell rang that evening, I let Mary get the door. I had quite deliberately neglected to mention Mr. Slovar's stature for fear of seeming mean-spirited. To my disappointment, she was not in the least disconcerted. She merely inclined her head towards him with a smile of genuine warmth and said, "Mr. Slovar, how lovely to meet you."

He stepped inside and held up to her a large bouquet of long-stemmed roses clearly purchased at a florist's and not, as is my habit when I remember, from a bucket at the supermarket. "Please. Call me Tony." Mary flushed with pleasure.

Extending his hand, he looked up at me with a disarming smile. "It was kind of you to invite me to dinner. It really wasn't necessary."

I was momentarily baffled. He had invited himself — or so I thought. "Oh," I mumbled. "Think nothing of it."

While Mary — face buried in the foliage and cooing at the scent — went to fetch a vase, I showed our guest to the living room. Unslinging a blue knapsack from his left shoulder, he sat on the sofa using his hands to fully cantilever himself back. His shoes, expensive leather with a fresh shine to them, barely touched the floor.

I offered a drink, but he raised a palm at me like a traffic policeman. "Business first," he said, reaching into the knapsack. "Here are all your papers as well as copies of my correspondence with the tax department. As you'll see, they were most accommodating."

"But how did you manage—"

He patted the papers. "It's all in here. Self-explanatory. You read it at your leisure and if you've got any questions, give me a call."

"Did you find something that escaped me?"

"No, I just lay the facts before them."

"But so did I, I thought."

"Ahh, professor — 's okay if I call you Alistair? — it's not just the facts, it's how you interpret them, what you do with them. Regulations are just words, and numbers can be magical. Nothing's written in stone."

"Well, if all you say is true, you certainly are a magician."

"As I said, you'll have the cheque in a month, two tops. Don't go expecting any apology, though." He laughed. His confidence was infectious. I found myself laughing along with him.

Mary came in, primping the roses, still snorting from them with all the avidity of a pollen-sucking bee. "Alistair," she said, "haven't you offered Tony anything to drink yet?"

"I have, Mary. But he chose to get business out of the way first."

"And now that it is," he said cheerily, "I wouldn't say no to a scotch on the rocks."

"I'm not sure we've got any—"

"Of course, we do, dear. You know — the good bottle you keep for that writer friend of yours."

"Ahh, yes. Of course." But I was astonished. Because of the price of good scotch, Mary had decreed that the bottle was to see the light of day only when Dan Mullen came by.

When I returned some minutes later with two glasses of scotch and a sherry, Tony was explaining his name to Mary. Sitting on the other side of the sofa, her expression was rapt.

His father, he was saying, had been born in Russia, a child of the revolution who fled his progenitors when it became clear that their idea of the New Soviet Man was one who did not eat. "And my father enjoyed his food, lots of meat and bread washed down with buckets of vodka and hot, sweet tea. He wandered around for a long time, looking for a cause." He found it, Antonio Gaudi Slovar said, in Spain. "My father didn't like the Reds, but he liked the fascists even less." And it was there, as a member of the international brigades fighting on behalf of the Republic, that he assumed the *nom de guerre* "Slovar" — the Russian word for 'dictionary'. "That tells you just about everything about my father."

It was while besieged in Barcelona that his father came to know and admire the work of the architect Antonio Gaudi. "My dad was a know-it-all but he wasn't what you'd call the artistic type. But this Gaudi guy just blew him away. Closest he came to a holy experience in his life, so when I came along many years later he decided to bless me with the name. He used to go all starry-eyed when he talked about the cathedral, the Sagrada Familia. You ever seen it? An awesome thing. Fantastical, grandiose. Built only with public donations. They've been building it forever. Dad always said it'd probably never be completed, it would probably always be a work in progress. He liked that. As for Slovar, he decided to keep it after the war."

Mary, enraptured, said, "And your mother?"

"My father always claimed she was an Hungarian countess. She lived with him for a year, until I was born. Then she left. I know nothing else about her."

Hungarian countess? Indeed . . .

Mary said, "Don't you even have a photograph?"

Tony shook his head. "All his life my father believed in living light. Easier to pick up and run, that way. He kept nothing. After his death, everything he owned except his clothes fitted into a single cardboard box, and not a large one either."

"He wasn't a conventional father, was he . . ."

"He wanted the best for me."

The ambiguity of his reply was, I felt, calculated. He wished to encourage Mary's quite uncharacteristic curiosity. So there was no reason for her to stop.

"Alistair and I have always wanted the best for our daughter," she said, "but I've never been quite sure what that meant."

"My father had a very precise idea of what that meant," he said, taking a gulp of his drink. "He wanted me to find my very own civil war and my very own Sagrada Familia. He didn't take kindly to my becoming a C.A. In fact, on the day that I learnt of my success in the exams — I just missed the gold medal, you know — on that very day, just a few hours after I gave him the news, he keeled over in the local tavern never to rise again."

Never to rise again? Oh God . . .

Mary pondered the words. "Never to rise again. How sad, but how poetic." Mary, it must be said, had been known to go teary over Mother's Day cards.

For me, however, Slovar's poetry was the last straw. "Tell me, Mr. Slovar, were your parents little people too?"

"Alistair!" Mary hissed.

Tony's eyes glided malevolent over to me. "My mother, I don't know. My father was six foot four." Then the malevolence passed from his eyes and his gaze turned sly. "And as for that other question you're too much of a gentleman to ask, nature has been quite generous to me, thank you. I've never had any complaints." He let his words float aound in the brittle silence that followed, then added, "Most people wonder, Alistair, but few have the balls to ask." He glanced at Mary. "Forgive me, dear lady. I'm told I'm sometimes quite short with people."

Mary burst out in the most delightful laughter.

Supper could not come soon enough for me, and as we approached the table I wondered how to handle the embarrassment I assumed to be only seconds away: What to do about the fact that when our guest sat at the dining table, he could comfortably rest his chin beside the water glass? I was nervously considering offering him a telephone book or two when Mary, with exquisite timing, swept up a large cushion for him to admire. It was of hand-tooled leather stuffed a foot thick with dense cotton wadding. "Isn't it beautiful?" she said. "Our daughter Agnes brought it back for us from a trip. A safari in Africa, with cameras, of course."

Slovar made the appropriate noises, turning it over in his hands. Then he passed it back to Mary who placed it on the chair towards which she waved him. The balance was precarious but I daresay that the fellow was quite accustomed to the necessary gymnastics. To my disappointment, he made nary a stumble.

Mary, bright-eyed and energetic, filled his plate with food while he lectured me on the intricacies of needlepoint, one of his passions. I wondered what his father had thought of *that*.

As we ate it came as a revelation to me that people — and here I mean myself — are as intimidated by a shortage of height as they are by an excess of it. Tony provoked conflict in me. His height aroused my sympathy and, to be truthful, my silent derision; yet his charm awoke my envy. I kept wishing for him to fall. Instead, I was the one to become clumsy, dropping my knife, then my fork, and spilling wine on my shirt. Mary fussed, but Tony, keeping up a constant patter of conversation, pretended not to notice — which made me feel all the more foolish, as if I were a troublesome child whose embarrassing antics guests chose to ignore.

Seeking to get a hold of my dignity, I heard Slovar's question only when he repeated it.

"Have you travelled a lot, Alistair?"

"Travelled? Oh, some. Not a great deal. I was in Europe during the war, you see. Got banged up a bit. I've preferred to stick close to home ever since."

"Have you ever been to Spain?"

"Spain. No. I'm afraid I'm not a fan of the Latin character. Spain. Italy. France. These are not places that interest me."

"Oh, I see."

The note of disappointment in his voice did not trouble me.

Mary said, "Have you been to the Latin countries, Tony?"

"Many times," he said with renewed enthusiasm. "My father used to say — and this was weird, coming from him: I'm not sure

whether he believed it or just thought it was a catchy thing to say
— he used to say, If you're gonna go, go first-class. I don't think
he ever went anywhere first-class in his life, but I think it's what
he wanted for me in his own oddball way."

"Was your father an oddball, then, Tony?"

"Good God, Mary, give the man a chance to talk. I don't know
about you, Mr. Slovar, but between the Latin countries, first-
class travel and your father's oddness" — not to mention your
own, I thought — "I've quite lost the thread of this conversation."

He laughed, and, to my consternation, so did Mary. Flashes of
my ill-temper usually spark flashes of her own.

"How silly of me," Mary said. "Alistair's got a point. Forgive
me? Now about the Latin countries . . ."

In all the years I'd known Mary, she had never once been
coquettish. Now, here she was, suddenly, shamelessly, displaying
this side of herself — to a *dwarf!*

The evening ended after midnight, rather later than our evenings
tended to do. I don't believe I uttered more than a dozen words
during the rest of dinner, perhaps a dozen more during the
glasses of liqueur Mary kept pressing on Slovar — and half of
those were to direct him to the bathroom.

Skipping back and forth through the years, he had regaled us
— or at least Mary — with stories of his travels on foot, by train,
by the luck of the thumb. He spoke of the pleasures of landscape
and architecture, of masterpieces of art, of sipping wine in a café
just off the Champs Élysée, drinking beer on the Ramblas and
wine in the shadow of the Prado, of tumbling into a Venetian
canal and dancing with Gypsies late one night in Granada. He
claimed to have belted out a garbled version of "Hello, Dolly"
from the top of the Leaning Tower of Pisa; other tourists, he
said, tossed him coins.

After we'd seen him off, my irritation tumbled out. Looking away, I said to Mary, "Well, you've taken quite a shine to him."

"I think he's the sweetest man. A delight. And he likes women."

"So do I, Mary. Besides, it never occurred to me he might be, you know, *that* way . . ."

"Oh, stop being silly. What I mean is, Tony enjoys the company of women. He flirts, of course, but he's not out to seduce. Oh, he could if he wanted to, but that's not his purpose. He's naughty but not dangerous. I suspect he's a very moral man. No, Tony's that rare man who simply feels most at ease, most himself, when he's with women. There's nothing more attractive. He's a kind of man who's very easy to love."

"Really, Mary, the man's a dwarf!"

"Yes. Imagine. And if he were six foot two, with broad shoulders and Clark Gable looks, he'd be no more attractive than he is now." Her thin smile grew wider, more mischievous; then it became a grin. "This is just killing you, isn't it?"

"Why should it?" I would not give her the satisfaction.

She shook her head as at an incorrigible child. "You haven't got anything to worry about, you know. I have no intention, or desire, to get to know Tony more — how shall I put this? — more intimately, the way some others have."

"What others?"

"Well — I shouldn't be telling you this."

"Come on, out with it."

"Do you want me to betray a confidence?"

"Not if you don't want to. But I think you want to."

"One of my friends has had an adventure with Mr. Slovar. It didn't last very long but apparently it was of unusual intensity. Tony is apparently quite the, umm, performer."

"One of your friends, eh? There's no point in being coy, Mary. Who else would it be but Martha the Amazon?"

"Granted, she's tall, Alistair — but she's hardly an Amazon."

"She's no leprechaun, either. Why, the top of Mr. Slovar's head probably wouldn't reach much beyond her waist—"

"Exactly." Mary raised what suddenly appeared to be an enormous eyebrow at me. "And if you ask no more questions, I shall offer no more details. But feel free to let your imagination roam . . ."

I shuddered at the thought.

The promised cheque arrived a month later, and while it was not a king's ransom, it was not insubstantial either. Uneasy at the windfall — I had wild fantasies of men in tight suits and sunglasses banging on our door after midnight and shouting, "Revenue Canada! Open up!" — I wanted to tuck the entire sum away in a safe investment. That way it would gather modest interest and be readily at hand should we be obliged to repay it.

Mary was less cautious than I. Slovar's reputation had made her confident. "Let's be extravagant for once," she said, and so we ended up at a spa in the Laurentians for several days of eating, sleeping and long afternoon walks together through the extensive surrounding woods. Mary availed herself of the sauna and massage services while I did a few undemanding laps in the pool before nodding off over one of Mullen's less engaging works.

Evenings were given over to leisurely dinners, followed — after two days of such self-indulgence — by what Mary playfully called "making the bed-springs squeak." (I, of course, pointed out that there were no bed-springs.)

On our last evening, too full from dinner to return to the room, I suggested a walk. The air was warm and fragrant, the night lit only by the stars. We knew our way even in the darkness, having trod this path through the woods several times during the day. We walked along in silence, arm in arm, until the lights of the spa were left far behind and the only sounds were those of leaves stirred by a light, high breeze.

After a bend in the path, Mary whispered, "One moment."
She let go of my arm and took a step or two away from me.

In the enveloping darkness, I immediately lost sight of her.
"Mary?" I said, with some anxiety.

"I'm here," she whispered back, and I caught sight of her
silhouette against the greater darkness. She seemed to be bending
over.

"Is everything all right? Have you got a pebble in your shoe?"

She did not reply — but as suddenly as she had disappeared,
her face now reappeared inches from mine. Her breath fell warm
and moist on my neck.

"Mary?"

She felt for my hand in the darkness, gently took hold of it,
and placed it on her hip. My fingers met warm, smooth skin.
"Oh, Mary."

Afterwards, giggling like naughty children, we searched for
our clothes. We eventually found them — everything except her
panties, which may still be there, somewhere, among the trees
and grass and flowers growing wild.

Mary was it who reminded me to telephone Antonio Gaudi
Slovar to thank him once more.

When he answered, I promptly identified myself and said I
was calling to let him know that the cheque had arrived and that
Mary and I were grateful for what he had done.

After a brief pause, he said, "Who did you say you are?"

"Alistair Mackenzie. You solved a problem I had with the tax
people. A little under two months ago."

"Mackenzie, eh? Name rings a bell, but—"

"You had dinner at our home."

"Go on. Remind me."

"You brought Mary flowers. Roses."

"Oh yeah, the professor."

"That's it."

"So, everything hunky-dory?"

"Yes, quite."

"Good then. Anything else?"

"No, we just wanted to thank you—"

"You're welcome. Look, gotta go now, I'm kind o' in the middle o' something." And he hung up.

After I had replaced the receiver, I said to Mary, "Mr. Slovar evidently did not find us — or at least me — as memorable as we found him."

"But why should he have?" she replied.

The thought cheered me up.

Antonio Gaudi Slovar then dropped out of my life and mind, until tax time rolled around once more

As I sat at the dining table on which I had neatly arranged all the implements of the annual larceny — the forms and booklets, stacks of receipts, freshly-sharpened pencils, new erasers, a calculator — I indulged in my usual, pre-calculation grumbling. I was (and remain) convinced that these forms are the products of inmates at some institution for the mentally deranged.

Mary, having heard my useless complaints for many years, said, "So why don't you call up Tony? I'm sure he'll be glad to do them."

"No need," I replied sharply. "I'll be done *short*-ly." Pride is the damnedest thing. I quietened down and resigned myself to the torturous task.

By the end of the day, it had come clear that Mary and I were owed a small sum by both the provincial and federal governments. Sitting back in satisfaction after having gone over the figures, I thought that things were, perhaps, after all, not so bad. I felt that in calculating a refund, I had quite legally trumped the tax people. Mary later dampened my euphoria by reminding me that the refund meant only that we had already paid out too much. When it comes to government, she said, all triumph is illusory.

Which is precisely why I had thought it would be prudent to secret away the sum Antonio Gaudi Slovar had obtained for us, but it would have been mean to mention this now. The money, after all, had brought us a pleasure far greater than the sum of its numbers.

Early one Saturday morning just over six months later, I awoke before dawn, as was and is my habit. I washed quickly, prepared the coffee brewer and, to the first of its promising sybillants, fetched *The Gazette* from the front porch. I recall the sharp fall air, the silhouettes of bared branches against the peacock-blue sky, the cleansing scents of a world girding itself for winter. The ground, both front and back, was carpeted with the last of the fallen leaves, my sense of well-being all the sweeter for knowing that I was free to enjoy their beauty. Mr. Frank the gardener would arrive at some point with his leaf-blower to gather up and bag them and those of other neigbours less physically inclined. This annoyed Tremblay no end. He objected to the whine of the leaf-blower, ridiculed the expense, suggested that we would all benefit from an hour or two of raking. Every fall, he spent a couple of days out back splitting logs for their fireplace. Our wood was, of course, delivered pre-chopped.

I took my coffee and the paper into the living room, sank into my favorite chair and, in the soft light of the reading lamp, savoured the moment, the house silent, the world at bay.

Some time later, after I had gone through the first sections, I heard Mary moving about. As I roused myself to go prepare a fresh pot of coffee, my eye fell on a familiar face staring back at me from the front page of the Business section. Antonio Gaudi Slovar.

Doing the Heart Good

The headline, the work of a playful, or perhaps vengeful, writer, read:

CLIENTS ASSESS DAMAGE
"Brilliant" accountant short-changes clients
Shrinks from sight

The city police, the story said, were investigating the sudden disappearance of an accountant in whose hands many of the city's richest professionals had placed substantial financial resources. Not only had A.G. "Tony" Slovar saved his clients several millions of dollars through "aggressive" accounting techniques, he had also taken charge of investing a large percentage of the savings for many of them. This money the newspaper described as being "unaccounted for" — as was, apparently, A.G. "Tony" Slovar himself. The reporter had found his office locked; the telephone had gone unanswered. There was little about the man apart from his accounting brilliance and his (to my surprise, considering his office) grand house, now empty and abandoned, just below Summit Circle, near the top of the mountain. There was, of course, no mention of his physical stature.

Mary, wrapped in her housecoat, came in yawning and batting her palm against her lips.

With some glee, I called out, "Come, take a look at this."

Just at that moment the telephone rang.

Knuckling sleep from her eyes, she mumbled, "Who in the world would be calling at this hour?" She picked up the receiver. "Oh, morning, Randolph," she said. "No, no, I'm afraid I haven't . . . Three days ago, perhaps. She was going shopping, but I had something on, I couldn't join her . . . Of course, I will. But don't you worry now, I'm sure everything's fine . . . Yes, of course, I will . . . Goodbye, Randolph."

Her hand still resting on the receiver, she turned slowly towards me. "Martha hasn't called recently, has she?"

215

I shook my head.

Martha, Randolph had said, had left home two days before to visit her younger sister in Niagara Falls, Ontario. Concerned that she hadn't called — which was so unlike her, she knew how much he worried — he had telephoned the sister. Not only was Martha not there but her sister claimed to know nothing of Martha's plans; she and Martha hadn't spoken in weeks and this was a most inopportune moment for a visit.

"Martha," Mary said, "seems to have disappeared."

"Disappeared?" The word struck me as overly Agatha-Christieish. "I wouldn't worry too much, Mary. Why, she's probably just—" And then it dawned on me where Martha was. I unfolded the newspaper and held it up for Mary to see.

She took a few cautious steps towards me, peering at the paper, forehead wrinkling.

A moment later, her jaw fell open in soundless astonishment.

Mary gazed wistfully at the postcard. It was nothing extraordinary — a nature scene as one might find in any of a dozen tropical countries — but retrieving it from the mailbox had altered her entire mood. Scribbled on its back, after all, were the first words she had heard from Martha in three months. *Just a quick note*, it read, *to let you know I'm fine. Of sound mind and body, altho you probably have your doubts about the former. Will be in touch again. Also, will be long gone from here when you receive this.* It had been mailed six weeks before, in Costa Rica.

"Do you miss her?" I asked.

Her head tilted. "Yes, of course I miss her. And I'm afraid for her, and I wish she'd come back. But you know, Alistair—" She raised her gaze to me, her pupils somehow vitreous. "—part of me envies her, too. No matter how much I wouldn't want her life — this life she's chosen — a mean little corner of my heart envies her. Envies the courage it took to drop everything — you realize she's lost it *all*! — and just follow her heart." She seemed mesmerized by the thought.

I hesitated before asking the question that then came to me, but I needed to know the answer. "So does this mean that you . . . Do you sometimes wish to just drop everything, Mary? And, as you put it, follow your heart?"

"Alistair," she said. "Sometimes, following your heart can lead you to wonderful places. I know. Following mine led me to you. But sometimes it can lead you to places you wish you'd never gone. Let me tell you what's probably going to happen to Martha.

"I'm sure it's all very exciting right now, but part of her is terribly, terribly afraid." She held up the postcard. "Look at her handwriting. It's hers, I'd know it anywhere, but it's already fraying. Do you see what I mean? Look at her Ss, for instance. She's already lost control of them. And look at her name. The t, h and a have practically merged, and I'll wager anything that within two months the M won't be that large or that confident. No doubt dear Martha was full of *frissons* when she ran off with Tony. She probably still is. But it won't be long before those chills grow less enticing. They're going to lose intensity. And I fear that one morning, maybe a year or two or three from now — or maybe even in a week — Martha's going to wake up and wonder what in the world she's done." Mary looked at that moment as sad as I'd ever seen her.

"Do you think she'll be back?" I asked.

"Yes, she'll be back. But it won't be the same Martha. It'll be a different Martha, and I'll have to get to know her all over again." She sighed. "I didn't think she'd fallen in love with him, you know. There's so much she never told me." Then she ripped the postcard in two.

I had no idea what the gesture meant. "Will she still be your friend?"

"Of course, Alistair. Why would you think otherwise? Don't you know? Martha and I are friends for life."

When Agnes returns to the living room sometime later, she has regained her composure. I have decided that with her — as with Mary, as with Jack — there are some demons best left undisturbed. She is more subdued than before, but it is Christmas. She is — we all are — trying hard. As she busies herself setting the table, she calls out, "You look sad, father."

"Do I?"

"Let's not let the centre—"

"I've said my piece, Agnes. That's forgotten."

"Nothing's ever forgotten, father."

How true.

Martha never did come back, leaving Mary to live out the rest of her life with a core of unresolved sadness. As for Randolph, he hired a private detective agency to track her down — bewildered, he was prepared to forgive all — but after a fruitless year he called off the search. He tried to carry on the business but without Martha's inspiration *ADAMANT EVE* lost its focus. The clientele began drifting away. Randolph, ever the prescient businessman, decided to cut his losses and sold out before the value of the store was too badly eroded. He played with a few new ideas, but his heart was no longer in the game. The last time we saw him, a week or so before his departure for a retirement community in Arizona, he was gaunt and dispirited, and his farewell handshake told me that pushups, too, were now well beyond him.

Agnes, rolling up a table-napkin, says, "What's on your mind, father?"

Martha, I want to say. Her absence. Her *absences*. But that answer would displease Agnes. She retains a fondness for her mother's friend, a soft spot, and to bring up my feelings now would be unseemly, for she would see that her willingness to forgive Martha — Forgive: Is that the word? Accept her, perhaps? Like Randolph, like Mary — strikes me as a betrayal of her mother.

So, to make her happy, I say, "Your mother."

And saying it makes it true. My trick turns back on me. Mary, my dear Mary . . .

Then I shake myself. This mood must not be allowed to prevail.

"Listen," I say, leaning forward in my chair, "do you remember when we met Mike Pearson in Ottawa?"

"Mike Pearson? You mean the prime minister?"

"Well, he wasn't prime minister at the time, this was before. You must remember. We'd just toured the parliament buildings and were making our way off the hill when all of a sudden there he was, in the flesh, striding across the lawn. His jacket was unbuttoned — it was a fine, warm day — and I remember you saying how silly his bow-tie looked, that no man who wore a bow-tie would ever amount to much. Hah! Shows how much you know! Within months he would have the Nobel Prize. No wonder you don't remember. Too embarrassed to, probably."

"But—"

"Silliest thing — I could have kicked myself for forgetting the camera. Don't you remember? He stopped and shook our hands and asked where we were from and wished us a good visit to the nation's capital."

"But I was so—"

"Don't you remember how hard you laughed when he shook Agnes's hand and declared that she looked like a good little Liberal? Don't you remember?"

"Agnes's hand?"

"Yes, yes. Why don't you remember?"

"But how could I? That would have been in fifty-six, fifty-seven?"

"Fifty-seven. Definitely fifty-seven."

"I was only five. I hardly remember anything—"

"Five? What d'you mean?" I am baffled. How can Mary not remember meeting the great man? How can't she—

A swift movement, intimations of alarm. A hand light on my shoulder. A soft voice. "Father? Father, it's me, Agnes."

Agnes? "Yes, of course. It's . . . Agnes. You're . . ."

Again, as so often, my heart aches.

Then the fear follows, shuddering through my body like a shower of ice.

Suddenly François clatters into the living room, his tough little body rambunctious with an enviable energy.

Taken by his joy, hungry for a taste of it, I open my arms to him. This brings him up short. A shadow of uncertainty crosses his face — but only for a moment. The joy blossoms again and he hurls himself onto me, crushing me back into the chair,

❧

knocking the wind out of me, embracing away the fear and sadness with arms that clasp the back of my neck in their rich
warmth. I am only vaguely aware of Agnes's gasp of surprise —
and then, as if from some great distance, of her laughter that
begins in anxiety before opening up in relief.

Agnes, my daughter, cannot imagine me as a man who will
fling his arms open to a child. She cannot imagine me doing anything, everything, for him. I have not been that kind of father to
her. I suspect that, despite the war, she sees in me, the man she
has known all her life, no possibility of heroism.

$\mathcal{H}e$ *pulls the chair so close to my desk,* his knees must be pressed hard against the metal front. His arms spread like eagle wings out onto the desk top, as if to embrace it. He is a short fellow, and stout — he comes within an inch of being rotund — and those arms, bared from the elbows, hardly look like arms at all, more like the muscled thighs of some furry animal. What hair he has left is drawn like a bar-code across his bald pate.

"Well, Frank," I say, trying to hide my wariness with a show of gaiety. "It certainly has been a long time." Until his retirement, Frank was our once-a-week gardener.

"To be precise, Mr. Professor, five years, three months and twelve days. Your place was the last one I did before giving it all up." He taps a thick index finger at his temple. "The date is written in my head. How is the lawn by the way?"

"In fair shape. I take care of it myself, you know."

He puffs up his cheeks and spits out the air with friendly scepticism. "I can imagine," he says.

"You should come by sometime, have a look for yourself."

A thoughtful look comes to him. "Maybe I will one of these days. Who knows?"

"And the business?"

"I sold it. There was no one to give it to."

I wonder what he is doing here — he has to have deliberately tracked me down — but to ask strikes me as awkward. So instead I say, "How did you know I'd be here?"

"I called your home. The missus told me where to find you. How is she, by the way? She sounded tired."

"Mary? Not bad. She has a heart condition, you know."

"Sorry to hear it. Give her my regards."

"I'll be sure to." I lean forward, my hand reaching to a stack of essays. "Well, Frank, it's been a pleasure seeing you again. Good of you to drop by."

But he doesn't stir. The arms remain where they are, splayed on my desk. "This is not just a social visit, Mr. Professor. After five years, three months and twelve days, that would be strange, don't you think?"

Indeed. "So what can I do for you, Frank?"

"A little favour, Mr. Professor."

"A little favour . . ." I repeat the words, knowing that after five years, three months and twelve days, there can be no *little* favour.

His eyes search my desk. He sees a writing pad and helps himself to a sheet of paper. "Not for me, Mr. Professor," he says. "For Boobie."

"Boobie? Who is Boobie, Frank?"

He does not answer. Instead, with great deliberation, he shreds the paper with his fingers. He holds the shreds up to me.

"Boobie, Mr. Professor," he says, "is a young man who has not yet learnt that you should never trust your fate to a piece of paper."

Then he releases the shreds and watches them flutter onto my desk.

Frank — Otto Steiglitz Frank — first saw Boobie and his elder brother on a summer's day a year ago. They were standing at the corner outside the apartment building where Frank has lived alone since the death of his wife three years after his retirement. When the building's superintendent was absent — ill or on vacation — Frank stood in for him.

On that hot summer morning, Frank had just set off to do some errands when he spotted them: Boobie, a petulant-looking sixteen-year-old; his brother, a year or two older, staring puzzled at a piece of paper in his hand. As he walked by, the brother said with almost obsequious politeness, "Good morning, sir. Forgive me for disturb you, but where is Concorde Street?"

Frank, who resents having his thoughts interrupted, replied, "Concorde? Never heard of it."

The brother, taller than Frank by a foot, assumed an ingratiating smile. "We are refugees, sir, from—"

"I don't care who you are or where you're from, I still never heard of Concorde Street. Good luck to you." But he was intrigued despite himself, and slowed his pace.

"Thank you in all case, sir," the brother said to him. And to Boobie he added, "Oh, Boobie, remove that thunderstorm from face. We will find Concorde Street and when we do—"

Boobie's face swelled with fury and he lashed out at his brother in a language unknown to Frank.

His brother cut him short. "Speak to me in the new language, Boobie. This other, it is of another life."

"We never find Concorde Street!" Boobie screamed. "Three

225

times you say, Look, let us ask that gentleman, he look like he live here, he must know. And three times, nobody know! Why you not listen to me? Buy a map, find Concorde Street, go there."

"Boobie, Boobie, calm yourself. You are too young to—"

"I am sixteen year old, you *balkash*! Two years more old and you think you have wisdom of the world!"

Frank saw his brother hang his head in shame. He saw Boobie's face soften.

Then he continued on his way and was soon out of earshot.

Later, Boobie's brother would say, "I do not mean to treat Boobie as child, but we have only each other left in this world, and it is my job to care for him. I want spare him worry, and if I treat him as child sometimes it is because I am aware, oh so painfully aware!, that he has been robbed of childhood. He was dodging mortar shells when he should be riding bicycle. He was hiding from sniper when he should be hiding with girl. You understand?"

And Boobie, making a face, would say, "Do not dramatize, brother. My childhood only little worry." And to Frank: "My brother, this *balkash*, he study two years Academy of Dramatic Arts. He learn English, French. But acting, he learn nothing! Dramatize, dramatize, all the time."

But then Boobie would confess that even here, in the street, he felt exposed and unshielded, that his backbone remained taut in anticipation of the hot bite of impact. That he saw the neat buildings as blackened ruins, apartments revealed through rubble, the school at the corner dismantled and smoking, the street pitted with shell holes. The corners of his eyes, he would say, wove constantly among the shadows, seeking movement and the glint of a rifle-barrel. And then a car might drive by or someone on a bicycle, and their leisurely pace would cause his pulse to quicken. And the sounds and sights at the park two streets over

— children laughing in the playground, boys whacking balls on the tennis courts; men and women stretched out sleepily on the grass or diving into the pool — were so unbearably carefree, he panicked for the people.

When Frank returned from his errands, he was not happy to see Boobie and his brother lounging on the lawn at the entrance to the apartment building. Averting his eyes, he headed up the walk. "I mind my business, Mr. Professor, and these young men were not my business. Besides, I didn't like the look of them. There was something desperate, and desperation is never pretty."

Boobie's brother leapt to his feet and, dusting the seat of his pants, ran over to Frank. "A great pleasure to see you again, sir," he said.

"Again?" Frank replied. "What do you mean 'again'? I've never seen you before in my life."

"Just a little time ago, sir. We are refugees. We are looking for Concorde Street but you said you don't know where it is."

"Told you — wasn't me. I know Concorde Street. I live here. This is it."

"I know, sir. I see the sign."

"So if you know, why're you going around asking people where it is, Mr. Smarty-pants?"

"Before, sir. Before to see the sign."

"Congratulations, then. You found it. Now, if you'll excuse me, my bags are heavy." As Frank made for the door, he saw Boobie impatiently jerk his head at his brother.

"Excuse me, sir," the brother called again, running up to open the outer door for Frank.

"What now?"

"We wait for superintendent, sir. I push button. No answer. Do you know—"

"What business you got with the superintendent?"

"For apartment, sir. For my brother and me."

Frank paused, eyeing Boobie then his brother. "You can pay rent?"

Boobie's brother released the door and reached into his coat pocket. "I have letter for superintendent, sir. Rent guaranteed for six month by church sponsors. Also, I have found work."

Frank considered this for a moment, then said, "You opening the door for me or not?"

The brother, reaching for the door knob, said, "The superintendent, sir?"

"He's back," Frank said as he entered the lobby. "Follow me."

Later, Boobie would ask Frank why he had not told them where Concorde Street was, and Frank would teach him a new word: "Cussedness."

When Boobie understood the word, he glowered at Frank. "Not nice, Mr. Frank."

"Nobody pays me to be nice, Mr. Professor."

Mary was it who once characterized Frank as tough-tongued. "He's loud about the little things," she said, "because he can't do anything about the big things." He had thrown a tantrum over the damage a neighbourhood dog had done rooting about in a flower bed.

Boobie would tell him about the excitement they felt when they saw the street sign, when they saw the number of the building they had been sent to by the man at the church group. He would tell of breaking into a trot. "From relief," he would say. To scamper from the openness.

His brother pressed long and hard at the red button labelled SUPERINTENDENT. Waiting for a response, he ran his eye over the walls, at the joints, along the aluminum frame of the main door. Boobie knew he was admiring the workmanship, the finesse with which the construction had been completed, even here in a lobby no longer new and haphazardly cleaned. He had been doing this since their arrival in this country, marvelling over the washroom at the airport, at the church basement where they were housed for the first month, at the university dormitory where they were housed for the second.

Boobie found himself growing increasingly impatient with this stream of wonderment. His brother had dreamt — and continued to dream — of being an architect. "Actor! Architect!" Boobie said to Frank. "Maybe he build scenery in theatre, no?" Before the troubles began, he had spent a summer labouring at a construction site, pushing wheelbarrows, hooking buckets of fresh cement to hoists. And now, here he was, talking like some expert. Sometimes he suspected that his brother was more pained by the destruction of their beautiful city than by the decimation of its inhabitants.

Once, invited by his brother to admire the craftsmanship of a small city park — the shaping of the flowerbeds, the style and placing of the benches — Boobie had said, "Home, too, look like this once, long time ago. Only better."

"Better, Boobie?" his brother had replied. "Different, yes, but better?"

"He need believe this," Boobie said to Frank. "That home not better, here better."

His brother pressed again at the button and when, after a minute, there was still no answer, he said, "Come, Boobie, he is absent, but that means he will return. Let us sit outside and drink the sunshine."

"Sit outside?" Boobie said. "Where? No benches."

"We sit on lawn," his brother said. "Remember, Boobie, in this country, grass is not just for admiration."

And so they sat out in the sun. It was hot, Boobie would tell Frank. They watched their shadows diminish and retreat and pool under them. He grew tired and thirsty, and thought they should return the following day. In all that time, no one entered or left the building.

His brother, discouraged by the long wait, gestured towards a pipe hugging the side of the building. "There is a tap, Boobie," he said in their language. "They must use it for watering the grass. I'm sure no one would begrudge you a few drops."

Boobie went over to the tap. The water gushed out hot, and when it had cooled down tasted of rust. Boobie drank a little, washed his face, splashed some on his neck.

The gestures felt familiar, he would tell Frank, and he was reminded of washing in similar fashion in the ruined city, an impatient queue behind him, people with buckets and pots and pans waiting to get the water that no longer flowed to their homes. Suddenly, crouched at the tap, the water grew frigid on Boobie's neck, and his ears filled with the echoes of long-ago screams, his mind slithering to images of the line dissolving behind him, people scattering in every direction, running to the scantest of cover as their utensils clattered to the cobblestones like metallic rain. And where before there had been clucks and mutterings of impatience, now there were only moans. Steps away, a toddler gripped the hand of her prostrate mother. Farther away, a kneeling man spouted purple from his chest.

Boobie barely made it back to his brother on legs gone wobbly.

"And then you come, and you played with us for cussedness," Boobie would say, resentful.

The windows of the apartment looked out over the tarred roof of a strip-mall across the street. Beyond the parking lot, on the other side of the main street, was the neighbourhood park: a playground busy with swings and slides; tennis courts; a volleyball court; and, beyond a knoll on which several people lay sunbathing, a large playing field.

Boobie's brother, standing beside him looking out, said, "Look, Boobie. A football field. We can play." And he did a little dance, arms upraised, one foot as if teasing an imaginary soccer ball.

Frank, waiting, watching, recognised the choreography. As a young man, he, too, had played.

But Boobie shook his head. "Football," he said. "No, no more football."

His brother went limp. "Boobie, you must let go," he pleaded. "What is done, done."

"You present, brother," Boobie replied quietly. "You present to see the soldiers play football with Adriana. For me, some things never done. Cannot."

His brother nodded. "No football, then." Then he shook his head. "I should not tell you. Was mistake."

Frank, impatient, tossing a set of keys from hand to hand, said, "Well, you like or not?"

Boobie's brother looked to him for the decision, and Boobie — aware, like Frank, that his brother's face said yes — took one last look around. The look on his face, Frank said, was plaintive. The place was small. A single bedroom, which they would have to share; a bathroom confined enough to present danger to elbows and toes; a kitchen in which two people could stand only in profile. It was clean, though, the furnishings well-used but serviceable — and it was, as Boobie's brother had said repeatedly to Frank despite his lack of interest, sturdily built.

"Well, Boobie," his brother said. "Home?"

At last, Boobie nodded. "Home," he agreed, but he pronounced the word as if it were strangling him, in a voice, Frank says, that committed itself to nothing beyond the white walls.

They moved in with one suitcase and a grocery bag each.

Frank says, "That was one grocery bag of possessions more

than I had when I came to this country."

"Where are you from, Frank?" The lightness of his accent has always made him unplaceable.

"I am, Mr. Professor," he says with great solemnity, "from the country of the past tense."

"Very poetic, Frank, but where on the map would I find it?" Europe, certainly, possibly eastern but more likely central.

"On no map, Mr. Professor, will you find it. But it is real, none the less, and is a country such as you have never conceived of. May you never see it, for there no one ever just visits. And what you must do to leave, well . . ."

Frank, clearly, is turning mystical on me. I have no patience with such things but his story of Boobie and his brother intrigues me. "English is not your first language, Frank."

"Not the one I heard when I left my mother's womb, no. But the one that became mine when, by a miracle, I was given a second life."

All right, I tell myself, he has a right to the mystery of his life. It is his life, after all.

"A second life, Mr. Professor," he says. "Not everybody is given one, but it is not so rare a thing as you might think. Everyday, you know, all over the world, people like Boobie and his brother arrive with their suitcase and their grocery bag, step timidly through a door that will never seem to them solid enough, and take possession of its key with a wonderment that tells you they are terrified — absolutely terrified, Mr. Professor! — of waking up."

For several weeks, Frank saw them leave together in the early morning and return separately in the late afternoon. Each carried a small brown paper bag in which, Frank assumes, was their lunch. He also believes, although he cannot prove this, that they used the same small brown paper bags day after day. This, says Frank, was a familiar frugality. In addition to the bag, Boobie, on his way to language classes, carried a textbook and a notebook.

Boobie rarely acknowledged Frank. His elder brother usually smiled and nodded. They never spoke.

At the end of the day, Boobie would return before his brother, his books in one hand, a grocery bag in the other.

Later he would tell Frank that this was their arrangement. They agreed in the morning on what they would eat that evening. On his way home, Boobie picked up "the necessaries". When his brother returned, they attempted — together, so that neither could blame the other — to concoct dinner. "We are not," his brother said, "adopt at cooking."

And Boobie, glowing, said, "Adept, you *balkash*, adept. We learned yesterday."

His brother, stung, said, "Boobie! How many times I tell you? The new language! Say no more *balkash*."

"Okay," Boobie said. "How you say *balkash* in new language?"

"No way to say it. Closest translation, perhaps, motherfucker-shithead."

"Okay, Motherfucker-shithead," Boobie said gaily.

Frank, alarmed, exercised a gentle diplomacy — "Not my strong suit, Mr. Professor, diplomacy never did much for me, but sometimes . . ." *Balkash*, he said, had such a nice ring to it. And then, to change the subject, he asked about their cooking.

"Gloom from one, Mr. Professor. Dismay from the other. A pathetic sight."

"We try," Boobie's brother said. "Fry porkchop."

"You can throw," Boobie said. "Like frisbee."

"Boil potato."

"Boil very long," Boobie said. "Become syrup."

"Bake chicken."

"Again very long," Boobie said. "Skin, bone. Meat hard like shoe. Finish, I say to brother. Just once, just *once*, I like to sit at table and be not aghast."

"Aghast?" his brother said.

Boobie translated for him and his brother nodded in sad comprehension. In frustration his brother ran to the supermarket and returned with an armful of frozen dinners.

Boobie said, "That night, before to go to bed, I not brush teeth. I fall asleep with taste of food in mouth, and a smile on lips."

For a week they voraciously devoured frozen dinners, two, sometimes three, at a time. His brother discovered that the flavour of the mashed potatoes was improved by mixing in the square of apple-pie beside it, but it was Boobie who took the credit for suggesting they also add in the peas and diced carrots.

At the end of the week, however, his brother calculated their food bill. In five days they had consumed almost three weeks of their food budget. This could not go on. Frozen dinners, they decided, would be saved for a Saturday evening treat, weekdays given over to experimentation.

There would come the day when Boobie and his brother would invite Frank to dinner. He would watch as Boobie concocted one of his inventions. A can of tuna and a can of mushroom soup mixed with rice cooked as prescribed on the package. Then a can of peas heavily sprinkled with black pepper and carefully stirred so as not to squash the peas. The result would be grey in colour and gluey in texture. Frank's stomach would heave slightly at the sight of it. But Boobie would glow with pride and there would be no way out.

"A surprise, Mr. Professor. It was rich, and satisfying. Who would know to look at it? I ate my fill. Then I went to my place to fetch a bottle of brandy. The boys are young, but after what they have been through, what harm in a little brandy?"

Over the coming months, the boys thrived on the routine — language classes for Boobie, work for his brother.

Frank could not say with any precision what was the nature of Boobie's brother's work — or, at least, he could not explain the purpose of the thing he made. He knew that he ran a machine which shaved curls from a minuscule daisy, giving shape to the stainless-steel petals. What happened to the daisies, what function they eventually fulfilled, was a mystery, even to Boobie's brother. Frank knew only that his hours were long and his pay good enough that they had no need to appeal to their church sponsors for the rent. They were proud of this, and genuinely taken aback when Frank suggested that they accept the sponsors' money and bank the difference.

This was when Boobie, visibly distressed, fetched his passport from the bedroom. "Look," he said, handing the passport to Frank. "Look. Passport. Papers. You see visa? That is like life. Need nothing else. Passport-papers-visa. Like gold. Brother has job. One day I have job. One day house, maybe. All possible now." Then he retrieved the passport from Frank and pressed it to his chest.

"And you know, Mr. Professor, believe it or not, the boy had tears in his eyes."

One afternoon, as Frank was raking up the last of the golden leaves that the wind had blown in from the park, he saw Boobie coming in from his classes. He was early, and was walking with unusual rapidity. Frank waved and called out. Boobie returned the greeting, but did not break his pace to the entrance. He was, Frank said, ashen-faced.

Later Boobie would tell him about his language class. He would tell him about the instructor, a young woman whose glasses refused to remain planted on the bridge of her nose. He would tell him that every thirty seconds or so — Boobie found

himself counting: a thousand-and-one, a-thousand-and-two . . .
— she would press the glasses back up into place with her right
hand as if anointing herself with the Father but choosing not to
proceed to the Son and the Holy Spirit.

The gesture both pleased and irritated Boobie. He liked its
elegance, the sweep of the arm, the light flick of the middle
finger at the gold frame and then, almost imperceptibly, at the
curl of dark hair that crept constantly down her forehead.

But the gesture offered, too, another association. It put him in
mind of Ingam — so long his best friend and now . . . someone
for whom he could find no word.

"Ingam!" Boobie's brother said. "*Balkash*, that one! Big
balkash!"

But Boobie only shrugged. Ingam had treasured the gesture,
this blessing of the self: before eating, before sitting an exam,
before putting boot to football and, always, after scoring a goal.
He was, in this, not unusual in his communtiy, only more intense
— or, perhaps, creative — than most. Ingam would cross himself
before diving into the swimming pool, and once again after he
had emerged from it.

There were those, of both his faith and Boobie's, who treated
him with a gentle derision. Hey, Ingam!, they would call out, do
you cross yourself before you take a piss? Hey, Ingam! Do you
plan to cross yourself before doing it with a girl? Boobie, though,
never participated in the teasing. This was, he would explain,
partly because they were friends, partly because he offered to
Ingam's faith the same respect he expected for his own, but
mostly because he was not certain that their friendship, even
though begun before their births when their mothers met in
their gynaecologist's waiting room, would survive even so light-
hearted a betrayal. So he had simply accepted the gesture as being
one of Ingam's mannerisms, like his own nail-biting or his
brother's habit of spitting on his palms and smoothing his hair

when he saw an attractive girl.

It was only later, when everything had changed, that the gesture struck Boobie as a marking of the cardinal points — north, south, west and east — in a world so violated that neighbourhoods had been churned into moonscapes, parks into cemeteries. Only later, after Ingam had chosen to join the armed gangs hunting down "rug-kissers", had the gesture turned sinister. He remembered the morning, just before Sunday lunch, when Ingam had looked at him through narrowed eyes and hissed, "Rug-kisser!"; remembered the moment the way he remembered the day he accidentally slit his palm open with a hunting knife, the skin peeling backwards, slowly filling with blood and with a pain that seared the nerves in his skull; remembered the same sensation coming to him at Ingam's hiss — only it felt as if his belly itself were being sliced in two.

Sitting there in the barren classroom with two dozen others struggling to acquire the new language indispensable to the new life, with the instructor pushing at her glasses and flicking at her curl every thirty seconds, all this had come back to him. Perspiration tickled from his hair, ran cold down his forehead. A drop pooled on his eyebrow, and he found that he could not wipe it away, his arm would not move.

Then the instructor pushed at her glasses, flicked at her curl and said in a patient voice, "Go on, Boobie, repeat after me. Home is where the heart is."

Home: a difficult word for Boobie. It sat unpronounceable on his tongue, defying him. Four letters stripped of meaning — or, rather, with so many meanings that he grew confused in a thicket of associations.

But there it was. The word. Obliging him to confront it. For a moment he felt the eyes of his classmates on him, expectant. He heard their sniffles of impatience tinged with derision.

And then he was no longer there. He was instead hurtling down a tunnel, the sensation not unpleasant, into the serene echoes of a dark and spacious apartment, into the embrace of shadows that he knew. Lemon-coloured walls, hardwood floors polished warm. There were suggestions of corners, alcoves; there were doors that barred no mysteries, the air thick with a familiar mustiness. In the distance, a window glowed white onto the street, beyond it, he knew, the city yet whole. And somewhere not far off, his mother hummed an air of Mozart, her hair hastily knotted into a bun, her pianist's fingers threading a needle or turning a page or thrumming distractedly on the arm of her chair . . .

It was the laughter of his classmates — an embarrassed, uneasy laughter: anyone of them would be next — that wrenched Boobie from the slender, rhythmic fingers back to the classroom, to its white light, unadorned walls, and the chalk-board on which the instructor had written in her beautiful script *Home is where the heart is.* Boobie followed her hand from the glasses, to the curl, to the sentence. A shimmer ran through his jaw. The instructor smiled encouragement, but when the drop of perspiration broke and splashed with a light burn into his eye, she turned from him and sought out another.

"New language, Mr. Frank," Boobie would say into the silence following his story. "But old memory like high wall. Words can not jump."

Boobie's brother placed a hand on his arm. "No, Boobie. Not so hard. Listen. Home is where heart is. See? No sweat."

Boobie thought for a moment and then, enunciating carefully, said, "Horses sweat. Gentlemen perspire."

"And Boobie smiled, Mr. Professor. Imagine. After all that, he smiled. I laughed and, although he didn't get the joke, Boobie's brother laughed too."

Frank says, "You remember the blizzard we had last February,

Mr. Professor? Thirty-six centimeters of snow, winds like a million devils beating the bushes, couldn't see more than ten meters in front of you?"

I nod, the memory still fresh. When I opened the door for the newspaper the following morning — the blizzard had begun the afternoon before and blown throughout the night — a chest-high wall of snow blocked my path, the flattened snow bearing the imprint of the door.

The evening before, Frank had been out shovelling the path to the front door of the apartment building. "Yes, the snow was still coming down in buckets but walk must be clear as possible, so you shovel five, ten times. No tenant falls, less snow in the lobby."

Just as he was scooping up the last shovelful, Boobie emerged from the whiteout, trudging through the drifts. He was hugging his books to his chest, and he looked cold and miserable. He was much later than usual.

Shaking himself free of snow in the lobby, ignoring Frank's glare of disapproval, Boobie said that he had had to walk home, an hour's trek through the blizzard. His brother had forgotten to give him his expense money and he had discovered too late that he had no bus tickets left.

"Nose frozen," Boobie said. "And hands and foots and ears. All this, for money! My grandfather rich man. Farmer. Many, many hectares of wheat. Every year good crap. Need twenty, thirty men to help harvest. Now my grandfather land take over. My grandfather dead. Grandmother. Father. Mother. And the land full of blood. Don't know if blood good for growing. What you think, Mr. Frank? Like poison, maybe? I think need many, many years before can have good crap there again."

"What would you have done, Mr. Professor? What the boy was saying was heartbreaking — but the way he said it, this crap-crop mistake of his, that was hilarious. Me, I said nothing. No point to puncture his emotion. And besides, I had to bite insides of my cheeks to stop from laughing. I feel bad about that but, as you see now, for me the humour is still stronger than the pain."

As it is for me. "That was good of you, Frank. To say nothing."

"Good had nothing to do with it," he says. "Not to be cruel — that was what I wanted. Not being cruel is not the same thing as being good, Mr. Professor."

Then came the day when everything changed — the day a new tenant moved in.

"He was a big man, built like a tree trunk. He had a meaty nose. And his eyes, Mr. Professor, they were pig eyes. Narrow and hooded, and always pink, never white. Not easy to read. You could take the half-shut lids for a kind of dimness — you know, thick in the head — whereas the truth is that they were sharp and watchful, like a security camera. Eyes that miss nothing because their survival depends on missing nothing. People like that, they were a dime a dozen when I was young, Mr. Professor. Here in this country we don't have too many like that but still you see them sometimes, in the rough parts of town, and in the financial district. In black leather jackets or three-piece suits. In my day, too, they usually wore uniforms."

"You're setting me up, Frank. You're describing a villain. You're showing me some sharpie in the shadows in a silent movie."

Frank sighs. "Okay, Mr. Professor, you're right. The description I just gave, that came later. At first, all I saw was this beefy guy who turned up one day, rented a bachelor apartment and paid for three months, up front, cash. Didn't talk much. But he was not just silent. He *surrounded himself in silence*, if you grasp my meaning. A word here or there, a grunt from time to time—"

"There you go again, Frank. A grunt. Really, now."

"You know another word for grunt, Mr. Professor? He didn't chirp, this guy."

"Perhaps he was merely a man of few words?"

"No doubt, Mr. Professor — and of many grunts. Now, if you will excuse me, time is beginning to grow short."

"Short, Frank?"

"Yes. May I continue?"

"By all means, Frank. Do."

Boobie would not be the one to come to him. Boobie's brother it was who came knocking at his apartment one evening, his face grim with shaken optimism. They spoke there, at the door, Frank guarding his privacy.

"Like a watch-dog, Mr. Professor. I was not too happy. It was late. The kitchen sink again, probably. Those boys don't understand — the sink doesn't eat garbage."

Boobie's brother got straight to the point. The new tenant, he said, what was his name?

"That's private," Frank snapped back. "If you want to know, ask him yourself."

"Then Mr. Professor, a terrible thing happened to the boy's face. A terrible thing. Every nerve in his face went haywire. It was as if, right under his skin, you understand, as if an entire ant-colony suddenly went crazy, scrambling here and there, crawling and jumping over each other. I have seen many ugly things in my life, Mr. Professor, but never this. The boy was unrecognizable for many seconds. He fought to control his face and when it settled down again, he said, 'The name, Mr. Frank. So I can tell Boobie who it is not.' Damnedest thing, eh, Mr. Professor? 'So I can tell Boobie who it is not'. And then he filled me in."

Her name was Adriana and she had been, along with Ingam, that *balkash*, Boobie's special friend — not his girlfriend, but the first friend he had made at kindergarten, the friend with whom he had moulded plasticine, studied mathematics, gone to the movies and splashed about in the communal swimming pool. Their mothers would say, only half in jest, that they would one day marry, which caused Boobie to turn red and mumble that Adriana was not his type, even though he was too young to have a type.

There had always been something boyish about Adriana, Boobie's brother would tell Frank. She enjoyed playing football and basketball and challenging Boobie to foot races. She was impatient with her hair, which she wore long at her mother's insistence. And her preference for pants over dresses prompted other girls, whose games she found dull and uninteresting, to call her Adrian.

But Adriana could not escape who she was, Boobie's brother would say. She could not hide her eyes, which were intelligent and frank and playful — and suggestive, to older boys like himself, of a great beauty that would soon shape itself around her cheekbones. She could not hide her lips which, beneath the sneer she used to belittle them all, seemed always to be smiling to herself. And when her hair came loose as she raced towards the goalposts! That was a sight that could bring the older boys' conversation to a halt, their words instantly leached of boasting, eyes glazed at the sight of the hair heaving like a lustrous cape around her shoulders. Boobie's brother was not the only one to think: Ahh, give her a few more years . . . — but he was probably the only one to have the thought chased by a light guilt. Adriana was, after all, his brother's special friend.

And then the war started. Life in the city grew hard. Taps ran dry, electrical wires lay curled on the asphalt like dead serpents. Walls disintegrated in the darkness. Soon their city itself was reduced to their neighbourhood. Tall buildings once a half-hour tram ride away became nests for the other side, the dark windows obscuring men with slender rifles and telescopic sights. The mountains surrounding the city, tamed for decades by hikers and picnickers, grew diseased with concealed mortars, heavy artillery, dug-in tanks. Everywhere, the stench of sulphur and burning rubber.

꿏

Then one morning, the men whose presence had kept the other side distant — weary, unshaven men in sneakers and mismatched uniforms, their skin yellowish from malnutrition — were found to have decamped. Snipers no longer targeted their neighborhood, for the streets were now theirs. They were better fed, these others, better dressed, with military insignia on their uniforms and silver crosses glinting at their necks. Within two hours, Boobie's brother would tell Frank, every man between the ages of eighteen and fifty had been rounded up and marched off at gunpoint, their father and uncles among them. It was said that they were still alive, held somewhere in underground prisons. Boobie believed this, but Boobie's brother did not. He believed they were underground, he said, but not in prisons.

Those left behind — girls and women, boys and old men — spent the day and the following night cowering in their homes. The next morning Boobie's brother, driven by a fiery thirst, convinced their mother to let him go in search of water. She would not let Boobie accompany him.

The streets were deserted, he said to Frank, the silence such that his own breathing sounded to him like the harsh winds that rushed down from the mountains every November. Uncertain where to start, the emptiness of the jug in his hand searing his parched throat, he decided to make his way through the back alleys to Adriana's house.

"He let himself in through the back door. It was unlocked, and that put him on his guard. He saw right away that the kitchen had been overturned. He called out softly but no one answered. Then he began making his way through the house. The dining room, the living room, everywhere destruction. Then he went to Adriana's father's study, and what the boy found there, Mr. Professor, human eyes should never see."

At first, Boobie's brother would tell Frank, he could see only the destruction in the morning shadows. The floor carpeted with books and scattered papers. Armchairs upended, paintings slashed. This all flooded the eye, he said, it made him dizzy. Which explained why it was only as he turned to go that he noticed the figure lying on the desk in the far corner in front of the shuttered window.

"The boy's left eyelid began to jump, Mr. Professor, tic-tic-tic-tic, like the wings of some panicky insect. You see, he recognised the clothes right away. The trousers that had been slit open between the legs, the blouse that had been pulled apart. He knew it was Adriana, and he knew something terrible had been done to her. It never occurred to him she would not be alive. He ran over to her and he—"

Frank falls silent, his throat leaping with tension, his eyes focussed unseeing on the middle of my forehead. I wish I had something to offer him to drink.

Finally he finds his voice. "The boy almost fainted, Mr. Professor. Right there, he fell to his knees. For Adriana, you see, Mr. Professor, had no head. It had been cut off. And her body — I will tell you as the boy told me. He said it was as if they had spat all over her with their semen."

Suddenly from the street came yelps of joy and the chatter of excited voices. Boobie's brother peered through the shutters and he saw a group of soldiers standing in a circle on the cobblestones. They were having a game of football, kicking the ball from one to the other. The ball was Adriana's head.

Looking on, impassive, was the man who commanded the troops. He himself took no part; he merely stood by eating peanuts from the shell, chatting quietly with those around him. Boobie's brother recognised him. He had been a well-known rabble rouser in their town before the war. He had seen him many times. The war had given him a reputation for imagination. It was said that he had dispatched entire villages without wasting a bullet; that his favourite technique for instilling obedience in

prisoners was having two of them fight barehanded, the winner
— whose life would be spared — being the first to succeed in
severing the other's testicles with his teeth. His men, it was
known, were permitted to cool their boiling blood between the
legs of enemy women.

"Their game did not last long, Mr Professor. I imagine a head
does not last long when pounded by army boots. The boy waited
for them to leave and then he himself left. He does not remember returning to his home."

Boobie's brother, Frank says, had begun to hiccup as he
got to the end of his tale. "He hiccupped after every word,
Mr. Professor, I was afraid he would throw up." Frank breathes
in hard, as if the telling of the story has robbed him of air. "And
that man, Mr. Professor, that man who calculated his savagery,
had just moved into our building."

Boobie, his brother said, had seen the new tenant. Boobie, his
brother said, was going crazy. "The name, Mr. Frank," Boobie's
brother pleaded. "I must have the name."

"So I told him the name. And I watched him turn grey, his
eyelids darkening like in death."

"Come on, Frank, are you saying the fellow used his real
name? Surely—"

"This kind of arrogance, I know it well, Mr. Professor. The
world is full of people who are not ashamed of having done their
duty, and who want nothing more than to live out their lives in
peace. There are many bakers today, Mr. Professor, who were
once butchers."

I nod in acknowledgement. "Sadly so, Frank. Sadly so."

Frank glances at his watch. "I beg your pardon, Mr. Professor,
for stealing so much of your time." He gestures at the stack of
essays. "I know you are a busy man."

"Quite all right, Frank. Those will wait. Is there more to your
story?"

"Much more, Mr. Professor, but time is growing very short. I will make it quick." Smiling slightly, he gathers in his arms and steeples his fingers between us, not a spiritual gesture but one suggestive, in its shape, of the heart of things. "Last night, Mr. Professor, I could not sleep. In fact, my eyes probably tell you I've been up all night.

"You see, it was four days ago that Boobie's brother came to see me, and after his visit I saw Boobie not once. His brother came and went as usual, but he would only nod at me, he had nothing to say. Then last night his brother came knocking at my door again. He was frantic. He could hardly speak. Something about Boobie. He wanted me to come. How could I not go with him? Giving him the new tenant's name, I had implicated myself, you see.

"Boobie was sitting on the sofa. He was hunched forward, staring at the floor. He had a large kitchen knife in one hand and a file in the other. His brother let me go forward. I didn't need to be told what was happening.

"I sat beside him. He didn't move. I said his name. He didn't react. I reached for the knife — and he tightened his grip on it. I tried speaking to him softly. Put down the knife, Boobie, this is no solution for you, it will get you in trouble, give me the knife, Boobie. I talked and talked, Mr. Professor, for half an hour, an hour. And Boobie said nothing. He would not give up the knife. His brother sat on the floor listening, with tears running down his cheeks. Then he said something to Boobie in their language, and when Boobie replied his eyes were a terrible sight — two wounds bloodied by a flaring rage. His brother trembled as he translated for me. Boobie, he said, wants the head of the *balkash*, nothing but his head. Then, hiccupping again, he told me that Boobie hadn't slept in four days.

"There are times, Mr. Professor, when words are not enough. There was only one thing to do. I stood up, pretending I was leaving and, without warning, kicked the knife from Boobie's hand. He growled like an animal and threw himself at me. I pinned him in my arms. He pounded at me, but feebly, he was weak from lack of sleep. He cried, sobbed, screamed. He tried to drive his fingers into my eyes, and that was when I released him from my grip and smashed him in the face. That was all it took. One blow. He went down for the count.

"I helped his brother put him into bed. He said he would keep watch. I examined the bruise on his cheek where I had hit him. It was not serious. He looked so young, Mr. Professor, lying there asleep. A child. When I left, I thought it prudent to take the knife with me.

"Back in my apartment, I could not settle down. Boobie was on my mind. I thought I could warn the new tenant. I thought I could call the police. But what good would any of that do? Boobie would be the one in trouble, a refugee intent on murder. The new tenant, what he did, that was somewhere else. We in this country do not concern ourselves too much with blood spilled elsewhere, but our own carpets, we like to keep them clean. Warning the tenant, calling the police — that was out of the question. So I sought another solution, and I was many hours, Mr. Professor, in understanding what had to be done. It would be dawn, and much thought later, before I could bring myself to act.

"When the first light gleamed in the sky, I wrote a note to Boobie with your name and telephone number and slipped it under their door. Then, after thoroughly washing Boobie's knife, I went to the new tenant's apartment and knocked.

"He was some minutes in opening it, still asleep, I guess, and when he did he was suspicious. Good morning, I said. He grunted. There's an emergency with the building's plumbing, I said, I have to check your kitchen taps. Come back later, he said. No, I said, it's an emergency. He swung the door wide and lumbered ahead of me into the darkened living room. I saw that in his hand he held a stretch of pipe — and I knew, Mr. Professor: A man with a clear conscience does not arm himself before opening his door.

"He stopped and swept his arm towards the kitchen. As I stepped past him, I turned quickly and drove Boobie's knife deep into his belly. It entered so easily I thought I had missed. So I did it again, and a third time. I had no thoughts then, and no feelings, but his surprise, Mr. Professor, was a wonder to behold.

"'For Adriana' I said uselessly as he fell to his knees before me. *Balkash.*

"Then I opened the drapes to the brightening sky. We had this morning a glorious dawn, Mr. Professor. Did you see it?"

Frank's steepled fingers lose their tension, rise so that they rest fingertip to fingertip. He stares into the oval they have shaped: as if into the depths of a transparent sphere. Or into the orb of the sun, rising.

I am left speechless.

What am I to do with this tale? How do I gauge its veracity?

"Frank," I eventually manage to say, "this story. It's incredible."

"Incredible?" He gazes hard at me. "You do not believe me, Mr. Professor. I hear it in your voice, I see it in your face. You think I am telling tales."

"Truthfully, Frank, I don't know what to think." How can he trust Boobie's brother's tale of brutality? And if it is true, what certainty is there that the new tenant is the same fellow? Has he considered the possibility of a fatal resemblance? Even the name is hardly conclusive. I am, I realize, terribly fearful for Frank.

"All I have told you is true," he says. "And Boobie and his brother are not wrong. There are faces you never forget, Mr. Professor. Never. Some faces gouge their way into your memory. Every hair, every pore, every flutter of a nostril. This I know."

His hands curl into fists, and he thrusts a forearm at me. The

fingers of his other hand brush the thick hair aside and I recoil at
the sight of the blue numbers tattooed into his skin.

In the vertiginous silence into which we have tumbled, he will not
speak of it. He will speak, he says, only of the aftermath.

"This you can understand, Mr. Professor."

There was, he says dismissively, no life to go back to.

"In the country of the past tense, Mr. Professor, the only place
to go, if you can, is to the future."

It was as simple, and as complicated, as that.

"I was like an orphan flung onto another planet. I could
remake everything. I began by changing my name. Otto Frank is
my name because it has been for so long, but it is not the name I
was born with. An easy enough matter. At the end of the war,
who had documents? So when they asked, What is your name, I
made one up, right there on the spot. I said, Otto Steiglitz Frank,
this is my name. Then they wrote it down, it became real, and it
found its way onto every document, making them real and itself
even more so.

"When I arrived in this country, I set about finding myself a
wife. A wife — and I was decided about this — who had not been
through what I had. A wife whose life had not been broken in
two. A wife whose greatest worry had been, perhaps, where to get
new nylons or which club to go to on Saturday night. I found her
easily enough, and our life of many years together was longer on
happiness than on sadness.

"But I will confess something to you, Mr. Professor. Having
this kind of wife was a miscalculation on my part. You see, many
of my fellow survivors felt a desperate need to have children, to
sew back some of the threads to the past by making a future of
flesh and blood. And despite my attitude I too felt that need to
some extent, not for yesterday, you understand, but for tomorrow. My wife, she felt no such need — none at all. And perhaps

because of this, she failed to conceive. Ever. We had a good life together, but this absence in our home, it was to her a relief and to me a dull ache. We never spoke of it."

As he speaks, his free hand brushes continually at the hair on his arm, pressing the strands back into place, returning the tattooed numbers to their obscurity.

"When the knife went into him, Mr. Professor, not once, not twice, but three times, I knew that I had lived fifty years just for this moment. I am not a religious man, Mr. Professor — how could I be after all I have seen? — but I knew that this moment redeemed everything."

"How so, Frank? How so?" My words emerge mumbled, lips barely able to move.

Frank says, "You see, doing what was necessary was no way for the young Boobie to start his new life. But doing what was necessary is a good way for me to end mine. Besides, Mr. Professor, a parent would willingly give his life for his child, no? Without thought? Even if not of his flesh and blood?"

I am not often dazed by words, but now I am. Then I think of my daughter, remember my unshadowed conviction that I would willingly trade my life for hers, and I am dazed again.

Frank gets to his feet. "Now, if you will excuse me, I must return home. The authorities must be notified."

"Just like that?"

"You know another way, Mr. Professor?"

My head spins. "Frank, is there anything I can do for you?"

"For me, nothing. I don't want to hear from you. You must stay away. I am an old man. Let them do what they will. But Boobie, he will contact you, and when he does, remember that he is young enough to think he can trust his fate to a piece of paper — a passport, a visa. Remember, Mr. Professor, that nobody can afford that illusion in this world."

꿎

When he leaves I remain rooted in my chair. I realize too late that I have not shaken his hand.

The following day, Frank's photo is in the newspaper, as is a photo of his victim. I recognise the pig eyes, the meaty nose. The story identifies Frank as a retired gardener, his victim as a man notorious in his country for his role in several massacres. There are international warrants out for his arrest.

On the television news there is a report about the killing and the arrest. There is a brief shot of Frank being led in handcuffs from a police cruiser. He looks tired but walks upright. On his lips is the drugged smile of a man relieved of a great burden.

Neither report makes mention of Boobie.

Some weeks later, as I am sorting through some books in my office, the telephone rings. When I answer, Frank's voice — at least, Frank's voice as it might have sounded over half a century ago — says, "Hello, Mr. Professor. I am Boobie."

We arrange for him to come see me.

François toddles in from wherever he's been. His eyes are bright, and the front of his shirt is damp. He announces that Ruth-Ann's awake. He's been cleaning the tub for the bath she wishes to take. Agnes gives me a baleful look — "Last minute brownie points for Santa," she says. "Taking no chances," I mumble back — and hurries to inspect the damage. She will see to Ruth-Ann, she says.

"Maman," François calls after her, "je veux écouter de la musique."

"Vas-y, mon chou," she calls back. "Mais pas trop fort, okay? On veut pas déranger papa."

He squats before the CD player. His fingers press here and there, confidently summoning lights in Christmas colours, a golden band splattered red and green. In an instant, a rising of strings. *I'll Be Home for Christmas.* The sound is sweet, full of longing, just an energetic step or two away from mournful. And it is distant. Barely within my reach. Wholly beyond my grasp.

I turn the contraption up as high as the volume will go.

Agnes has complained that she knows almost nothing of my life. She has not made these complaints in dramatic fashion; they have been lobbed in passing. And, truth to tell, I have shared little with her beyond a few rudimentary stories. Once, when she was in high school, she sat me down before a tape-recorder for a class project. Five minutes later it was all over. I did not, apparently, give a good interview. Agnes was left with the feeling — this I learnt from Mary — that I do not trust her.

And she's not wholly wrong.

Not that she's not a fully trustworthy individual. Even the bank has recognised that by making her a manager. No. The distrust I learnt of my daughter I learnt when she was a child.

In my earlier years, I was subject to a bad habit. If Mary criticised me for something — Couldn't I be gentler with the dishes? Hadn't I fixed the kitchen faucet yet? — I'd swallow the sharpness that came to my tongue in order to avoid a squabble. An unhappy Mary was a blunt Mary, and riposte merely made her blunter. So I'd wander off somewhere and mutter away my vexation, venting steam through words. After they'd passed my lips, I'd find that the annoyance too had departed with them, or so I told myself. Mary cured me of that habit, mostly — the vexation never really left the tongue; it was merely absorbed into the flesh — but for a long time, when Agnes was a child, I remained a mumbler. My words were intended only for myself. They were not keepsakes. They were offerings to the wind. Unfortunately, twice the wind carried them to young Agnes's ears — and twice she carried them to Mary's. There was hell to pay.

Agnes was a young child at the time, five or six. Her actions were those of innocence. But it was then that I learned discretion in her presence, a discretion that has cast a wide and long net.

So if Agnes feels that her father is something of a stranger, or at least an unknown quantity, she's not wrong. She also feels, though, that she has the right to rummage around in my head. Yet Agnes, growing through adolescence into adulthood, was uncompromising in claiming her independence. She demarcated her territory, she drew boundaries around a life of which I had, and still have, only the vaguest idea. A life of vanishings and breathlessness. Inviolable. Mary was never bothered by it, and so I felt free not to be either.

It was around her fourteenth birthday that Agnes began slipping away from me, or at least that her alienation became manifest. Since our child would bear my family name, I'd insisted that he or she be named for Mary's parents, Arthur or Agnes. Our daughter had always known the provenance of her name, but it was on this particular day that she learnt that it had been at my insistence and not Mary's. I remember her inexplicable fury when she turned on me and demanded to know why I had hobbled her with such a name. "Agnes! No one's named Agnes these days! It's musty, it's tone-deaf, it's got no ring!" For several months afterwards, her friends would telephone and ask to speak to Sunbeam — a name which endured until the day she realised she'd named herself after a line of kitchen appliances. I saw in Agnes's character so much of the mother, so much of the aunt, and so little of the father. We have lived our lives in consequence, as familiar strangers.

All of this I hope she avoids with her own child. And if she cannot avoid it, I hope she will ensure that the blank pages are one day sketched in. We do not owe our children rummaging rights. We do owe them a sense of our and their yesterdays.

François taps my arm, pulling me from my reverie. There is a look of distress on his face. "Regarde, grand-papa," he says, pointing to the tree. A string of lights at the very top has gone dead. The red bulb beneath the angel no longer glows, the angel herself now baleful, cast in shadow.

I check the plug, but it's secure in its outlet. "Oh, dear," I say, "we have a little problem, don't we, François?" I take him by the hand. "I'm going to need some help fixing it. Could you be my helper?"

His face shines up at me. He nods vigorously. We go off together to the cupboard where Jack stores the Christmas decorations and extra bulbs. The string of lights is old, one of those I passed on to Agnes so many years ago, when they became useless to me. One blown bulb will darken the entire string. So it may be that the problem is simply a bulb that needs changing, or it may be that the wiring is thoroughly worn out, the string good now only for the memories of when it shone.

The first snowfall always makes Agnes cautious behind the wheel. Staring ahead as if the moist, deserted highway might at any moment present a hazard, she says, "Maybe I should come with you this time, father."

Beyond her profile, the industrial landscape, newly whitened, slides by through the grimy glass of her window. "Whatever for, Agnes?"

Her fingers tug at the slender arm of the windshield-wiper control. Blue fluid splatters onto the glass, foaming and flattening out, runnels rushing for the edges as the rubber blades arc after them.

"I just thought you might prefer some company. This time."

"Thank you, Agnes. But this time won't be terribly different from every other time. Ruth-Ann — and I say this with regret — is who she has become. Any news I bring seems to find no hook within her. I could tell her the world is about to end and she might ask how popcorn is made. For the most part, we have conversations of *non sequiturs*."

My eyes moisten unexpectedly. My view, of the interior of the car, of the world outside, grows blurry.

I am fragile. I have been fragile for just over a month. I expect I shall be fragile for some time to come.

That day began early for me, and it began with disagreement.

I hadn't been sleeping well, not insomnia in the classic sense but more a kind of restlessness. I slept in fits and starts, which left me with a disposition that was, to use Mary's term, unarguably grumpy.

Squirming in the bed in search of a seductive nest, I woke her for the umpteenth time. Her response was to slug me in the arm, a protest most unbecoming — but which, for that very reason, drove home her point. Miffed, I arose and, without taking pains to be silent, left the bedroom.

It was neither as late nor as early as I had surmised. I found myself torn between the sofa and the kettle. I opted for the kettle. Waiting for the water to boil, I stepped out to clear my head with a breath of air. The morning was cool, still smoky with night. Dawn would be some time in coming, but it was close enough that the stars, in their diminished intensity, hinted at their own frailty. I could smell the sharp, fresh odour of newly fallen leaves. Even though dressed only in my bathrobe, I was tempted to wander farther out, to steep myself in the breathless street, but the leg was a touch sensitive and my sense of propriety precluded a public appearance in night clothes.

As I busied myself preparing coffee, the newspaper thudded onto the porch. I hurried for it, hungry for word of the world —

even if indifferently written, hastily edited and a day late — arriving on my doorstep. It is one definition of luxury, this sinking back into a familiar armchair, with freshly brewed coffee steaming its heady aroma and the morning paper fragrant with ink and fibre, still folded machine-tight — all this and a solitude, arising from the false sense that much of the world still sleeps, that is serene and composed and capacious, *sanctum sanctorum*. These are exquisite moments, rich with sensuality, demanding to be savoured because life will soon resume, another rhythm will impose itself and the tranquillity they offer will be a thing of memory.

I had just taken the last sip of my coffee when Mary began stirring around in the bedroom. I put aside the paper, brought the water to a boil and made her a cup of tea.

She was sitting at her make-up table brushing her hair with languid strokes of her brush. Her eyes were gazing — but sightless, her thoughts somewhere distant — into the oval mirror mounted on the wall in front of her. Although the morning was crisp and sunny, she had not opened the curtains. The light from the table-lamp fell from her left, and in the mirror, she was like a glowing apparition, half-awake, the lines of sleep still marking themselves on her face.

I put the cup of tea on the table and kissed her on the crown of her head, in the little space where her hair, all silvery in the light, had thinned. Her eyes found mine in the mirror. She smiled tiredly. I said, "Did you sleep well?"

"Off and on. More off than on."

"I'm sorry."

"So you should be."

"My arm still smarts."

"As it should."

I went over to the window and drew the curtains apart. Sunlight flooded the room, smothering the light from the table lamp, revealing the disorder of the bed. A moving sight: She had thrashed around in search of reluctant Morpheus.

The tea cup clinked as she replaced it on the saucer. I watched from the window as she pulled her hair back into a ponytail and secured it with a black band: every movement precise and purposeful, her fingers limber, blessed still with a dexterity now denied the rest of her body.

She stood, stepped over to the closet, paused before the serried clothes as if bored by everything she saw — by the simple daily act of selecting and dressing. Finally she lifted out a white blouse and, after a moment's more consideration, a peach-coloured skirt. An unprepossessing outfit. An outfit chosen with an eye not to style but to comfort. An outfit that would have caused the younger Mary to toss restlessly around for the accoutrement — the brooch, the necklace, most often the scarf — that would turn shop-paper into parchment. This was an alchemy, though, that she practised with lessening frequency. Her clothes would never be tasteless, but she seemed to have disengaged that part of her that instinctively defied the prosaic.

She placed the skirt and blouse on the bed and, facing away from me, eased the nightgown over her head, the material billowing in the balletic sway of her arms and the clasp of those nimble fingers. Then the nightgown was off, her back given by the light a pleasing tension of momentarily rippled muscle, her neck flowing into the skirt of her shoulder-blades, her spine as delicate as a finely-turned necklace. At the base, like a concave buckle on her trim waist, was an indentation I knew well, a spot of great sensitivity which, in our younger days, had often been the focal point of my initial ministrations. I wondered whether that sensitivity remained, whether the touch of my fingertips might still elicit the gasp and shudder and feline unfolding of her body.

But my curiosity went no further, for the indentation had for

years been hidden beneath an acquired fleshiness. Now, it had
returned, a reminder not just of long-ago pleasure but of the
mystery that Mary had, in the last three months, lost a great deal
of weight, due perhaps to her heart condition. Or perhaps not.
The doctors would not commit themselves.

Suddenly Mary turned around, and I saw that, in this light —
in this light — she was almost breastless, almost hipless. I saw too
many bones cast in awkward relief.

"What are you gawking at?" she said, her tone not one of
displeasure. She ran a hand across her breasts and down her belly.
"I could use some fattening up, couldn't I."

"And I could stand to lose a few pounds," I replied.

"So together, our weight should be just about right?"

"Just about," I said as, drawing me with her eyes, she slipped
back into bed.

Mary and Agnes both had a firm grasp on the nature of the problem with Mary's heart.

It had first appeared some years before, the doctors reassuring
as they fine-tuned its operation with at first a few, then gradually
very many, daily pills. My mind proved incapable — "Not
incapable," Mary once said angrily. "Unwilling, is more like it."
— of retaining the technicalities of the problem. I would hear
them, I would understand them, and minutes later I would have
forgotten them.

Deterioration was the word I settled on. I saw her heart crum-
bling, dissolving, tiny bits flaking off at the edges, but at a glacial
pace. Hers was a big heart, I assured myself; a thousand years
would pass before it was brought down. When people asked,
I said that Mary had a heart condition, and left it at that.

She sat at the kitchen table, hunched over a second cup of tea.
With the sleep lines cleared from her face, her hair arranged with

less dispatch, she had reclaimed the dignified beauty of the weary but unravaged older woman she presented to the world.

"Shouldn't you be putting on a cardigan?" she said, tugging the cuffs of her own sweater flush with those of her blouse.

"Are you cold?"

"Aren't you?"

"No."

"You'd look better if you did."

I glanced down at myself. I have never been, by any stretch of the imagination, a fashion-plate. Apart from the summer months, when the heat justifies short-sleeved shirts of reasonable colour, I rarely stray far from the professional leftovers I was wearing: a white shirt buttoned at the wrist, grey or brown trousers with matching belt and socks, and the slip-ons Agnes gave me upon my retirement so that I would no longer have to endure the strain of dealing with shoe-laces. (That winter, Mary and I acquired zippered winter boots for the same reason.)

"You look," Mary said, "a trifle drab. That cardigan Agnes gave you for Christmas, for instance. It's a lovely burgundy. Just what you need to—"

For no apparent reason, her words ended there, as if the rest of the thought were self-evident, or as if something unshared had distracted her. And precisely because of this, I retrieved the cardigan in question from the chest of drawers where it had lain for months enfolded in crêpe paper. When I returned to the kitchen, Mary looked up bright-eyed at me and said, "Oh my. Alistair. You make my heart dance."

Precisely at ten o'clock, the doorbell rang.

"That'll be Wendy," Mary called from the bedroom. She was in the midst of sorting through a molehill of freshly washed clothes. "Would you mind letting her in?"

Wendy was an acquaintance of Mary's from the neighbourhood group she had joined devoted to the promotion of human rights in obscure, far-off countries. "Hi!" she'd said brightly the first time she came to our home. "My name's Windy." Her pronunciation of the name seemed particularly suitable. There was to her something distinctly windswept — her crisp, straw-coloured hair, which brought to mind a windsock in a stiff breeze; her baggy clothes which flapped about at the slightest movement. She looked as though she had struggled through some unrelenting wind-tunnel to get here. She was vaguely familiar to me as I was to her, and we were not long in establishing that, many years before, she'd spent a few miserable months as the receptionist in my department at the university.

Windy and Mary would sit at the dining room table with an old typewriter, an orange folder to which they referred from time to time, a stack of white bond, a packet of letter-sized envelopes, several cards of postage stamps, a pot of tea and a plate of cook-ies. Their involvement in human rights was labour-intensive, but perfectly suited to Mary's physical limitations. They received each month a newsletter — all of which were preserved in the orange folder — updating the effect of the organization's efforts on behalf of various political prisoners and detailing, in some-times gruesome detail, fresh outrages. Each newsletter also contained the prison addresses of those unlawfully detained, and the names and addresses of the heads of state who had ordered their detention.

Once a month, beginning three months before, Mary and Windy spent the better part of a day typing out a sheaf of letters, always one of personal greeting to the prisoner ("Dear Exotic Name: Greetings from Canada!") and a more formal letter of protest to the head of state ("His Excellency General Exotic Name, President of Exotic Place, Sir: We are writing on behalf of . . ."). The addresses would be typed on the envelopes, stamps affixed, letters folded and inserted and, flap-glue moistened with a damp cloth, envelopes firmly sealed. It was, in their hands, a process of great precision. Mary and Windy's sense of satisfaction was palpable once this labour was done. Their sighs, their languorous stretching of stiffened muscles, showed that they felt they had performed good and useful work.

Once, taking a short break during their second session, they sought to seduce me into joining them by sharing with me some of the sordid stories from the newsletter: reports of tortures both manual and electrical, public decapitations, premeditated rape, murder by machete and machine gun, butchery of the most elemental kind. It was a peculiar kind of poetry. Names, dates, places, sometimes photos — and, always, the dispassionate relating of fates.

But what was the point?

The prisoners, if they received their letters, likely evinced some measure of comfort from knowing they had not been forgotten, but it was more difficult to imagine the reactions of the heads of state. Hard to imagine any of them seeing the name *Mary Mackenzie* scrawled beneath the respectful sentences and breaking out in a cold sweat.

Mary scoffed at my question as if it were undeserving of an answer, but Windy leaned forward in her chair, her face marked by a quiet intensity. "We don't expect to change these guys," she said calmly. "And they're always guys, by the way. We just want to remind them that we're here, we won't go away, and we know what they're up to."

I did not join them, but I did agree to mail the letters. It was the least I could do, considering the envy that came to me as I returned to Dickens's evocation of the darknesses of another age.

Windy was subdued that morning when I let her in. She was as storm-tossed as ever, but clearly preoccupied. Clutching her slender briefcase to her chest, she stepped inside almost gingerly

— quite uncharacteristic for someone who habitually blew in with all the energy of a medium-sized gale.

"Is something amiss, Wendy?" I said.

"No, no, it's just that— Is Mary here?"

"She's expecting you. She's dealing with some laundry in the bedroom. She'll be right out."

I showed her to the dining table and offered to make some tea. She was pale around the lips, and her eyebrows were fluttering at alarming speed.

"Tea'd be great," she said, sounding strangely breathless, "though if it wasn't this early I'd go for something stronger."

I was about to offer something stronger — was she envisaging a cup of coffee or a glass of whisky? — when Mary bustled from the bedroom. "Alistair," she said somewhat officiously, "would you be a dear and make us a pot of tea?"

Feeling like Jeeves, I bowed stiffly — "Yes, m'um!" — and left them to their conversation of urgent whispers.

When, some minutes later, I returned bearing teapot and cups on a tray, Mary said, "Alistair, do you know how we should go about sending a telegram?"

"A telegram? Do people still send telegrams?"

"Don't be foolish, Alistair. This is important. A matter of life and death. One of our adoptees has disappeared. That is, Wendy's been told that he was removed from his prison cell last night and no one seems to know what's happened to him. We're terribly worried."

Windy extracted the orange folder from her brief case, then extracted a sheet of paper from the folder. She held it up to show me the grainy photograph of a man in his mid-thirties, with a shock of uncombed hair crowning Asian features. "He's a poet," she said. "He's been in prison for three years."

"What did he do?"

"He wrote some poems the government didn't like."

"Bad poetry a crime? There's hope yet for humanity, I daresay. We'd need to build more prisons in this country, though."

"Alistair," Mary said wearily, "must you be such an ass?"

"Just joking, my dear." I put the tray on the table. "Now, why a telegram?"

"A massive intervention," Windy said. "We want to send a telegram to the general in charge of the government. We want him to know we're—"

"You want to send a telegram to the fellow who imprisoned your poet?"

"We want to inundate him with a blizzard of telegrams from all over the world," Windy said. "We want to make him think twice. If it isn't already too late."

I poured them each a cup of tea and promised I would find out how one went about sending a telegram to a dictator in a distant land.

Sending the telegram turned out to be a rather simple affair. Mary patiently dictated the text over the telephone, the telegram people apparently quite unfazed at the prospect of dispatching the "expression of extreme concern" to His Highness General So-and-so, Emperor of the People's Democratic Republic of So-and-so. Once the task was done, Mary and Windy neatly arranged their materials on the table and set to work.

I was, I must admit, impressed by their industriousness.

They worked steadily for over two hours, the clickety-clack of the typewriter driving me to seek the silence of the kitchen.

They paused for a brief lunch of tuna-fish sandiches and sliced tomato, which we had together on the small porch at the back. A strong midday sun warmed us enough that I removed my cardigan and Mary her sweater. "What a lovely fall," she said.

"Isn't it," Windy concurred.

After a while, Mary said, "It's such an invigorating season, isn't it?"

"I know what you mean," Windy replied.

It was an inane conversation. Somewhat irritably, I said, "You're both thinking about your poet, aren't you?"

Mary, fanning herself with her napkin, nodded. "I must admit, at times like this, I don't quite know if what we're doing makes any sense. I mean, this General-fellow can do whatever he pleases, can't he? And the world be damned. It makes you feel so . . . insignificant. For all we know, our poet, as you call him, might already be lying lifeless in some field somewhere." Suddenly her eyes bristled with tears. "It all seems so lonely somehow, to end up like that."

Windy's gaze was lost in the sun-drenched garden. The grass was mowed short and the narrow flower-beds had been cleared of vegetation; beneath the soil, weeded and tilled in preparation for the snows that would soon come, tulip bulbs — which I have always imagined as nuclei of warmth cocooned at the heart of an onion — prepared for a winter of hibernation. Windy was, I could see, pained by Mary's words. She sat there, beside Mary and across from me, still and stiff-backed in the fraying rattan chair. I suspected that Windy shared the feelings of despair fringed with hysteria that Mary had expressed, but that she would not — through pride, perhaps, or through fear, through a sense that they might amount to a kind of heresy or betrayal — admit to having them.

Her eyes rose from the garden and, unexpectedly, met mine. And I saw in that instant that I had read her right — and that she knew I had. I saw too, though, that *that* — indeed, that I — was beside the point. Fingers clutching at the rim of her plate which sat with a half-eaten sandwich on her lap, she murmured, "You haven't been at this very long, Mary. The fact is — and you never get used to it — that you win some and you lose some. We're like doctors or lawyers in that way."

"Doctors or lawyers!" Mary's emotion drained away in pique at what she clearly took to be Windy's condescension. "Wendy! We're letter-writers. We're stamp-lickers. We address ruthless criminals as if they were the denizens of Mount Olympus and entreat them not to commit murder. We're supplicants. Maybe the gods will grant our wishes, maybe they won't. Doctors or lawyers! My dear, you do overstate your case."

I was taken aback at Mary's outburst — it seemed a tad extreme — but, at the same time, I couldn't help admiring the acuity with which she punctured Windy's more romantic vision of the task they had assumed.

Windy, however, remained unfazed. "Perhaps. But the fact remains: you win some, you lose some."

"I know," Mary said, suddenly weary. "The problem is, I don't want to lose any."

And suddenly, with a swell of pride that remains mysterious to me, I no longer knew which of them was the romantic.

That evening the weather turned blustery. The last of the leaves on the trees slipped their moorings, whipping downwind into the greater darkness. Humid air impregnated the house, insinuated itself through cardigan and shirt and undershirt so that my skin felt clammy and chilled. It was as if the world had turned surly.

Mary and Windy had persevered with their typing for most of the afternoon, although there was a distracted air to them, the typewriter less vibrant than usual, as if the machine itself doubted the usefulness of its purpose. I busied myself with the household tasks, cleaning up after lunch, doing a little dusting, a little straightening, nothing too vigorous. Around mid-afternoon I dozed off over Dickens in my armchair and awoke just as Mary

268

was seeing Windy out. The afternoon had turned dull.

High in the sky, grey clouds were vigorously knitting themselves together.

We had an early dinner — leftover lasagne, a simple salad — and when we were done Mary put on her flannel pyjamas, wrapped her padded, pink housecoat around her — a bulky affair that caused her to appear bloated — and asked me to get the fireplace going.

The living room was not long in warming up. The logs were as dry as coal, and required only a few sticks of kindling and one newspaper section ("Lifestyle") to set them ablaze. Mary, yawning, tuned the television to a soap opera she had been quite shamelessly following for some time. I commented only once or twice on her choice of viewing, for she responded to my initial ridicule by pointing out that the tales told were hardly more melodramatic than, as she put it, "the fictions that fetch up in the works of Mister Dickens." Mary, it must be said, remains unmoved by Oliver, unconvinced by Scrooge, unamused by Mrs. Malaprop. Why the people of the evening soaps — where the world glitters with fine cars, showcase homes and enough jewellery to fill a Spanish galleon; where cosmetics are as ubiquitous as extra-marital affairs; where the men are as pretty as the women and happiness is merely a foreshadowing of disaster — should hold her interest remains a mystery to me. But I let her be.

I puttered about for a bit, aimless and restive. Mary's condition had circumscribed our modest activities to a fair extent. She was easily fatigued, and even a walk to the supermarket required an hour-long rest afterwards. Going out to the cinema, which we would do on the cheap-matinée afternoons, was now out of the question, not that it was dangerous but it drained her sufficiently that any pleasure she might have derived from the movie would be quickly effaced. The effort simply wasn't worth the trouble — not for the meagre pleasures offered by today's movies, I mean.

My pointless meandering irritated Mary. "For Heaven's sake, Alistair," she called out above the jingle of an advertisement. "If you must dillydally and lollygag, please do it outside. Go for a little toodle around the block or something."

When Mary began using terms such as *dillydally*, *lollygag* and *toodle*, it was advisable to pay close attention. "Are you sure you wouldn't mind, Mary?"

"Mind? You'd be doing me a favour."

She, however, had done me an ever bigger favour, for the truth was that I felt no small measure of guilt over Mary's inability to partake in the "toodle around the block" which, just a few short months before, had been a staple of our evening routine. Unwilling to wound her by going off on my own, I had for the most part abstained. Although the leg needed regular stretching and even though some fresh air (or, at least, air as fresh as possible) would stand me in good stead at bedtime, I restricted my exercise to trips to the bank and the supermarket, the vegetable store and the fishmonger's. The necessity negated the guilt — just as Mary had to some extent by inviting me to, so to speak, take my agitation to the streets. To some extent only, though, since she invited me to leave because I had annoyed her in the first place.

"I won't be long," I said, doing up the buttons on the cardigan. And I wouldn't be. I never was. I couldn't allow myself to be.

It had been a shock, the sudden appearance of Mary's condition, I mean. She had always been so healthy, so vigorous, and as we sat together holding hands in the specialist's office, her measured medical voice explaining Mary's situation, my mind slipped back to the day decades past when I first saw her on the street, being harangued by a stranger for wearing an outfit with too many buttons. The world was still chaotic with war then, my damaged leg a fresh souvenir of that chaos. Mary, full of self-possession even as the fellow foolishly accused her of impeding the war effort, was a haven for another man who, until that moment, had not suspected that he was in need of one and who, even then, remained unaware of the depths of his own need. It would take the near loss of that haven for him — for me — to learn the frankness by which to treasure it.

But now, faced with my fears and my guilt, I lost that frankness. How could I confess to Mary that my walks were short because I feared being too far from her for too long, feared being away at the critical moment? If we live life blessedly ignorant of the means of our demise, having these means made explicit is to confront a paralyzing starkness. Knowledge is power, they like to say, but this was a knowledge with the power to unravel.

I had just taken my windbreaker from the closet when there was an urgent rap at the front door. At this time of the evening it was likely to be Tremblay or his wife asking for the loan of an egg or some flour or sugar for the baking that seemed to go on at their place at all hours. These loans were always repaid, with interest as Mary liked to say, in the form of the finished product: muffins, meat pies, sugar tarts.

Expecting Marie-Angèle, I was not a little surprised to see Windy standing there looking like her name. She was flushed and out of breath. "Is Mary in?" she said, gasping.

She knew the question to be useless. Mary, these days, was almost always in. "She's watching television," I said, standing aside to let her enter. And for the second time that day I asked her if something was wrong. Also for the second time that day, she ignored the question. She apologized for the lateness of the hour and for turning up unannounced. Then, bustling towards the living room, she called out: "Mary! I have big news. Wait till you hear."

Mary sat up alarmed and confused in her chair. Wrenched unceremoniously from her fictitious world by Windy's interruption, she was like someone suddenly roused to a midnight darkness by the sounds of cacophony.

271

Windy, practically hopping from foot to foot, seized Mary by the arms and pulled her to her feet. "I've just had a call!" she said, speaking in exclamation marks. "From London!"

"London?" Mary said, still puzzled.

"Yes, London, England! He's free! He arrived on a plane just hours ago!"

"Your poet?" I said.

"Apparently he doesn't have a thing with him, except a notebook full of poetry! Isn't that astonishing?"

Then she did something even more astonishing — to me, at least. Grasping Mary by the shoulders, she began whirling them both around the living room in an arching, overwrought waltz, her hair and clothes billowing a full second behind her, Mary — a bundle of pink padding — swirling awkwardly in her slipstream, the two of them blurring at the edges as Windy swirled them faster and faster, their laughter erupting and entwining like twin melodies, Mary — feet actually leaving the ground — bobbing and floating before my eyes with all the weightless momentum of a full-sail schooner caught in the delirium of a whirlwind.

Watching them, I found myself growing unaccountably happy, as if I, too, were caught up in the gale of unheard music sweeping them along. A great sweetness filled the air, as if the manic-edged chuckle that arose now from Windy now from Mary were giving off a rich and peculiar fragrance.

When, finally, they stopped, Mary was rosy-cheeked and breathless. She pressed a hand to her chest and let herself fall back, luxuriating, into the armchair. Windy stood at the centre of the living room, hands on her hips, smiling down at her.

"And what happens to your poet-fellow now?" I said to Windy.

The smile left her lips. She cocked her head, stared back at me with large, oval eyes. The question, I saw, had startled her.

Later, after Windy had left, Mary would tell me that my

～

question had been unfortunate. Inopportune. It had taken the wind out of Windy — had becalmed her, as it were. "You see," she said, "she's been at this game for quite a while, and there aren't that many opportunities for celebration. Far more for mourning, in fact. But, well, it's afterwards, after the little triumphs, that things sometimes turn — what's the word? — problematic."

And she told me about Windy's first experience of a triumph. It had occurred mere months after she had signed on with the organisation. "There was this woman," Mary said. "Myriam was her name. She lived in one of those countries where, you know, the capital's main throughfare keeps getting renamed for the date of the latest military coup—"

These words did not sound to me like Mary's; they sounded acquired: like a gift of jargon.

"Well, anyway, Myriam was a feminist and a writer and a social activist and a human-rights campaigner and a birth-control advocate all rolled into one, sort of a jill-of-all-trades. Which, of course, really endeared her to the fellows in the camouflage suits. It took years of letter-writing and string-pulling and ego-stroking to get her out of solitary, and years more to get her out of the country. But miracles do happen — and one day Myriam turned up in Toronto, just like our poet in London."

Mary yawned, her eyes watering. The return of the fatigue was inexorable. It was fast replacing the animation in which Windy had engulfed her.

"Wendy met her a few weeks later, when she was visiting to attend a fund-raiser downtown. There'd been some national media publicity, so she turned out to be an okay pull across the country. Wendy was a little uneasy about the whole thing. She said it was as if Greenpeace decided to raise donations by sending some whale it had saved on a cross-country tour. She admitted the tour had its glamorous side — the audiences and the journalists and the cameras and the hotels — but still felt that perhaps Myriam was just our saved whale. Still, what could you do? Every organisation needs money, and when you won't compromise yourself with goverment hand-outs, you do what you have to, especially when you've got someone as dynamic and personable as Myriam at your disposal."

Mary rubbed at her eyes with her knuckles, the gesture of a sleepy child. But her face was not that of youth; it was that of an old woman whose seams were being undone. Watching her, my throat went tight, trapping in my chest fear and sadness and the rise of a crippling disbelief.

"But the upshot came some months later, when Wendy walked past Myriam on the sidewalk in Chinatown. She hadn't known that Myriam had decided to settle down here. In fact, once the tour was over, Myriam just kind of disappeared. A normal life, you know. Unfortunately, normal life didn't seem to be have been very kind to Myriam. Wendy saw a woman who was gaunt and exhausted, with dark, concentric circles under her eyes, which she said were yellow and haunted. And while her clothes weren't threadbare, they were ill-fitting, a couple of sizes too big, probably bought on the cheap. Wendy couldn't even bring herself to say hello and walked on by. To her relief, Myriam didn't recognise her. She did some asking around and was told that Myriam had 'problems', that she now kept very much to herself. In fact, someone said that poor Myriam was probably more alone now than when she'd been in solitary. I mean, after all, at least in prison she'd received the letters, at least she'd had that contact with other human beings. Now that she was free, she shunned everyone, and everyone had learned to keep their distance. This was quite a blow to Wendy, and for some time she didn't write any letters, she couldn't see the point. Eventually she returned to it — obviously — but she avoids follow-ups. She doesn't particularly want to know how they get on afterwards. Too often, there's pain. They end up broken, like Myriam, or become stock-brokers, for God's sake, or insurance salesmen. And Wendy doesn't ever want to have to ask herself why again."

The story troubled me — for did it not suggest that Windy was interested more in the human condition than in the human? And was it not peculiar that she valued her own satisfaction more than the ultimate fate of those she laboured to help? The entire thing struck me as odd. But Mary was exhausted, so I let it pass. There would be ample time in the morning to pursue it.

We went together to the bedroom. I helped her out of her housecoat and she curled up on the bed. Before I could fully tuck the comforter in around her, she had fallen into a profound sleep.

Just after two in the morning, my bladder woke me. I eased out of bed and tiptoed to the bathroom. The relief, as always, was a blessed event, replete with shivers of pleasure and stifled moans.

I exercised greater caution in returning to the bed. The bathroom light had induced night-blindness and I could hardly distinguish the shadows. More than once on other nights I had accidentally encountered some object or piece of furniture, drawing protest from either it or myself and, invariably, from Mary.

She was a deep sleeper, and nothing diminished her habitual subtlety quite as effectively as being roused for no good reason in the middle of the night. It brought out her family's seafaring traditions: her grandfather, who had enjoyed a long and reasonably distinguished career in the Royal Navy; her father, a civilian ship's officer, who had survived the sinking of *The Empress of Ireland* in the St. Lawrence in 1914 and three more ship-sinkings during the Great War only to drown in a placid lake just days prior to the outbreak of the Second World War, when Mary was sixteen. It was this naval heritage, I felt, that emerged on those disrupted dark nights in our bedroom by turning her language distinctly salty.

On this night, I had been successful in manoeuvering back to the bed without mishap. I eased myself onto the mattress with all the control and precision of a gymnast on a balance beam. Slowly I drew the covers up to my neck — and only then, safely ensconced, did I dare allow myself a deep breath.

I suppose it was then, as I let the breath out, the exhausted air spewing from between my lips with a muted hiss, that the peculiar quality of Mary's slumber caught my attention.

"You awake?" I whispered.

She did not stir.

"Mary?" I touched her shoulder.

Then I shook her. "Mary?" She rocked on the bed, inert. I sat up, my breathing seized, my chest suddenly seared by jagged ice.

My hand brushed her cheek. Despair, desolation: She was no longer even warm. Mary, my dear Mary, had drifted away alone into the night.

I turned on the reading lamp and in its light saw that, somehow, her seams had been redone. She had shrugged off many years. Even her hair appeared to have darkened. I drank in every detail of her face: the rise of every eyelash, the curve of the eyelids, the shape of the parted lips. With my eyes I traced the intricacies of her ear and the line of her jaw. I took her hand in mine, read with my fingertips the shape of her nails, memorized the accordion of skin at every knuckle, stared for the very first time at the lines on her palms: was startled to see that the palms were like photocopies of each other. I wondered whether she had ever noticed that. Forgetting myself for a moment, I spoke the question out loud. To her. Then, for uncountable moments, I struggled with the silence into which my question had fallen.

With her hand wrapped in mine, I turned off the light and sat with her.

When I finally rose to call Agnes, the sky was growing bright, bringing to me the dawn of a new life, a life at that moment too terrible to imagine. After all, solitude is sweet only when it is finite.

Discretion, someone later whispered to me in an attempt at compassion, had always been her strong suit.

She was sixty-four years old. She had spent forty-three of those with me.

Agnes does not understand why the headstone I commissioned at a handsome sum is graced not only with her mother's names and dates but also with a beautifully rendered etching of a three-masted schooner in full sail when her mother never once revealed the slightest interest in sailing. "I like it," I said, unwilling to explain further even at the risk of seeming a foolish old man. Agnes let me be, assuming — I assume — that the mystery was merely the product of the unpredictability of grief. I was content with this. I had my reasons, and no one, not even my daughter, had a claim to them.

"Ruth-Ann, I have some bad news. It's Mary. You remember Mary? My wife?"

She blinks at me, and I take hope from a sparkle in her eyes.

"I'm afraid Mary's dead. She had a heart-attack. She liked you a great deal, and I know you liked her, too. I thought you should know."

Unexpectedly, she puts her hand on mine, the lightest touch, and says, "I offer you my deepest condolences at this difficult time."

The words are so proper, so formal, I cannot read the emotion behind them — indeed cannot tell whether there is any emotion. Does she remember Mary? Is she truly touched by the news I have brought?

She says, "Will you get another one?"

꙳

"Pardon?"

"Will you get another one? Another Mary, I mean." Then: "I need new shoes, you know."

The next moments are a struggle: with her question, with her failure to understand, with her wish, nevertheless, to sympathize. "No, dear," I finally manage to say. "I shan't be getting myself another Mary. But as for shoes, I'll take care of it, I promise."

She smiles, uncertainly at first and then with great assurance.

I take her hand, curl my fingers around its pliant softness, and hope that the constriction in my throat will one day ease.

$\mathcal{T}$he year of Mary's death is, in my mind, one of roiling event and mangled time.

In the year of her death, an American navy missile shot down an Iranian airliner over the Persian Gulf. 290 people were killed. It was called an accident. In that year, too, a bomb destroyed an American airliner over Lockerbie, Scotland. 270 people were killed. It was called terrorism.

In the year of Mary's death, in Sao Paulo, Brazil, a skydiver plummeted to earth without the benefit of a functioning parachute. He landed square on the oldest and heftiest samba dancer in the land. In gratitude, he paid her funeral costs.

In that year, fire-storms raged on the sun, Pluto was found to have an atmosphere (unlike, declared the newspaper's restaurant

279

critic two pages on, a toney new restaurant whose decorator probably couldn't distinguish a salon from a saloon), brain cells were transplanted for the first time, and Superman turned fifty. Moscow, for so long the purveyor of nuclear nightmares, got its comeuppance when an American fast-food chain opened twenty outlets to flood Russian stomachs with hamburger facsimiles. Capitulating utterly, the beleaguered city elected its first beauty queen.

In the late fall, some newspapers gave many column inches to a man from Memphremagog who claimed to know the precise location of Samuel de Champlain's long-lost grave. Little amusement was apparent when, a week and extensive media coverage later, he led a solemn group of reporters to the final resting place of his beloved collie, named for the great explorer because of his wandering ways. Outrage was muted when careful vetting of the man's words revealed that he had not compromised himself. He had promised nothing beyond the grave of "Samuel de Champlain" who, he said, had been loyal and fearless. "He had a nose for new territory". The newspapers had cast the web of history around themselves, and the fellow had not deigned to relieve them of it.

In the week of Mary's death, a shoplifter was caught at our local supermarket. He was a tall, skeletal man wearing too big a coat on too warm a day. Store employees closed in on him at the exit. An animal cornered. Eyes protuberant with panic, back stiffened, arms waving before him like a dancer underwater: at the doorway two strides too far, at the hefty young men in purple aprons gesturing warning and temperance back at him. He drew back, drew away. But there was no place to go.

On the day of Mary's death, three poets were arrested in a busy downtown square. They were charged with indecent exposure. Their poems, declaimed in the poetic monotone that lends gravity to the vacuous, had sunk unremarked into the cacophony of car-horns and urban buzz. Frustration led them to unzip their props. They pleaded not guilty on the grounds of literary licence. The judge, in dismissing the charges, issued the young men a warning.

> *How laudable it is that youth*
> *Wish not to be locked in a booth.*
> *They have things to say*
> *And dragons to slay*
> *But if I may*
> *A word of caution*
> *Find youselves a more honourable profession*
> *Like street-sweeping or garbage-collection.*

The Union of Poets was not amused and for several days the young men and their union supporters were to be found through-out the media denouncing the judge and demanding his removal. Through my heartbreak, I could hear Mary laughing heartily at the story. I could hear her mumbling in pointed amusement: *The paltry section.*

At the end of the year of Mary's death, Canada was put up for sale when parliament approved a free-trade agreement with the United States. Windy, in a rare moment of bitterness, said that the country was like a whore greedy for greenbacks. Then she turned red and clapped a palm to her cheek. Her eyes watered. She said, "Oh, I miss her so."

At the end of the year following Mary's death, a gunman whose name everyone remembers brutally murdered fourteen female university students whose names few people remember. Agnes remarked that not even her husband could look her in the eye for days.

The world altered. Walls came down, big ideas whispered themselves away into history.

≈

There are events I wish Mary had lived to see, and events I'm glad she never witnessed. I remain staggered by the world already so reshaped that a countless number of her references would be useless. She would hardly recognise the world that is becoming François's, just as the boy I once was hardly recognises the world that became his, just as the man I am hardly recognises the one that flame has made mine.

"*Hey, you up there!*"

I am shouting. I know that I'm shouting because my mouth yawns wide at every word, my jaws strain at the joints, the muscles in my throat vibrate.

"Hey! Tremblay!"

But my own words come to me through the intermediary of technology, through circuitry miraculously miniaturized that thins and bleeds them of stature. Each vibrates an unheard echo from the top of my throat into the chamber of my skull — echoes that serve only to underscore that I am growing deaf even from within.

"What now, M'sieur Mackenzie?" Tremblay's head pokes out over the porch railing, gazes down at me, all innocence.

❧

"*Mister* Mackenzie to you!" I lean farther out over my porch railing, the better to see him, the better to gauge the manner of his words. "You know I won't take that *miss-your* shit from you, Tremblay." But looking upwards to his puffy face, the leaves behind him dark against the soft blue sky, vertigo hits and I must turn away, to the trim patch of lawn just feet below.

After a moment, Tremblay says, "All right, t'en, *Mister* Mackenzie, what I can do for you?"

"You can stop that infernal banging, that's what you can do." Turn away: to the sidewalk and the street quiet with shadow and parked cars. "It's not even ten o'clock—"

"If my banging derange you, take out your ear."

"I decide when I take out my ear, Tremblay. I need my ear. What if my phone rings?"

"You take me for an imbecile, *calice*? Your ear, it's not completely bad, eh? Beside, who's going to call you?"

My daughter, that's who. Nevertheless, I shout, "None of your business."

He goes silent. And then — the arrogance of the man — the morning reverberates with the renewed bang-bang-bang of his hammer.

"Tremblay!"

"This is my house, M'sieur Mackenzie." Bang-bang-bang.

"Like hell it is!" His is the upper floor, mine the lower. We have been uneasy neighbours for longer than I care to remember. We have watched each other growing infirm. "Tremblay! Tremblay! You stop that racket now, you hear me?"

His response is more bangs of the hammer. The porch trembles with the shock of the blows.

Blood surges into my head. In a fit of exasperation, I snatch the earphone from my ear and retreat into the house. I slam the door shut. I know that I slam the door shut because I see the violence of my action. The sound comes only seconds later, with the faded force of a single echo.

In the kitchen, I lift the dripping teabag from the cup into which I had placed it when his banging began. The tea is dark and, when I sip it, thick and bitter on the tongue. Tremblay has even managed to ruin my cup of tea.

This living beneath Tremblay: It does my heart no good, no good at all.

Today is Wednesday. Agnes will be coming by at some point, either during her lunch break, if she's not too rushed, or after work on her way home. She'll bustle about the kitchen assuring herself I'm not facing imminent starvation. She'll run her fingertips along the furniture and complain that the cleaning woman she pays isn't worth the money but what other choice is there? I don't have the strength and she, Agnes, doesn't have the time, not with all her other obligations — her job, her family. Then she'll make us each a cup of tea and sit with me in the living room, scalding her tongue and trying to make conversation. Conversation, I say, but that may be too generous a word for what transpires between us. An interview, rather, question and answer. Heated questions, muted answers.

Do not misunderstand me. Agnes is a good daughter, just not the daughter I had expected. Was I wrong to have dreamt of an angel who would mimic the manner of her mother, God bless her soul? Am I wrong to be disappointed in having had a daughter who inherited the ways and heaviness of her father? Perhaps it's the wrong word, disappointment. Perhaps disenchantment would be more accurate. Or disillusionment. But none of this has prevented us from being father and daughter to each other. I saw to her needs to the best of my abilities, as she now sees to mine. And yet it must be admitted that there are situations in life when one's best is, quite simply, not good enough. This is the reason, I believe, that, in spite of the contraption, my daughter continues to shout at me.

The house is growing warm. The windows are shut, as they are on all except the hottest of days, to protect me from the draughts Agnes says could be the death of me. The weather has not been all that it should be for the fourth week of June. Clear skies and sunshine have proved insufficient to warm the air, the chill of early spring reluctant to relinquish its grip. It has rained infrequently and in the main at night, the occasional deluge crackling down through the trees and at the windows with a ferocity that awakens me even though I do not wear my ear to bed.

Tremblay's banging has ceased, for the moment at least. I replace my ear and now there is nothing to hear but the breathing of the house, a low, steady pulse of which I remained unaware until the contraption revealed it to me. Now, little effort is required; my fingertips detect it in the furniture, the walls, the polished floorboards. On sunny afternoons, when the sun brightens the living room, I fancy that it can even be perceived in the dust-laden air.

I prepare a fresh cup of tea and consume the last of the cookies Agnes brought over on Saturday. They're good cookies, sweet, with chunks of white and dark chocolate. They taste homemade but are not. Agnes doesn't have time to bake and buys cans of them at a place not far from where she works. I have contemplated telling her that they are probably responsible for the extra weight that lends her a somewhat ponderous gait, but Agnes is sensitive about her size and there seems little point in underlining the obvious. I don't know whether my daughter is happy. I don't know whether she even asks herself the question.

The tea, sipped steaming hot, causes me to break out in a light perspiration. My undershirt, shirt and unbuttoned cardigan acquire a certain weight and I decide there will be no harm in admitting some fresh air. As I limp over to the window, I marvel at the feeling that comes to me, a feeling of naughtiness, a sense of minor defiance. Agnes, I am fully aware, would have a cow — her habitual expression — at my foolishness. Agnes has, through her forty-seven years, given birth to several herds. And yet I wonder how it is that age has turned the opening of a window into an indiscretion.

My fingers grasp the latch and are tugging at it when my eye is attracted to a car slowing in front of the house. A blue car. Agnes drives a blue car. And indeed, there she is, sitting erect behind the wheel. My hand flees the latch as if from pain: what in the world is she doing here at this time of day? She rarely does this, arriving unannounced. The last time she did, three years ago or so, the bank had been robbed and she'd needed to get away to settle her nerves. Only two things seem to rattle Agnes, guns and her father, and yet it was here, to this house, that she had come in search of tranquillity. She had spent an hour or so alone in the bedroom that had once been hers. It has long been a place for storing odds and ends but I suppose she made herself comfortable behind the closed door. I said nothing at the time out of consideration for the exceptional circumstance, but my daughter knows that unexpected visits do my heart no good. So what in the world, I wonder again, is she doing here when she should be at work?

I watch her parallel-park in a perfectly executed manoeuver. Agnes drives well, drives — why not admit it ? — like a man. It is something her mother never even considered doing, driving. Agnes has done many things Mary never considered doing.

She heaves herself from the car, locks the door and waves to someone out front. I press my face to the window and see Tremblay standing on the patch of lawn. He says something to Agnes and points towards my porch with an upraised finger —

not, I note, the middle one. Agnes stands on the sidewalk looking upwards. She smiles and responds to what he has said. In
all likeliood, she is speaking his language, a sign of the times. He,
in response, gives a graceful bow of his shaggy head. Then she
sees me at the window and waves. Tremblay, too, turns in my
direction, gives me a little smile and a nod of the head.

We are men of approximately the same age but he is in better
shape than me. And why shouldn't he be? He never had to face,
as did I, the savagery of enemy guns. I volunteered for an overseas battalion to protect king and empire, which were precious to
me. He volunteered for a home battalion to protect this land,
which was precious to him. A question of courage is how I've
always seen it. Agnes does not agree: a question not of courage,
she's said, but of vanities. I've never really understood what she
meant by that. I chose to face the Nazis. He chose to face a parade
ground. So why, then, should he not be in better shape than me?

Agnes lets herself in. "Hi, father," she says, heavy grocery bags
hanging from one hand. "Did you see M'sieur Tremblay's flag?"

"Miss-your Tremblay's what?"

"His Fleur-de-lys," she calls more loudly, accommodating her
voice to my ear. "Oh. Guess you haven't been out yet, eh? He was
just telling me he put it up this morning."

"Now why would he do a darn fool thing like that?"

"It's June twenty-fourth, father. St. Jean-Baptiste, remember?"

"Oh that."

"Yes, *that*. Why are you so peevish? Are you all right?"

"I'm fine." So it's their public holiday, their day for painting
themselves blue and white and enshrouding themselves in the
flag. The bank's closed. That explains what she's doing here at
this hour.

"You haven't shaved," she says.

"I would have if I'd known you were coming."

"You should shave anyway. You don't want to go around looking like some old boozer, do you?"

Some old boozer: Had she thought before speaking, she might have used a less sensitive simile. She knows I have been wary of alcohol for some years now, ever since the day her mother — no teetotaler herself — gave the evil eye to my growing fondness for the sherry bottle. *Some old boozer*: I remain proud of having avoided this occupational hazard of middle-aged literature professors, the scourge of the department that I have come to think of as the Sherry-and-Dickens syndrome. I have, within reason, resisted the delights of sherry, and my daughter has, despite my best efforts, resisted the delights of Dickens. It is no surprise, then, to find that she fails to avoid wounding similes.

I follow her into the kitchen, where she is hurrying through her habitual pantomime.

"That M'sieur Tremblay's such a delightful man," she says absentmindedly as her eyes forage through my refrigerator. She opens the milk carton, sniffs at the milk, puts it back.

"He spent the morning banging with his hammer," I say, and I hear the peevishness in my own voice.

She checks the orange juice, but the carton is unopened. "He was just putting up the flag, father. That hardly took all morning."

"It was loud."

"Why didn't you open the radio or the tv, then? Drown the noise out."

"Idiot boxes to drown out an idiot. I asked him to stop. He wouldn't."

"Did you ask nicely?"

"You know me, Agnes."

"No wonder he didn't stop." She says this without humour, the tips of her fingers pinching a blackened, half-eaten banana from the depths of the refrigerator. She holds it up, as if challenging me to examine its ugliness. "Really, father," she says with a shake of the head.

"I was saving it."

"What for? We haven't had a rainy day in weeks." She drops the banana into the garbage can.

"A witticism, Agnes?"

But she has already turned her attention to the crisper. A head of wilted lettuce and a furry carrot join the banana before she's satisfied that nothing else is threatening to take root in the refrigerator. She turns her attention to the pantry. Here, as usual, the contents have diminished, but that diminishment elicits a sigh from Agnes. She is about, I think, to have a little cow. "How many times have I told you, father? You've got to have fresh vegetables, too."

"Cans are convenient."

"Yes, well, that's all very nice but you don't get vitamins from canned soup and canned spaghetti."

"So why do you buy them, then?"

"Because you'd starve if I didn't." She shakes her head more vigorously, a sign of her going into labour. "You're just like François, and he's only six. For goodness sake, father, you're an adult, adults are supposed to understand about eating well."

I remain silent. It is the only way to arrest Agnes's contractions. I once made the mistake of asking her if she was going to have a cow — and a bull was born.

"If things continue like this, we'll have to look seriously at other options."

I maintain my silence. It's been a while since Agnes has brandished the threat of other options.

"If it's the only way I can get you to take better care of yourself . . ."

Her threat is not as ominous as it appeared to me when she first mentioned it two or three years ago. I had stumbled while descending the stairs outside, a little tumble that resulted in a slight sprain to my ankle. Tremblay, who happened to be returning from the supermarket just at that moment, helped me back into the house. Despite my protestations, he telephoned Agnes at the bank. "It's humiliating, Tremblay," I said to him as he looked up the number in the telephone book. "M'sieur Mackenzie," he replied, "you know not'ing about humiliation." I admit to being shaken and sought to master myself through a dignified silence, letting Tremblay do as he would. He removed my shoe and sock, fashioned an ice-pack from a plastic shopping bag and placed it on my swelling ankle. He asked if I wanted something to drink. I shook my head in refusal. Tremblay ministering to my helplessness: I know about humiliation . . .

He remained with me until Agnes arrived, harried from having to leave work, anxious about my condition. She was particularly concerned about my hips — they snap so easily in the aged — and insisted on wasting the better part of the day having me poked and probed and x-rayed. My ankle was back to normal by the following morning.

A few days later, Agnes mentioned what she considers other options. She said, "I think we should consider moving you to a home, father, it'll be safer for you." That, in any case, is what I heard. It's not unreasonable to say that we then exchanged harsh words before Agnes accused me of not listening to what she had said. "I said, we should consider moving you to *my* home, father." Well, that was a little better but, for various reasons, it remained an unappealing alternative. Other options are infrequently mentioned now, and usually only as a weak threat easily disarmed by silence.

"Well, father, what do you have to say for yourself?"

I have nothing to say for myself, but I know I must say

something. "I will try harder, Agnes. You know other options just aren't possible for me."

She shuts the pantry door, closes her eyes and pinches the bridge of her nose between thumb and forefinger in a gesture of fatigue. "Why do you resist, father?"

I have never defined my obstinacy for my daughter, for to delineate my reasons beyond a not unreasonable desire to die in the house in which I have so long lived would be to wound her. And I have no desire to wound Agnes. The very idea is repellant to me.

"What is it, father? Can you explain it to me?"

No, I cannot explain it to her. She would think me senile were I to begin talking about the breathing of the house, about its rhythmic palpitations which, in their steadiness and predictability, offer a nourishment far more vital than vitamins. And she would think me petty were I to mention my reservations about living in a house in which my language is infrequently spoken and where cultural references are lifted from a world unknown to me. Yes, Jacques speaks fluent English, and he accepts with good humour my calling him Jack. But it is little François who causes me more than a modicum of distress. At six years of age, he has already acquired a remarkable body of language — a language I am not versed in, there never having been any need. Although he regularly watches "Sesame Street" — learning to say x-y-zee instead of x-y-zed — and so understands much English, his refusal to speak it erects an inevitable barrier to our communication. Agnes assures me this will change as he grows older, but for the moment I find the situation difficult — not being able to converse with my grandson, I mean. So I respond lamely to Agnes's question: "It's not the thought of moving into your house, Agnes, it's the thought of moving out of mine."

"You're not getting any younger, father. One day we'll all have to learn to be practical." She turns away from me and makes herself busy with the grocery bags she's brought.

Feeling myself dismissed, I return to the living room and sit in my armchair, resting my leg and sighing my inadequacies away.

From the kitchen come the sounds of tea being prepared: the kettle being filled, teacups clinking onto saucers. Agnes takes it for granted that I will join her in a cup, and although I have drunk my fill I will not disappoint her.

"Strange weather we're having this year," she says, helping herself to a third cookie from the new can.

"Indeed. But so was last year's as I recall, and the year's before that. We always seem to think our weather strange in this country. A sign of desperation, don't you think?"

"But last year was hotter than usual, father. This year's cooler."

"Yes, but every year has its own characteristics from which . . ."

And so Agnes and I pass the time, munching on cookies and sipping at tea, bartering in meteorological perceptions.

I grow even warmer as we speak, sufficiently so that Agnes takes notice of the shine of perspiration on my forehead and suggests that we open a window or two. Before doing so, though, she obliges me to move from my armchair to the sofa, which is off to one side and therefore sheltered from the draught. The interruption brings an effective end to our exploration of the whys and wherefores of the weather and it is a few minutes and another cookie before Agnes's search for conversational inspiration prompts her to invite me to supper with her family. The invitation, I suspect, is occasioned simply by the need to say something and so I have little compunction about easing out of it, pleading fatigue, saying I am not up to it: perhaps another time.

And yet, to my surprise, the idea appeals to Agnes. She repeats it, with a tone best described as the sincerity of revelation. They are having Jack's family over for a barbecue, people I have encountered fewer than a dozen times — at their wedding, at Christmas festivities — and Agnes thinks it would be "fun" were I to agree to swell the numbers. "François would be so thrilled!"

She makes it hard, my not disappointing her, and I shape this refusal with greater care, putting a little more zeal into my fatigue, as it were.

She assures me that this little excursion — they live in Pointe Claire, hardly thirty minutes away — is precisely what I need: get out a bit, see some people. "Clear the cobwebs away."

Only her sincerity prevents me from asking: "So what shall we do this evening, then? Shall I clear the cobwebs while you have cows?" A question of a certain comic potential, but I suspect Agnes would find it inappropriate, perhaps even objectionable. She really is trying to be kind.

"Let me guess," she says to my lack of response. "You don't like Jacques's family, right?"

"Don't be silly, Agnes. They're fine people. A touch rustic perhaps, but one can't hold that against them. The fact is, though, that communication is a bit of a chore."

"Now who's being silly. You don't speak their language and they don't speak yours. There's no communication, so where's the chore?" The tension in her voice has mounted a notch or two, and I see that I am justified in not having raised with her this very conundrum as regards my grandson.

"But that's precisely it, Agnes. Sitting in the midst of a party unable to participate, sitting there excluded — it's the most difficult thing in the world."

Agnes reflects on this for a moment. Then she shakes her head and emits a tired laugh, a private laugh, a laugh that hints at a humour in my own words that is inaccessible to me. "As you wish, father," she says. "As you wish."

I accompany her outside. It is almost midday, the sun at its most

potent, and even in the shaded porch the frigid undercurrent of
the air is diminished. We proceed down the stairs, my right arm
gripped by Agnes's hand, my left preoccupied in bracing myself
with the stick. The stick is all I need — my tumble had resulted
from a worn rubber cap — but I do not protest Agnes's aid. It
makes her feel useful; it soothes her fears.

At the end of the concrete path that leads to the sidewalk,
Agnes insists that we pause to catch our breath. Mine has not
escaped me but I see no reason not to comply. It is a fine day,
one perfect in all respects for a lengthy stroll, on the mountain
perhaps, but that is a trek well beyond my resources now.

Agnes opens her purse and, while she fishes around in its
depths for her keys, I take the opportunity to sneak a glance at
Tremblay's porch. Although I know the sight will do my heart no
good, I am nevertheless curious about the reason for all his banging. The flag turns out to be large, one edge nailed to the railing,
its white on blue field extending a foot or so down past the floor.
I could, if I so wish, protest that that foot or so is infringing on
my space. I could, if I so wish, stand on a chair and trim it back
with scissors. Instead, I flick my stick at the thing and say half-
heartedly, "He can't do that, that's my porch."

"Father," Agnes says, "the ceiling of your porch is his floor.
He can do whatever he likes."

"He's blocking my view."

"Don't be absurd. Maybe if you were ten feet tall . . ." She
laughs, disarming me enough that I join in her laughter. The fact
is, I don't really care, not even for the principle. The truth is this:
If I react to certain situations in certain ways, it is because this
is what is expected of me. Playing the game has become a kind
of reflex, but sustaining it presents a greater challenge. Life's
nuisances, I have concluded, are in the end deserving of no more
than a shrug: indifference wisely deployed is a potent weapon. So
I gaze steadily at Tremblay's flag and perform a luxurious shrug.

Agnes jingles her keys. "You won't stay out too long, will you, father."

"I won't." Two cups of tea and an ageing bladder will see to that.

She glances at her watch. "I can spare a few more minutes."

"Don't let me keep you."

"Are you sure you won't change your mind about supper? You can spend the night and I'll drive you back on my way to work in the morning."

I shake my head in refusal. "See you next week."

She nods and strides across the street to her car that is the same shade of blue as Tremblay's flag. I watch her get in, fumble with the seatbelt and, with a brief wave, drive off.

I turn around and make my way back up the path. As I am about to mount the first step, Tremblay's voice calls out from above: "Hey, M'sieur Mackenzie, what you think of my flag?"

"It's blocking my view, Tremblay." I do not look up at him.

"About time somebody block your view, you don't think?"

I know he is merely teasing, but my blood races nonetheless. A shrug of any kind is beyond me. Seeking an appropriate response, I am prey to momentary inattention. My stick, reaching for the second step, misses its mark and I stumble, my right hand arresting the fall by seizing the railing.

"M'sieur Mackenzie?" Tremblay calls in a voice full of anxiety. "Take it easy t'ere."

I steady myself. "No harm done. No cause for alarm, Tremblay. Thank you for your concern."

He makes no response, but I feel his eyes heavy on me, measuring my progress.

"Have a good afternoon, Tremblay."

"You too, M'sieur Mackenzie."

Miss-your Mackenzie: but I am too chagrined to object.

Back inside the house, I spend a few moments leaning on my

stick, letting my equilibrium reestablish itself. Bad luck, that —
being seen stumbling by Tremblay, I mean. There is, however,
nothing to be done about it now. At least I managed to retrieve
the situation somewhat. His concern for my welfare is genuine,
but I would rather not give him cause to exercise it.

I go to the kitchen and prepare a sandwich from the supplies
Agnes has provided, slices of cheese and ham between two slices
of margarined, whole-wheat bread. I prefer butter and white
bread, but she claims neither is good for the health. Agnes, I
believe, fears my death more than I do. The meal, such as it is, is
dry but satisfactory. My tastes have never tended to culinary subtleties. I was, for most of my life, a meat-and-potatoes man. Red
meat, baked potatoes: the memory still intrigues my palate but
my stomach tightens at the mere thought of accommodating the
heaviness it once relished.

Once the dishes have been rinsed, I shut the windows — the
temperature has grown quite comfortable in the living room —
and settle into my armchair. My afternoon routine is really quite
simple. First I ascertain whether there is a baseball broadcast on
the radio. If there is none, and there appears to be nothing today
but the static of popular music and mindless chatter, I spend a
few hours with Charlie, working my way through his repertoire
for the umpteenth time. There's no established order, although I
have in the past pursued my reading chronologically. To date,
this time round, I have completed *Great Expectations*, *Bleak
House* and *Hard Times*. I shall now, for no reason other than it
happens to be next on the shelf, leap into *A Tale of Two Cities*.

A chill wakes me. The living room is dark, the windowpanes
reveal the street sombre in early dusk. The book lies open on my
lap. I have a vague memory of my eyes growing tired, of my letting them shut just for a moment — a moment that has stretched
into hours.

I put the book aside and stir myself, a slow flexing of stiffened muscles. I have not dreamt, or at least I have no memory of having dreamt, and that is good. For when sleep overcomes me in the daylight hours I am frequently prey to nightmares of the most vivid sort, nightmares that shape the waking minutes with the sweet ache of their impossibility: I dream that Mary is alive, that our life together continues with the gentleness and consideration that marked our final years. And then I awake to the frightful knowledge of her absence. It is in the aftermath of sleep that the nightmare comes.

Today, though, I have been spared. I feel refreshed, view the evening ahead with a certain optimism. Perhaps I shall watch a baseball game on the television, or listen to the classical music station on the radio, or push on with Charlie. Perhaps all three at the same time: words from the book, sound from the radio, pictures from the television. It was in this way, I suspect, that most of my former students did their essays, with the dexterity of inattention.

First I must insert my ear, which has slipped out. Then put on some lights and consult the tv guide that comes with the Saturday paper, the only one with which I bother. Indeed, there is a baseball game on tonight, on an Ontario channel, the local stations being all consumed with the holiday. The broadcast is to begin in a few minutes, enough time to prepare something to eat, my choice — spaghetti, stew — made simple by opening whichever can first comes to hand. The task is quickly accomplished, the stew quickly consumed. These are not meals over which one is encouraged to linger.

Before returning to the living room, I change into my pyjamas, the maroon pair, cotton with blue piping, a Christmas gift from Agnes. Before my retirement she gave me shirts and ties; now I receive pyjamas and slippers, a sign of the times. My times, I mean. Knotting the tie of my bathrobe, I turn on the television set just as the first inning is coming to an end. The Toronto team has already scored twice. I have no need of commentary and so turn the volume all the way down. A beer advertisement shimmers across the screen and I take the opportunity to fetch from the credenza the polished wooden box within which lies the tangible affirmation of my wartime efforts, the medals with which I have been graced.

They are not numerous, four in all: I was no Russian general. The men who planned the fighting all seem to have received greater consideration than the men who did the fighting. I feel no resentment, though, for it is a reality that has had curious reflection in my civilian life: those who study the writing are usually more handsomely rewarded than those who do the writing. The world is full of people who build careers on the labour of others.

My medals are not for me, as medals have become for so many others, icons of my life. I do not meditate on them but cherish them the way I would any other sign of esteem. They are removed twice a year for cleaning prior to the only days on which I wear them: Dominion Day or, as some have taken to calling it, Canada Day, seven days hence; and November 11th, the western world's version of the Day of the Dead. Only once did I join the ceremonies at the cenotaph in Ottawa: a profoundly depressing experience, standing at attention among old men slowly dying adorned with the pretty relics of a brutal time. I swore then I would not return, and I have not, but this was never meant as a rejection. I continue to remember, and to honour, in my own way.

The balls are flying as if alive from the hand of the Toronto pitcher. They avoid the Boston bats as if guided by radar, and I am reminded of the pictures we saw from the war in the Persian Gulf of Cruise missiles dodging the trees and buildings of Baghdad on the way to their targets.

I lay out my implements on the side-table: the cans of polish, the soft cloths. I once showed Tremblay my medals. He'd been sent by his wife to borrow sugar or flour or some such thing from Mary and I happened to be polishing them at the time. He examined them with a feigned disinterest and commented that he'd already seen such medals at a flea market. Then he said, "It was wort' it, M'sieur Mackenzie? For t'ese t'ings?" I saw no point in going into the matter; Tremblay would never have understood.

Each of the medals enfolds its own little tale, none so dramatic as to merit retelling. They are in the main for showing up, for facing fire, for getting wounded: a minor, and incidental, heroism. My war memoirs would take the form of a lengthy memo. So it is not my military experiences that remain most vividly with me from that time, but rather what came later, as with my nightmares, in the aftermath.

The Boston batters swing mightily at the ball but success eludes them. They return to the dugout one after the other with the same determined vigour they brought to the plate. I apply polish to the first medal, wrap it in the cloth reserved for cleaning and gently rub it between thumb and forefinger.

My wounds were hardly life-threatening but my significant discomfort kept me in the hospital for some time, surrounded by the sightless, the armless, the legless. I counted myself lucky to have lost just an ear and partial use of a leg — or at least that is what I like to tell myself today. At the time, the ear was the cause of some distress: I seemed to have lost a great part of the world. The nurses were considerate, but Marie-Claude Dupont was the only one who remembered to address me from the right side. She had introduced herself as Guard Dupont, which led me to ask whether I was under arrest. Another nurse, who was changing my neighbour's bandages, laughed and corrected me. "Not guard. *Garde*," she said. "That's how you address the French-speaking nurses, soldier."

I tried out the word. My effort caused *Garde* Dupont to break out in thoroughly charming laughter. She said something in rapid

French to the other nurse who, grinning, translated for me: "She says you sound as if you're gargling." Then a cry of pain from the far end of the ward sent them both scuttling off.

Over the coming weeks, *Garde* Dupont's voice, the sound of it, was a reassurance and I listened gratefully through the buzz that filled my head as she told me in halting English about various episodes of her life: her early years in Rivière-du-Loup or some such place, the move to Quebec City after the death of her mother, the struggle to rise out of poverty. I suppose she thought it would do an Anglo good to acquaint himself with some of the realities beyond our presumed world of privilege and affluence. She was young, she was pretty, and it was probably inevitable that I — like most of my companions sufficiently restored to feel the stirrings of desire   should believe myself to be falling in love with her.

Toronto comes up to the plate. A hit, a walk, another hit. I replace the first medal and remove the second, repeat the procedure with the polish and cloth.

But, unusual for a nurse, she was married. Although she wore no ring   none of the nurses did — she had spoken often of her mother-in-law, a woman she held in some esteem despite the inevitable tensions in their relationship. I therefore made no effort to reveal my attraction to her and sought, while continuing to enjoy her companionship, to impose restraint on myself. It seemed the only honourable course of action.

Another Toronto hit brings in two runs. The Boston manager, spitting once and hiking his belt up over his belly, marches out to the mound to confer with the pitcher and the catcher. I wrap the third medal in the cloth and my ear picks up the sounds of voices in the street. They are loud. I know they are loud because I hear them even through the closed windows. As the Boston manager signals for a new pitcher, I go over to the windows and look out. In the glow of the streetlamp I perceive activity at the house across the street, adolescents gathered on the sidewalk and in the porch. They are probably having a party. The holiday is an excuse for parties across the city. I am surprised, but only mildly, when close attention reveals English being spoken, or shouted rather: It is, like Agnes's mastery of her husband's language, either a sign of the times or merely a sign of youth. When a few moments later I return to my chair, the new pitcher has forced a double-play and rattled the following batter into a simple pop-up.

One day, as the end of my hospital convalescence approached, *Garde* Dupont failed to turn up for her normal shift. And when neither of the two following days brought her return, I enquired of another nurse what had become of her. The nurse informed me that she was on her honeymoon, a generous one to be sure, considering the times we were living in. She would be back in two days.

I didn't understand. Why would a woman already married for some time merit such consideration?

But she'd only got married three days before, the nurse replied. To a Frenchman, a liaison officer of some kind. She'd attended the wedding, a modest affair. It had been a whirlwind romance: one day they were being introduced; two weeks later they were being wed. She only hoped that Marie-Claude knew what she was doing.

As I work on the final medal, Boston begins to show some life. A stand-up double is followed by a home-run. The Toronto pitcher, apparently imperturbable, reveals his anxiety by removing his cap and fingering perspiration from his forehead.

The rest of that short exchange with the nurse has remained more vividly with me than any other event grand or insignificant from that time. I remember saying, "But she told me about her mother-in-law."

"She couldn't have. At the wedding Colonel Leclerc said that his parents were both—" And then the nurse paused in her task, put a finger to her chin and said, "Marie-Claude's English isn't very good, is it? *Belle-mère*. Sometimes it means mother-in-law, sometimes it means step-mother. I'll bet she mixed them up, that's all."

That's all.

When *Garde* Leclerc returned to her duties, I offered her my best wishes and, as a gift, a volume of Dickens undoubtedly still unread. Not long afterwards, I left the hospital and the army for good. I met Mary and the rest, as they say, is history.

By the eighth inning, Toronto has amassed a six-run lead. The Boston team is visibly weakened, the players' hearts no longer fully in the game.

I shut the box on my medals, securing the lid with the little brass clasp. After a moment's deliberation, I turn off the television — close it, as Agnes would say. A Boston uprising is unlikely and the game retains little intrigue for me in its drama softened into inevitability.

Across the street, the party has caroused onto the lawn and the sidewalk. The young people, scruffily dressed, stand about with beer bottles and cigarettes in their hands. Two boys, whooping in delight, skateboard down the street. Off to one side, a couple is wrapped together in public intimacy, the passion of their embrace blending their bodies into a subtle undulation of arms and legs. Two boys and a girl, sitting cross-legged on the sidewalk, guzzle beer and set fire to one sheet of paper after another — an essay, I presume, their English literature teacher in metaphoric effigy. All the activity forms a tableau of an awkward age: they are neither adults nor infants but flit uneasily between the two. New passions exploring themselves against old urges: It is, too, I decide, a tableau of a frightful unpredictability.

I turn off the lights and head off to bed. I am in the bedroom before I notice that, in my absorption with the ways of youth, I have absent-mindedly brought my medal box with me. I decide to leave it on the night stand, there will be time enough tomorrow to put it back into the credenza. My ear goes on top of it, my dentures into a glass of water beside it. When, in the silent darkness, I climb into bed, my body makes intimate contact with the pulse of the house. My skin prickles at the feel of it, my flesh is tautened by its gentle energy. My heart, losing its diffidence, settles into a strong, steady beat.

It is as usual some time before sleep comes to me, and when it does it is not relly sleep at all. It is more like a shallow descent into unconsciousness, a grey and unsteady glide through the long hours, feeling the house, listening to the silence, surviving the embrace of the night . . .

Rain.

The harsh downpour has reached through the tunnel of my ear to nudge me into wakefulness. With a touch of panic I wonder whether the windows are closed, and only an effort at recollection brings me the reassuring memory of watching through glass the young people at play.

I lie back, eyes closed, enjoying the distant, crackling sound. The sound of rain at night has always pleased me, comforted me, made me glad to be in a dry bed. It's a sensual pleasure, one of the few not nullified by the academic life of the mind. The simple sound of rain manages to cut through the thickets of my life and return me to a time when I still believed the world to be a warm and safe place. Would it be unbecoming for a man of my age, the not undistinguished although now retired Professor Mackenzie, to admit that the sound of rain causes his toes to curl with pleasure under the blanket?

But now there's another sound. A voice calling through the rain. I listen hard, hand cupped to my ear: "Mackenzie! M'sieur Mackenzie!" Tremblay? Why would Tremblay be calling to me in the middle of the night? I think: I must be dreaming. And I am reminded of my first night as a war casualty when a voice, penetrating and crystal-clear, called my name in an empty room. I had been chilled then by what I thought the voice of death.

My arm reaches up through the darkness to the bedside lamp. My fingers find the switch, turn it. Nothing. The hydro must be down, a not infrequent occurrence during storms. My fingers find my ear, insert it — and I know I'm not dreaming when I hear my name again.

"M'sieur Mackenzie! Vite! Get up!"

I sit up in bed as my door flies open and a man who may be Tremblay stands silhouetted by a thin light filling the doorway. The beam of his flashlight cuts dizzying swaths through the darkness. "Quick, M'sieur Mackenzie!"

What the devil is Tremblay doing in my house? Has he gone mad? How did he get in? But he gives me no opportunity to react. He scurries over to me, grasps my arms and tugs me unceremoniously out of bed. The dread of urgency in the dark: I fight back, but my disadvantages render resistance futile. He gruffly bundles me towards the door. "Tremblay! What do you think you're—"

He mumbles a reply, too low for my ear to pick up.

"Eh? What? Say again?" We are out on the porch now, stumbling down the stairs. The crackling of the rain fills my head and I expect to be drenched because of Tremblay's madness. But I am not drenched, I'm not even sprinkled: there is no rain. Instead, the stench of burning pervades my nostrils.

Multiple hands reach out to me in support, lead me away from the house, into the street that is a confusion of neighbours looking up, faces lit by a strange yellow light. In the distance, sirens piggyback on other sirens.

I turn around, look back to the house, and my vision blurs at the sight. Tremblay's porch is obscured by smoke. A tide of blue

~

flames seethes along the roof, yellow sheets billow high into the sky. The air pops and crackles with the sound of old wood avidly consumed.

Policemen, running, clear the street. Fire-trucks roll in, disgorging men and hoses with feverish control.

The air is hot, suffocating. The flames roar into a ferocity such as I have not seen since the war: the house is disappearing before my eyes. Vertigo hits. My knees buckle. Unknown hands catch me, lower me to the ground. My ear falls out. My hand reaches up to find it but all my fingers clutch is grass.

Other hands restrain me now, the hands of men in uniform: one pressing a stethoscope to my chest, the other lowering an oxygen mask to my face. Looking up past their absorbed faces, past neighbours standing with faces turned to the light, all I see is the tops of trees gilded and flickering.

The oxygen fills my lungs, sharpens my brain to giddiness. Strong arms lift me, place me on a stretcher, strap me in. Then I am being wheeled and I must shut my eyes to the movement, to the flashes of trees and flames and anxious faces.

The journey to the ambulance lasts only a few seconds and, as I lie there waiting, the tunnel of my ear continues to offer me the distant sound of rain, the sound converted now into the terror of conflagration.

I think: What is happening?

An object is placed gently on my belly, some medical implement, I assume. Curious, I open my eyes. And I see, to my astonishment, that my medal box has materialized on the orange blanket. And I see that, standing beside me, is Tremblay. His face is drawn; his eyes are wet, his cheeks tear-stained. He says, "M'sieur Mackenzie, they put . . ."

But his voice falls off and the rest of his sentence is lost to me. I cup my hand to my ear.

He leans in close, his mouth widening in a shout: "My flag,

M'sieur Mackenzie, they put fire to my flag."

Dear God . . .

The stretcher begins rolling once more, and the body of the ambulance swallows me. I struggle to raise my head. "Miss-your Tremblay!" I shout. "Thank you, Miss-your Tremblay!" But the oxygen mask is in the way, it obscures my words. He cannot hear me, and I can hear only the cranial echoes of my futile effort. The last thing I see as the doors are closed is Tremblay's anxious face mouthing unheard words at me.

The ambulance moves off.

I think: Other options . . .

Then: What page was I on in Charlie's book?

Then, severely: Your thoughts are disordered, Mackenzie.

My hands reach for the medal box, fingers clutching at the wood, and it strikes me as curious that it should be there, safe with me: Why should Tremblay have thought of rescuing it? In the confusion of the moment, it occurs to me that I may never see him again. The tragedy of folly will cause us to go our separate ways.

And to my surprise, the thought does my heart no good, no good at all. The thought of not seeing Tremblay again, I mean.

$\mathcal{L}$ed by François, Ruth-Ann emerges holding herself as if entering a ballroom. Draped on her shoulders is the pink woolen sweater that in no way matches her navy-blue dress but which is, nevertheless, as much a part of her as her hair, her nose or her fingers. She glances at me as at some benign alien and says, with prim friendliness, "Hello, how do you do? So pleased to meet you." She looks happy, but all I can see is that misshapen sweater and Mary's fingers busy with the wool.

I follow Agnes into the kitchen, leaving François shuffling through a stack of CDs, Ruth-Ann, perched on the sofa, gazing bright-eyed at him. The flavours of Jack's turkey thicken the air. The counters are clean. The sink sparkles beneath its fluorescent bulb. A single orange light glows on the stove. I stand there in the semi-darkness, suddenly at a loss, driven by the music heard now only in my head, by the sense it imparts to me of the lateness of the hour. The hour of my life, I mean.

Agnes looks quizzically at me. Is everything all right? Am I hungry, thirsty? She places a gentle hand on my arm. "Father, do you know who I am?"

The blood mounts to my head, a tidal surge through my veins. She has found the right question. "No, I don't, Agnes."

"Father?"

"What I mean is . . ." My voice goes raucous, as if seized from within by some phantom hand. I cough it away, resentful of its imposition. I do not wish to mumble. "What I mean is, I take it that some things have happened in your life that I do not know about. Some hard things. That you do not wish me to know about."

I search her face for a reaction, for confirmation or denial. She offers neither, only chews at the inside of her cheeks. But her eyes soften onto me with uncertainty, an uncertainty becoming in one so strong-willed. What a mystery she is to me, my child! I have watched her shape her life, making unanticipated choices, following her own internal logic, seconded always by her mother, with me, her father, somehow incidental. I wonder still out of sheer puzzlement why she chose this man — a good man, yes, a man of serious intent, of depths that go beyond the glow of his professional lights, but still not a man to my eyes unique — over any of her previous boyfriends. Over, for instance, Philip, who had a passion for environmental causes. I liked Phil, I enjoyed his company even if his politics were a tad extreme. He would grow out of the received feeling, I felt, he would mature, become a man grounded in a life anointed by ideals. Mary, though, perhaps sensitive to Agnes's hesitations, referred to him behind his back as Land Phil. Agnes did not choose Phil, and the last we heard he was riding inflatable rafts to rescue whales from Japanese fishing vessels.

"I'm not going to ask you about those things, Agnes, they're your business and you have your reasons, I'm sure, for keeping them to yourself. I accept that. But, Agnes, but—"

And I think incongruously about my writer friend who protected the innocence he claimed was vital to his work by pinning on the wall a sign that read *Sceptics are a pain in the but.* He mentioned this many times to me. Each time it felt like a warning, well-meant but undeserved, and so irritating. Each time I disregarded it, dismissing it as merely a bad pun.

"There's always a but," I continue. "But I think it's important, if not for you then for the boy, that those things whatever they may be, those stories, not disappear, because once they do it'll be as if they've never been, and so, with time, as if a large chunk of you has never been. We narrate ourselves, you know, Agnes, to ourselves and to others. But when they write the history of our times, you and I won't be there, we're not important enough in the larger scheme of things. It's up to us to ensure we aren't completely effaced, the little people."

I have gone too far. I have fallen into my professor's voice, slightly officious, slightly didactic, but I do not know whether it is this — the tone which Agnes has long found unflattering — or the idea I am submitting to her that triggers her frown.

"The whole truth and nothing but the truth, father?"

Her question, even if merely a challenge, quickens my pulse. "Maybe not the whole truth, Agnes. I'm not talking about baring your soul. God knows, it's the one thing that belongs exclusively to us. I mean enough of yourself, all those stories you haven't told, snapshots of your life, portraits of events, so that when your son is an adult, perhaps after you are gone, he will know that his mother had a full and rich life. That she had hesitations and doubts and bouts of foolishness. That she made choices, suffered regrets, was blessed with triumphs and happiness. So many people end up as just cyphers, Agnes, names and dates in a family tree."

"Father, life can be such a mess sometimes, maybe that's not such a bad thing."

"Has your life ever been such a mess, Agnes?"

A smile comes slowly to her lips, like waves unfurling on a placid surface long after the passage of some distant ship. "We all have our accounts to settle, father, with history or with whatever. But we all see the terrain in our own way, so we've got to settle those accounts in our own way, too, don't we."

She speaks with a finality that puts a period to the conversation. With a nod of my head I concede the point, soothed by a memory of eavesdropping decades old.

Agnes was seven or eight, perhaps nine, and spring that year was particularly wet. Every morning and afternoon brought showers with the occasional drenching at night, so that it seemed the world would never be dry again. Agnes, restless indoors, was let out between downpours. Several times the rain beat her to the door, not always, her pleasure indicated, by happenstance. We had been hectoring her endlessly about removing her soiled shoes on the porch before entering the house, but our appeals and pointless threats — the floor would have to be washed yet again; there would be no more excursions outside — had little effect. One afternoon, as yet another deluge began, she clattered to the door with some of her friends. Mary and I, to our astonishment, heard her intone, "Shoes off, everybody. We don't want to give my mom more housework." We knew then that she would be all right. The prospect of our own inevitable twilight, whatever form it may take, no longer seemed quite so terrifying.

"Of course, Agnes. Of course." I turn to go. Her fingers tighten on my arm. Without warning she lays her cheek on my chest and for an interminable moment listens to the beat of my heart.

With a click — the sound startling me: rarely setting the volume of the contraption at maximum, I have lost so many simple sounds of the world — the orange light on the stove winks out.

Agnes lifts her head. Her eyes are closed. Then she turns and bustles away.

When I return to my chair in the living room, François directs a lengthy and mischievous glance my way. How, he wants to know, have I wet my chest?

My fingers find a damp spot. A wondrous thing.

Stigmata.

I turn the volume down on the contraption. No, no longer so terrifying, that twilight.

On the sofa, Ruth-Ann and François sit close together folding sheets of paper into airplanes. Her fingers work with the skill of a finely-calibrated machine, no movement superfluous. His are less nimble, less skilled. His airplanes have mismatched wings; the halves of the fuselage do not fit flush. They perform death spirals the moment he releases them from his grip. He watches in admiration as hers glide through the still air, alighting like butterflies on the carpet, on the plexiglass turntable cover, even on the branches of the tree. Reaching for new paper, they begin again, Ruth-Ann working away with unchanging precision, while François eyes her fingers and tries to replicate her movements. On their faces is a concentration that eliminates the world. François, I would wager, has even forgotten about Santa Claus. For the moment at least.

In the dining room beyond, the ceiling lights are turned low. The table is finely turned out, the tablecloth green, the red napkins rolled into silver holders. China and more silverware than I know what to do with gleam in the light of a dozen red and green candles rising from a candelabra of Mexican silver, a memento of Jack and Agnes's honeymoon.

They are standing at the liquor cabinet, Jack shuffling through the forest of bottles, Agnes whispering urgently into his ear. He has just emerged from his labours downstairs — a first draft of the article is done; like all first drafts, it is unsatisfactory — and I suspect she is telling him about Mike Pearson. My intuition is confirmed when they toss simultaneous glances my way. Agnes's eyes shift sharply away, but Jack holds my gaze, his eyes tired and soft. He smiles. Is he thinking of Ruth-Ann and me? Of the ways in which the future might bring us together, living side by side but mostly unaware of one another? Is he thinking that time might work some kind of trick, returning us in our final years to our early days of hermetic parallel lives? If he is, I can forgive him. After all, this is what I too have been thinking.

"How are you feeling, Professor?" Jack asks.

"All right, Jack. Thank you for asking." And because I wish there to be no pretence between us — not anymore — I add: "This forgetfulness, it's not unusual, you know."

"I know."

"Damned embarrassing, though."

"I know that, too. We'll all be there some day, God willing."

"God willing, did you say?" The expression surprises me enough that I suspect I've misheard him. Jack is not religious beyond the conventions. He wishes his son to go through the entire Catholic rigmarole and, if asked, he would say that he believes, but there would be a shrug to his voice. *God willing* is an old expression, expressive of another time. From his lips, it somehow acquires weight and meaning, seems to circle in on some mystery.

"God willing," he repeats. "Considering the alternative, I'm willing to exchange a little memory for old age."

My eyes draw his attention to Ruth-Ann, who is firing off another paper airplane. I do not have to state my question.

"So long as you can still have a little fun," he adds. Ruth-Ann is the only person permitted to smoke cigarettes in his house. He holds the sherry bottle up. "A drop or two more?"

"Make it three, Jack, before I forget how much I enjoy the stuff."

Doing the Heart Good

Jack and Agnes both acknowledge my bravado with smiles, his genuine, hers somewhat sickly. She's not sure whether such a remark — ghastly, perhaps, or gruesome — deserves approval. I'm not interested in her approval, however. It's like combat. Away from battle, thoughts of yesterday and tomorrow crowd into the mind, bracketed by the realization of how much you have to lose. Fears manifest themselves, bringing in their wake a kind of paralysis. Once in the thick of the horror, though, there is only the moment, a cold calculation of one's situation, and the readiness to do whatever you must to survive them. Yesterday has been lived. Tomorrow will take care of itself.

A warm glow seeps throughout my body. Jack has carried his glass of champagne — "the real thing" which, sadly, does not agree with my stomach — into the kitchen. He is seeing to the final preparations of his bird, which will emerge decorated with cranberries and puffs of filigreed white and aluminum paper. It will be accompanied by a bowl of his mother's cranberry sauce. François and Ruth-Ann have been given tumblers of cola. He tilts his head back and carefully dribbles the liquid into his open mouth. She stares intently into her glass, as if fascinated by the conglomeration of bubbles and ice-cubes.

Outside, the snow continues down in steady fashion. Jack will be up early tomorrow morning, working his snow-blower along the driveway so that his family will have space for their cars when they arrive for the Christmas Day gathering.

It is now, in this pause before the feast that will begin with Jack's ceremonial carving of the turkey, that Agnes comes to my chair and perches on the arm. She holds her electronic agenda. Its green display reveals what she wishes of me. "Not now, Agnes," I mutter. "I'm not really up to it."

But her other hand grips the receiver. She's already dialling. She presses the phone into my hand and steps away. Flustered, I

315

nevertheless find myself pressing the implement to my ear. Agnes is right to insist. I have procrastinated long enough.

"Allo?"

"Tremblay?"

"Oui?"

"It's Mackenzie."

"M'sieur Mackenzie?" He is shouting. I know he is shouting because I hear him clearly. I detect astonishment — and is that an undertone of excitement? — in his voice.

"Yes, Miss-your Tremblay. Mackenzie."

"You are well?"

"I am well. And you?"

"We are well, me and my wife. You are comfortable living wit' your daughter?"

"Quite. And you?"

"We like it here. It's *tranquille*. You must come, M'sieur Mackenzie. Make us a visit."

"I don't get around very easily, Tremblay. It's very kind of you, though."

"You will come? Your daughter and her family, too."

"Perhaps. Yes, I would like that. Very much."

"Good."

A silence falls between us, but unlike the old days, it is not charged. We each, I suspect, have tallied our losses, mourn them, would like to make whole again what we can. Too much has been wasted in mindless bickering. Still, I can think of nothing else to say. "Well, Tremblay, it was good hearing your voice. I should go now. I just wanted to wish you and your wife—"

"You want to hear somet'ing funny, M'sieur Mackenzie?" he says.

"Go ahead."

"I am learning Spanish. Si, sen-your. Evening course. My wife and me, we plan a big voyage next year. To Espagne."

I find myself chuckling. "Maybe I should take Spanish lessons, too."

"You come with us!" He laughs.

"No, no. I was just thinking about you and me, Tremblay. We need a new language, a new way of speaking to each other."

He is silent again for a moment. Then he says, " We have not need of Spanish, M'sieur Mackenzie. You come, make a visit. We will find the new language, you and me."

Now it is my turn to fall silent. "How far is it to your new home, Miss-your Tremblay?"

"Not far," he says.

I suddenly know that it doesn't matter how far it is, I will find a way to get there. "Listen, Miss-your Tremblay, talking on the phone takes quite an effort. My hearing, you know."

"I remember."

"I must go now. We will talk again?"

"Bientôt, M'sieur Mackenzie."

"One more thing. Joyeux Noël, Miss-your Tremblay. And joyeux Noël to your wife, too."

"Merry Christmas, Mister Mackenzie. *Hasta la vista!*"

There is a click and the connection is broken.

Ruth-Ann swivels her head towards me as if she's only just become aware of my presence. "Was it good for you, too?" she asks.

Addendum

Not long after completing his language course, Boobie discovered in himself a passion for computers. Passion is not the same as talent. Boobie was long on the one and a little short on the other, but he persevered. "What choice I have, Mr. Professor?" he said to me. He struggled through a difficult private-college course, which provided the only instance when he sought my help in any concrete fashion. I arranged and paid for some evening tutoring. During this time, Boobie turned his bedroom — after the drama, the brothers moved to a larger apartment in another part of town — into a layman's nightmare of the interior of a computer. Every corner contained banks of equipment — some of it borrowed, some of it castoffs, a few items purchased — that blinked and beeped for no apparent reason. To get to his bed, he had to step over strands and coils of wire, discarded parts, the carcasses of cannibalised components. His brother refused to clean the room, but Boobie did so assiduously every weekend; dust was bad for the machines. After graduation, he secured a well-paid position with Hydro, repairing computer equipment. After a few short years there, he moved to the United States, to a lucrative position and a more promising future in California. He did not inform me of his move, he was too ashamed to. He felt he was somehow letting Frank and me down. I don't know what Frank thought, but Boobie misjudged me. It was not for me to condone or condemn his choice. I learned early, from Ruth-Ann and then from Mary, that we must all make the choices necessary to us. And I learned from Martha that those who judge the desires and actions of others do so in the main on the basis of their own narrow prejudices. Through his brother, I sent Boobie a letter offering him my best wishes.

As for his brother, he progressed in the company from making daisy-wheels to the lower echelons of management. He has dreams of rising higher. He married a local girl and now rents a small house not far from the airport. They have two children, a boy and a girl, and plan on having several more. When I took my letter to him, he proudly displayed his little brood — the dark-eyed little girl they named Adriana, the boy for his father whose name escapes me — and said with a hint of sadness, "There is a lot of people to replace, Mr. Professor." Never before had I felt like blessing someone.

Frank spent a few years in a penitentiary before the authorities decided to release him due to his declining health. We did what we could to ease his life, sending him the occasional care package. Mary and I joined several of his well-wishers — his trial had naturally garnered much publicity, all of it sympathetic — in preparing a small flat for him in his old neighbourhood. Enough money was collected through donations that he would not, modestly, want for money. The night before his release, as he was packing his belongings in his cell, he was felled by a heart-attack. The donated money was used to establish a small prize in his name at my former university, to be given to the writer of the best master's or doctorate thesis on the subject of war crimes.

Elliot has disappeared completely from my life. The last I heard, the partial restoration of his sight did not last. He adjusted, though, and found himself a tenure-track position at a university out west. In all probability he now has his hands full with all the duties of a tenured professor — the lectures, the seminars, the committees, the administrative work, the supervision of theses. I do not expect him to end his days in academe, behind some cheap and functional desk, surrounded by books which he has not read in years. There is an underlying restlessness to the boy, a restlessness that is innate and which does not go away, that will drive him out of the world he dreamt of for so long. He will, I am convinced, go off in thrall to some challenge that defies prescription. He will find it in himself to seek out the stars. Such, at least, is my hope for him.

Dan Mullen continues to write. He fills magazines and newspapers with acerbic columns and churns out a novel every three or four years. They are always well received and spend respectable time on the bestseller lists. I have read them all. His energy and imagination have never flagged. After each I wrote him a letter. None of them has been mailed. He has been given several important prizes, and his fame now reaches well beyond the borders of our country. I glimpse him on television and see his photos in the newspapers. He looks the same, only older and more fatigued. His wife never appears beside him. She is still rarely mentioned, the devoted and loving Kathryn ever in the background.

Thrush, or at least an urn with his ashes, is buried on the mountain. The photograph was never made public. Following the announcement that cleared his name without citing the evidence, grumblings of a whitewash echoed through the corridors of the university. There were letters to the student newspaper, and several instances of particularly nasty graffitti. But tongues were held, speculation ignored. Thrush's reputation remained stained, unforgiving memories of him fading only slowly. But, of course, memories of the man himself faded too, slowly but inexorably. Today, it is as if Thrush has never existed. Professor de Vasconselos is retired and lives abroad, in more temperate climes. Professor Goldman is now dean of the faculty and is said to be eyeing the rectorship.

Slovar, like Martha, perhaps with Martha, never materialised again. It is hard to imagine that he could live in anonymity, unremarked, but he has managed to pull it off. He is not the first man to engineer his own total disappearance, although he has not achieved the mythic status of the Toronto millionaire Ambrose Small, or that skyjacker fellow with the parachute, DB Hooper or Cooper or whatever he called himself. But Antonio Gaudi Slovar's name remains cursed by many a person of faintly reduced fortune in this city. I for one cannot believe entirely in *his* good fortune. He left, after all, with Martha in tow.

During Mary's funeral fourteen years later, I kept scanning the mourners for Martha's face, I kept listening for her voice. I couldn't shake the feeling that she would somehow know what had happened, she would hear the news or she would have a dream, a feeling, she would be taken unawares by a shudder or a sadness that she could not explain. *Friends for life*, Mary had said.

But she never came. By the end of the service, as I watched the casket being slid back into the hearse, I found myself harbouring a hatred for Martha that Mary herself would never have felt, or forgiven in me. But Mary, not I, had been Martha's friend. At that moment, I could afford to despise her.

A long time after Mary's death, when frivolity still seemed to me obscene and laughter inconceivable, Windy became for me once again, and for all time, Wendy.

She had visited once not long after the funeral. Thereafter she avoided the house, and therefore me, for many months. The emptiness with which I surrounded myself — echoes could be *sensed* like whispers against the skin — would have been to her unbearable. Inertia was anathema to Wendy. She felt, quite rightly, that such was my state. Such it would be for a long time and, perhaps, to some extent, still is.

Still, perhaps about a year later, she did venture by. She brought a pound cake. In no mood for companionship — What would we talk about? Mary? But I wished to be alone with my memories. — I nevertheless went through the motions of brewing a pot of tea. She sliced the cake. We ate, we drank. She shared news of a detainee released, of another moved from prison to house arrest. Meagre victories, but they animated her. Exotic names fell like tasty morsels from her tongue. Then, suddenly in a bustle, she gathered up her scarf and handbag and was gone, overwhelmed, I sensed, by my airlessness.

I received a postcard from her some months after. She had moved back to Chicago, where she had been born, to care for her ailing mother. We entertained a brief and inconsequential correspondence. She described her mother's ailments, the medications required, the constancy of the labour. I wrote in the main about the weather. In the four or five letters I received from her, she never once expressed a longing for the life she had left behind. It was this, more than anything else, that in my eyes returned to her her rightful name, this absence of longing for the irretrievable that earned her my admiration.

Agnes calls everyone to the table. François carefully places his empty glass on the carpet, takes Ruth-Ann by the hand, and leads her to her chair. He is astonishingly, touchingly, solicitous of her. Once we are seated, Jack, wrapped in a white apron with red trimmings, brings in the brown and gleaming bird on a silver platter. He places it in the middle of the table and after a brief contemplation accompanied by discreet oohs and aahs — the cheerleading led by François — turns his attention to pouring the wine that has been sitting, already uncorked, beside his plate. He gives a little to Ruth-Ann, generous amounts to Agnes and me. I appreciate this. Too often, people as old as I are treated like children: a little of this, a little of that. Jack has never treated me like an old man.

When people describe me as being "seventy-five years young", I am simply reminded that I am irretrievably old. They mean well, they think they're being clever, but it's a little like having a bayonet thrust into your belly. I am inevitably reminded that somewhere out there a woolly-headed boy awaits me. We have for all intents and purposes never met. We are strangers. Yet I know that when finally he turns to face me, it will be as if we have been the closest of companions all our lives.

But before then, there is a great deal of weather to be got through. This winter just beginning will be one of hibernation. I have reading to do, wounds to heal, strength to gather. Come spring, I shall take up my stick, ask Agnes for a ride downtown or explore the mysteries of the public transportation, and seek out the corners and alleyways of my life. The gin joint and the greasy spoons, the ice-cream parlour and the cinema, the low-rise where my parents brought me up and the field now a supermarket where Kevin died. I shall visit once more that place on the mountain where I fell before Mary, and that house rendered to cinders where for so long we made a life. None of them is left. Or at least they are all, in one way or another, phantoms now. But find them I shall: by their scents, their odours, their emanations from within. And, when I do, whole lives will flow.

Jack, standing at his place, raises his glass to me. "Joyeux Noël, m'sieur le professeur."

Agnes, sitting in her seat, does the same. "Merry Christmas, father."

"And to you both." I acknowledge each with a tip of my glass — "Agnes" — and with a quick intake of breath: "*Zhack.*" To his pleased smile I add, "With profound apologies to Miss-your Molière, of course."

We all take a sip of the wine and Jack, hefting his instruments, sets about carving the turkey. The blade of his knife flashes in the candle light.

Have I learned anything through this long life of mine? Yes. Unequivocally yes. A certain measure of humility that has been decades coming to me. I was born to a people to whom a sense of entitlement was innate. Even if my family were not among the blessed with mansions and chauffeured cars, there were always others, like Tremblay, who were below us. Even in our modest circumstances, we came from among the winners. It's not as if we lived every day with this sense, not as if we awoke every morning energised by the knowledge of our supremacy. We were, rather, unconsciously shaped by it. We felt ourselves to be special by virtue of history, by the levers of power some within our community controlled.

Yet how very human this is, always having someone to look down on. We begin and end each day with the belief that we are the centre of the universe. We still insist that the sun rises and sets when we know fully well that the sun is immobile, our earth — *we* — rising and dipping and spinning in obeisance to it. Dan Mullen once said in a newspaper interview, "So what's really changed over the years? I don't know. Today, he grows a pony-tail and she gets a crew-cut. That, it seems to me, is the extent of it." I don't share Dan's pessimism — *Mullen is so full of shit sometimes* — but the thought discomforts me. After all, the sun rises every morning, doesn't it? There was a time not so long ago when I would have taken that notion for granted.

Already, as I sit here before this splendid table in this splendid company, with coloured lights darting through the tree beside the window and with the knowledge that from the stereo sounds immemorial are calling up ancient mythologies, I smell spring in the air, fresh winds, rich earth and awakened greenery announcing a renewal older than time itself.

For no reason at all, François sets his eyes on me. He smiles, and it is like the dawn of a thousand suns, shining its light into a future, his and mine, which I know to be there even though I cannot see it.

He has his mother's eyes. A breathless silence.

So everything changes, again.